A TASTE OF PASSION

"Why are you holding me like this? Why don't you let me go?" Kristina cried.

"No man in his right mind would let you go." Cole pressed her supple curves snugly against his hard frame.

She didn't resist.

"You're very beautiful," he murmured huskily. Then, suddenly, his lips were on hers, and his demanding kiss left her breathless with wonder.

Kristina gazed thoughtfully into his dark-blue eyes, which were studying her with deep, tender longing. Once he learned the truth about her, those sensual eyes would regard her with cold fury. She recklessly threw all reason to the wind. She might be destined to lose this man, but before that happened, she would experience the pleasure of his embrace . . .

ROCHELLE WAYNE

MIDNIGHT ANGEL

ZEBRA BOOKS
KENSINGTON PUBLISHING CORP.

ZEBRA BOOKS

are published by

Kensington Publishing Corp.
475 Park Avenue South
New York, NY 10016

First printing: June, 1990

Printed in the United States of America

*This book is dedicated to my
sister-in-law and loyal fan, Sharon Kemp*

Prologue

Clay County, Missouri
1862

Cole Barton sat in the shade of a tall elm, staring blankly into space. The boy felt a pang of guilt, for he shouldn't sit idly when there was work to do—work that never let up. He sighed deeply. Farm work was demanding. He glanced at the gray mare waiting in the nearby field, the plow still hitched to her strong back. There was soil to break and furrows to cut, and he wasn't getting the job done sitting here daydreaming.

He decided to stretch out and relax for a few minutes, reluctant to abandon the cool shade. Folding his arms beneath his head, he looked up at the elm's sweeping limbs. A warm breeze stirred, rustling the smaller branches. For a moment he watched the leaves sway in the wind. Then, closing his eyes, he allowed his mind to drift.

He thought of the farm. Cole knew he didn't want to be a farmer. It was a fact, however, that he had kept to himself. He figured his parents wouldn't take him seriously, but would probably remind him that he was only fifteen, and at his age, disliking farm work was natural. When he was older, he'd feel differently, they'd say. Cole didn't think so.

Nevertheless, for the time being, he was resigned to his way of life. He had no choice but to remain on the farm. A year had passed since Cole's father had joined the Confederate Army. Before his departure, Cole had given him his promise to take care of the farm. Cole was an only child, and there was too much work for his mother to handle alone. Cole intended to abide by his promise, but it nonetheless plagued him. If the war were to drag on for an extended period, he'd soon be old enough to join the Army. Could he stay here, safe and protected, while other boys his age were fighting for the Confederacy? Although Cole had never tested his courage in a live or die situation, he was certain of his own valor. But if the war continued, and if he stayed on the farm, would others think him yellow? The possibility that he might someday be branded a coward greatly disturbed Cole. At his young age, it seemed a fate worse than eternal damnation.

Cole sat up and raked a hand distractedly through his dark hair. Maybe the war would end soon, his father would come home, and then he could start planning for his own future in earnest.

Cole had been twelve years old when he and his parents had moved to Missouri from their farm in Tennessee. Clay County was settled mostly by southerners, and living here wasn't much different than living in Tennessee. Cole was determined that someday he'd leave Missouri. He had nothing against the state, or against Clay County. If he and his folks were still residing in Tennessee, he'd still be feeling this same restlessness to move on. He was

8

anxious to fly from the nest and sow his wild oats. More than anything, he longed to travel to the untamed West. Cole was eager to explore the wilderness, and to help conquer the challenging land. His knowledge of the West consisted entirely of what he had learned from books, and he had read every book on the West that he could find.

With a heavy sigh, he got slowly to his feet. His westward journey would have to wait until after the war. In the meantime, he had a field to plow.

Suddenly, Cole heard the distant sound of horses' hooves, and shading his eyes with his hand, he peered back toward the house. The log-constructed home sat in a small clearing surrounded by verdant woodland. Smoke billowing from the chimney floated skyward, then dissipated before reaching the white, scudding clouds. Several hens, along with a rooster, were loitering in the yard, but as the four riders charged into view, the startled chickens squawked, flapped their wings, then hurried to safer ground.

Although Cole was a good distance from the house, he could see that the intruders were Union soldiers. Anger flickered in his blue eyes, and his hands unconsciously balled into tight fists. Damn the bastards! In Cole's opinion, the men's blue uniforms didn't make them soldiers. They were still hated Jayhawkers from Kansas!

Hostility had existed between Kansas and western Missouri years before the onset of the War between the States. Kansas citizens, considering Missouri a hotbed of pro-slavery elements, had organized roving bands known as Jayhawkers. Determined to keep Kansas free of slavery, these Jayhawkers would often ride into western Missouri and harass families who had southern connections.

Now, with the country at war, the Jayhawkers had become Union soldiers. Western Missouri had struck back by organizing small bands commanded by men such as "Bloody Bill" Anderson and the infamous William Quantrill. Thus, as the War between the North and the South continued to rage, Kansas and Missouri fought their own war—a merciless war dictated by years of violent hate.

Cole frowned testily. This wasn't the first time soldiers had come to the farm—they had been here once before, demanding William Quantrill's whereabouts. These soldiers had erroneously assumed that Cole's father was fighting with Quantrill's men. Cole and his mother had tried to convince them that he was a Confederate soldier riding with the Tennessee troops.

Now, standing in the distance, Cole couldn't make out the Jayhawkers too clearly. He could see, however, that they weren't the same ones who had harassed them once before.

Cole considered returning to the house, then discarded the notion, for he didn't think the four soldiers posed a threat. Also, certain his mother could handle the situation, he decided to go back to work.

Cole had been plowing only a few minutes when he heard his mother's sudden scream. He bolted quickly from the plow. As he ran toward the house, fear for his mother sent his heart hammering.

Another scream pierced the air, this one filled with stark terror. Cole ran even faster, but it seemed to him that he was living some kind of nightmare, for his legs felt as though they were made of lead, dragging him down. Panting heavily, his lungs exhausted, the boy pushed onward, his thoughts racing as speedily as his strong, young legs. Were the soldiers threatening his mother, perhaps even striking her? No! Her screams had been too horrifying for that! Cole's mother was a beautiful woman, and a possible reason behind her screams suddenly hit him with the force of a sledge hammer. God! If those bastards had dared to touch her, he'd kill them!

Cole was now driven by a crazed anger, and reaching the house, he bounded up the porch steps, shoved open the front door, and rushed inside.

A pistol wielded by an unseen attacker instantly slammed against Cole's head. Stars flashed before his eyes, his knees buckled, and he dropped limply to the floor. Losing consciousness, he sank into black oblivion.

A long time passed before Cole was able to open his eyes, grimacing against the pain throbbing in his head. He was still on the floor, and he made a feeble attempt to rise but was too groggy to manage the simple feat. Catching a movement out of the corner of his eye, he turned his head to the side, the motion costing him severe discomfort.

The sight confronting Cole was so horrible that for a moment, his mind refused to accept it. A soldier, his shirt ripped open, was standing over Cole's mother. She was lying on the bed, naked, her body drenched in blood. The man held a knife in his hand, its blade painted scarlet-red.

A low, guttural groan escaped Cole, causing the soldier to turn toward the sound. Lying flat on the floor, Cole couldn't see the man's face. His gaze was now leveled to the soldier's knees, but, slowly, the boy raised his eyes. He took in the tall Jayhawker's blue trousers, then the man's exposed chest. There, Cole's gaze froze. Three branded R's in the shape of a pyramid stood out blatantly on the stranger's flesh. It

11

was a shocking sight, and before Cole's eyes reached the soldier's face, his vision suddenly blurred and a cloak of darkness descended as, once again, Cole lost consciousness. Helplessly, he plunged into an endless void.

Cole awoke to the smell of smoke, but his mind was too muddled to react, and he lay motionless. First, he became aware of a hammering pain, and with effort he raised a hand and gingerly rubbed the bloody lump at the back of his head.

The air grew heavier with smoke, and suddenly regaining his senses, Cole sat up with a start. He was in the front yard. He got quickly to his feet, then his eyes darted to the hitching post. The soldiers were gone.

He turned swiftly to the house, and was alarmed to see smoke drifting thickly from the open windows. The damned Jayhawkers had torched his home!

With a powerful jolt, Cole's full memory returned, and, panic-stricken, he looked wildly about for his mother. When he didn't find her, he ran frantically toward the burning house. God, the bastards had left her inside!

The front door was closed, and, as he pushed it open, he was engulfed by black smoke. Dropping to his knees, placing himself below the suffocating fumes, he crawled across the threshold. Remaining close to the floor, he made his way to the bed, where he had last seen his mother. The smoke was so dense he could barely see, and his outstretched arms groped blindly.

He found her—she was still on the bed, a crumpled, blood-soaked quilt tossed over her body.

Cole had to stand up in order to lift her, causing the smoke to fill his nostrils and burn his throat. The hot fumes stung his eyes as he wrapped the cover securely about the woman, then picking her up, he crossed the room as quickly as possible.

Reaching the door, he stumbled onto the porch, down the steps, and to the front yard. Carrying his mother to the edge of the clearing, he laid her down carefully.

A shred of hope existed in Cole's heart that she would still be alive, but that hope dissolved as he gazed down into her lifeless face. A heartrending sob emerged from the boy's throat, and a flood of tears gushed from his eyes as he cradled his mother's body close to his chest.

By now, the log-constructed house had become a blazing inferno. Leaping flames burned their way through the roof and darted crazily toward the sky as fire raged through the windows. The wooden front door was suddenly ignited, burning like dry kindling.

Cole couldn't bear to watch the destruction, but the crackling of flames consuming his home echoed in his ears, the sound as dismal as his spirits. Grieving, his face turned away from the conflagration, the boy continued holding his mother's lifeless form.

The house had burned down to smoldering embers before Cole gently placed the woman on the ground, then drawing up the bloodstained quilt, he covered her body completely.

A cold, murderous rage filled Cole's heart as his thoughts turned to the man with the branded chest. The three marked R's in the shape of a pyramid were a positive identification. Solemnly, he swore he'd find this man who had raped and murdered his mother. He would not rest until this man, and the other three, had paid for their crime. They would pay with their lives, for Cole was determined to kill them. It was a determination he knew wouldn't lessen with time. He'd hunt them down if it took him a lifetime!

"Someday, I'll find that murdering bastard!" Cole uttered viciously. "I swear to God, I'll find him!"

Chapter One

"Kristina, wait a moment," Mary Johnson called to her daughter's maid.

Kristina Parker had crossed the spacious foyer and was starting up the marble staircase. Now, pausing, she saw Mrs. Johnson emerge from the parlor.

The woman approached Kristina with long but graceful strides. Though her looks were austere, she was elegantly attractive. Her auburn hair was arranged in a chignon, and her conservative gown fit her tall, slim frame flawlessly.

She handed Kristina a sealed envelope. "This came in the morning mail," she said tartly. "Give it to Samantha, please."

The woman's acrimonious tone didn't surprise Kristina—she knew the passing years hadn't mellowed Mary Johnson's hostility. The woman still bitterly resented Drake Carlson's letters, though they had just the opposite effect on Kristina.

The prized envelope in hand, Kristina climbed the spiral stairway. A bright gleam shone in her jade-green eyes, for Drake's letters always lifted her spirits.

Knowing Samantha would show no interest in her father's latest correspondence, Kristina walked past Samantha's room and headed for the servants' stairs at the end of the hall. Bounding lithely up the steps, she went to the third floor and to her own room.

She stepped to her bed, sat down, and anxiously opened the envelope. She drew out the one-page letter, and as she unfolded it, a few loose bills fell onto the bed. She looked at the money with puzzlement. Why was Drake sending Samantha cash? Her curiosity was racing, causing her to read the letter with haste. Finishing, she refolded the paper, then returned it and the bills to the envelope.

The sparkle had left Kristina's eyes, and they now reflected sympathy for Drake Carlson. Drake wanted his daughter to visit him, even going so far as to send her money for passage. Kristina knew Samantha wouldn't visit her father; she was going to Europe.

Kristina released a long sigh. Even if Samantha weren't leaving, she knew the young woman still wouldn't journey to Drake's ranch in Texas. His feelings meant nothing to Samantha.

Placing the envelope on the bedside table, Kristina rose. She passed through the meagerly furnished room, went to the open window, and gazed outside. She stared vacantly down at the quiet street that meandered through one of Philadelphia's most exclusive neighborhoods. She drew a small rocker up to the window and sat down. Leaning her head against the chair's high back, she began to rock gently.

Kristina wished fervently for the chance to visit Drake Carlson. She was anxious to meet the man and found the prospect of visiting a Texas ranch exciting. A tear escaped from the corner of her eye, but she promptly brushed it aside. She would probably never meet Drake Carlson, or see his ranch.

She wondered what the future held in store for her. *Well, my future certainly doesn't lie here in the Johnsons' home*, Kristina thought, determined to find a way to leave. She had no intention of remaining Samantha's maid and companion for the rest of her life.

While the Johnsons and Samantha were in Europe, Kristina had already decided to use the opportunity to find new employment—preferably a job that would take her westward and bring a taste of adventure and excitement into her life.

Kristina Parker had been a small child when her father had deserted his wife and daughter, leaving them destitute. Desperate to find employment, Mrs. Parker had found domestic, live-in work in the Johnsons' home. She and Kristina had shared a room in the servants' quarters.

The Johnsons' daughter, Samantha, was the same age as Kristina. Mrs. Parker, wanting her daughter to receive an education, boldly asked her employers if Kristina could join Samantha in her school lessons. The Johnsons, deciding that the obedient and diligent Kristina would be a good influence on their daughter, instructed Samantha's tutors to educate both girls. The couple's generosity continued, and when Samantha reached the age to attend a finishing school for young ladies, the Johnsons also enrolled Kristina.

Kristina was an astute, intelligent student and graduated at the top of her class. Samantha, however, barely made it through school with passing grades. Unlike Kristina, she had no interest in an education and considered studies a waste of time.

The girls, now young ladies, had been home from school for only a couple of months when Kristina's mother passed away, following a short illness. Mrs. Parker's death devastated Kristina, for she had loved her mother dearly.

The day after the funeral, Mrs. Johnson offered Kristina employment as Samantha's maid and companion. Having no place to go and no relatives to turn to for help, Kristina accepted.

Now, leaving the rocking chair, Kristina returned to the bed and picked up the envelope containing the money and Drake's letter. She knew she should go to Samantha and let her know about the letter, but postponing the task, she lay back across the bed and hugged the envelope to her bosom. For a few moments she'd press Drake's written words to her heart and pretend. . . . pretend that he was her father, and not Samantha's.

Malcolm Johnson was Samantha's stepfather. Her parents had been divorced when she was an infant. Although her estranged father had made no attempt to see her, he had nonetheless written to her for years. She had received her first letter from him when she was eight years old. Samantha, having no real interest in her father, and finding letter-writing tedious, had always asked Kristina to correspond with him and sign the letters "Samantha." In the beginning, Kristina complied simply as a favor. Soon, though, she was thoroughly enjoying receiving and answering Drake Carlson's letters. Through the man's written words, Kristina had found a substitute father for her. At first, she had felt guilty about writing Drake and signing the letters "Samantha." Letting the man believe he was corresponding with his daughter was terribly unfair. But Kristina buried her guilt, surrendered to her vivid imagination, and pretended that she was truly Carlson's daughter. As she grew from a child into a young woman, she still

18

adhered to her fantasylike dream. Her own father had deserted her—although Drake didn't know it, his daughter had deserted him. Through their letters, though, she and Drake had found each other.

She rose from the bed, slipped the envelope into her pocket, stepped to her vanity, and peered at her reflection. Picking up her brush, she began to run it vigorously through her curly ash-blond hair.

Kristina had always found the silky mass of curls annoying. Her constant attempts to style her hair into an orderly fashion always failed. Finally, deciding the obstinate locks had a will of their own, she put down the brush and gave up.

At the age of twenty-one, Kristina was exceptionally pretty, and her unruly blond tresses, cascading over her shoulders, were her crowning feature. Her heart-shaped face was enhanced with high, pronounced cheekbones and dark-green eyes shadowed by long, thick lashes. Her full lips were sultry, and she unknowingly presented a very sensual vision. Kristina was too modest though, to be aware of her own astounding sensuality and the breathtaking effect it had on men.

Moving away from the vanity, she left her room, descended the stairs, and went to Samantha's door. She knocked softly, and receiving permission to enter, she stepped inside.

Samantha was giving her elaborate quarters a last-minute check, making sure she and Kristina had packed everything she intended to take on her European tour.

"Did we forget anything?" Kristina asked.

"No, I don't think so." She gestured casually toward a stack of garments piled haphazardly on the bed. "Kristina, I've decided I don't want those. You can have them."

Kristina went to the bed and looked over the articles. "But, Samantha, most of these things are practically brand-new."

"I must make room in my closets for the wardrobe I'll bring back from Europe." She tossed her head haughtily. "Besides, I never especially cared for those clothes. They aren't my style." Her gaze swept over Kristina's slim form. "They'll look better on you. You're not as full-figured as I am."

Samantha stepped to the long mirror that hung between her two massive closets. Turning this way and that way, she studied herself closely. "Do you think I'm plump?" she asked Kristina.

"No," she answered truthfully.

Samantha's face screwed into a sullen pout. "I do envy you. You're so naturally slim." The young woman's envy, however, was short-lived, and still peering at her reflection, she said with a smile, "But men prefer women who are voluptuous."

A little amused, Kristina looked on as Samantha continued to study herself. Like Kristina, Samantha's hair was light in color, only it was golden-blond, whereas Kristina's was ash in hue. Both women had dark-green eyes framed by long lashes and arched brows, but there the resemblance ended. Samantha's oval face was full, and her cheeks were somewhat chubby, lending her cherubic charm. Although she was shorter than Kristina, her frame was more fully endowed.

Samantha turned away from the mirror. "Has Mother ordered the carriage yet?"

"I don't know," Kristina answered.

"Well, I'm sure she has. It's almost time to leave for the depot." Samantha and her parents were taking a train to New York, and from there, they would sail to Europe.

Samantha studied her companion thoughtfully for a moment, then asked, "Are your feelings hurt because you aren't going to Europe with us?"

"No, of course not," she replied, meaning it.

Samantha wasn't convinced. If she were Kristina, she would be absolutely crushed. Excusing her mother's decision to leave Kristina, she said hastily, "You know Mother doesn't want the problems of traveling with a large entourage. Father's valet and Dolly will be quite sufficient. Also, they are married and can share the same quarters." Dolly was Mrs. Johnson's personal maid. "Mother is certain that Dolly can tend to both of us."

"Believe me, I'm not upset," Kristina said patiently.

"Yes, but we'll be gone six months. What will you do with so much time on your hands?"

"I already told you that I plan to look for another position."

Samantha frowned irritably. "Honestly, Kristina! I can't believe you still plan to find a job that will take you out west, where you'll probably fall prey to savage Indians or wild animals."

"The West isn't as uncivilized as you might think."

Samantha seemed exasperated. "How do you plan to find this job?"

"I'm not sure, but I know there are several western towns in need of schoolteachers, and I'm well qualified."

"Surely you don't plan to send your qualifications to western newspapers?"

"Why not?" Samantha questioned archly.

"A lady doesn't publicly advertise herself!" Samantha eyed her companion reproachfully.

Kristina suppressed a smile, and let the subject

drop. She and Samantha were so different.

Slipping a hand into her pocket, Kristina withdrew Drake's letter. "This came in the morning mail. It's from your father."

Samantha waved it away as though it were of no importance. "I don't have time to read his letter."

"I already read it," Kristina told her. "He wants you to pay him a visit. He even sent money for the trip."

"I'm not going to Texas. I'm going to Europe! When you answer his letter, make up some excuse why I can't visit him, and send back the money."

Kristina agreed to do so.

A couple of knocks sounded on the door, followed by Dolly's voice, "Miss Samantha, your mother wants you to come downstairs. It's time to leave."

"I'll be right there," Samantha called. She turned to Kristina. "Now, remember, Father gave Raymond Lewis a key to the house, and he'll be overseeing things during our absence."

Kristina cringed inwardly. She loathed Raymond Lewis. He and his parents visited the Johnsons often. More than once, Raymond had caught her alone and made advances, but she had always managed to avoid his overtures and make a quick escape. A cold chill ran up her spine. She would now be alone in this huge house with only the butler and his wife. The coachman had his own quarters out back. The butler's wife was the cook, and she and her husband were getting on in years. Kristina was afraid that her elderly chaperones' presence might not deter Raymond Lewis, should he decide to compromise her.

The first time the young man had made advances, Kristina had gone to Mary Johnson and told her what had happened. But as the Johnsons and Lewises were good friends, and since Mary held

Raymond in high regard, she had subtly turned the unpleasant event completely around, making it seem as though Kristina was at fault. In a stern manner, she had informed her young employee that she had apparently tempted Raymond; innocently, perhaps, but that didn't make her less guilty. Henceforth, she must never say or do anything to entice Raymond, or any other man. Then, Mary Johnson had brusquely closed the subject, and she soon conveniently forgot the entire matter.

Thereafter, Kristina saw no reason to reveal Raymond's overtures. To do so would be futile, for the blame would surely fall on her.

"Well!" Samantha exclaimed, drawing Kristina from her troubled reverie. "I guess it's time to say good-bye. I wonder if you'll still be here when I return."

"Probably. Finding employment by mail will take a long time." She smiled warmly. "I'll walk you downstairs and wave good-bye from the front porch." As she followed Samantha to the door, she remembered to thank her for the lovely clothes.

A pert smile crossed Samantha's face, placing a deep dimple in her rosy cheeks. "Even wearing my cast-offs, you'll still be the best-dressed schoolmarm in the West!" she giggled.

Kristina found no humor in Samantha's thought-less remark. She hated accepting the woman's handouts, though she held her pride in check. She had been wholly dependent on the Johnsons since childhood, and such dependence galled her pride. She blamed her father for her impoverishment. The unfeeling scoundrel had abandoned his wife and daughter, leaving them penniless. She despised the man with a passion. She lifted her chin proudly. Soon she would find a new job and be totally independent. Then, even if it took her years, she'd pay back the Johnsons every cent they had spent on her education.

As Kristina followed Samantha into the hall, the young woman chattered gaily. "I'm so excited! I can hardly believe I'm actually going to Europe! Maybe a handsome Frenchman will fall madly in love with me. I've heard they are very debonair, and terribly romantic!"

As they were descending the spiral stairway, Kristina was unnerved to see Raymond Lewis poised at the bottom, watching her intently. Her steps faltered, and she gripped the banister so tightly that her knuckles whitened.

"Raymond!" Samantha declared cheerfully. "Did you come to see us off?"

"Yes, I did. I want to wish you a bon voyage."

Avoiding Raymond, Kristina brushed past him and stepped out to the front porch. She inhaled deeply in an effort to calm her shaken nerves. The mere sight of the man upset her terribly. Suddenly, sensing another's presence, she whirled about.

Raymond, standing close behind her, was grinning expansively.

She tried to move away, but his hand shot out and grasped her wrist, holding her firm. Boldly, his lust-filled gaze raked over her. His lewd scrutiny was making her feel physically ill. She was about to try to wrest free, but hearing the others coming outside, he released her. Then, wishing the travelers a safe and happy journey, and promising to keep an eye on Kristina, he left.

Raymond's brougham, equipped with driver, was waiting. As he stepped inside, and settled himself on the upholstered seat, a large smile was on his face. As the carriage moved away from the Johnsons' home,

24

his smile grew even larger. Raymond Lewis was not a handsome man, and the calculated grin spreading his wide mouth made him even less attractive.

His quick visit to the Johnsons had merely been a pretext. He true reason for stopping by was to secretly present the butler and his wife with choice tickets to tonight's opera. The couple had been thrilled. Raymond had asked them not to tell anyone that he had given them the tickets. He didn't want Kristina to know he was responsible, for she'd surely realize his reason for getting rid of the pair. Tonight, Kristina would be alone, and he had a key to the house. He'd simply let himself in, then the beautiful woman would be his for the taking.

Raymond Lewis desired Kristina so powerfully that she had become an obsession. He had no qualms about forcing himself on her, for if that was the only way he could have her, then, so be it! Tonight he'd enjoy her naked beauty to the fullest! By God, he'd relish every inch of her lovely body!

Chapter Two

Cole Barton had visited Austin on business numerous times, but as he left the sheriff's office, his thoughts turned to relaxing at Ramón's Cantina. Late-afternoon shadows were darkening the town as he untied his gray Appaloosa and walked the horse the short distance to the cantina, the loud music from inside drifting outdoors. A piano, accompanied by a guitar, played a toe-tapping melody.

The town was fairly crowded. Cole spotted several familiar faces, and a few men acknowledged him with congenial nods, some even waving an affable hello. They believed Cole was the kind of man one didn't approach without invitation. The men in town who weren't personally acquainted with Cole paused to watch as he moved slowly toward the cantina. Some recognized the well-known bounty hunter and they stared at him with awe. Others merely regarded him cautiously, for Cole exuded a somewhat threatening appearance. The women in town, impressed with his good looks, cast him admiring glances.

If Cole was aware that he was the center of attention, one couldn't tell by his indifferent manner. His tall, lithe frame was totally relaxed as he continued his unhurried trek to the noisy saloon. He was dressed in black, in a snug-fitting shirt that emphasized his strong shoulders, and trousers that clung tightly. A Peacemaker .45 was strapped about his hips, the holster's leather thong tied securely about one leg. Cole's hand brushed against the gun's ivory handle as though he were reassuring himself that it was there if he needed it. The Peacemaker was a popular weapon with law officers and gunmen across the West, for it could be modified for fast draws. Some were decorative, others plain, but all were lethal.

Cole wore a black, weather-worn hat, its wide brim shading his deep-blue eyes and covering his thick, sable-brown hair. He sported a well-trimmed mustache that tapered attractively to the corners of his lips. Cole Barton was indeed a striking figure of a man.

He chewed absently on one end of an unlit, partially smoked cheroot as he tied his horse in front of the saloon. Removing a match from his shirt pocket, he struck it and lit his smoke.

A shadow of a smile crossed his face as he suddenly recognized the palomino tied at the other end of the hitching rail. The horse's owner was a good friend, and anxious to see him, Cole went quickly inside the cantina.

The place was crowded, and as Cole nudged his way past the patrons, he caught sight of his friend sitting alone at a corner table.

Ramón, the proprietor, was tending bar, and Cole asked him for a bottle of his best whiskey and two glasses. The large Mexican knew Cole, and, happy to see him, he gave him his order and told him that it was on the house. Cole uttered a sincere thanks before picking up the bottle and glasses and heading across

28

the congested room.

His friend saw him coming, and pushing back his chair, Josh Chandler got to his feet. A bright smile curved his full lips and a twinkle shone in his brown eyes. He was a handsome man, and his tall, muscular frame was well-proportioned. He removed his hat to reveal wavy black hair, worn to collar length. Pitching the discarded hat onto an extra chair, he extended a hand to Cole. "When did you get to town?" Josh asked cheerfully.

Cole placed the whiskey bottle and glasses on the table, then shook his friend's hand. "I got here a short time ago. I stopped by the sheriff's office, but he didn't have any new work for me."

The man's disapproving scowl was imperceptible. Josh Chandler was opposed to his friend's profession. He had tried for years to convince Cole to give up bounty hunting, buy himself a ranch, and settle down.

As they sat down, Josh asked, "Were you going to leave town without visiting the ranch?"

"No, of course not. I planned to have a couple of drinks before riding out to your place. I wasn't expecting to find you in town."

"How long are you staying?"

"I have to leave in the morning."

"Have you seen Drake Carlson within the last few days?"

"No. Why do you ask?" Cole asked with interest, for he and Drake were close friends.

"I received a letter from him a short time back, and he said that if you showed up at my place, to tell you that he needs to see you."

"Is anything wrong?"

"Not that I know of. You'll go see him, won't you?"

"Sure, but first I have to go into Mexico on business. Tell Drake I'll see him as soon as I can," Cole said, putting out his cheroot. Regarding Josh closely, he asked, "How have you been? I haven't seen you in months."

"I'm fine," he was quick to answer. "Why wouldn't I be? Unlike you, I don't confront death on a daily basis."

Cole uncorked the bottle and filled the glasses. Josh's remark rankled him, but he held back a retort. He preferred to avoid an argument. He knew the man disapproved of his profession, but he also was aware that Chandler's opposition wasn't a threat to their friendship. Cole loved him like a brother, and his feelings were deeply rooted. It would take a lot more than a disagreement to alter his loyalty.

Handing Josh a glass, Cole asked, "Have you heard of a man named Sam Wilkes?"

"Not that I can recall. Is he your reason for going to Mexico?"

Cole nodded. "He was last seen headed for the border."

"What did he do?"

"He murdered three people, including a woman. I was in Albuquerque a few weeks ago, and the sheriff gave me the lowdown on him. He said he's heard talk that Wilkes has a scarred chest."

Josh scowled. "The odds that this man is the one who attacked your mother are too numerous to count." He took a big swig of his whiskey, then slammed the glass on the table. "Cole, when are you going to stop chasing ghosts? It's been sixteen years since your mother was killed. Sixteen long years! The men who attacked her are probably dead!"

Cole's response was calm. "Josh, we've had this same discussion more times than I care to remember.

It always ends the same . . ."

"With you getting your dander up," Josh completed, "and with me ultimately apologizing."

"Well?" Cole eyed him expectantly, a teasing note in his voice.

His companion smiled. "All right, I apologize. I'll refrain from sticking my nose into your business." But he couldn't help from adding, "At least for the present."

At that moment two skimpily clad señoritas descended the stairs leading from the second floor. The young prostitutes, who worked for Ramón, were very attractive, and their services contributed largely to their employer's thriving business.

The women had captured Cole's attention, and his blue eyes swept over their seductive curves. "I've been on the trail a long time," he said to Josh. "Before riding to your ranch, why don't we . . . ?" He let his meaning drift as he indicated the prostitutes with a slight nod of his head.

"You must've read my mind."

As Cole was motioning for the women to join them, Josh refilled his glass. His thoughts were safely hidden behind an inscrutable countenance, but seeing Cole Barton never failed to put him on edge, and it always took him a little time to adjust. As he lifted his glass to his lips, the slight trembling in his hand betrayed his outward composure.

The betrayal went unnoticed by Cole, for his concentration was solely on the two women. Josh drew a long, steadying breath, which put him back in full control.

Alone in Adela's room, Cole drew the pretty prostitute into his embrace. She eagerly lifted her lips

31

to his and kissed him fervently. The handsome gringo had her pulse racing with desire. She didn't often entertain a customer quite so good-looking, or so blatantly virile.

It had been weeks since Cole had enjoyed a woman, and his passion was quickly aroused. The pair were anxious to consummate their union, and they hastily shed their clothes and climbed into bed.

As Cole's lips branded Adela's in a heated exchange, his hand blazed a fiery path over her responsive flesh. She was soon writhing and asking him to take her completely.

He was more than ready to accommodate her, and their bodies came together passionately. Adela, her arms wrapped about her partner's neck, moaned with genuine ecstasy. Squirming in the throes of passion, she arched wildly beneath Cole's thrusting hips.

Later, as Cole was achieving fulfillment, Adela was cresting her own breathtaking apex. She usually faked a climax, but this one was for real, causing her to cry aloud with intense pleasure.

Cole gave her a gentle, lingering kiss, then moving to the edge of the bed, he reached for his discarded clothes. Lustful bouts with prostitutes always left him physically satisfied but emotionally distressed. Such encounters were a painful reminder that his life lacked a woman's true love. Deep within the recesses of his heart, he longed for a wife and children, but there was no place in his life for a family. His vow to find his mother's killers still ruled his very existence. Visions of his mother's death haunted him with such clarity that he could remember it as though it had happened yesterday. The sixteen intervening years hadn't dimmed his memory—or his determination to kill the man with the branded chest.

Meanwhile, down the hall, Carlota's large brown eyes were glazed with satisfaction as she watched Josh leave her bed to slip into his trousers. The young woman had bedded Chandler several times before, and she always enjoyed their times together, for he was a gentle, considerate lover. Also, he never failed to treat her courteously. In her profession, such gentlemanly behavior was rare indeed. Furthermore, Josh Chandler was exceptionally handsome, and the woman in her invariably responded to his ardent caresses. Yes, he was perfect, except for one annoying quirk: the man refused to remove all his clothes. It bothered Carlota to make love to Josh and have a piece of clothing between them. Regardless of her entreaties, he always insisted on wearing his shirt. When she first questioned him about it, he told her that during the war he had suffered a severe chest wound. It didn't heal correctly and had left an ugly scar, one so ghastly that he didn't want her to see it.

Now, leaving the bed, Carlota stepped to the water basin, and sponged herself thoroughly. It was growing late, and she needed to get back downstairs and solicit another customer. Ramón didn't like it when she spent too much time with one man. "Time is money, Carlota!" he always said.

Dressed, Josh went to the door, opened it, then looked back at Carlota. She was still naked, and, for a moment, he gazed admiringly at her silky flesh. "I'll be in town next week. I'll see you then."

"I hope so, Señor Chandler. You are a wonderful lover."

"So are you."

"*Gracias, señor.*" She smiled sincerely.

As Chandler stepped into the hall, Barton was leaving Adela's room.

"We'd better get out to the ranch," Josh said.

"Rosa is expecting me for dinner, and if I'm late, all hell will break loose."

Cole grinned. Rosa, Josh's housekeeper and cook, reigned with a firm hand. Not even Chandler was beyond her reproach.

"I hope she cooked enough for two," Cole remarked. "I'm as hungry as a bear."

"You know Rosa, she always cooks extra."

The men had started toward the stairs when Josh remembered that he had left his hat in Carlota's room. He told Cole he'd meet him downstairs.

Barton descended the steps quickly and went to the bar for one last drink. The saloon was crowded now, and he didn't notice the three men loitering close to the entrance. They, however, were very aware of him.

The Caldwell brothers had been looking for Cole Barton for several weeks, and their search had finally brought them to Austin. They watched as their intended victim downed a shot of whiskey. They advanced stealthily, surprised that killing Barton was going to be so easy.

Cole had acquired an uncanny ability to sense danger, and as the Caldwells approached, a chill prickled the back of his neck. He whirled about, ready to draw his revolver, but was dissuaded by three pistols aimed at him.

Meanwhile, the customers standing close to Cole had scurried to the far end of the bar. The other patrons, realizing trouble was about to erupt, watched raptly as silence descended over the cantina.

"Do you remember me, Barton?" the oldest Caldwell uttered gruffly.

"I never forget an ugly face. You were at your brother's trial. That was weeks ago. It was in . . . in . . . ?" Cole played for time. Where the hell was

Josh? If he didn't show up soon, Cole knew he'd be eating the Caldwells' bullets for dinner instead of Rosa's cooking. "Now I remember, it was in Tucson."

"You're damned right it was Tucson! After Johnny was convicted, I told you that I'd hunt you down and kill you." A vicious gleam radiated in his cold eyes. "You bastard, you're the one who caught my little brother and turned him over to the sheriff. Now, my other brothers and me are gonna send you to hell! If it wasn't for you, Johnny would still be alive. But 'cause of you, he got hung!"

"He deserved it. He raped and killed a fifteen-year-old girl."

The saloon was deathly quiet as everyone stared at the three brothers holding Barton at gunpoint. One customer tried to leave so he could fetch the sheriff, but one of the Caldwells told him to stay put.

"Hurry up, Frank," a brother said anxiously. "Let's kill this son of a bitch, then get the hell out of here 'fore the sheriff shows up!"

Frank wasn't overly concerned about the sheriff. If necessary, he and his brothers could shoot their way out of town.

By now, Josh had started down the stairs, but the ominous silence confronting him gave him good reason to pause. A Colt revolver was strapped to his hip, and he drew it before cautiously moving farther down the steps. He could hear Frank's deep voice.

"Barton, you're gonna die."

Moving incredibly fast, Josh leapt the remaining steps and opened fire, eliminating one Caldwell. Frank froze, but only for a fleeting moment. It nonetheless gave Cole time to draw his gun as he dove to the floor, barely escaping the bullet Frank fired in his direction. The man didn't have time to shoot again, for Cole killed him with one accurate shot. The third brother, surrendering, threw down his gun and held up his hands.

As Cole got to his feet, Josh hurried over, "Are you all right?" he asked.

"I'm fine," he answered, then added with a grin, "It took you long enough. I was beginning to think you'd decided to go another round with Carlota."

"I considered it," Josh replied lightly. He gestured toward the two dead bodies and the man left alive. "Who are these bastards?"

"The Caldwells. I collected a bounty on their brother. The law hung him for rape and murder. His victim was fifteen years old."

Sheriff Canton had heard the gunshots, and as he barged inside, the saloon was buzzing with voices. The customers, all speaking at the same time, were moving in closer to gawk at the dead Caldwells.

"Barton!" the sheriff grumbled. He was a burly man in his late forties. "I suppose you're involved in this."

The lawman's tone didn't anger Cole. He liked and respected Canton. "It was self-defense, Sheriff."

Ramón and the majority of his customers were quick to verify Cole's claim.

"Who are they?" the sheriff asked.

Cole identified the Caldwells and their reason for coming after him.

Canton sighed heavily. "Barton, when are you leaving?"

"In the morning."

"Good," he responded. "Trouble follows you as close as your own shadow. There's always someone gunnin' for you. In the morning, before you leave, stop by my office so you can sign a statement. Did you kill both of 'em?"

"I got one of them," Josh told him.

"Then you'll have to sign a statement, too. I'll see you both in the morning." He looked at Cole. "Now, will you please go away before someone else gets killed?" There was no anger in his voice, for he sincerely liked Cole.

Cole obliged readily, and he and Josh left Ramón's, eager to sit down to Rosa's cooking.

Chapter Three

Kristina sat alone in the Johnsons' parlor, the clothes Samantha had given her stacked neatly at her feet. She opened her sewing basket and removed a needle and a spool of thread which matched the shade of the dress she planned to alter first. Samantha's old garments had to be taken in and the hems lowered to accommodate for Kristina's slimmer, taller frame.

The butler and his wife had already left for the opera, and the huge house was unusually quiet. Kristina was finding the stark silence a trifle unnerving. Deciding the sound of her own voice was better than total silence, she began to sing one of her favorite melodies. She failed to hear the front door open, then close softly.

Raymond Lewis, moving furtively across the foyer, slipped the house key into his pocket. Following the sound of Kristina's voice, he crept toward the parlor. Reaching the threshold, he paused, his presence still undetected. For a long moment he adored Kristina with his eyes as his mind envisioned the lustful pleasure awaiting him. This sensuous, beautiful woman would soon be his to do with as he pleased.

Suddenly, Kristina sensed that she wasn't alone. Her singing stopped abruptly, and fear rose within her. She turned her head sharply, and glancing over her shoulder, she saw Raymond coming toward her. She leapt to her feet, and the dress she'd been altering fell soundlessly onto the carpet.

"What do you want?" she gasped.

"You know what I want," he uttered. A lewd gleam shone in his small, close-set eyes.

Every nerve in her body leaped and shuddered. "Stay away from me or I'll . . . I'll—"

"You'll what?" he taunted. He came closer.

"I want you to leave at once!" she ordered harshly. "If you don't, I'll scream so loudly that the coachman will hear. His quarters are directly out back."

Raymond's smile resembled a sneer. "This is Friday, and I know he visits his favorite barroom on Friday nights. Scream all you want, my beauty, no one will hear you."

His words hit Kristina with a terrible force. The coachman was gone, and the neighboring houses were spaced so far apart that her screams would go unheard. Although she had feared that Raymond might try to compromise her, she hadn't believed he'd stoop to rape. Terror coursed through her. She was alone, defenseless, and totally at this evil man's mercy!

She turned to flee, but Raymond lurched forward and grasped her arm, jerking her into his imprisoning embrace. She fought wildly, but her struggles were futile against his superior strength.

His mouth, wet and demanding, pressed against her lips, and his vile kiss turned her stomach. Somehow, she managed to draw her lips away from his. She gagged, and, for a moment, she thought she

40

might actually become ill.

She was still crushed against his chest, and his mouth again swooped down on hers, his kiss painfully brutal. Kristina was determined to fight, and she tried desperately to squirm out of his confining arms. A demonic chuckle sounded deep in Raymond's throat as he wrestled her to the floor, while Kristina pounded her fists against his chest and shoulders.

He grasped the bodice of her dress, ripping the material down to her waist. Then clutching her thin chemise, he tore at it ruthlessly until her breasts were exposed. His eyes widened as he ogled her naked bosom. His hand cupped a breast as his tongue flickered over the nipple.

"No! No!" Kristina cried, repulsed. The fight hadn't gone out of her, and grasping a handful of his hair, she jerked his head upward and away from her breasts.

Lewis was anxious to take her completely, and impatient with her relentless struggles, he growled, "Stop fighting me, bitch! If you don't lay still, I'm going to knock you senseless!" To prove his point, he slapped her soundly. The solid blow sent a ringing through her ears and left her temporarily dazed.

Hopeful that she would now submit, Raymond groped for her skirt and began shoving the long folds, along with her petticoat, up to her waist. As he was reaching for her final undergarment, Kristina's senses returned and she began fighting him frantically.

Carrying out his threat, Raymond's large fist plowed into her fragile face, his hard knuckles cutting her bottom lip. Blood gushed, then flowed down her chin in a steady stream.

Still, Kristina refused to surrender, and bringing

41

up a knee, she jabbed it strongly into his groin. The excruciating pain that ensued shot through him like a thunderbolt.

He grew limp, motionless, and taking advantage of the moment, Kristina pushed him aside and scrambled to her feet. She ran through the foyer to the front door, flung it open, and was about to escape, when she felt Raymond's hand grab her hair. Entangling his fingers into her long tresses, he suddenly jerked her head back so roughly that she cried out with shock as well as pain.

He shoved her back into the parlor. Losing her balance, Kristina collided with the small table that held her sewing basket. As she fell to the floor, her arm knocked over the basket, and its contents scattered in various directions, the scissors landing close to her side.

Raymond's body was suddenly on hers, pinning her to the floor. "I'm going to beat the hell out of you!" he yelled viciously. "I'll teach you to be so damned insolent! After I have you properly humbled, you'll be humping me like a whore! You uppity, low-class bitch! You know you want it as much as I do!"

Kristina was beyond rational thought, and it was instinct that guided her hand to the nearby scissors. As Raymond raised up to his knees, his arm drawn back to deliver a vicious blow, Kristina grabbed the scissors and jabbed the sharp blades into her attacker's shoulder.

The shears remained buried in Raymond's flesh, as he released a beastly howl, the guttural wail sounding inhuman. Kristina, frozen with terror, watched as he withdrew the scissors from his shoulder. Blood spewed from the gaping hole, flooding his white shirt and turning it scarlet-red.

Thoughts of rape had flown from Raymond's mind, replaced with murderous ones. He'd kill this bitch! A rage filled the depths of his evil being, and a demented gleam came to his eyes.

Kristina knew he was going to kill her; she could read her fate in his bloodthirsty gaze. Fear struck her numb, and she lay as though paralyzed.

Raymond snarled vindictively as he raised the scissors. He was about to plunge the bloodstained blades into his victim's heart when, suddenly, a man's voice called out.

"Kristina . . . Kristina?"

For a second, Raymond froze. Then, throwing down the scissors, he jumped to his feet. Holding a hand to his wounded shoulder, he brushed past the coachman who had rushed into the parlor. Stumbling from the room, Raymond looked over his shoulder, his crazed eyes meeting Kristina's frightened ones. "I'll have you arrested for attempted murder! You'll spend the rest of your life in prison! That's no threat, bitch, that's a promise!"

With that, he staggered across the foyer and out the front door.

The coachman started after him, but concern for Kristina drove him back into the parlor. She was gathering her torn dress about her naked breasts as he came to her side. Carefully, he helped her off the floor.

"Ted!" she cried shakily. "Thank God you showed up when you did!"

"I wasn't feeling well, so I decided to come home early. The front door was standing open, and I thought something might be wrong."

"I almost escaped," she explained, her voice weak, rasping. "I had just opened the door when he caught me. Apparently, he forgot to close it . . . thank God!"

A sudden wave of dizziness washed over her, and she stumbled to the chair and sat down.

Kneeling at her feet, Ted asked, "Did Lewis . . . did he . . . ?" He didn't know how to put it delicately.

"No," she replied. "He didn't, but he was going to, and when I stabbed him with the scissors, he decided instead to kill me." A violent shudder coursed through her.

"I'll break that son of a bitch apart with my bare hands!" Ted raged, standing upright.

"No! Please! Don't become involved! Ted, if you harm him, you'll go to prison! Raymond and his family are important people in this town. The law won't care if you had just cause to attack him!"

Kristina watched Ted closely, hoping he'd succumb to reason. He was a huge man, and she didn't doubt that he could tear Raymond apart.

He didn't speak for a moment as he studied her battered face. Then he said quietly, "Why don't you tend to your injuries while I fix you a cup of hot tea? Then we need to talk."

"Talk?" she repeated blankly.

"We have to find a way to get you out of town. Lewis will most likely go to the doctor before going to the police and insisting on your arrest. So we probably have a little time. But you've got to leave town tonight."

"But where can I go?" she questioned, her eyes staring into his.

"I don't know, but I'll think of someplace where you'll be safe. Go on, clean up. While I fix your tea, I'll come up with a plan."

She hurried from the parlor and up the stairs to the servants' floor. As she rushed into her room, the full impact of tonight's violence hit her forcefully. Her whole body trembled as though a chilling wind had

44

seeped into her very soul. She moaned, falling across the bed, and released some of her tension through a flood of tears.

After a moment, her common sense intruded, reminding her that she didn't have time for tears. She must hurry back downstairs. Ted was right—if she didn't leave town, she'd find herself in jail. The Lewises were a prominent Philadelphian family, and they had a lot of influence. To make matters worse, Raymond's uncle was a judge. If she were to stand trial, she'd have no chance against Raymond. The court wouldn't believe her side of the story or Ted's, but would take Raymond's word over theirs.

Leaving the bed, Kristina filled the basin and washed her face, carefully cleaning her bruised lip. Then she removed her torn gown and put on another one.

Her movements quick, precise, she left the room and sped down the narrow hall. As she descended the stairs, she thanked God for Ted Cummings. She was profoundly grateful for his help.

Ted had come to work for the Johnsons six months ago. Although he was hired primarily as a coachman, he also worked as the Johnsons' gardener and handyman.

Kristina had taken an immediate liking to the man, for she thought him gentle and kind. Although he was twenty years her senior, a warm friendship had quickly developed between the two, which led Kristina to confide in him. He was an avid, sympathetic listener, and she had even talked to him about her father, admitting that she despised the man for deserting her and her mother. She had also spoken to Ted about Drake Carlson, letting him know that she always answered the man's letters as though she were Samantha. She even confessed that

45

she wished Drake Carlson was truly her father.

In the kitchen, Ted had finished preparing Kristina's tea. He was seated at the table, waiting for her to join him. His expression was filled with rage, and he barely had his temper under control. His large hands, knotted into fists, were itching to wrap themselves around Raymond's neck. Ted was exceptionally strong, and he knew he could break the horny bastard's neck with one quick snap.

He drew a calming breath. He'd get his revenge on Lewis, but he'd have to wait for the right time. Now he must concentrate on helping Kristina.

Tears glistened in his eyes as his thoughts centered on Kristina. He wished he had the right to take her into his arms and hold her close, but he had forfeited that privilege years ago. On the day that he had abandoned Kristina and her mother, he had given up all claim on his daughter.

After years of wandering and searching his heart, Ted had returned to Philadelphia with hopes of finding his family and somehow making amends. He made inquiries in the neighborhood where they had once lived and learned that his wife had gone to work for the Johnsons. He also learned of her death. Ted had gone to the Johnsons' home under the pretext of looking for work—he had really hoped to catch a glimpse of his daughter. He was sure she wouldn't recognize him. She had been only four years old when he had left. Furthermore, the years had drastically altered his appearance. His hair, which used to be thick, was now thin and had receded, and he had gained weight.

Ted hadn't expected the Johnsons to hire him as a coachman, but needing employment, he accepted the job readily. He had been at his new job two days before seeing Kristina. As he had figured, she didn't recognize him. His real name was Theodore, which had prompted him to use the nickname Ted—Cummings had been picked at random.

As the weeks passed, he and Kristina began to build a warm relationship. Bolstered by their intimacy, he seriously considered revealing his true identity. It was at this time, however, that Kristina admitted to him how deeply she despised her father. He was then reluctant to tell her the truth, for he'd rather she loved him as a friend than hate him as a father.

Now, as the kitchen door opened, Ted glanced up quickly. As Kristina entered, he drew out a chair and asked her to sit down.

"Drink your tea," he ordered gently.

Lifting the cup, she took a tentative sip, but the hot liquid burned her cut lip. She set the cup back on the table. "I'll wait until it cools," she murmured.

"Kristina, you need to pack your things," he began briskly, for a plan was quickly forming. "I'll hitch up the carriage and drive you to the next town. From there, you can take a train."

"Take a train to where?"

"San Antonio."

"What?" she gasped.

"Drake Carlson's ranch is outside San Antonio, isn't it?"

"Yes," she replied.

"You've been writing to him for years. You know he's a good man. I'm sure he'll let you stay with him."

"I haven't been writing to him as Kristina, though, but as Samantha."

"When you see him, tell him the truth. If he's the kind of person you've led me to believe he is, then he'll understand."

"Maybe," she said lamely.

47

"Kristina, you must leave Philadelphia. Carlson's ranch is the most logical place for you to go." He arched a brow, favoring her with a tender smile. "Besides, you told me you've always wanted to go westward. Here's your chance. Once there, you can look for a job teaching school. I have a little money put away. I don't think it's enough to pay for your passage but—"

"I have money for the journey," she interrupted. "This morning, Samantha received a letter from Drake. He wants her to come visit him, and he sent money for the trip. I can use it, then pay him back when I find a job."

"Good!" Ted exclaimed. "Now, drink down that tea, then get packed. I'll get the carriage."

"But why are you taking me to another town? Why don't you take me to the train station here?"

"You might have to wait awhile for a train. Lewis will go to the police, and when they don't find you here, they'll check the station."

The fear of being arrested propelled her into action. She gulped her tea down, then bounding from her chair, said quickly, "I'll pack quickly and be ready to leave within the hour—if not sooner!" She rushed out of the kitchen.

Ted stood and headed for the carriage house. The rage he had managed to suppress surfaced again, a murderous scowl on his face. He would bide his time, then, when the right moment arose, he'd kill Raymond Lewis for attacking his daughter!

Kristina went straight to the parlor, and quickly put the spilled contents back into the sewing basket, except for the scissors. She couldn't bear to look at them. She had an extra pair in her room to take their place. She then gathered up her dresses, along with the basket, and hurried upstairs.

As she began to pack, her thoughts raced speedily. She could hardly believe that she was going to San Antonio. She would see Drake Carlson! At long last, she'd meet the man face-to-face. She hoped he wouldn't be too angry when he learned that she had been the one writing to him all these years.

Kristina was almost done packing when she heard a knock on her door. "Are you ready?" Ted called.

"Come in," she said. "I'm about finished."

She put the last article into the suitcase, then Ted closed and fastened it.

"When you learn your schedule . . ." Ted began, "you should send a wire to Drake, letting him know when you'll arrive. It'll make matters simpler if you sign it 'Samantha.' You can explain everything when you see him."

Kristina agreed. She stepped to her vanity, opened a drawer, and withdrew Drake's latest letter. The money was still inside the envelope, and she slipped it into her purse. Then, turning to Ted, she said with a calmness she didn't truly feel, "Well, I'm ready to go."

"I'm gonna miss you," he murmured, meaning it more sincerely than Kristina could imagine.

She moved to stand before him. Gazing warmly into his dark-green eyes, she replied softly, "I'll miss you, too. Ted, I don't know how to thank you."

"There's no need," he replied.

Tiptoeing, she reached up and kissed his cheek. His arms went about her, drawing her close. He hugged her tightly for a moment, then released her with reluctance. He wondered despairingly if he'd ever hold his daughter again. Knowing time was critical, he grabbed her suitcase and said tersely, "Let's go."

She followed him out of the house through the rear

49

entrance, to the waiting carriage. Ted placed her suitcase in the carriage, then helped her in before he climbed quickly onto the driver's seat and laid the reins against the pair of horses.

As they rode down the pebbled path, then past the house, Kristina gazed out the carriage window. She watched the Johnson mansion fade from view, then disappear into the dark night. She had lived there for seventeen years, but leaving the house that had never been her home did not depress her.

She wondered what the days to come had in store for her. She didn't know what lay ahead, but she knew what she was leaving behind—a prison sentence!

Chapter Four

Cole had spent days in Mexico looking for Sam Wilkes. When the quest proved futile, he decided the man hadn't crossed the border after all. He intended to resume his search, but first he'd make the promised visit to Drake Carlson. Crossing the Rio Grande, he headed toward San Antonio.

He was curious about Drake's reason for wanting to see him but wasn't overly concerned. If anything was seriously wrong, Drake would have said so in his letter to Josh.

Carlson's ranch, the Diamond-C, was located five miles north of San Antonio. It was a colossal spread, its grass-covered range covered with cattle. As Cole rode across Carlson's extensive holdings, the cowhands recognized him and called out greetings.

Cole's search in Mexico and his journey to the Diamond-C had been tiring, and when the ranchhouse came into view, it was a welcome sight. As he rode up to the house, the sun was dipping into the west, casting long shadows across the pastoral landscape. The two-story Colonial house sat majestically atop a small hill, overlooking the corrals, the barn, and the large bunkhouse.

Cole dismounted and turned his horse over to a waiting stablehand, then ambled up the wide front steps and knocked on the door.

He was admitted by Drake's butler, an elderly black servant named Joseph. A large grin crossed the servant's face. "Mista Cole, come in. Mista Drake's gonna be mighty happy to see you. He's been a-wonderin' when you was gonna show up." Joseph took Cole's hat, then said, "Mista Drake's in the study."

Cole went to the study and rapped softly on the closed door.

"Come in," Drake called.

Carlson was sitting at his desk, going over his ledgers. The books had his full attention, and his guest was halfway across the room before he glanced up.

"Cole!" Drake exclaimed, beaming. He moved to his friend and shook his hand vigorously.

Following warm amenities, Drake poured two brandies and handed one to Cole. Returning to his chair, he gestured for his guest to sit down.

Taking the chair facing the desk, Cole said, "Josh said you wanted to see me. Is anything wrong?"

"No, quite the opposite. Things couldn't be better." He explained quickly. "I wrote Samantha and asked her to come for a visit. I even sent her money for the trip. I wanted you to know because I'm anxious for you two to meet each other."

"Do you think she'll pay you a visit?"

He smiled expansively. "I received a wire from Samantha. She'll be in San Antonio tomorrow. She's arriving on the afternoon stage."

"I'm real happy for you, Drake," Cole replied, sounding less emotional than he felt. But a slight tension had come over him. Samantha! After all these years, he was finally going to meet her. He wondered why it made him so apprehensive.

"I thought you'd express a little more enthusiasm," Drake remarked, clearly reproachful. "You've waited a long time to meet Samantha." A framed photograph was on his desk, and he turned it around so that it faced Cole. It was a picture of Kristina, taken two years ago. When Drake had written, insisting on a picture, Kristina had sent him one of herself in lieu of Samantha's.

Cole's blue eyes softened with admiration as he studied the picture. He had seen it several times, but the young woman's image never failed to move him. Her face was enchanting, but he was taken with more than her beauty. There was a sadness in her eyes that touched a tender chord deep within his heart. Her sadness totally mystified him, for she was beautiful, young, and had everything money could buy.

"Cole . . ." Drake began. "I've seen the way you study this picture. You look at my daughter the way a man looks at the woman he loves."

"That's ridiculous," he scoffed. "How can I be in love with a woman I don't know?"

"But you do know her. You've read every letter she's written to me."

Cole was willing to agree, up to a point. "Knowing her through letters, and knowing her personally isn't quite the same thing."

Drake waved aside his reasoning. "She knows you, too, Cole. I've written to her about you time and time again." He took a large swallow of brandy. "It's always been my dream that you and Samantha would fall in love, get married, and fill this house with my grandchildren."

"Drake, I didn't know you had such an imagination." Cole spoke lightly, but he had a feeling that

Carlson was totally serious.

"Drink up," Drake said, "and I'll refill our glasses."

Cole quaffed down his brandy. He watched as Carlson went to the liquor cabinet to pour the drinks. Drake was fifty-three years old, but his build was still strong and solid. Cole was used to the man moving energetically, but as he returned with their brandies, his steps were somewhat sluggish.

"Are you all right?" Cole asked, accepting his drink.

Drake moved around the desk and sat back down before answering. "I've been having some chest pains."

"Are you in pain now?"

"A little, but it'll pass. It always does." He sounded unconcerned.

"Have you seen Dr. Newman?"

"No, not yet."

Cole was worried. "I think you'd better see him as soon as possible."

"I'll be in town tomorrow to meet the stage. I'll go in early and stop by the doc's office. You're coming to town with me, aren't you? I'd like you to be there when Samantha arrives."

"You're damned right I'm going with you. I'm gonna make sure you see Dr. Newman."

Drake got to his feet. "I'll go tell Autumn Moon to prepare your room."

"How is Autumn Moon?"

"She's fine. The woman amazes me. While I grow older, she grows more beautiful."

Drake left the study to find Autumn Moon, the full-blooded Comanche who had been Drake's housekeeper for over twenty years, and the woman he loved.

54

Cole's eyes returned to Kristina's picture as he pondered Carlson's observation. Did he really look at this picture like a man in love? He shrugged off the possibility. The idea was absurd. He wasn't in love with Drake's daughter—somewhat infatuated, perhaps, but nothing more. When he fell in love with a woman, she'd be flesh and blood, not just a pretty face in a picture.

He reached over and picked up the framed photograph. For a long moment he gazed thoughtfully at Kristina's lovely features. His attention was soon drawn to the note of sadness in her eyes. "Samantha Carlson . . ." he whispered. "Why does your image always linger in my mind? And why do your beautiful, sad eyes torture me so?" He set the picture back on the desk.

Clearing his thoughts of Drake's daughter, he sipped on his brandy and concentrated on Sam Wilkes. The man frequented New Mexico, and Cole decided to search for him there. He'd cut short his visit with Drake, then head out for New Mexico.

The study door opened. Entering, Drake said, "Autumn Moon is preparing your room. When she's finished, I'm sure you'll want to bathe before dinner."

"That sounds great. I'm coated with dust." Cole had his own room at Carlson's home, complete with wardrobe. Because of his work as a bounty hunter, always on the move, Cole didn't have a permanent residence, and since he always traveled lightly, he kept most of his possessions at the Diamond-C.

Drake stepped to his desk and picked up the photograph. He looked at it for a moment, then said to Cole, "You know, I'm a little nervous about seeing Samantha. I've waited such a long time." He grimaced, but Cole sensed it was from pain, not nerves.

He stood and grasped Drake's arm. "What's wrong?"

The discomfort passed. "Nothing—probably just a touch of indigestion."

Cole frowned in concern, more determined than ever to personally deliver Drake to Dr. Newman's office.

The inn was overheated and stuffy, and the smells of dinner lingered heavily in the cramped quarters. Kristina, badly needing a breath of fresh air, stepped outside.

A gentle breeze was stirring, and she welcomed its cooling caress as she walked across the front porch and down the steps. Strolling leisurely, she moved to the corral, and resting her arms on the fence, she watched the horses. The stagecoach stood close by. Tomorrow it would take her and its other passengers to San Antonio.

Kristina released a long, weary sigh. The exhausting journey from Philadelphia had seemed to take forever. For the most part she had traveled by train, but the final leg of her journey was to be completed by stage.

She turned away from the corraled horses and glanced back at the inn. The log-constructed building sat alone on the vast Texas plains. It not only offered room and board to travelers but was also used as a relay station where the stage's tired team was relieved by a fresh one.

The inn's front door was creaked open, and Kristina watched closely as a man crossed the porch, then sauntered in her direction. The night was well lit by a full moon, and she recognized him as a fellow traveler. He had been at the inn when her stage arrived. During dinner, he mentioned that he'd been on his way to San Antonio when his horse had stumbled badly and broken a leg. The man had been forced to destroy the animal. Then, lugging his saddle and other belongings, he had trekked to the inn.

"Evenin', ma'am," he drawled politely as he drew near. "I came outside to have a smoke." He reached into his pocket and withdrew a cigar. "Do you mind?"

"No, I don't mind," she replied. Preferring not to be alone with a strange man, she moved to leave.

"Don't go," he said quickly. "I didn't mean to scare you off."

He was young, not much older than herself. He certainly didn't seem threatening, so she decided to stay a little longer. She wasn't sleepy, and the night air was indeed refreshing.

He lit his cigar, then said, "My name's Billy Stockton."

She knew he was waiting for her to return the courtesy and introduce herself. Because she was traveling under Samantha's name, she replied, "I'm Samantha Carlson."

"Carlson?" he repeated. "You wouldn't be kin to Drake Carlson, would you?"

She swallowed heavily, then forced out the lie. "Yes, he's my father."

Billy was obviously amazed. "I heard that Mr. Carlson had a daughter living in the East."

"I'm from Philadelphia," she murmured. "Do you know my father well?"

"No, not really. I used to work for your pa. But I got tired of bein' a cowhand and moved on. I tried my luck at bounty huntin', but I failed miserably. So, here I am returnin' to San Antonio. I'm hopin' Mr. Carlson will give me back my job." He smiled broadly. "Your pa's a fair man and a good boss. I should never have left." He took a long drag from his smoke, then asked, "Is this your first visit to the Diamond-C?"

"Yes, it is. I'm anxious to see the ranch. I've heard so much about it through Dra—through Father's letters." She studied Billy somewhat inquisitively. "Why in the world did you decide to become a bounty hunter?" To Kristina, he seemed entirely too young and unintimidating for such work.

"Cole Barton's a bounty hunter, and is a good friend of your pa's. When I worked at the Diamond-C, Cole visited Carlson a lot, and I really did admire him. I guess I was hopin' to be as good a bounty hunter as he is. But I almost got myself killed more than once. That's when I decided to quit and return to bein' a cowhand."

"Father's written to me about Cole Barton and his line of work." There was a disapproving edge to her voice.

"Cole ain't your ordinary run-of-the-mill bounty hunter. Unlike most of 'em, he's real choosy 'bout who he goes after. Most bounty hunters chase a man strictly for the reward. They don't care what kind of crime he committed. But Cole only tracks vicious killers. There's no man I admire more than Cole Barton. I like him a lot, and he's always been real nice to me. But Cole ain't no man to cross. There's a coldness in those blue eyes of his that can chill a man to the bone."

"He sounds ruthless."

"No, ma'am. He ain't ruthless. He just ain't the kind of man other men cross, not if they value their lives."

Kristina wasn't convinced. Cole Barton still sounded ruthless to her. She thrust him from her thoughts. Though Drake mentioned him frequently, she probably wouldn't come into contact with him during her brief stay at the Diamond-C. Kristina had decided on a short visit, for she planned to be completely honest with Drake right from the start, then find a job teaching school. More than likely, her future job wouldn't be in San Antonio but in some remote western town in dire need of a schoolmarm.

"Well, it's getting late," Kristina murmured. "It was nice meeting you, Mr. Stockton."

"Good night, Miss Carlson." He touched his hat's tattered brim.

She smiled warmly, then headed back to the inn. Tomorrow she would reach San Antonio! The thought sent her heart pounding. Although she was anxious to meet Drake, she dreaded telling him the truth. Learning she wasn't his daughter but his daughter's maid would undoubtedly upset him. She hoped he wouldn't be too angry. Alone in this vast wilderness, she was wholly dependent on Carlson's compassion. If he refused to help her, what would she do? The possibility was too terrifying to even consider. She forced the thought from her mind, telling herself she'd cross that bridge when, or if, the time came.

Since she was the only female passenger, she had a room to herself, furnished with a large double bed. Undressing, she extinguished the lamp and slipped between the cool sheets. Her window was open, its drawn curtain allowing the full moon to cast a soft, golden glow over the room.

Kristina tried to put her fears and uncertainties to rest, but they refused to go away. Troubled, her thoughts in a turmoil, she tossed and turned restlessly. Despite her serene surroundings, she could foresee a long, sleepless night ahead.

*　　　*　　　*

Hundreds of miles away, Josh Chandler was also having trouble sleeping. As Kristina was lying awake in the remote Texas inn, he was pacing his bedroom floor, also plagued with fears and uncertainties. Sleepless nights, however, were common to him, for he had suffered through them for years.

Stepping to his dresser, he poured himself a full shot of whiskey and downed it neatly. He promptly refilled the glass. He knew from experience that the only cure for his insomnia was liquor. He finished off the second drink, then foregoing the glass, he lifted the bottle and drank from it.

A mirror was hanging above the dresser, and lifting his gaze, he glared at his reflection as though he were his own worst enemy. A look of self-loathing distorted his features as he grasped his shirt and ripped it open, the buttons scattering to the floor.

He stared bitterly at his exposed chest, watching it rise and fall with his now-rapid breathing. He raised a trembling hand to the three R's branded grotesquely across his flesh, brushing his fingers lightly across the letters.

Then, as though he could no longer stand the sight, he whirled away from the mirror. Taking the whiskey bottle with him, he moved lethargically to his bed and sat on the edge.

Leaning forward, he rested his arms on his knees, letting the bottle dangle between his legs. His wide shoulders slumped, and bowing his head, he stared vacantly at the floor.

He stayed that way for a long time, then bringing himself out of his trancelike state, he proceeded to get drunk.

Much later, he sank peacefully into a whiskey-induced sleep.

Chapter Five

Autumn Moon was an excellent cook, and Cole heaped his plate with biscuits, eggs, ham, and fried potatoes.

Amused, Drake remarked, "Cole, I don't know how you can eat so damned much."

"I don't usually get good home-cookin'." He glanced at Drake, who was merely picking at his food. "What's wrong with your appetite?"

The man shrugged, pushed aside his plate, and murmured, "I'm not hungry. Maybe I'm too excited to eat. In a few more hours my daughter will be here. God, I've waited a long time for this day!"

Autumn Moon was seated at one end of the table, Drake at the other, their guest was between them. Taking a sip of her coffee, Autumn Moon studied Drake over the rim of her cup. She was gravely worried about him. He didn't look well, his face was pallid, and there was a tautness about his mouth.

Autumn Moon and Drake lived together as though they were man and wife, and sharing his bed, she knew he had been restless last night. This morning when she had questioned him about it, he had told her that he was anxious over Samantha's arrival. She believed him in part, for she was aware that his daughter's visit meant a great deal. She suspected, however, that his fitful night was also due to illness. She knew he had recently been experiencing chest pains, and she had tried several times to convince him to see Dr. Newman. To her dismay, Drake had balked at her suggestion. He refused to take his condition seriously.

Drake's eyes met Autumn Moon's, and reading her thoughts, he said with an understanding smile, "I plan to go into town early and stop at Dr. Newman's office."

The woman's relief was evident. "Good," she murmured.

He favored Autumn Moon with a loving wink. Drake was completely devoted to her, and he would have married her years ago if she had agreed, but Autumn Moon had refused. The passing years hadn't changed her mind, and she still held steadfastly to her resolve. She loved Drake Carlson with all her heart, but he was an important, prosperous Texan, and his fellow citizens held him in high regard. Autumn Moon knew a Comanche wife would not only slander his reputation, but would ultimately wedge an impenetrable gap between Drake and most of his friends. Hostility between the whites and the Comanches had run rampant over the Texas plains, and there were very few Texans who hadn't lost a loved one to a Comanche's arrow. Although the proud Comanches were now subdued and placed on reservations, the Texans who had fought them still harbored hate and bitterness. That Drake had a Comanche woman as housekeeper and mistress didn't offend his fellow comrades, but if he were to marry her, they would shun him, and their wives would be mortified.

Carlson, considering his life no one's business but his own, had begged Autumn Moon to marry him. He knew his true friends wouldn't desert him, and the others could go straight to hell. Despite his earnest pleas, Autumn Moon held tenaciously to her decision. She would clean his house, share his bed, and be his lifetime companion—but under no circumstances would she be his wife. Years ago, when Autumn Moon became pregnant with their child, Drake had believed that she'd relent. Still, she adhered to her vow to never marry him. Finally, giving up, Drake had stopped pressuring her and had reluctantly bowed to her wishes.

Now, as Drake admired her from across the table, he studied her lovely, ageless face. Although she was forty-one years old, her golden-brown complexion was youthful, and her large, dark eyes shone with vitality. Her slim figure was still firm and curvaceous. In his opinion, time hadn't tarnished Autumn Moon's beauty. Instead, she grew more lovely.

Autumn Moon, aware of Drake's loving scrutiny, smiled at him before lowering her gaze to her plate. She picked up a fork and began to eat. She ate mechanically, barely tasting her food. She knew Drake was thrilled about seeing Samantha, and she was sincerely happy for him. Samantha's approaching visit, though, made her feel her own daughter's absence more acutely. Nineteen years had passed since Autumn Moon had borne Drake a beautiful, healthy daughter. Drake had named her Alisa, after his mother. The baby had been a joy to her parents, and they had doted on her extravagantly. As a child, Alisa had been happy and well-adjusted. As she grew older, however, the shame of her illegitimacy and the term "half-breed" shattered her blissful existence. She soon became determined to leave Texas and move someplace where no one knew about her past. Following unrelentless pleading and cajoling on her part, her father finally agreed to send her to St. Louis to live with his cousin and her husband. Alisa had been sixteen when she left home: that was three years ago, and she had refused to come back for a visit.

Finishing his coffee, Drake pushed back his chair and got to his feet. He looked at Cole. "If I'm gonna stop at the doc's office, we'd better leave."

Cole agreed and was rising from the table when, all at once, Drake doubled over with pain. Gasping, he grabbed at his chest. His body weakened, causing his legs to buckle beneath him, and he would have fallen had Cole not caught him in time.

Carefully, Cole eased him to the floor. The man's breathing was erratic, and his face had turned deathly pale. He was obviously suffering a great deal of pain.

As Autumn Moon rushed over, Cole told her quickly, "Order my horse saddled so I can ride to town for the doctor." When the frightened woman stood as though paralyzed, he yelled impatiently, "Go on! We can't waste a minute!"

Cole sat at Drake's desk, holding a half-finished glass of brandy. Worry was etched deeply on his face. His eyes, reflecting his inner fear, were staring across the room, his gaze fixed on nothing in particular.

Dr. Newman, along with Autumn Moon, was still upstairs tending to Drake. He had heard nothing from either of them for over an hour. He was growing impatient, and decided if one of them didn't come to him soon, he'd go upstairs and find out for himself how Drake was doing. Cole tried to avoid thinking of Drake's possible death. He loved Drake Carlson

64

like a father, and imagining life without him tore painfully at Cole's heart.

Cole had been fifteen when he met Drake. Following his mother's death, he had abandoned the farm and wandered into Tennessee. He had tried to join the Confederate Army but was considered underage. Because he had always longed to go westward, he headed into Texas. Broke and homeless, he finally decided to lie about his age and join General Hood's Texas Brigade. After passing himself off as seventeen, he enlisted in the Army and was assigned to Major Drake Carlson's regiment. The major took an instant liking to the young soldier and befriended him, and Cole had ridden under Carlson's command for two years before admitting his real age.

Lost in thought, Cole was somewhat startled when the study door suddenly opened and the doctor stepped inside, his expression revealing nothing about Drake's condition.

Dr. Newman took the chair facing the desk. "I don't think Drake's going to make it," he announced gravely. "He's had a severe heart attack."

Anguish gripped Cole, tearing into him powerfully. "God, no!" he groaned.

"I'm sorry," Newman said.

"Are you sure he's . . . he's dying?"

"Well, I've done all I can do. Now it's in God's hands." The doctor sighed wearily, his eyes touching on the framed photograph of Drake's daughter. He reached out a hand and turned the photograph so that it was facing him. For a moment he studied the lovely woman in the picture, then said with a heavy sigh, "You might consider sending a wire to Drake's daughter. She should be notified of her father's condition."

Suddenly, Cole tensed. Placing his glass on the

65

desk, he exclaimed, "Samantha! Damn, I forgot!" He glanced quickly at the clock on the mantel. "Her stage got in an hour ago!"

Newman was confused. "Her stage?"

"She's arriving today." Cole leapt to his feet. "I'll hitch up a buckboard and ride into town." He rushed from the room, cursing himself for leaving Drake's daughter stranded.

Kristina paced back and forth in front of the clapboard building that served as the stage depot, post office, and telegraph office. The sun's scorching rays slanted over the dusty street, which, due to the afternoon heat, was nearly deserted. The town was quiet, except for the saloon across the street. Voices from within drifted outside, but they were not overly loud or rambunctious.

Kristina took a seat on the wooden bench in front of the stage depot. Twisting her hands in her lap while tapping her foot impatiently, she peered down the street, hoping to catch a glimpse of an approaching buckboard. She was disappointed.

Kristina's stage had arrived nearly two hours ago. She had spent the first hour waiting anxiously for Drake's appearance. When he failed to show up, she began to wonder if he had received her wire announcing her time of arrival. She had questioned the man who handled incoming and outgoing wires. He had remembered the telegram she sent to Drake and assured her that he had received her message. He had then suggested that she hire a driver to take her to the Diamond-C. Not knowing what else to do, she had agreed. Remaining helpful, he had sent his young employee to the livery to fetch a buckboard and driver.

Now, waiting for her ride, Kristina rose from the bench and resumed her restless pacing. The driver was at least thirty minutes late. What was keeping him? Her nerves were shattered, and her patience was quickly waning. Furthermore, the Texas heat was unbearable. Kristina was miserable, tired, and was growing more apprehensive with each passing minute.

Drake's unexplained absence had her terribly uneasy. Why didn't he meet her stage? If, for some reason, he couldn't make it, then why didn't he send someone in his place? Why did he leave her stranded? There were no answers to these questions, and pondering them merely increased her anxieties.

The warm air was so humid that Kristina's constant pacing soon had her short of breath, so she returned to sitting on the hard bench. She was wearing a traveling gown that had belonged to Samantha. It had been among the clothes that she had given to Kristina. The dress was not suitable for this hot, desertlike climate. The material was entirely too heavy, and the long sleeves and high-necked bodice blocked off what little breeze was stirring. A straw bonnet, trimmed with a salmon ribbon matching the color of her dress, sat atop her blond curls. Her long tresses were pulled back away from her face, caught at the back of her neck in a mass of cascading ringlets. Despite the heat, and Kristina's fatigue, she was a fetching sight.

As a buckboard with a lone driver came into sight, Kristina stood up quickly and stepped to the edge of the street. Her mood was testy. In her opinion, the driver's tardiness was not only inexcusable but a very rude way to treat a paying customer.

Meanwhile, as Kristina's temper was reaching flash point, Cole was guiding the buckboard toward the stage depot. He was still upset with himself. He should've remembered to meet the stage. He felt bad about doing such a thing to Samantha, and as if he had somehow failed Drake.

He saw the young woman waiting at the edge of the street. Wondering if she was angry, he tried to discern her expression, but he was still too far away to see her that clearly.

Kristina, hands on hips, waited petulantly for the buckboard to reach her. The moment it came to a stop, she cast its driver a cursory glance, muttering sharply, "Well, it's about time!"

"Miss Carlson—" Cole began, intending to apologize.

She cut him off abruptly. "If you don't mind, I'm in a hurry." Without waiting for assistance, she hefted her long skirt and climbed up onto the seat. "My suitcase, please," she clipped, gesturing at it tersely.

Her arrogance was perturbing, but Cole bit back a retort. Jumping lithely to the street, he stepped to the walkway, lifted the huge piece of luggage, and placed it in the back of the wagon. He returned to his seat, took up the reins, and turned the team around.

They rode in silence for a long time, then Kristina suddenly questioned. "What took you so long? I sent for you over thirty minutes ago." She drew a calming breath. "Please forgive me for being so abrupt. I'm sure you have a good reason for being late. I'm just so tired, hot, and miserable."

"Ma'am, you may have sent for someone, but it wasn't me."

For the first time, she looked directly at him, instantly struck by his good looks. "Don't you work at the livery?" she asked.

"No, ma'am," he replied, finding her even more

beautiful than her photograph. Her closeness had a disturbing effect on him, but he kept it well concealed.

"I ordered a driver and buckboard to take me to the Diamond-C. Oh, dear!" she sighed. "I made a terrible mistake. I thought you were my driver. Please forgive me for imposing on you."

"That's all right," he replied, grinning. "I came to town to pick you up."

"Do you work at the Diamond-C?"

"No, I'm just visiting."

"I wonder what happened to the driver from the livery?"

"He's probably at the stage depot wondering where you are."

"Yes, probably," she murmured vaguely, her gaze sweeping over the man at her side. She looked thoughtfully at the gun strapped to his hip, and then to the rifle propped at his feet. "Do you always travel so heavily armed?"

"Usually," he answered. "By the way, ma'am, my name's Barton—Cole Barton."

"So you're Cole Barton!" she blurted out. "Father's written about you several times, but I didn't think you would be so . . . so . . ." She wanted to say so handsome, but she couldn't bring herself to speak so boldly.

"So what?" he coaxed.

"Never mind," she said quickly. Eager to change the subject, she asked, "Why were you so late picking me up? And why didn't Dra—Father come to town with you?" She groaned inwardly. She hated pretending she was Samantha. She was anxious to tell Drake the truth.

Cole brought the buckboard to a stop. He dreaded telling Samantha about her father. "This morning,

Drake had a heart attack," he said softly. His soft tone didn't cushion the terrible blow.

"A heart attack!" she cried. "Is he . . . is he—?"

"He's alive," Cole assured her.

"Will he recover?"

"The doctor doesn't think so. Samantha, you need to prepare yourself for the worst."

Tears gushed from her eyes. She loved Drake Carlson. Although she had never heard his voice, his laughter, had never touched him or felt his embrace, she still loved him!

Placing the reins aside, Cole drew her into his arms and held her close. Resting her head on his shoulder, she cried heartbrokenly.

"Drake's strong, and he's a stubborn cuss—he'll pull through this," Cole murmured, trying to give her hope, as well as himself.

Kristina's sobs abated somewhat, and she left his embrace with reluctance. His arms had been comforting and she had enjoyed his closeness. The revelation was a little unnerving. She didn't especially approve of Cole Barton, for she found his line of work disgraceful. She took a handkerchief from her purse and wiped her eyes.

"Drake's gonna make it," Cole said, his deep voice breaking with emotion. "He's got to make it!"

Kristina heard the sorrow in his voice. "You love him very much, don't you?"

He didn't reply, but the grief in his eyes answered her question.

Leaving Dr. Newman alone with Drake, Autumn Moon went in search of Joseph. She found him in the kitchen, sitting at the table. An untouched cup of coffee sat before him.

At Autumn Moon's entrance, Joseph stood up quickly. "Mista Drake ain't . . . he ain't gone, is he?"

"No, he's still holding on. Joseph, I want you to go to town and send a wire to Josh Chandler and one to Alisa. They need to know that Drake is seriously ill."

"Yes'm, I'll go at once."

She handed him a slip of paper. "I wrote down the information you'll need."

He took the paper, then hurried to do her bidding. Her steps sluggish, Autumn Moon moved to the stove and poured a cup of coffee. Then, stepping to the table, she pulled out a chair and sat down.

She wondered if Alisa would respond to the telegram and return home. A cold chill coursed through her. She wasn't sure if Alisa even cared if her father was alive or dead. Autumn Moon knew her daughter harbored ill feelings toward both of them. She had bitterly resented her parents for bringing her into the world. She hated being illegitimate, but she hated her Comanche blood even more.

Tears ran down Autumn Moon's face as she got slowly to her feet. She picked up the cup of coffee— she would offer it to the doctor, for she was too upset to drink it herself.

As thoughts of Alisa continued to disturb her, Autumn Moon considered stopping Joseph and telling him not to send the wire. Undecided, she paused for a moment. An overwhelming desire to see Alisa made the decision for her, and she didn't go after Joseph.

She started up the stairway and to the bedroom she had shared with Drake for over twenty years. A sense of impending doom washed over her, but she wasn't sure if it was brought on by Drake's illness, or her daughter's possible arrival.

Chapter Six

Cole slapped the reins against the team—the buckboard lurched and rolled into motion. Out of the corner of his eye, he studied the lovely woman at his side. She was still using her handkerchief to dab at her tears. Her sorrow had touched him deeply, and he wished there was something he could say to lighten her grief.

Fighting a sudden desire to draw her into his arms once more, he gripped the reins tightly. Samantha! God, how was it possible for her to be even prettier than her picture? He had admired her photograph for the past two years and had thought her extremely lovely. Now, here she was in person, and more beautiful than words could adequately describe.

Cole thought about the letters she had written to Drake through the years. He had either read them himself, or Drake had read them to him. As a result, he felt as though he knew Samantha, had known her since she was eight years old. Through her written words, he had seen her grow from a child into a young woman.

Meanwhile, as Cole was deep in thought, Kristina's own thoughts were in turmoil. That Drake might die had her gripped with grief, as well as fear. She tried not to consider her plight, should he pass away. But against her will, the terrible possibility flashed across her mind. Envisioning herself alone and practically destitute in this unfamiliar land was frightening. She knew she couldn't return to Philadelphia, for the police would surely arrest her on sight. If Drake should die, where could she go? Who could she turn to for help?

Deciding it was selfish to worry about her problems with Drake seriously ill, she quickly cast aside these plaguing questions. If worse came to worst, she'd find a way to survive. She wasn't a helpless shrinking violet but a determined woman with a strong will of her own.

She moved her hands to her lap and toyed absently with her wadded-up handkerchief. She cast a furtive glance in Cole's direction, trying to recall some of the things Drake had written about this man. She remembered that during the war Drake had been Cole's commanding officer, and that their friendship had continued through the intervening years. Drake had often written that he loved Cole like a son. He had also made it quite clear that he disapproved of Cole's profession.

Kristina thought it somewhat strange that, even considering Drake's remarks concerning Cole Barton, she didn't really know that much about him personally. It was as though Drake had guarded his comments about Cole. Perhaps he hadn't felt free to give personal information, so he had kept details of Cole's life mostly confidential.

She was still studying Cole from the corner of her eye. He was indeed a striking figure. His tall, lithe frame exuded masculine strength, and his dark hair and mustache made him devilishly handsome.

Feeling her scrutiny, Cole's gaze suddenly met hers. For a long momemt his blue, penetrating eyes held her mesmerized. She was the first to look away, and overcome with a strange sensation she couldn't analyze, she glanced about distractedly at the surrounding landscape.

The passing scenery was mostly grazing fields with intermittent trees and clumps of shrubbery. The countryside, however, escaped Kristina's notice, for her thoughts were elsewhere. Should she end her masquerade and tell Cole who she really was? She hated pretending she was Samantha. A feeling of uneasiness came over her, and she nervously twisted her handkerchief. Could she possibly bring herself to make such a startling confession to this man who was practically a stranger?

She turned her head cautiously and looked at him through half-lowered eyes. There was a threatening aura about Cole Barton that she found unsettling. She didn't think her confession would provoke a physical anger, but she believed he'd most certainly react unfavorably. Somehow she sensed that he wouldn't tolerate such deceit, especially against someone he liked as much as he did Drake.

As the sound of an approaching horse arrested her attention, she cleared her thoughts and watched as the rider came closer.

"It's Joseph," Cole said, "your father's butler."

Fear knotted in Cole's stomach as he halted the team and waited for Joseph. He hoped, prayed, that the man wasn't a bearer of bad news. Was Drake still alive? Or had he lost the friend he loved like a father?

The moment Joseph reined in, Cole asked apprehensively, "Is Drake dead?"

"No, suh, Mista Cole."

"Thank God!" he sighed in relief.

75

"Autumn Moon asked me to ride into town and send a wire to Mista Josh and one to Miz Alisa." Joseph looked at Kristina and said movingly, "Miz Samantha, seein' you is gonna be good medicine for Mista Drake. If anyone can pull him through this, you can. Just your being there will give him strength."

A pang of guilt cut into Kristina so sharply that she came close to telling these two men that she wasn't Samantha. But she was too ashamed to bring herself to make such a declaration, and the words remained stuck in her throat.

Joseph rode away, and she and Cole resumed their journey. They had traveled a couple of minutes before Cole remarked, "We're now on your father's land."

"How much farther to the house?"

"Fifteen, maybe twenty minutes."

"My fa—" referring to Drake as her father was difficult—"my father has written to me about Josh," she stammered, thinking of the wires Joseph planned to send. "But who is Alisa? I don't recall him mentioning anyone by that name."

Cole tensed. He knew Drake had never told Samantha about Alisa. He had believed it was wrong for Drake to keep such a secret. Although he had advised him to tell Samantha that she had a sister, Drake had chosen to do otherwise.

Now Cole didn't feel it was his place to reveal such information. "When Drake gets better, I'm sure he'll tell you about Alisa."

"If he get's better," Kristina murmured sadly. Alisa's existence didn't arouse her curiosity, for she knew Drake must have several close acquaintances whom she knew nothing about.

Cole and Kristina said very little during the

remainder of their trip, and Kristina was buried in thought when the ranchhouse came into view.

Sitting up straight, her eyes filled with the impressive sight, she exclaimed, "It's even more grand than I imagined!"

At first sight, she loved the magnificent house sitting proudly atop the hill. It was surrounded by a white picket fence, and an arch had been erected over the open gates with the Diamond-C painted on it in large letters.

Kristina gazed around with interest. Drake's letters had described his ranch in such detail that she had always managed to see it in her mind. But her imagination had failed to do justice to the reality before her.

She spoke somewhat breathlessly. "My father must be more more successful than I thought."

"He's the most prosperous rancher in these parts."

Kristina envied Samantha, her envy laced with bitterness. Someday, the Diamond-C would belong to Samantha, and Kristina knew she wouldn't cherish such an inheritance. Knowing Samantha, she'd sell the ranch, and never give it another thought. A depressing shadow fell over Kristina. The Diamond-C should belong to Drake's loved ones, not to strangers. How could strangers honor the memory of the man who had made all this possible?

Cole guided the team to the house, then alighting from the buckboard, he reached up and assisted Kristina. He led her quickly across the porch and into the front foyer, then ushered her to the study.

"Wait here," he said, "while I go upstairs and check on Drake."

Left alone, Kristina walked slowly across the spacious room. It had been decorated to suit a man's taste. Large pieces of furniture filled the room, and an amply supplied liquor cabinet stood in one corner. An oil painting of an Indian buffalo hunt hung over the fireplace. A beige rug, matching the shade of the drapes, covered the center of the highly polished floor. It was a comfortable room, and Kristina could imagine Drake spending a lot of time here.

Stepping to the desk, she saw her photograph. She lifted the framed picture, gazed at it for a moment, then put it back.

Kristina eased her tired body into Drake's leather armchair, her gaze returning to the photograph. It had been wrong for her to send Drake a picture of herself. When he had insisted on a photograph, Samantha had told Kristina to choose one and send it to him. Samantha had several pictures of herself. Kristina had chosen one she was sure Drake would like and had every intention of sending it. Even now, she wasn't sure why she had sent one of herself. He had written that he wanted to gaze upon her photograph as he wrote to her. Was that why she hadn't mailed him Samantha's picture? Could she not bear Drake writing to her while looking at Samantha? Had her deceitful act stemmed from jealousy?

Kristina looked away from her picture and fixed her gaze across the room. She had regretted switching the photographs, but once the picture had been mailed, she couldn't undo the action. She had considered telling Samantha, but she had found herself too overcome with shame to admit to such selfish behavior.

The study door opened, and Kristina got quickly to her feet. As Cole entered, she asked anxiously, "Is he better?"

"No," he answered. "I'm afraid not, but Dr.

Newman said it's all right for you to see him."

Cole took her arm and guided her from the room. As he led her down the hall, then up the staircase, Kristina's heart was pounding irregularly. God, she couldn't pretend to a dying man that she was his daughter! She couldn't! She just couldn't!

I'll tell him the truth! she decided desperately. *I must tell him! I must!*

Dr. Newman was waiting in front of Drake's closed door. His gentle eyes swept over Kristina appreciatively.

"Samantha . . ." Cole began. "This is Dr. Newman."

"Is my father conscious?" she asked. She couldn't very well make a confession if he wasn't.

"He drifts in and out," the doctor replied. "Miss Carlson, before you go in to see him, I must emphasize that you say nothing to upset him. He's barely holding on to life, and even a mild disturbance could bring on another attack."

"Damn, Newman!" Cole uttered gruffly. "She doesn't plan to upset him!"

The doctor quickly apologized. "I'm sorry, Miss Carlson. I didn't mean to imply . . ."

"I understand," she answered, her voice almost inaudible. Now she couldn't possibly tell Drake the truth—such a declaration might kill him! She swallowed her guilt, for she was stuck with it.

The doctor opened the door, then stood back for Kristina to precede him. The heavy drapes were drawn, and the room was lit by two lamps, the luminous glow casting a soft light.

Autumn Moon was sitting at Drake's bedside. As the others came inside, she got up wearily. She looked closely at Kristina, surprised to see that she was even prettier than her picture.

79

Kristina smiled timidly. "You must be Autumn Moon," she said quietly. Although Drake had written that Autumn Moon was his housekeeper, he hadn't revealed that she was also his lover and the mother of his second child.

"Your father is awake," Autumn Moon murmured softly. "Talk to him, Samantha. Your being here could be the miracle he needs."

Miracle! Kristina reflected bitterly. She was no miracle, she was a fraud! How intensely she despised herself. She had fallen into this trap with no harm intended—had planned to be completely honest with Drake—but that didn't lighten her self-condemnation.

She moved haltingly to the chair placed beside the large four-poster bed and sat down. Through a blurry haze of tears, she gazed upon Drake Carlson. Death's hovering shadow hadn't dimmed the man's virile good looks, and only his shallow, gasping breaths attested to his illness.

Cole moved over and stood beside Kristina's chair. "Drake?" he said gently. "Can you hear me?"

The man's eyes were closed. He attempted to open them, but it seemed too much of an effort. "I hear you, Cole," he whispered.

"There's someone here to see you. It's Samantha."

Slowly, Drake's eyelids fluttered open. "Samantha?" he called, his voice terribly weak.

Kristina was too overcome to utter a word. Cole nudged her gently. "Please say something," he encouraged.

Kristina reached out a hand and placed it on Drake's. "I'm here, Father," she murmured, tears flowing. Oh, she did love this man! And deep within her heart, he was truly her father!

With effort, Drake turned his head and gazed

lovingly into Kristina's tear-streaked face. "Saman-tha, honey, I'm sorry . . . I had made so many plans for us. And now . . ."

"Please, Father! You must save your strength. When you recover, we'll do all the things you planned."

"No," he moaned raspingly. "I'm not gonna make it. But I thank God that I got to see my little girl. I love you, sweetheart . . ."

Kristina's shaky composure crumbled, and hard sobs tore from her throat. "I love you, too! I've always loved you!" she cried piteously.

As Dr. Newman moved hastily to Drake, he motioned for Cole to take Kristina away. He was worried that the emotional scene had been too exhausting for his patient.

Grasping Kristina's shoulders, Cole urged her to her feet, then out of the room. He kept an arm supportively about her waist as he led her down the stairs to the study.

He guided her to the sofa, and when she was seated, he stepped to the liquor cabinet and poured a sherry.

Returning, Cole sat beside her. "Here, drink this," he said, handing her the glass. She accepted the offered sherry numbly. "Come on, now drink it all down. It'll make you feel better."

Drawing a deep breath, she did as she was told. The warm liquor was soothing and had a calming effect on her tattered nerves.

She set the empty glass on the coffee table, then turned and looked directly into Cole's watching eyes. She could no longer bear her guilt alone—she had to tell someone! As she continued to gaze into Cole's kind eyes, she decided to make a full confession.

"Cole . . ." she began apprehensively. "There's something I must tell you."

81

At that moment, however, Autumn Moon suddenly entered the room. She spoke to Cole. "Drake has asked for Reverend Scott. He knows he's dying, and he wants the reverend to pray with him."

The painful certainty of losing his friend hit Cole forcefully. His body tensed as grief ripped through him. Rising from the sofa, he managed to reply, "I'll ride to town and get the reverend."

"No, I'll send one of the hands," Autumn Moon told him. "Drake has insisted on seeing you."

As Autumn Moon was leaving the study, Cole turned to Kristina and said, "Try to relax. I'll be back as soon as I talk to Drake."

She watched as Cole hurried from the room. Tears threatened again, and powerless to hold them in check, Kristina lay across the sofa and wept uncontrollably.

Exhausted, she drifted into a light, restless sleep. Minutes later, Cole's entrance brought her awake.

As he came toward her, she sat up and asked, "Why did he need to see you?"

Pausing to stand before her, Cole answered, "He made a dying request. There's something he wants me to do."

"You agreed, didn't you?"

"Not yet."

"But why not?" She couldn't imagine Cole denying Drake's last request.

"I couldn't commit myself because you are also involved."

Kristina rose quickly. "Cole, whatever he wants, we'll do!" She spoke strongly, unalterably.

"Are you sure?"

"Yes, I'm sure! I'll not deny his last wish! What does he want?"

"He wants us to get married . . . tonight."

82

Chapter Seven

"Married!" Kristina gasped, her face paling. Her knees weakened, and she sank back onto the sofa.

Cole sat beside her. "It's always been Drake's dream that we marry and live here at the Diamond-C."

"But why?" she asked breathlessly.

"I'm not sure, but I can make a guess. He loves this ranch, and he also loves both of us. This land is the most precious gift he can give. Also, he knows me as well as I know myself, and through your letters, he knows you very well. He believes we're the perfect match, and our falling in love is inevitable."

She studied him expectantly. "Do you agree with him, that we'll fall in love?"

He thought for a long moment, then said softly, "Samantha, I feel as though I've known you since you were eight years old. I've read every letter you've written to your father and they have reflected your personality. I know you're a very kind, sensitive, and honest young lady."

Kristina tensed. Honest! The word tore through her conscience.

Cole continued. "From the first moment I saw

83

your picture, I was totally infatuated. Now that I've met you, I find you even lovelier than any photograph. I also see that you're just as kind, sensitive, and as honest as the letters revealed. I think falling in love with you would be very easy."

She was touched by Cole's declaration, and found his words thrilling. For some reason, imagining this man in love with her sent her pulse racing. She felt that she could also fall in love with him, but she kept the revelation to herself. Cole believed he was discussing marriage with Samantha Carlson, not Kristina Parker.

Cole had been waiting for her to say something, but when she remained noncommittal, he explained. "Samantha, if we decide to grant Drake's wish, you won't be committed to your marriage vows. We can have the marriage annulled."

"But if we marry knowing we're going to have it annulled, then we aren't really granting his last wish, are we?"

"Not necessarily," he replied. "We can give ourselves time to get to know each other better, to see if we will fall in love. If it doesn't work out, then we can have the marriage dissolved." He reached over and held her hand. "But I have a feeling I'll learn to love you very deeply." He grinned wryly. "Maybe I'm already a little in love."

"Cole . . ." she began emotionally. "Why do I have the feeling that love and marriage are two topics you've always avoided?"

He grasped her hand more tightly. "You must know me better than you realize."

She withdrew her hand. His touch was too pleasant, and his tender words were carrying her away from reality. She couldn't marry Cole Barton! It was Drake's wish that he marry Samantha, not

Samantha's maid!

"But . . . but we can't get married," she stammered.

"Why not?" he questioned. "We have nothing to lose, and maybe everything to gain."

"You don't understand," she replied wearily.

"They why don't you explain?"

She swallowed nervously, drew a calming breath, and was about to tell him who she really was when, unexpectedly, the study door opened.

Autumn Moon entered. "I'm going to fix a light supper." She looked at Kristina, her expression tender. "I'll bring you a tray." She turned her gaze to Cole. "Will you please show Samantha to her room?"

Cole said that he would, and, as Autumn Moon left for the kitchen, he helped Kristina from the sofa.

As she walked beside Cole down the hall, then up the stairs, her mind rehearsed the scene that had to take place. She had no choice but to tell Cole the whole truth. She dreaded his reaction, and she tried to think of the best way to break the startling news. She had a sinking feeling that he'd be furious.

Cole took her to the guest room that had been prepared for her visit. He opened the door, and as she stepped inside, he told her he'd fetch her suitcase from the buckboard.

Kristina, her mind in turmoil, gave the tasteful decor a cursory glance as she went to the canopied bed and sat down. It was a lovely room. In honor of her arrival, Autumn Moon had hung brightly toned curtains, and multicolored throw rugs were placed about the floor. A yellow spread covered the bed, and a vase filled with yellow roses was placed on the nightstand. It was indeed a cheerful room, but it failed to lighten Kristina's gloomy spirits.

She felt trapped in a tangled web, and to escape she had to be perfectly honest with Cole. The moment he returned with her suitcase, she would tell him the truth.

Meanwhile, Cole was having second thoughts. The buckboard had been taken to the barn, Kristina's suitcase still inside. He lifted the heavy piece of luggage, then set it at his feet. Reaching into his pocket, he withdrew a cheroot and lit it. Leaning back against the wagon, he went over everything he had said to Kristina.

Cole was finding it hard to believe that he had actually tried to persuade Drake's daughter to marry him. He had always avoided matrimony. A wife and children would interfere with his way of life. He was a bounty hunter, a loner, and a wanderer. He relished his independence, for it left him free to search for his mother's killers. But if he and Samantha were to grant Drake's request, and then if they were to fall in love, Samantha would expect him to quit his profession, give up his search, and stay at the Diamond-C. It would be no more than any wife would expect.

A hard, determined coldness came to Cole's piercing blue eyes. He'd not abandon his quest! Not even for Samantha!

As her face flashed before him, the expression in his eyes softened. He wondered why Samantha had such power over him. When he was with her, his heart and not his common sense ruled his feelings.

Cole's thoughts churned turbulently. Could he deny Drake's last wish? He supposed he should resent the man for putting him and Samantha on the spot. Drake's request was unreasonable, but then a dying man didn't always think rationally.

Picking up the suitcase and walking out of the barn, he dropped his cheroot, stepped on it, and smashed it into the ground.

The white, six-columned home stood grandly in the distance. Pausing, Cole glanced up to the second floor, his gaze resting on Drake's bedroom window. The curtains had been drawn aside, admitting the cool breeze that had arrived with the approaching dusk. Despite Drake's unreasonable request, there was no resentment in Cole's heart. He felt only love for this man who had befriended him so many years ago.

Kristina had lain across the bed while awaiting Cole's return. Tired, and emotionally drained, she had fallen sound alseep.

Her door had been left open, and, as Cole brought her suitcase into the room, he saw that she was sleeping. He put down the bag, then moving soundlessly, he went to the bed and gazed down at her.

She was beautiful in repose. A few wayward ringlets had fallen across her brow, the unruly curls lending her an impish charm. He admired the long, dark lashes veiling her eyes, and the sensual shape of her lips. He allowed his gaze to roam over her young, ripe curves. The heavy traveling gown hid much from his view, but it didn't stop him from conjuring up a vision of her lying seductively naked. He quickly erased the picture from his mind, for it was too arousing.

He whirled about as Autumn Moon, carrying a dinner tray, walked softly into the room.

"Is she asleep?" the woman asked quietly.

Moving away from the bed, Cole answered, "She's sleeping like a baby."

"I'm sure she's very tired." Autumn Moon placed the tray on the bedside table, then followed Cole who was on his way out of the room. As they stepped into the hall, she asked, "Do you think I should awaken her?"

"No, let her sleep. I'm going to the bunkhouse and have a talk with the men. I also need to go over tomorrow's work with the foreman." He moved away, then turned back around. "If there's any change in Drake's condition—?" he started.

"I'll send for you," she assured him.

Much later, when Kristina awakened, she was surprised to find that night had fallen. Except for the moonlight shining through the window, her room was shrouded in darkness. She lit the bedside lamp. As her gaze fell across the dinner tray, her stomach reminded her that she hadn't eaten since morning. Autumn Moon had fixed her a light supper and a cup of tea. The tea was cold, but Kristina drank it anyway.

She was wondering how long she had slept when she suddenly spotted her suitcase. If only she hadn't been asleep when Cole had brought it! She decided to freshen up, then go in search of him. The sooner she made her confession, the better she'd feel.

Her movements quick, precise, she went to the suitcase and opened it. She took out a summer gown and carried it to the bed. She undressed hastily, then filled the washbasin and sponged her face. Anxious to find Cole, she slipped quickly into the clean dress, then peered at her reflection. Her hair was mussed, and removing the pins, she let it fall freely. A hairbrush was on the dresser, and she ran it briskly through her curly tresses.

She was on her way to the door when a sudden rap sounded on it. "Samantha?" she heard Cole call.

"Come in," she greeted with anticipation. Now she could get the truth in the open!

Kristina's fetching beauty struck Cole full force as he stepped into the room. His eyes, filled with desire, swept over her summer gown, which clearly defined her feminine curves. His vision climbed upward to her curly, ash-blond hair, and he wished he had the right to run his fingers through the long tresses.

Kristina was acutely aware of his stare, and his intense examination was making her flush in excitement. Her eyes, with a will of their own, returned his scrutiny and traveled intimately over Cole's masculine frame. His beige shirt and tan trousers fit him like a second skin, emphasizing his strong chest and long, muscular legs. The gun holster strapped about his hips made him appear somewhat dangerous, but excitingly so. Kristina's gaze went to his handsome face, and as she looked into his eyes, she felt as though she were drowning in their blue, fathomless depths.

The attraction between them was so strong it was palpable, and it began to draw them to each other like an invisible magnet.

Cole moved lithely toward her and Kristina, spellbound, took a tentative step in his direction. Then, without warning, she whirled about and retreated. Going to the open window, she pretended to gaze outside. She breathed deeply in an effort to calm her jumbled emotions.

She had wanted desperately to go into Cole's embrace and to feel his lips on hers. But until she told him the truth, she didn't have the right to be in his arms. Suddenly, she felt very despondent. The truth might set her free, but it might also free her forever from Cole's affections.

Cole crossed the room and came to her side. He was puzzled, for he knew she had wanted his embrace. What had caused her to have second thoughts? He considered questioning her, then changed his mind. Tonight was not the time for delving into her moods, nor was it the time for romance. At the moment, only Drake mattered.

"Reverend Scott has arrived," Cole said, breaking the uneasy tension.

She turned her gaze to his. "How long did I sleep?"

"A couple of hours."

"So long!" she exclaimed. "Has there been any change in . . . in Father's condition?"

"No," he replied. "He's the same."

She looked away from him and returned to staring out the window. It would be easier to make a confession if she weren't gazing into his face. "Cole . . ." she began, her voice timorous. "I must talk to you. Will you please listen to what I have to say without interrupting? This is very difficult for me, and I want to get it over with as quickly as possible."

She had his full interest.

Cole had left the door open, and, at that moment, Joseph stepped into the room and announced gravely, "Mista Cole, Miz Samantha, the doctah's a-wantin' you. We's losin' Mista Drake!"

Cole moaned, then, grabbing Kristina's hand, he led her from the room, down the hall, and to Drake's room where Dr. Newman was waiting.

The physician's face was etched with sorrow, for Drake Carlson was a good friend. "Go on in," he said to Cole and Kristina.

"Is he . . . is he—?" Kristina cried brokenly.

"He's still alive, but he's very weak," the doctor murmured.

Kristina, her heart breaking, followed Cole into the room. Dr. Newman and Joseph trailed close behind. Autumn Moon was seated at Drake's bedside, her hand holding his. The reverend was standing at the foot of the bed, uttering a silent prayer.

Cole and Kristina moved to the bed and gazed down upon Drake's pallid face. His eyes were closed, and his breathing was so ragged that he had to fight for each breath.

A rasping, grief-stricken moan came from deep within Cole's throat, and Kristina turned to look at him. She was profoundly touched by his sorrow. Clearly, Cole loved Drake Carlson very much.

"Drake?" Cole called, his voice hoarse. He leaned over the bed, repeating, "Drake?"

Carlson responded to Cole's voice. His eyes opened, and he gazed at the man he loved as a son. "I was dreaming," he whispered. His words were so weak that only Cole could hear. "I was dreaming you and Samantha had given me a grandson."

Cole's reaction was impulsive. He was driven by a compulsion to grant this man his dying wish. Grabbing an extra pillow, Cole slipped it under Drake's head, elevating him. The others, confused, looked on incredulously.

"Drake," Cole remarked strongly, "I'm raising you up a bit so you can see the ceremony."

Dr. Newman decided to interfere. "Cole, what the hell do you think you're doing?"

Cole ignored the man's intrusion, turned to the preacher, and said briskly, "Reverend, I want you to marry Samantha and me—right now!"

"Now?" the reverend exclaimed. "But, Mr. Barton,

91

this is highly unusual."

"I don't care how unusual it is! Just marry us! You can fill out the license later."

Kristina, too shocked to voice an objection, stared at Cole as though he were completely out of his mind.

Cole grasped Kristina's hand, pulling her to his side. "Reverend Scott . . ." he said impatiently. "Start the ceremony. I don't know how much time Drake has, so make the ceremony short and to the point." He leaned close to Kristina and whispered, "We must go through with this for your father's sake. It's not only his last wish, but, God, it just might keep him alive."

Kristina was torn in two—a part of her demanded that she flee the room at once, but the other part wanted to remain. If she could save Drake's life, then she would do so, even if it meant marrying Cole Barton! Afterward, when she told Cole her reason for going through with the ceremony, he would understand. Surely, he would!

As Kristina's emotions churned, Dr. Newman turned and looked at his patient. He was astounded to see a small, satisfied smile fall across Drake's lips. Newman was suddenly filled with hope. This unexpected marriage could be the miracle his patient needed. It might give him added strength to fight off death. The doctor set his gaze upon the reverend. "Don't just stand there like a bump on a log! Get these two married!"

The physician's command compelled the preacher into action. With his Bible in hand, he moved over to stand before the intended couple.

"Dearly beloved," Reverend Scott intoned, "we are gathered here to join this man and this woman in holy matrimony . . ."

92

Kristina's better judgment refused to accept what she was doing, causing her to drift into a trancelike state. Her spirit seemed to be hovering above the group, looking down as she recited her sacred vows. Suddenly, though, she tried to will her spirit back into her body, for without it she was powerless to stop this travesty. She almost found the willpower, but before she could pull herself together, the quick ceremony was over.

"I now pronounce you man and wife. What God has brought together, let no man put asunder."

Cole didn't kiss his bride, but turned his full attention to Drake. The man had remained conscious throughout the ceremony, but the effort had tired him considerably. He was able to summon up an approving smile before his eyes closed. His head lolled to the side of the pillow.

Dr. Newman checked his patient, then quickly announced, "He's fallen asleep."

Cole had feared he was dying, and he now sighed with relief. Then, he turned away from the bed to look at his bride. Kristina's face was deathly pale, and she seemed about to collapse. He stepped quickly to her side. "Are you all right?" he asked anxiously.

Kristina stared blankly at this man who thought he was now her husband. But they weren't really married, for the whole ceremony had been a farce. The marriage license would state that he was married to Samantha Carlson, not to Kristina Parker.

As the full impact of what she had done hit her with a startling force, her knees buckled and the room began to sway beneath her feet. A loud ringing reverberated in her ears, and a cloak of blackness fell over her vision.

She fainted into oblivion, but Cole's arms caught her before she sank to the floor.

Chapter Eight

Kristina came awake slowly and her thoughts were muddled at first. She was confused to find herself lying on her bed with Cole sitting beside her. His blue eyes were watching her with concern. Then, as their hasty marriage flashed across her mind, she groaned, "Oh, no!"

Cole mistakenly assumed she was mourning her father. "Drake's still alive," he told her quickly, then favored her with a tender smile. "How do you feel?"

"All right," she replied hesitantly. "Did I faint?"

"You sure did." He was still smiling.

"I've never fainted before in my life."

"I shouldn't have pressured you into marrying me."

Kristina knew it had been more than their marriage. The tangled web she had woven was suffocating her.

"I'm sorry," Cole continued. "But, at the time, all I could think of was granting Drake his last wish." He brushed his fingertips across her cheek. "Samantha, you aren't committed," he said kindly. "We can have the marriage annulled."

"Is that what you want?" she asked. The question

had emerged from her heart, for she knew the marriage wasn't even legal—she wasn't Samantha Carlson. It wouldn't have to be annulled, it could simply be discarded.

Cole's reasoning told him to agree to a quick annulment, but, as he continued to gaze into her jade-green eyes, he was overwhelmed with such tender emotions that he almost changed his mind. He fought back against his weakness and said evenly, "We'll see about an annulment as soon as possible. All things considered, it's for the best."

"But earlier, you said we should give ourselves a chance to fall in love." Kristina reproached herself. Why was she questioning him? What difference did it make? He'd had a change of heart, but if he knew the truth about her, he'd have more than that—he'd be furious.

Cole considered his answer carefully. "Samantha, I still think I could very easily fall in love with you, but due to my way of life, I'd make a lousy husband. I'd be away from home too much, and my job is dangerous. I wouldn't want to make you a widow."

Kristina managed a shaky smile. "I understand, Cole. But it's all immaterial." He was sitting on the edge of the bed, and she reached out and placed a hand on his. "There's something I must tell you."

Clasping her hand, he drew her toward him. Kristina knew she should pull away, but she was powerless to do so. Furthermore, she longed for Cole's kiss. She'd experience the joy of his lips on hers before telling him her true identity.

Cole's thoughts were as reckless as Kristina's. Her beauty had him so enraptured that his independence fled his mind as he brought her into his arms.

His lips touched hers with featherlike softness, the contact a teasing invitation for more. Kristina, her

96

heart pounding, locked her hands behind his neck, urging him onward. Bolstered by her response, his mouth then claimed hers in a fervent conquest that sent her mind swirling. Cole's demanding, questing kiss caused a wild surge of pleasure to course through Kristina. She had never imagined that a man's kiss could be so wonderful. Back in Philadelphia, Kristina had occasionally allowed a beau to kiss her good night, but their kisses had been lukewarm compared to Cole's.

Cole released her with reluctance. With effort, he held himself in check. He longed to draw her back into his arms and relish her completely, for her sweet kiss had stirred his deepest passion. He was suddenly reminded that she was his wife, and he had every right to make love to her—but, if he did, then he'd be making a real commitment. His vow to find his mother's killers was still as strong as the day he had made it. Not even a wife such as Kristina would deter him from his quest. He gazed tenderly at her, but rose from the bed. Hereafter, he must avoid her closeness, for this beautiful woman weakened his resolve. He mustered a veneer of composure and said calmly, "I think we should be with Drake. He might not make it through the night."

Kristina, still feeling the exciting effect of his kiss, had to breathe in deeply to settle her emotions. Cole's lips on hers had been so stimulating, she wondered if she was falling in love. Could love happen so quickly? The memory of his kiss assured her that indeed it *could* happen. She routed the disturbing revelation from her mind, and turned her thoughts to Drake. Cole was right, they should go to his room and be with him. First, however, she was determined to tell Cole who she really was.

"Before we go to Dra—Father's room, I have

something to tell you."

"Can't it wait?" he asked impatiently.

"No," she replied. "It's too important."

Cole was anxious to be with his dying friend. "All right," he said somewhat testily. "Tell me whatever it is, but make it fast."

"It's not something I can say in a few words."

"Then it'll have to wait until later." He took her hand and urged her to her feet.

Kristina started to insist that he listen, but she understood the need to be with Drake. She sighed defeatedly, and made no objection as Cole led her to the door. After all, did it really matter if she confessed now or later? The result would be the same—Cole would despise her.

Drake awoke with the break of dawn. Autumn Moon was seated at one side of his bed, Kristina and Cole on the other. Joseph and the doctor were on the sofa, and the servant was dozing lightly. Reverend Scott had returned to town shortly after performing the marriage ceremony.

"Autumn Moon?" Drake whispered. His eyes fluttered open, closed, then opened again.

"I'm right here, Drake," Autumn Moon said, taking his hand.

"Cole? Samantha?" he called, his voice hoarse.

"We're here," Cole replied softly.

Drake swallowed with difficulty, then murmured, "I'm so thirsty."

Autumn Moon looked questioningly at Dr. Newman. "Give him a drink of water," he told her. He rose from the sofa, and stepped toward the bed.

Carefully, Autumn Moon lifted Drake's head and placed a glass of water to his dry lips. He managed a couple of swallows.

Kristina and Cole moved away from Drake's bedside, giving the doctor room to examine his patient. They watched silently as Newman listened to Drake's heartbeat through a stethoscope. He then checked his patient's pulse.

The doctor smiled. He looked at Autumn Moon, then turned to Cole and Kristina. "His heartbeat is regular, and his pulse is much stronger."

Drake, listening, asked weakly, "Does that mean I'm gonna live?"

"I certainly hope so," Newman replied. Cole took a step toward the bed, but the doctor held up a warding hand. "You can talk to Drake later. Right now he needs rest." His gaze went over the group. "We all need some sleep."

Leaving Autumn Moon to sit with Drake, the others left the room.

"I'll fix some breakfast," Joseph said as they stepped into the hall.

"Don't fix anything for me," the doctor said. "I need to check on a few patients, then get some sleep. I'll be back this afternoon."

He started to walk away, but Cole detained him. "Is Drake going to make it?"

Dr. Newman shrugged. "I don't know, but I'm more hopeful now."

"I'll walk outside with you," Cole told him. "I need to go to the bunkhouse, then I plan to work with the foreman for a few hours—"

"Cole," Kristina interrupted. "Please, don't leave. I must talk to you."

"We'll talk later." He reached over and gave her hand an affectionate squeeze. "All right?"

"Yes," she acquiesced. She watched as Cole and the doctor moved down the hall and to the stairs. She

99

wanted desperately to tell Cole the truth, and these continual postponements were beginning to fray her nerves.

"Are you feelin' poorly, Miz Samantha?" Joseph asked. He thought she looked a little drawn.

"I feel fine," she replied, forcing a smile.

"I think Mista Drake's gonna recover, don't you?"

She smiled again, but this time it wasn't forced. "Yes, I do. Thank God!"

The afternoon sun was declining when Cole returned to the house. He had worked all day alongside the ranch hands. He came through the back door, which led into the kitchen. Autumn Moon was standing at the stove, cooking supper.

"How's Drake?" Cole asked.

"He seems much better," she was happy to say. "He even drank a little broth."

Cole sat down at the table, and Autumn Moon brought him a cup of coffee.

"I think he's gonna make it," Cole remarked, grinning.

"So do I," Autumn Moon murmured. She pulled out a chair and sat down.

"Where's Samantha?"

"She's asleep. She waited all day for you to return, then a few minutes ago she went to her room. When I checked on her, she was sleeping."

"She wants to talk to me, but I guess it can wait." He took a drink of coffee, then asked, "Do you remember Billy Stockton?"

"Yes, I do."

"He's here. He wants his job back."

"Billy's a nice boy and a good worker. I don't think Drake would object if you were to let him come back

100

to work."

"That's what I figured. I told him to move into the bunkhouse and start work in the morning. The sheriff sent me a message through Billy. He wants to see me as soon as possible."

"Did Billy know why?"

"It has something to do with a stagecoach robbery." Cole finished his coffee and got to his feet. "I guess I'll ride into town and see what he wants."

"But dinner will be ready soon!"

"I'll get something to eat in town." Cole headed to the back door, and turning to face Autumn Moon, he said, "Tell Samantha we'll talk when I get home."

Kristina was upset that she had missed Cole. She was beginning to feel as though she'd never free herself from her deceitful web.

She had taken only a short nap and had awakened before dinner. Hurrying to find Autumn Moon, she had learned that Cole had gone into town. Her nerves on edge, she had eaten very little supper, and then had gone to the front porch to await Cole's return.

She was pacing restlessly when she spotted a buggy approaching the house. As it drew closer, she recognized Dr. Newman.

He tied his horse to the hitching rail, then with black bag in hand, he walked to the house. Seeing Kristina, he smiled congenially, "Good evening, Samantha."

This was the doctor's second visit within hours. Kristina was impressed by his dedication, and noticing he seemed quite fatigued, she murmured, "Dr. Newman, if you don't start taking better care of yourself, you're going to need a doctor."

He chuckled. "You just might be right." Two cane

rockers and a lounge were on the porch, and gesturing toward them, he suggested, "Let's sit down, shall we? I have something to give you."

When they were seated on the lounge, the doctor reached into his suit pocket and removed a sheet of paper. Handing it to Kristina, he said, "Reverend Scott asked me to deliver this. It's your marriage license."

Kristina's hands trembled as she unfolded the official document. The name "Samantha Carlson" seemed to jump out at her. She quickly folded the paper.

"Is something wrong?" Newman asked, noting her reaction. When she didn't answer, he asked kindly, "Samantha, what's bothering you?"

Kristina could stand no more, and losing her self-restraint, she blurted out, "Don't call me Samantha!"

"I'm sorry," the doctor replied, somewhat non-plussed. "I didn't think you'd mind if I called you by your first name." He continued stiffly. "My apologies, Miss Carlson—or should I say Mrs. Barton?"

Newman started to leave, but Kristina's hand was suddenly on his arm, keeping him at her side.

"I don't want you to call me Samantha, because I'm not Samantha Carlson! My name is Kristina Parker!" A long sigh of relief escaped her lips. She felt as though a heavy burden had suddenly been lifted from her shoulders.

The doctor gaped at her. "But . . . but I don't understand," he stammered.

"I'll explain," she replied.

"Please do," he said sharply.

Kristina made a full confession. She let the doctor know that it was she, and not the disinterested Samantha, who had always written to Drake. Then she told him about Raymond Lewis's attack, and the reason why she and Ted Cummings had decided she should come to Drake Carlson.

"I want to tell Drake the truth," she continued. "But he's so ill that I'm afraid to upset him."

"You're right not to tell him. The shock could very well bring on another attack. You can't tell him until he's stronger."

"I hate living this lie," she groaned.

"I'm sure you do," he answered sincerely. "But, for now, you have no other choice." He watched her closely. "Does Cole know?"

She fought back tears. "No, I haven't been able to tell him."

"But you actually married him!" Newman exclaimed.

"He didn't give me any other alternative. If you'll remember, I was pressured into that ceremony."

Newman spoke apologetically. "I'm as guilty as Cole. I insisted on the marriage also. I thought it might help Drake recover."

"Apparently it did," she murmured lamely.

"We'll never know for sure." He reached over and patted her hand gently. "Kristina, you must tell Cole everything."

"I will, as soon as he comes home. I also plan to tell Autumn Moon and Joseph."

"I don't think you should say anything to Autumn Moon or Joseph. At least not yet. They might inadvertently let it slip to Drake. He mustn't know the truth until he's strong enough to take the shock."

"But I hate deceiving them!" Kristina rose abruptly and moved to the porch railing. Her back was turned to the doctor.

Newman placed his hands on her shoulders and turned her so that she was facing him. Gazing down

103

tenderly into her tear-filled eyes, he murmured, "If Drake's life means as much to you as I think it does, then you'll live this lie a little longer."

"I love Drake!" she exclaimed. "I've loved him for years. He's always been like a father to me."

"Then for his sake, keep pretending you're Samantha. As soon as I'm reasonably sure he's well enough to hear the truth, I'll let you know. I promise."

Kristina was despondent. "He'll hate me."

"No, he won't. I'll be with you when you tell him, and I'll help you explain. Drake will understand that we kept this secret for his sake."

"I hope so," she sighed helplessly.

The doctor picked up his bag. "I need to check on my patient."

Kristina went to the door and held it open for him. "Dr. Newman, thank you for listening, and most of all, for understanding."

He smiled warmly. "You're very welcome. But, Kristina, don't put off telling Cole."

"I won't," she assured him. "I intend to tell him the moment I see him."

"Did you want to see me?" Cole asked, walking in to the sheriff's office.

Sheriff Bickham was seated behind his desk. At Cole's entrance, he pulled open a drawer and withdrew a bottle of whiskey and two glasses. "Sit down, Barton."

The sheriff filled the glasses, then handed one to Cole.

"The stagecoach was robbed this morning," Bickham began. "It happened about ten miles north of here. It took place out of my jurisdiction.

Otherwise, I'd be tryin' to track down the robbers. The man ridin' shotgun and one passenger were killed. The driver recognized one of the hold-up men. A couple months back, Wells Fargo posted a large reward on him. I thought you might want to pick up his trail."

"It's tempting," Cole replied. "But with Drake still sick, I don't feel free to leave." Cole finished his whiskey. "Thanks for the drink. Have you had supper yet?"

The sheriff said he hadn't.

"I'm going to the hotel for dinner. Why don't you join me?"

Standing, Bickham replied, "I think I will." He returned the bottle to the desk drawer, then pulled out an oversized sheet of paper. "Here, you might want this. It's a poster on the same man who robbed the stage."

Cole looked at it. "Sam Wilkes!" he exclaimed.

"You know him?"

"I know *of* him." Cole folded the paper and stuck it in his pocket. "If Drake's still improving, I might go after this bastard."

"I wouldn't wait too long. You need to leave before his trail gets cold."

"I'll leave in the morning, if possible."

Chapter Nine

Kristina remained determined to see Cole the moment he arrived. She returned to the lounge and waited impatiently. The gray shadows of dusk finally gave way to night's full darkness. The moon appeared in the cloudless sky and bathed the landscape in a soft golden hue.

She was still on the porch when Dr. Newman left his patient. They discussed Drake's condition in earnest before he bid her good night. Time continued to drag slowly, and Kristina had no idea how long she had been waiting.

Suddenly the front door opened, and Autumn Moon stepped onto the porch.

"Samantha, Drake wants to see you."

Kristina tensed. She dreaded having to face Drake alone and pretend she was Samantha. With a calmness she was far from feeling, she rose from the lounge and said, "If Father is asking for me, then he must be a lot better."

The woman smiled radiantly. "His recovery is like a miracle."

Kristina regarded Autumn Moon. *She's in love with Drake*, Kristina realized. She wondered if Drake

107

shared her feelings.

"You better hurry to your father," Autumn Moon encouraged. "He can stay awake only a short time."

Kristina hurried into the house and climbed the stairs quickly. As she started down the hall, her steps grew somewhat hesitant. She and Drake would be by themselves for the first time. She hoped her love for this man wouldn't affect her emotions and cause her to break her promise to Dr. Newman. Before his departure, the physician had emphasized to Kristina that her pretense was imperative—Drake was not strong enough to handle the shock of her true identity. Kristina had promised that she would continue her deception.

Reaching Drake's door, she knocked softly before entering. She stepped quietly to the chair placed beside the bed. Drake's eyes were closed, and she was wondering if she should awaken him when he suddenly looked at her.

"Samantha," he murmured. "Newman thinks I'm gonna make it. I guess this old ticker of mine isn't quite ready to give up."

She slipped her hand into his. "You'll soon be as good as new."

His gaze lingered on her face. "You're a very beautiful young lady. You make me so proud."

She swallowed heavily. "Thank you."

"Where's Cole?"

"He went into town."

"Are you mad at me for manipulating you two?"

"You didn't manipulate us."

"Of course I did. How could either of you deny a dying man's last wish? I was not only manipulative but also a cheat. I didn't even die."

"If that's cheating, then I hope you continue to

cheat." She couldn't help but smile.

"Seriously, my dear, I'm sorry about pressuring you. But will you take some advice?"

"I might," she responded warmly.

"Give your marriage to Cole a chance to succeed. I've always had the feeling that you two belong together."

She skirted the subject. "We'll discuss my marriage when you're stronger. Now you must concentrate on getting well."

He squeezed her hand weakly. "I wish I didn't tire so quickly. I'd like to talk to you longer but—"

"That's all right," she replied. Standing, she leaned over the bed and kissed his brow. "We'll talk again soon. Get some rest."

He was asleep before Kristina crossed the room. Stepping into the hall, she was surprised to find Autumn Moon waiting.

"I thought you might like a bath . . ." the woman began. "Joseph will bring up the tub, but I don't know if he should take it to your room or to Cole's."

"My room, of course. Why would he take it to . . . ?" A sudden blush colored her cheeks. "Cole and I shared marriage vows, but we don't plan to share a marriage bed."

"I understand," Autumn Moon replied, her cheeks coloring in embarrassment.

"If Cole should arrive while I'm bathing, will you please let him know that I must talk to him? It's imperative that I see him as soon as possible." Kristina's brow furrowed. "I wonder why he hasn't returned?"

"He went into town to see the sheriff," Autumn Moon explained. "They're good friends and are probably at the Branding Iron Saloon together."

"But Cole knew I wanted to talk to him. How can he leave me waiting like this?" Kristina was growing irritated.

"If you decide to remain married to Cole, you will spend a great deal of time waiting for him. Cole comes and goes as he pleases. We who love him have learned to accept it."

Kristina knew, if she were truly Cole's wife, she would never learn to accept his absences. She disregarded the notion—she wasn't Cole's wife and never would be.

Kristina was immersed in the large tub, thoroughly enjoying her bath when a knock sounded on her door.

"Samantha?" Cole called.

"Just a minute," she replied. She stepped out of the tub, grabbed a towel, and dried off quickly. As she slipped on her robe, she considered telling Cole to meet her downstairs so she could get decently dressed before seeing him. Preferring to avoid another postponement, however, she discarded the idea. Wrapping the silk robe about her tightly, she tied the sash securely, then hurried to the door.

As Cole closed the door behind him, his gaze etched a fiery path over her delectable beauty, which her silk robe clearly enhanced. Her curly blond tresses were falling freely about her shoulders in seductive disarray.

Kristina, reading the intent in his blazing scrutiny, took a tentative step backward, but Cole's hand shot out, grasped her wrist, and pulled her into his arms.

She could smell liquor on his breath. "You've been drinking," she remarked in annoyance.

"I've had a few drinks, but I'm not drunk. I know exactly what I'm doing."

"Then why are you doing this? Why don't you let me go?"

"No man in his right mind would let you go." He pressed her supple curves snug against his hard frame.

She didn't resist.

"Mrs. Barton, you're very beautiful," he murmured huskily. Then, suddenly, his lips were on hers, and his demanding kiss left her breathless with wonder.

Teasingly, his warm lips moved down to the hollow of her throat, the contact whisper-light. The tingling effect sent a tremor of desire through Kristina. She shifted closer to Cole.

Despite Kristina's intoxicating beauty, Cole was still in control. He knew if he made love to his bride, he would then be bound to his marriage vows. Did he really want to make such a commitment?

As he gazed down into Kristina's face, he was filled with conflicting turmoil. Deep within his heart he longed to pledge a commitment, but the untamed side of him rejected the ties of matrimony.

Kristina's inner strife was as turbulent as Cole's. She wanted to surrender completely to this man who had such power over her heart and body. If she were really Samantha, she would give him her love with no reservations, but she wasn't Drake's daughter. Kristina still believed Cole would be furious when he learned the truth.

She gazed thoughtfully into his dark-blue eyes, which were studying her with deep, tender longing. Following her confession, though, she knew those sensual eyes would regard her with anger. She

111

recklessly threw her reasoning to the wind. She might be destined to lose him, but before that happened, she would experience the pleasure of his embrace.

Driven by an overpowering need to love him fully, Kristina laced her arms about his neck and urged his lips down to hers.

Kristina's ardent gesture drove Cole's doubts from his mind, and surrendering to his fervent feelings, he kissed her passionately.

"Darlin'," he murmured. "I think Drake is right. We belong together."

Kristina agreed. Drake had the right lovers paired, he merely had her name wrong.

Cole swept her into his arms and laid her down gently on the bed, then moving to the lamp, he lowered the wick to a romantic glow.

He removed his gunbelt and boots. Then, returning to Kristina, he lay beside her and drew her intimately close. He kissed her deeply. Her response was instant, almost shameless. She became conscious only of his closeness and his lips on hers.

Anxious to relish her unclad beauty, Cole untied the robe's sash, then pushed the silky material to the side. His lips moved to her breasts, kissing one taut nipple then the other.

His intimate caress made Kristina flinch, but her reaction was momentary, for Cole's fondling soon had her swept away on tidal waves of pleasure. Suddenly, his mouth was back on hers, his urgent kiss so brutal that it seemed a punishing sweetness.

Her passion unleashed, Kristina returned his kiss totally, her tongue exploring his mouth with an urgency that set Cole's desire blazing.

He hurriedly removed her robe. As Kristina lay naked before his raking gaze, her better judgment tried to reason with her passion-filled mind, warning her that this man would take her innocence, then desert her. But she was beyond such logic, for Cole had her totally at his mercy. She was his to do with as he pleased.

Cole's roving hands mapped a fiery path over her flesh, touching and stroking her intimately. Fire shot through every nerve in her body as she succumbed to the burning passion his caresses were evoking.

"Sweetheart," Cole murmured thickly as his lips sought hers in a demanding exchange. Then, he left the bed to shed his clothes.

Kristina, feeling no modesty with Cole, watched boldly as he disrobed. She was fascinated by his lean, muscular physique. As her eyes came to rest on the dark hair covering his strong chest, she felt an undeniable urge to run her fingers through the curly mass.

When he was left standing before her totally unclothed, she lowered her gaze to his erect manhood, which incited her untutored passion to greater heights. She held out her arms to him, and he went into her embrace eagerly.

Her hands moved over the muscular planes and hard-muscled ridges of his superb body.

Kristina's exploring caresses were electrifying, setting fire to Cole's already raging desire. His need was now burning out of control, and capturing her lips to his, he moved over her delicate frame.

Suddenly, though, he was gripped with a sense of fairness, and it cooled his fiery passion. Tenderly he kissed Kristina's brow, then gazing into her eyes with loving concern, he murmured, "Sweetheart, if we consummate our marriage, we'll truly be husband and wife. I won't take my commitment to you lightly. I'll love you, cherish you, and treat you with the utmost respect. But you'll have to take me as I am, or not take me at all. Do you understand what I'm saying?"

She understood only too well, but she also knew his loving warning was not of significance. Consummating their love wouldn't make them husband and wife, for their marriage was not a valid one. She came close to telling him who she really was, but his lips were suddenly on hers, drowning her confession.

"Do you understand?" he asked again, his voice husky with passion.

"Yes," she whispered timorously. "But, Cole—"

Cole's mouth smothered her lips urgently, and, as she surrendered to his amorous kiss, all thoughts of confession departed her mind.

He parted her legs with his knees, and slipping his hands beneath her buttocks, he lifted her thighs to his. He entered her quickly, and she gasped softly as he took her innocence.

Hesitating, he waited until her discomfort abated, then he pressed himself even deeper into her moist depths.

Wondrous sensations began to sweep through her body, and holding him tightly, she whispered raspingly, "Cole . . . Cole, love me."

He kissed her fiercely, then as his hips started moving rhythmically, she matched each driving thrust. Engulfed totally in passion's splendor, Kristina writhed and moaned as Cole's fervent love-making carried them into a world all their own.

Time and reality ceased to exist for Kristina. This moment was forever, and only her undying love for Cole Barton seemed real—nothing else mattered.

Kristina lay quietly in Cole's arms, wrapped in the

afterglow of their union. She had never imagined that lovemaking could be so ecstatically exciting. She had a feeling, however, that only Cole had the power to take her to such rapturous heights, for she was hopelessly in love with him. A rush of apprehension came over her, destroying her mood. She had to tell Cole the truth. Now, before she lost the courage!

She lifted her head from his shoulder, so she could see his face. His eyes, their expression loving, gazed into hers. She became so lost in the azure depths that her confession temporarily faded into oblivion.

"Darlin' . . ." Cole began. "Did Drake write to you about my mother?"

"He said that she was dead, but that was all. Why do you ask?"

Fluffing his pillow against the headboard, he sat up and leaned back. "You need to know why I don't intend to stop being a bounty hunter. Not even our marriage will change that."

"Cole, before you say anything more, there's something I must tell you."

"No," he replied strongly. "Let me finish, then you can have your turn. Please?"

She consented reluctantly.

Cole spoke quietly as he explained his mother's death in detail, but the pain in his eyes revealed that the memory still tortured him. "I learned that those Jayhawkers deserted and headed west. That's why I eventually decided to become a bounty hunter. Men as vicious as the ones who killed my mother never change. They remain murderers. As a bounty hunter, I come into contact with killers all the time, and one day, I'll meet up with the man I saw leaning over my mother's body."

"The one with the branded chest," Kristina clarified.

115

"When I find him, I'll kill him," Cole remarked coldly.

"What happened to your father?"

"When I left the farm and went to Tennessee, I learned that he was killed in battle."

Kristina sighed sympathetically. "Cole, it's been sixteen years since your mother was killed. The chances of you finding the man who attacked her are slim."

"Don't you think I know that? But I've got to keep trying!"

"Does revenge mean that much to you?" Her tone was pleading.

Cole shrugged aside her question. "I didn't think you'd understand."

"Even if you find your mother's murderers, killing them won't bring her back. What will you have gained?"

"Justice," he answered bluntly. A vision of the Jayhawker's branded chest flashed in Cole's mind, and the expression in his eyes turned deadly cold.

Kristina now understood Billy Stockton's description of Cole: "There's a coldness in his eyes that can chill a man to the bone." The expression was indeed chilling!

Cole noticed she seemed a little frightened. "What's wrong?"

"I'm afraid for you."

He smiled tenderly. "Are you afraid I'll be killed?"

"Yes, but I'm more afraid of what you are doing to yourself. You live with so much hate that I'm afraid someday you might become as cold-hearted as the killers you track."

"Not as long as I have friends, especially friends like Drake and Josh Chandler." He brushed his fingertips across her cheek. "And a sweet, loving wife

116

like you." His grin askew, he murmured, "How about a kiss?"

Responding to his light-hearted mood, she cuddled into his arms and pressed her lips to his. The kiss, initially tender, soon bloomed into one of passion.

Surrendering to their rekindled desire, they made love again. With each kiss and thrust, the lovers climbed closer to their ultimate peak. Their moment of fulfillment surged powerfully, and they trembled with wondrous, breathtaking release.

Cole kissed Kristina softly, then moved to lie at her side. He was totally exhausted. He'd had no sleep the night before and had stayed awake all day. He closed his eyes and was near sleep when Kristina sat up in bed.

"Cole . . ." she began. "I can't keep putting off talking to you. There's something I must tell you."

"All right, sweetheart. I'm listening." He stifled a yawn and forced his eyes open. He wished he wasn't so damned worn out.

Kristina was too filled with guilt and worry to look at him, and she turned her face away. Her heart started pounding anxiously. She hoped Cole would understand and forgive her for deceiving him. If he turned on her furiously, it would break her heart. With a quick intake of breath, she blurted out the truth, "I'm not Samantha Carlson. My name is Kristina Parker, and I was Samantha's maid and companion."

She didn't dare breathe as she awaited Cole's response. God, would he hate her? With her tension rising and her anxiety increasing, she girded herself for Cole's outburst. She was, however, confronted with total silence. Was he too enraged to say anything?

Cautiously, she turned and looked at him and was shocked to find that he was sound asleep.

"Damn it, Cole!" she moaned miserably. "I finally tell you the truth, and you sleep through it."

He stirred in slumber, came barely awake, and reached out to draw her to his side. "What were you sayin', sweetness?" he asked drowsily.

"Never mind," she replied. "It can wait until morning."

"I love you, darlin'," he whispered before falling back asleep.

Kristina extinguished the lamp, then drew up the sheet and snuggled against Cole's warm body. *I may as well look on the bright side,* she thought, knowing her confession was again postponed. *This way, I get to spend the night in his arms.*

Chapter Ten

The sun was a bright red ball cresting the horizon, and as the early-morning rays filtered through the open bedroom window, Cole came awake.

Kristina was snuggled next to him, her head on his shoulder, an arm resting across his chest. For a moment, Cole cleared everything from his mind and concentrated fully on his beautiful bride. A warm, tender smile curled his lips as he recalled her sweet, wild passion.

With a somewhat reluctant sigh, he moved away from her tempting body and left the bed. Stepping to the water pitcher, he filled the small basin and carried it and a washcloth to the bedside table.

Sitting on the edge of the bed, he leaned over Kristina and placed a kiss on her forehead. "Wake up, sweetheart," he murmured.

Her eyelids fluttered open, and then with a graceful, catlike stretch, she came fully awake. She smiled a sweet "good morning" at Cole.

Kristina's curly tresses fell seductively about her face and Cole lifted a silky lock and caressed it between his fingers. "Do you always wake up looking so damned desirable?" he asked.

119

"I must look dreadful," she replied, certain he was teasing. "Why are you up so early? Are you planning to work with the ranch hands?"

"No," he answered. He was feeling slightly uneasy. He still planned to pursue Sam Wilkes, and he had a strong suspicion that his bride wouldn't take his leaving in good humor.

"Then what are your plans for today?"

He wrung out the washcloth. "Well, first I intend to wash your lovely thighs."

Kristina was stunned. "What?"

He drew down the sheet covering her. "I took your virginity, my little innocent. Now I'll wash away the telltale signs." Gently, he parted her legs, then he carefully washed her between her thighs.

Kristina wasn't embarrassed lying vulnerable to this man's scrutiny. She felt no shame with Cole, and as he continued his tender ministrations, she allowed her gaze to roam over his bare physique. Apparently, he also had no modesty in her presence, and their closeness was thrilling to Kristina.

She was suddenly struck anew with how desperately she loved Cole Barton. Her feelings were so powerful, so passionate, that they overwhelmed her.

Cole returned the cloth to the basin, then, as their eyes locked, both could sense the other's intense desire.

She held out her arms, murmuring, "I want you, Cole. I want you now."

"The feeling is quite mutual," he replied in a soft, husky tone. He went into her loving embrace, drew her close and pressed his lips to hers.

Their fiery, questing kiss fueled their passion, and their bodies came together urgently. Kristina gave herself to Cole with total abandon, loving the feel of his hardness deep within her. Her hips, meeting

120

Cole's in love's erotic rhythm, sent exultant sensations wafting through her in fervent waves.

Cole's demanding passion took her to ultimate fulfillment, and she cried out throatily as she was engulfed in complete ecstasy.

Achieving his own breathless release, Cole sent his seed deep within her. Moments later, he kissed her endearingly before moving to lay at her side.

An uneasy silence followed their rapturous union, for they were both plagued with troublesome thoughts. Cole was dreading telling Kristina that he was leaving and Kristina was trying to gather the courage to admit that she wasn't Samantha Carlson.

Cole spoke first. "Darlin' . . ." he began. "When I was in town yesterday, Sheriff Bickham said the stagecoach was robbed. The man riding shotgun and a passenger were killed, but the driver recognized one of the robbers—Sam Wilkes. I've been trackin' Wilkes for weeks, but somehow he always manages to elude me."

He didn't need to say more. Kristina understood. She sat up quickly, exclaiming, "Cole, surely you aren't going after him!"

"As soon as I get dressed and pack a bag, I'm leaving," he said with an indifference he hardly felt.

"But, Cole, I love you!" Kristina cried. "And I thought you loved me!"

"I do love you," he replied calmly, moving off the bed and pulling on his clothes.

Kristina was speechless, as she watched him with disbelief. How could he be so unfeeling as to leave her? Didn't their love mean anything to him? She had given him her body, as well as her heart, but, obviously, Cole couldn't care less. He was as heartless as her father! He had no qualms about taking a woman's love, then abandoning her!

Comparing Cole to her father touched a raw nerve. She bounded from the bed, ablaze with anger, and slipped on her robe. "Cole Barton," she spat, "if you leave me to chase down Sam Wilkes, then don't bother to come back!"

But as the words left her lips, Kristina's logic surfaced, reminding her that she had no right to pass judgment on Cole, let alone give him an ultimatum. He might be a scoundrel, but *she* was a fraud!

Her harsh terms disturbed Cole, and he responded in turn, but his anger was aimed mostly at himself. He strapped on his gunbelt, then turning a cold gaze in Kristina's direction, he said irritably, "I should've listened to my common sense and not made a commitment to you. Damn it, I can't be the kind of husband you want! But, darlin', last night I said you'd have to take me as I am, or not take me at all." Rage flickered in his piercing eyes. "I warned you, didn't I?"

"Yes, you did," she conceded.

"And you chose to take me as I am. So, the way I see it, you know what you were getting. I told you I'd make a lousy husband."

The hurt in Kristina's eyes tore at Cole's heart, but he nonetheless held himself aloof. He was determined to find Sam Wilkes, and not even his treasured bride was going to stop him. At last he felt close to the truth about his mother's death. Rumor had it that Wilkes had a scarred chest, and no power on this earth could keep him from tracking the man down!

Struggling against a need to draw Kristina into his arms, Cole crossed the floor, opened the door, then turned back to face her. "I don't know when I'll be back. It might be days, maybe even weeks."

Kristina held back tears. She probably wouldn't be here when Cole returned. The moment she received the doctor's permission, she intended to tell Drake the truth. After her confession, she was sure she would feel too uncomfortable to stay in Drake's home. She didn't know where she'd go, but she was hoping that Dr. Newman could assist her. Perhaps he could help her find employment as a teacher.

Cole stood poised in the doorway, but when Kristina remained unresponsive, he turned to leave.

She was surprised when he suddenly whirled around to face her. There was nothing left to say. Finding Sam Wilkes meant more to him than her love.

"Last night there was something you wanted to tell me, but I fell asleep." Cole spoke calmly. "Do you want to tell me now?"

Kristina almost laughed. She had tried so desperately to be honest with Cole, but he had always evaded her confession. Now that he was ready to listen, she hadn't the heart to tell him.

"It doesn't matter," she said, her tone despondent. "When you return, you'll find out."

He didn't question her evasive answer but with a stern expression, he remarked, "You're my wife, and I'll expect you to be here when I return." With that, he left the room.

Cole paused outside Kristina's door. He had an urge to barge back inside, take her into his arms, and make her understand his leaving had nothing to do with his feelings for her. He turned toward the door and was about to enter when he suddenly changed his mind. If he tried to reason with her, his efforts would most likely fail. She was a bride whose husband had deserted her—at least, that was the way she saw it.

Deciding to leave things as they were, Cole headed toward his own room.

Kristina moved sluggishly to the bed and sat on the

edge, trying to control her tears. She hoped she would be gone when Cole returned. Seeing him again would only make her love him more. Also, she felt it would be easier for her to get over Cole if she didn't see him again.

Troubled, she rose from the bed and began pacing. She wanted desperately to tell Drake who she really was. Surely, the doctor would soon give her permission to do so. Then, if he did help her find a position, by the time Cole returned, she'd be gone. Would learning the truth about her enrage Cole? He would probably be more relieved than angry, for he didn't want a wife, nor did he need one. Finding his mother's killers meant more to him than her love.

Kristina once again sat on the bed. She loved Cole, and she had a feeling she always would. Regardless of what the future might bring, even if she should legitimately marry someday, she believed that no man would ever take Cole's place in her heart. She sighed disconsolately. After having loved Cole Barton, how could she truly love another?

Cole moved quietly into Drake's room. Joseph was sitting beside the bed, but when he saw Cole, he left so the two men could be alone.

The curtains had been drawn aside, and the early-morning sun shone cheerfully into the room. Going to the bedside chair, Cole sat down and smiled at Drake. "You look a lot better."

"I'm determined to live to see my grandchildren." He grinned teasingly. "Although I don't have anything against girls, I'd like the first one to be a grandson."

Cole laughed lightly. "I'll see what I can do."

Drake studied Cole closely before asking, "Where

did you spend last night?"

"You prying jackass, you already know." There was only warmth in Cole's retort.

"Autumn Moon went to your room last night to tell you I wanted to see you. Since you weren't there, it didn't take much to figure out where you were."

It was a moment before Cole answered. "Drake, this is what you want, isn't it? Samantha and I are married now in every sense of the word."

"Yes, it's what I want. But I also want you to love her."

Cole leaned back in his chair and stretched out his long legs. "I love her, Drake," he answered evenly.

The man smiled happily. "Does she love you?"

"I think so."

"Good! Cole, I know you relish your independence, but I'm hoping that you and Samantha will decide to live here at the Diamond-C."

Cole shrugged. "I haven't made any future plans. This marriage was kinda sudden, you know. But I hope you don't mind if Samantha lives here until I decide what to do about the future. I have a tidy sum of money saved. I might invest in my own ranch."

"What do you mean about Samantha living here? Aren't you going to live here with her?"

"Not right now," he answered.

"Damn it, Cole! You aren't leaving, are you?"

"I plan to leave in a few minutes. I'm tracking a man named Sam Wilkes. The sheriff in Albuquerque said that this man has a scarred chest. Yesterday he robbed the stage a few miles north of here. I hope to pick up his trail."

Drake frowned, but he didn't argue with Cole. He knew it would be a waste of breath. "I don't suppose my daughter is too happy about you leaving."

"No, but I told her she'll have to learn to accept me

as I am."

"Marriage is a fifty-fifty proposition, Cole. You're gonna have to change your lifestyle."

"Maybe," he replied, standing. "I'll be back as soon as I can. Take good care of yourself."

"You do the same. I'd hate to see Samantha be a bride one day and a widow the next."

"So would I," Cole replied with a hesitant chuckle.

Dr. Newman arrived at midmorning, examined Drake, and announced that he was still making considerable improvement. Kristina walked outside with him, and he assured her that Drake would soon be strong enough to hear the truth.

Remaining on the porch, Kristina watched as the physician's carriage moved farther away from the house. She started to go back indoors when she noticed a lone rider approaching. He pulled up his horse, said a few words to the doctor, then resumed his approach.

She continued to look on as the man's palomino galloped up to the hitching rail. He swung down from the saddle, secured his horse, then ambled up the porch steps. Tipping his Stetson hat, he greeted her with a "Good morning, Miss Carlson."

Kristina was quite impressed with the man's startling good looks. "Good morning," she replied.

"In case you're wondering how I know who you are, I recognized you from your picture. I've seen it on Drake's desk." He smiled charmingly. "I'm Josh Chandler."

"Mr. Chandler, we've been expecting you."

"I left as soon as I received Autumn Moon's telegram. Dr. Newman just told me that Drake is improving and that certainly is good news. I think a

126

lot of your father."

"I'm sure he'll be happy to see you, but the doctor's examination tired him. Maybe you should wait and see him after lunch."

"That'll be fine. Is Cole here?"

"He was," Kristina answered. She tried to keep her tone indifferent, but a note of bitterness leaked through.

Josh picked up on it immediately. "You seem disturbed."

At that moment, Autumn Moon came out and onto the porch. Seeing Josh, she went into his opening arms, welcoming him with a warm hug.

They discussed Drake's condition, then with a wide smile, Autumn Moon asked, "Did Samantha tell you that she and Cole are married?"

Josh was dumbfounded. "Married!" he exclaimed, turning to look at Kristina. "But if you two are married, where the hell is Cole?"

"Tracking down a man named Sam Wilkes," Kristina replied flatly.

"Well, I'll be damned!" he remarked. "Are you telling me that he married you, then took off?"

Suddenly embarrassed, Kristina lowered her eyes from Josh's level gaze. Damn Cole for putting her on the spot! There was no telling what Josh must be thinking.

Reading her thoughts, and sympathizing with her, Josh was quick to say, "Cole oughta be strung up and whipped. The stubborn, hard-headed ass!"

Kristina couldn't help but smile. "Maybe you shouldn't be so hard on him. After all, our marriage was sort of forced on him."

Josh's brow furrowed with puzzlement.

As Kristina moved over to sit on the lounge, Autumn Moon told Josh why the two had married.

Then, deciding to prepare a room for their guest, she went back into the house.

Josh stepped to the lounge and sat beside Kristina. He spoke gently, "You're in love with Cole, aren't you?"

"I didn't know it was so obvious," she murmured.

He smiled at her with kindness. "Be patient with him. You can't expect a man like Cole to change overnight."

They were interrupted by Joseph. "Miz Samantha, your pa's a-wantin' to see you."

She stood. "Excuse me, Mr. Chandler."

"Please call me Josh."

He watched as Kristina followed the butler into the house. A smile touched his lips. He didn't blame Cole for marrying such a beautiful lady. His smile widened and his expression grew hopeful. A good woman's love might persuade Cole to stop his sixteen-year search, hang up his gunbelt, and settle down.

For more reasons than one, Josh certainly hoped so.

"Samantha, dear, sit down," Drake remarked, gesturing toward the bedside chair.

She looked closely at him. Color had returned to his face, and his eyes were bright. She thought him a strikingly handsome man. "Josh Chandler is here," she said.

"Yes, I know. Autumn Moon told me. I plan to see him in a few minutes, but first I wanted to talk to you."

"About what?" she asked, although she was certain she already knew.

"Cole," he replied. As he regarded her thoughtfully, he found himself searching for a resemblance between them. She had blond hair and green eyes similiar to his own, but there the likeness ended. He could find absolutely no resemblance between her and his first wife.

"What about Cole?" she questioned, wishing she could avoid discussing him.

"Are you upset over his leaving?"

"No, not at all," she replied, hoping he believed her.

Drake smiled tenderly. "You're a very poor liar, Samantha."

Hearing him call her Samantha made her groan inwardly. *I'm a much better liar than he knows,* she thought bitterly.

Drake looked at her with concern. He knew she was trying to put up a brave front. Cole's departure had probably broken her heart. His eyes swept over her lovingly. She was extremely fetching in her pastel, short-sleeved dress. As his gaze traveled over her bare arms, he suddenly stiffened and drew a sharp intake of breath.

Worried, Kristina exclaimed, "Are you all right?"

He strove to calm himself. "Yes . . . yes, dear, I'm all right. I guess I'm overly tired. I think I'll sleep now. We can talk later."

She rose from the chair, leaned over, and kissed his forehead. "I'll see you this afternoon. Do you want me to ask Autumn Moon to come sit with you?"

"No, that won't be necessary."

Drake's eyes followed her as she crossed the room, opened the door, and left. Then, expelling a deep, troubled sigh, he murmured aloud, "Who the hell is she? She's not Samantha, that's for sure."

129

Chapter Eleven

"You must've ridden day and night to get here so quickly," Drake said to Josh.

Sitting in the chair beside the bed, Josh replied, "I didn't waste any time, that's for sure."

Autumn Moon was also in the room, standing beside the open window, gazing blankly outside.

Josh sensed an uneasy tension. "Is something wrong?" he asked.

Drake's answer was a simple nod.

"Is there any way I can help?" Josh offered.

"A couple of problems have come up."

Josh arched a brow. "For instance?"

"Autumn Moon sent a wire to Alisa. We haven't received a reply."

Turning away from the window, Autumn Moon said a little harshly, "Drake is her father! She should care enough to at least send us a response."

Josh tried to soothe their hurt feelings. "It's still early. You'll probably hear from her." He looked questioningly at Drake. "You haven't told Samantha about Alisa, have you?"

"If you are referring to the young woman who is pretending to be my daughter then, no, I haven't

131

told her.''

"What are you talking about?"

"The woman is an impostor."

Josh was incredulous. "But she's the same woman in the picture."

"I know that!" Drake barked impatiently. "My heart attack didn't affect my sight!"

"Then how can you think she's an impostor?"

"When she came to see me earlier, she was wearing a short-sleeved dress. I happened to look closely at her bare arms. Samantha has a birthmark on the inside of her arm, above the elbow. There's no birthmark on this woman."

"You haven't seen Samantha since she was three years old. Maybe the birthmark faded away."

"The doctor told Mary and me that it would fade with time but that it would never completely disappear."

Josh was totally perplexed. "But if she isn't Samantha, then who is she? And why do you have her picture instead of Samantha's?"

"I don't know, but I intend to find out. And I plan to confront her now," he said firmly.

"Do you want me to be here while you talk to her?" Josh offered.

"No, but thanks. You and Autumn Moon go downstairs and tell the girl that I need to see her."

Josh was uncertain. "Drake, this might prove to be too much for you. Maybe you should let me talk to her."

"I'll be all right. Don't worry."

"Don't worry?" he questioned. "Drake, you're still seriously ill."

"Maybe so, but that little gal isn't going to bring on another heart attack. I wish all of you would stop treating me like I'm about to break. Now, do as I say

132

and send her to me."

Josh and Autumn Moon conceded reluctantly.

They found Kristina in the kitchen talking to Joseph. Josh let her know that Drake wanted to see her.

Kristina left immediately, dreading another session with Drake. Pretending to the others that she was Samantha was extremely difficult, but with Drake it was doubly so.

She entered his room, went to the chair, and sat down. She smiled and was about to ask him how he was feeling when, suddenly, he cut her off.

"I don't know what kind of game you are playing, young lady, but it's over."

Kristina paled. *He knew the truth! But how?*

"Why don't you tell me why you're pretending to be my daughter? I'd also like to know why your picture is in my study instead of Samantha's."

Kristina was actually relieved that the farce was finally over. She looked at Drake attentively. He seemed in complete control. Realizing she wasn't Samantha apparently hadn't endangered his health.

"How did you know?" Kristina asked, calmly.

"Samantha has a birthmark on her arm."

"Of course!" she declared. "I completely forgot!"

"Then it's still quite noticeable?"

"Yes, it is. Samantha always wears long-sleeved dresses, even in the summer."

"Are you a close friend of my daughter?"

"I was her maid and companion."

"Why do I have your picture?"

"I sent it to you myself."

"But why?"

"I didn't want you to gaze upon her picture while

133

you wrote to me."

Drake was totally confused. "While I wrote to *you?*"

"All these years you have been writing to me, not to Samantha."

Kristina rose from the chair, and began pacing beside the bed. Slowly, and in vivid detail, she explained everything to Drake. She let him know that, from the very beginning, Samantha had no interest in corresponding with him. As her story continued to unfold, she elaborated on her life before moving to the Johnsons' home. She admitted to Drake that she had used him as a substitute father. Her own father had abandoned her, and although he didn't know it, his daughter had abandoned him — but through their letters, they had found each other. She gave him a full account of Raymond's attack and explained why she and Ted Cummings had decided she should come to the Diamond-C.

Returning to the chair, she continued. "I planned to tell you the truth the moment I saw you. Even when I learned about your heart attack, I still intended to be truthful. But when I came to your room, Dr. Newman was waiting in the hall. He warned me not to say anything that might upset you. That's when I became entangled in my own lies. Believe me, I wanted so desperately to tell you the truth. I finally admitted everything to Dr. Newman, but he said that I shouldn't tell you until you were stronger. He also warned me not to say anything to Joseph or Autumn Moon because they might inadvertently let it slip to you. More than once, I was about to tell Cole the whole story, but a couple of times we were interrupted. And the other times . . . well, the moment was never right."

Kristina fell silent. She had been talking nonstop

for a long time. Drake, listening avidly, hadn't intruded on her confession. Tears came to Kristina's eyes, but they were tears of relief. The pretext was over!

It was quite a while before Drake spoke. "So you are the 'daughter' I've been writing to for thirteen years."

Afraid he didn't believe her, she said quickly, "I can prove it. I'll write something for you, and you can check my handwriting."

"That isn't necessary. I believe you." He paused, then went on. "I can understand why, as a child, you did something so foolish. But when you grew up, why did you continue to write me as Samantha?"

"Because I needed your letters!" she cried, her tears now falling freely. "You and my mother were my only family. When Mother died, I had no one but you. Your letters meant the world to me."

"And yours meant the world to me," he murmured.

Kristina broke down, and weeping heavily, she cried, "Please don't hate me! It was never my intention to hurt you!"

He reached over and took her hand in his. "You've told me everything except your name."

"Kristina Parker," she whispered.

"I don't hate you, Kristina. Right now, I feel only sadness."

She controlled her tears. "Why are you sad?"

"All these years, I thought Samantha loved me as much as I loved her." He sighed wearily. "As a father, I'm a miserable failure."

"You can't blame yourself because Samantha's the way she is. Mr. and Mrs. Johnson have spoiled her terribly."

"No, my dear, I am a failure. You see, I have two

135

daughters, and neither one of them gives a damn about their father."

Kristina stared at him with surprise.

"Autumn Moon and I have a daughter named Alisa. She's nineteen years old and living with my cousin in St. Louis. I'll tell you about her later, but right now, we need to discuss you . . . and your marriage to Cole. It isn't legal, you know."

"Yes, I know."

A flicker of a smile crossed Drake's lips. "Cole's not going to take this in good humor. I hope you realize that. But after he's had time to cool down and come to his senses, he'll understand your actions. You two can get married again."

"He won't marry me," Kristina replied. "Cole doesn't want a wife."

"Nonsense!" he rebuked. "He loves you."

"I don't think so."

"He told me he does, and Cole always means what he says."

Kristina wasn't convinced, and, uncomfortable discussing Cole, she changed the subject. "I'll have one of the ranch hands drive me into town. I can stay at the hotel." She didn't bother mentioning that paying for a room would quickly drain her limited finances. "I'm hoping Dr. Newman can help me find a job teaching school."

"He probably can. He has a lot of friends in a lot of towns. But, Kristina, I don't want you to leave so soon. We've written to each other for years, and through your letters I've learned to like you very much. Of course I thought you were Samantha. But liking someone and loving them isn't the same. A parent can always love a child, but a parent can't always like one. That's why I held you in such high regard. I not only had a daughter who I loved, but

136

one I liked. That made you very special to me."

"But it was all a farce. It wasn't your daughter you liked, but your daughter's maid."

Drake was still holding her hand, and squeezing it gently, he replied sincerely. "You've been more of a daughter to me than the two I have. Apparently, Samantha couldn't care less, and Alisa is too embittered to care."

"Why does Alisa feel that way?"

"She was born out of wedlock."

"But why didn't you marry Autumn Moon?"

"She wouldn't marry me." He quickly explained Autumn Moon's reasons for refusing.

"She was wrong to feel that way. Furthermore, her child's birthright should have meant more to her than anything else."

"Kristina, you have to realize that Autumn Moon is a full-blooded Comanche. She was raised with her people, and she wasn't familiar with the white man's customs. The Comanches would never brand a child a bastard, or look down on that child." He sighed heavily. "Even if Autumn Moon and I had married, Alisa still would have been an outcast. She's a half-breed, and most people in these parts don't look upon her sort kindly."

"Is that why she moved to St. Louis?"

"Yes, she wanted to get away from here. She might never come back."

"Have you gone to see her?"

"No. She doesn't want to see me or her mother. She harbors ill feelings toward us. I can't really blame her."

"Why didn't you come to Philadelphia to visit Samantha?"

"I did. I visited her twice. Once when she was two, then again when she was three. She was too young to

137

remember those visits." He smiled reflectively. "She was a beautiful little girl with golden curls and big green eyes." He turned his gaze to Kristina. "You also have blond hair and green eyes. That's why I wasn't suspicious until I noticed you didn't have a birthmark."

"Why did you stop visiting her?"

"Not long after my second visit, the war started. After it ended, I returned to my ranch to find it falling to ruin. Even before the war, it wasn't the prosperous spread it is now. Autumn Moon, Alisa, and I lived in a log house with four rooms. A short time after returning home, I made a trip to Philadelphia and talked to Mary. She had remarried, and her husband adored Samantha. She convinced me that my presence would disrupt Samantha's life. I told Mary that I wouldn't attempt to see my daughter if she'd allow me to write to her. She agreed with strong reservations.

"A couple of months after I was back home, Cole and Josh dropped by. I didn't know Josh at that time, but he and Cole had become close friends. We hired on a few hands and headed farther south to look for wild cattle. Years ago, these animals had escaped from Spanish missions in southern Texas, and they eventually cross-bred with American cattle. They were free game. We hazed as many as we could out of the brush and drove them back here to the Diamond-C. These cattle are variegated, lean-flanked, and hardy. You probably know them as the longhorn. They made me a rich man. Josh took his share of the cattle up to Austin. Cole sold his and stashed away the money. He wasn't ready to settle down."

"Why did you decide to send Samantha money to come see you?"

"In my agreement with Mary, I promised her that

I wouldn't try to see Samantha until she turned twenty-one."

"I used the money you sent to make this trip. When I get a job, I'll pay you back."

Drake smiled warmly. "That isn't necessary. That money was sent to pay for my daughter's journey to the Diamond-C. And, now, you're here." His eyes turned misty.

Kristina's tears flowed again. "Thank you, Drake."

"I thank you, my dear, for all those sweet letters you wrote to a lonely father."

Kristina was alone in the kitchen, sitting at the table drinking a cup of coffee. Her spirits were high. The charade was over, and she could now be herself. But even more important, Drake had understood and forgiven her! His kindness hadn't really surprised her, for she had known from his letters that he was a compassionate man.

Drake had sent for Autumn Moon, Josh, and Joseph. Kristina knew he was at this moment telling them about her. She hoped they would be as forgiving as Drake.

As her thoughts turned to Cole, a heavy shadow fell over her spirits, sending them plunging. She didn't doubt that Cole would be furious with her. If only she had told him the truth right from the beginning! She had married and bedded him as Samantha Carlson, and there was no excuse for such deception.

She spoke her thoughts aloud, "I can only hope that Cole loves me enough to forgive me."

"I hope so, too," a man's voice sounded from the open doorway.

She looked up quickly. "Josh!"

He stepped to the stove, poured a cup of coffee, then joined her at the table. "I didn't mean to eavesdrop."

Kristina was blushing. "I should keep my thoughts to myself."

"Don't be embarrassed. I'm on your side."

She was somewhat amazed. "But you know I'm a fraud!"

"So?" he asked, grinning wryly.

"So, why are you on my side? Cole's a good friend of yours."

"That's true. And because he is such a good friend, I hope he realizes what a prize you are." Learning the truth about Kristina hadn't lowered Josh's opinion of her. Moreover, she had his full understanding, for unknown to her, Josh was hopelessly entangled in his own deceitful web.

Kristina was a little flustered. "Thank you, but I'm not really a prize."

"You're entitled to your opinion," he answered, still smiling.

He was watching her closely, and she began to feel uncomfortable under his scrutiny.

Sensing her discomfort, he apologized. "Forgive me for staring, but you're so beautiful I can't take my eyes off you. I envy Cole."

"Josh . . ." she began impulsively. "Tell me about Cole. Drake wrote to me about him, and Cole himself has told me some things about his life, but there's still so much I don't know."

"For instance?"

"Why is he so relentless in his search for the man who killed his mother?"

Josh sighed deeply. "I wish I knew."

"Cole told me that the man was branded with three R's on his chest. Why three R's? What does it mean?"

140

"If you were a southerner, you wouldn't have to ask. Some slave owners used to brand a slave with an R if he tried to run away. It stands for 'Runner.'"

"But this man had *three* R's. Does that mean he tried to escape three different times?"

"It would seem that way," Josh mumbled, fidgeting. He was uncomfortable with the conversation.

"But Cole said the man was a Jayhawker, not a Negro."

Josh explained hastily. "Cole learned that the man was a quadroon who had escaped into Kansas. When the war started, he joined the Union Army. Most of the soldiers were ex-Jayhawkers."

"Exactly what is a quadroon?" she questioned.

"A quadroon is one-fourth Negro. They look more white than Negro. In fact, some of them are so light that their Negro ancestry is undetectable."

"Do you think Cole will ever find this man and the others?"

"I don't know," he answered, his tone bleak. "But I have a feeling he won't give up until he finds them — or gets himself killed trying."

His grave prediction tore at Kristina's heart. She found the possibility of Cole's death too painful even to discuss, and she abruptly steered their discussion to a different course.

Chapter Twelve

The days passed quickly for Kristina, and she truly began to enjoy her visit to the Diamond-C. She and Drake talked often, and their friendship deepened. Kristina also grew very fond of Autumn Moon and Joseph. Josh extended his visit, and he and Kristina spent a lot of time together. A warm camaraderie developed between them.

Kristina began to think of the Diamond-C as home. The large Colonial house was impressive as well as comfortable, and although elaborate, it wasn't ostentatious.

Alisa had left her western-style riding clothes, and Kristina often borrowed one of the outfits to go riding with Josh. Occasionally, they would take a lunch basket and have a picnic. Kristina was amazed by the size of the Diamond-C—she and Josh could ride for miles and still be on Carlson land. During these outings, she and Josh often stopped to chat with the ranch hands, and Kristina soon learned to know the men by their first names. The cowboys were impressed with her beauty and warm personality.

Kristina was content with her new life, and pleased to be surrounded by people she had grown to love.

Still, Cole hovered over her thoughts like a dark cloud. She hoped desperately that he'd be as understanding as the others. She couldn't shake the feeling, though, that he'd be furious with her.

Although Kristina was apprehensive about Cole's return, deep inside, she couldn't wait for him to come back. His absence had left an aching void in her heart, and she missed him terribly. It was as though a part of her was missing, and only Cole's presence could make her whole again.

Josh and Kristina, returning from a brisk ride, handed their horses's reins over to a drover. They were about to climb the porch steps when a buckboard approached the lane leading up to the house. They watched as it came closer.

Josh knew the driver, who worked at the livery in town. A young woman was seated beside him, and Josh turned his gaze to her. Although he hadn't seen her in three years, he nonetheless recognized her instantly.

"Alisa!" he exclaimed, hurrying forward to greet her.

The driver brought the buckboard to a stop, and Josh helped Alisa to the ground, hugging her eagerly.

She returned his enthusiastic embrace, then stepping back, she lifted her gaze to his smiling face. "Josh, you're still too handsome for words." Her outward composure concealed her inner feelings, for Josh's closeness was causing her heart to race.

"You've grown even more beautiful," he replied, meaning it sincerely.

Kristina, looking on, studied Alisa closely. The young woman bore a strong resemblance to her

144

mother. Alisa's coal-black hair was worn in an upswept style, and a dainty green bonnet was perched atop the ebony tresses. Her fashionable olive-green traveling gown enhanced her trim, supple curves.

"Why didn't you send a wire and let us know you were arriving?" Josh asked Alisa.

"I decided the black sheep of the family should make her appearance unexpectedly." Her voice was laced with bitterness.

Josh let her remark pass without comment. He removed her luggage, set the pieces down, then paid the driver. As the buckboard moved away, he slipped an arm about Alisa's waist and led her to Kristina.

"Alisa . . ." he began. "This is . . ."

"An impostor!" Alisa cut in sharply. Her dark-brown eyes pierced Kristina with contempt. "The telegraph officer told me all about you. It seems you are the talk of the town. I was told that you arrived here pretending to be Samantha Carlson, and that Reverend Scott actually married you and Cole. Now rumor has it that you aren't really Samantha. Tell me . . . exactly who are you?"

"Kristina Parker," she answered, meeting Alisa's gaze without flinching.

"This misunderstanding can easily be cleared up," Josh said with haste. "Kristina was Samantha's maid. Drake asked Samantha to come for a visit, but she couldn't make it. Kristina wanted to come westward, so she came in Samantha's place. She didn't intend to impersonate Samantha. But Drake's heart attack was so serious that Dr. Newman asked Kristina to pretend she was Samantha."

It wasn't necessary to explain why Drake had Kristina's picture, for it had arrived well after Alisa's move to St. Louis.

145

Finding Josh's explanation highly suspect, Alisa regarded him skeptically. "That doesn't explain why she married Cole."

"Her reason for marrying Cole is nobody's business but hers and Cole's," Josh remarked.

"I think you're covering for her."

"Miss Carlson . . ." Kristina spoke up, bristling. "I wish you'd stop discussing me as though I'm not present."

Alisa turned to her. "Why are you still at the Diamond-C?"

"I'm here at your father's invitation."

Her eyes swept over Kristina. "I see you're wearing my clothes."

"You're very observant," Kristina retorted coolly.

"Are you also using my room?"

"Your room is still unoccupied," Josh intruded. "Why don't you go inside and see your mother? She's probably in the kitchen preparing lunch."

Complying, Alisa brushed past Kristina and went into the house.

Alone with Kristina, Josh attempted an apology. "I'm sorry Alisa was so rude. She has a lot of problems. I was hoping she had learned to deal with them, but she apparently hasn't."

Kristina was touched to see a deep sadness in Josh's eyes. "You must care about Alisa very much."

"I've known her since she was a child. She's always been very special to me."

"She's very beautiful, and she has a striking resemblance to Autumn Moon."

Josh was silent for a long moment, then said somewhat ruefully, "Yes, she's grown into a beautiful young woman."

He turned about and picked up Alisa's two suitcases and carried them into the house. He reminded himself that Alisa's age hadn't changed anything. He hadn't been free to love her when she was sixteen, nor was he free to love her now. He would never be free, for the three R's branded across his chest had him forever enslaved.

Autumn Moon was standing at the stove, her back turned toward the doorway. She wasn't aware of her daughter's presence until Alisa called softly, "Mama?"

For a moment, the woman froze. Then, whirling about swiftly, she gazed at Alisa with surprise. "You're home!" she cried, her voice timorous.

Alisa moved forward as though she were about to rush into her mother's embrace. She caught herself in time, though, and as her steps faltered, she said indifferently, "Yes, your wayward daughter has returned."

She groaned inwardly. Obviously, her daughter's three years away from home hadn't improved her disposition.

Alisa sat down at the table. "How's dear Papa?" Her inquiry was unmistakably flippant.

"He's doing very well. He'll be so happy to see you. He's missed you so much . . . We both have."

Alisa regarded her mother thoughtfully, then began with intentional spite, "Your English is still flawless. One would never imagine that you were born and raised in a Comanche village. You not only speak like a white woman, but you also dress like one. We're so much alike, Mama. I talk and dress like a white woman, too. But, just like you, my diction and dress don't fool anyone. My Comanche blood is so obvious that only a blind person could miss seeing it."

"What point are you trying to make?"

"I'm telling you that I wasn't accepted in St. Louis any more than I was accepted here."

Autumn Moon drew out a chair and sat down at the table. "Then why didn't you come home?"

"The first year I was gone, I came close to coming home a couple of times. Papa's dear cousin Eva was a fat, ugly pig, and a real bitch."

"Alisa, such language!"

"It's the truth, Mama. She pretended to welcome her half-breed relative, but her fawning was as superficial as she was. She didn't introduce me to her friends, but flaunted me like some kind of freak. Believe me, if she hadn't died, I'd have come home."

"Died!" Autumn Moon gasped. "But when?"

"The first year I was there."

"How did she die?"

"She just keeled over one day. She probably ate herself to death."

"Why didn't you let Drake know that she was dead?"

"Because I was afraid he would come to St. Louis and bring me home. I didn't think he would allow me to stay with Eva's husband."

"Why did you stay with him for two years?"

"John, Eva's husband, was a lot younger than she. Remember, she married him shortly after her first husband passed away. John admitted to me that he married Eva for her money. She was a very rich widow. John was passionately attracted to me, and I encouraged his affections. After Eva died, we became lovers."

Following her revelation, Alisa went to the stove and poured two cups of coffee. Returning to the table, she placed one of the cups in front of her mother. Sitting, she asked calmly, "Have I shocked you, Mama?"

148

Autumn Moon's face had seemed to age. "Why, Alisa?" she cried brokenly. "Why did you become that man's lover?"

"I thought he loved me and wanted to marry me. As John's wife, I'd be just as good as any white woman. I'd also be just as wealthy as the wealthiest. I foolishly believed as soon as a proper mourning period had passed, he'd ask me to be his wife."

Alisa paused to take a drink of her coffee. Her eyes filled with bitterness as she continued. "He never intended to ask me to marry him. He merely used me. On the same day I received your wire about Papa, John informed me that he was through with me. He planned to become engaged to a beautiful, light-skinned socialite. He wanted me out of his house, and out of his life. I didn't come home because I want to be here, nor because of Papa's health. I'm here because I have no place else to go."

Autumn Moon's hand struck out, slapping her daughter across the face. The sharp whack reddened Alisa's cheek and brought stinging tears to her eyes. "How dare you speak so coldly of your father's health! He almost died!" Her anger turned into desperation, and she pleaded heartbrokenly, "Alisa, don't you have any feelings at all? Can you love no one but yourself?"

Alisa brushed aside her tears, stood, and stoically faced her mother. "May I go to my room, Mama? I'm tired, and I'd like to rest for a while."

"Yes, by all means, run away to your room. You're very good at running away. You've been doing it for years."

Alisa turned to leave, but Autumn Moon deterred her.

"Wait! I'm warning you, Alisa. Don't say anything to your father about your affair with Eva's husband."

"Of course not, Mama," she replied caustically. "We must protect Papa—at any cost. I mean, you even let your child be born a bastard to protect Papa's reputation. Don't worry. I won't tell him that his daughter is no better than a whore." With that, she left the kitchen.

Alisa was lying on her bed when she was disturbed by a soft rapping on her door. Hoping it was Josh, she hurried to admit him. She was, however, sorely disappointed to find Kristina.

"I'm returning your clothes," Kristina said, handing her the garments.

Taking them, Alisa replied, "Come in, won't you? I think we should get to know each other."

Kristina complied hesitantly.

Pitching the outfit onto the bed, Alisa said with a friendly note, "Feel free to borrow my riding clothes any time you wish."

Kristina watched her warily. She didn't trust the woman's sudden congenial manner.

Alisa, discerning her companion's distrust, remarked honestly, "I apologize for my earlier behavior. But I was tired, on edge, and learning that some woman was impersonating my sister was upsetting. Not that I give a damn about Samantha, for I don't." She gestured to a chair. "Sit down, please."

Kristina did so, and as Alisa sat on the bed, she asked, "How long were you Samantha's maid?"

"Not all that long. But my mother worked for Samantha's parents, and we lived in the servants' quarters. So Samantha and I grew up together."

"Papa absolutely cherishes her letters."

Kristina drew a long breath, then explained to Alisa that she was the one who had written to Drake.

She gave her a full, detailed account.

After Kristina finished, Alisa was speechless. Then, all at once, she threw back her head and laughed uproariously. Finally, controlling her hysterics, she declared jubilantly, "This is marvelous, absolutely marvelous! All these years, Papa thought his darling Samantha was so sweet and considerate. Although he never said anything, I knew he was comparing me to her and finding me lacking." Alisa laughed again. "It wasn't even Samantha who was writing to him, but her maid!"

Kristina rose from her chair. "I don't think it's a laughing matter," she said sternly.

Alisa controlled her mirth. "No, I don't suppose you do. But you can't imagine how bitterly I resented those letters." She shrugged as though suddenly unconcerned.

Kristina crossed the room. "Are you coming downstairs for lunch?"

"No, I think I'll take a long nap. The trip was very tiring." Watching Kristina walk to the door, Alisa called out, "How long is Josh planning to stay?"

"I don't know. He hasn't said anything about leaving." She went out of the room.

Alisa stretched out on the bed, and as her thoughts lingered on Josh, tears filled her eyes and rolled down her face.

Alisa napped for a couple of hours, then washed, changed clothes, and left her room to visit her father. She knocked softly on his door and received permission to enter.

Drake was sitting up in bed, and as his daughter crossed the room, his eyes followed her. He had always thought Alisa was exceptionally pretty, and he was amazed to see that she had grown even lovelier. Her pale-yellow dress, V-necked with short puffed sleeves, revealed her slender form and her shiny black tresses were unbound, cascading beautifully past her shoulders and down to her waist.

"Alisa," Drake murmured warmly, "I'm so glad you're home. But you've been here for hours. Why didn't you come see me sooner? I've been waiting anxiously."

She sat in the chair beside his bed. "I was so tired that I took a nap." Her vision roamed over him. "You know, Papa, I can't recall ever seeing you abed before."

"Well, that's because I've always been as healthy and as strong as a bull." He turned a beseeching gaze in her direction. "Don't you have a kiss for your father?"

Alisa, her reluctance evident, placed a quick kiss on his brow.

Drake's expectations were crushed. He had hoped that his daughter's temperament had improved, but obviously, her three years away from home hadn't mellowed her bitterness.

"How's Cousin Eva?" he asked.

"She's dead," Alisa replied bluntly.

"What?" he exclaimed.

"She died two years ago. The doctor said it was a stroke."

"But why didn't you tell me?" His tone became reproachful. "You did manage to write your mother and me a few times during the past two years. Did Eva's death slip your mind?"

"I didn't tell you because I was afraid you'd come to St. Louis and make me come back home." She feigned a light-hearted smile. "Eva's husband assured me that I was welcome to stay for as long as I wanted."

"Were you alone with him?"

"Of course not, Papa. His widowed sister lived with us." She was telling the truth—John's sister did reside with them—but she didn't mention that the woman didn't dare interfere in her brother's life, let alone chastise him for having an affair with his young ward.

Alisa rose abruptly. "I slept through lunch, and now I'm feeling a little hungry. I think I'll go to the kitchen and fix something to eat."

Drake almost asked her not to leave but to stay and talk to him. Now that she was a grown woman, surely they could resolve their problems. She was his daughter, and he loved her dearly. He wanted them to find a way to build a close relationship. But he watched silently as she left the room. He felt if he had asked her to remain, she still would have found another excuse to leave. That she could barely tolerate his presence was a heavy cross for Drake to bear.

On her way to the kitchen, Alisa passed the study. The door was open, and catching a glimpse of Josh sitting at the desk, she changed her course and stepped inside the room.

Josh was going over Drake's ledgers, keeping them up to date. Aware of her presence, he lifted his gaze.

She went to the liquor cabinet and poured herself a glass of sherry, downed it, then prepared another.

"You'd better go easy, or you'll find yourself tipsy," Josh remarked.

Alisa turned and faced him. "I'm quite capable of handling my drinks." With glass in hand, she stepped around the desk, then sat on the edge facing

Josh. "When are you leaving?"

"In the morning. I've already been here way too long. I have my own ranch to run."

"You don't have to leave on my account. What happened between us before I left won't happen again." She studied him keenly. "You do remember that night, don't you?"

Josh, mustering a carefree smile, tried to make light of the incident. "Of course I remember. I was very flattered."

"Flattered?" she repeated. "Yes, that's the same word you used three years ago." She took a long drink of sherry, watching him over the rim of her glass. Although she was sure his memory was vivid, she nonetheless recited to him the events of that evening. "It was a few days before I went to St. Louis. You had come here to visit Papa. After dinner, you went outside to have a smoke, and I followed you. I convinced you to go to the stables with me under the pretext of seeing my mare's new colt. Then, once I had you alone, I tried to seduce you. I made a complete fool of myself. I literally begged you to make love to me. You, however, behaved as a true gentleman. You held off my advances, but assured me that you found my infatuation very flattering."

"Alisa, you were only sixteen. It's not unusual for a girl that age to have a crush on an older man."

"It was more than a crush," she declared firmly. "Furthermore, you felt the same way I did. You wanted me! Even at sixteen, a girl knows when a man desires her. Why did you turn me away? Was it my age? Or was it my Comanche blood?"

"You were entirely too young for me."

"Do you still consider me too young?"

"I'm fifteen years older than you."

"You're skirting my question."

Josh slammed the ledgers shut, pushed back his

154

chair, and stood. "Alisa, what do you want from me?"

"The truth."

He looked at her quizzically.

"Can you look me in the eyes and tell me that you still think I'm too young for you?"

"This entire discussion is ridiculous. If you'll excuse me, Alisa, I need to find the foreman. I have some business to talk over with him."

He started to move past her but was impeded by her hand grasping his arm. "It's not my age, is it? It's my Comanche blood. You don't want a half-breed as a wife."

Josh gazed into her face. He found her more desirable than words could tell and he had to call upon all his willpower to keep from kissing her. Her Comanche blood? If only it was that simple! Her hand was still gripping his arm, and he pried her fingers loose, then headed quickly for the door.

"Josh . . ." she called after him. "You don't have to run away from my feelings for you. I have them under control, and I'll not pressure you like this again."

He didn't answer, but simply left the room.

Josh wasn't running away from Alisa's feelings, he was escaping his own. He decided that, hereafter, he must endeavor to avoid Alisa Carlson. She might have her feelings under control, but his were dangerously precarious. He loved Alisa, but he believed she could never be his. She wanted a white, aristocratic husband, not a quadroon who was once a slave. Also, he was the man Cole had been trying to find for sixteen years—the indisputable evidence was branded across his chest! If Alisa were to learn his secret, would she be so repulsed that she'd tell Cole? Josh couldn't be sure, but he did know that it was a chance he couldn't afford to take.

Chapter Thirteen

Kristina stood at the porch railing and watched as the sun sank over the horizon. The approaching dusk began filling the distant hills with purple mist, and a sudden, gentle breeze rustled the cottonwoods bordering the lane leading up to Drake's home.

Kristina's thoughts were filled with Cole. She suddenly released a long, audible sigh.

Drake, no longer bedridden, was sitting on the porch lounge. "Is something wrong?" he asked.

She moved over and sat beside him. "I'm worried about Cole. He's been gone two months. I don't think he intended to stay away this long."

"You've got to learn not to worry about Cole," Drake replied. "If you don't, he'll make you grayhaired before your time. I used to worry about him until I finally realized that worrying didn't help."

"But if he's been detained, why doesn't he send me a wire and let me know?"

"Cole's been on his own since he was fifteen. He's not used to keeping a wife notified of his whereabouts. It's going to take some time for Cole to change his ways."

Kristina was exasperated. "How can he be so inconsiderate?"

"He doesn't mean to be," Drake replied. "Be patient with him."

"That's the same advice I received from Josh."

"He knows Cole as well as I do."

"The three of you must be very close."

"I love Cole like a son, and Josh is a good friend."

"How did Cole and Josh meet?"

He looked at her with a note of surprise. "When Josh was here, you two spent a lot of time together. Didn't he tell you how they met?"

"We didn't discuss Cole very much. I always got the feeling that Josh preferred not to talk about him. I guess he was afraid that he might tell me something Cole would consider confidential."

"He probably figured it was up to Cole to tell you about his life. But I don't think he would care if I told you how he met Josh. When the war ended, Cole went back to Missouri. He hoped to learn something more about the man who killed his mother. Right after the murder, the Union had investigated the incident and had informed Cole that the men were deserters. But Cole was hoping that the Union had found the killers. They hadn't, of course. So Cole left Missouri, and was heading here to the Diamond-C when he was waylaid by three desperadoes. Cole didn't have much money, but he was riding a fine-looking horse. I'm sure it was his horse that the men were after. Fortunately, Josh happened to come along. He's damned good with a gun, and he saved Cole from being robbed. In fact, it was Josh who taught Cole how to use a handgun and to be quick on the draw. But that's another story.

"Josh was in between jobs and wasn't headed anyplace in particular. Cole invited Josh to accompany him to the Diamond-C. By the time they arrived here, they had become good friends—been the best of friends ever since."

"Josh told me that he didn't fight in the war. Cole didn't hold that against him?"

"Josh said he was born and raised in San Francisco and didn't consider the war his concern. Cole agreed with him." Drake emitted a deep sigh, then changing the subject without warning, remarked, "I've been giving my last will and testament a lot of thought. It needs to be changed."

"Changed?" Kristina repeated blankly.

"Samantha inherits the Diamond-C. I altered my will a few years back and left the ranch to her. Before then, it was left to Cole. When I told Cole about it, he said it wasn't right that he inherit Samantha and Alisa's rightful property. I pointed out to him that they would probably sell the ranch. Cole finally accepted on one condition—he'd take the Diamond-C but pay Samantha and Alisa the full value of the ranch. He insisted I put his condition in my will. If he didn't pay the girls an agreed-upon sum, he couldn't claim the title to the Diamond-C."

"Why did you change the will and leave the ranch to Samantha?"

"Because of your letters," he replied heavily. "I could tell by your keen interest in the Diamond-C that you would never sell it."

"But you were thinking of Samantha, not me."

"True. But now, considering Samantha's disinterest in me, I'm sure she would sell my home and never give it a second thought."

Kristina didn't argue, for she knew it was true. "When you changed your will and left the ranch to Samantha, didn't you feel you were being terribly unfair to Alisa?"

"The title goes to Samantha, but the profits from the ranch go to both of my daughters, as well as to

Autumn Moon. The will clearly states that one-fourth goes to Alisa, one-fourth to Autumn Moon, and one-fourth to Samantha. The remaining one-fourth goes back into the ranch. Now, however, I intend to leave the ranch to Cole."

"Instead of leaving it to Cole, why don't you leave it to Autumn Moon?"

"She's a full-blooded Comanche. If Samantha were to contest the will, she'd have no problem taking the ranch from Autumn Moon. The law doesn't recognize Indians as having any rights. Even if the will wasn't contested, Autumn Moon would have a hell of a time finding cowhands willing to take orders from an Indian."

"Considering all you've said, I suppose leaving the ranch to Cole is a wise decision."

"Since I'm feeling so much better, I'll ride to town in the morning and have my lawyer make the changes."

"You aren't strong enough to make such a ride. You can send for your lawyer."

Drake smiled at her fondly. "You fuss over me more than my own daughter. I wish Alisa cared as much as you do."

"I think she does care," Kristina told him. "Alisa and I aren't close friends, but I understand her. She's built a wall of self-pity around her so thick it can't be penetrated. Behind that wall lies a very unhappy young woman. Also, despite her bitterness, she loves you and Autumn Moon. But she blames you two for her misery because you brought her into this world. Alisa wishes she had never been born."

"Yes, I know," he murmured, his face anguished. He fell silent for a long moment, then began somewhat pensively, "I used to believe that she would find happiness with Josh Chandler. She's

160

loved him for years, I think she even loved him as a child. She doesn't know, of course, that I'm aware of her feelings. But when she's with Josh, she wears her heart on her sleeve. It's obvious that she utterly adores him."

"Josh doesn't share her feelings, does he?"

Drake shrugged heavily. "I don't think so. Before she went to St. Louis, I'm sure he considered her too young for a serious relationship. But she's now a grown woman. Josh was here when she arrived, and I was hoping that they might . . ." His words drifted, and he sighed deeply, then continued. "He left the day after she arrived. Apparently, he simply loves her as the daughter of his good friend. His departure dashed my hopes. I actually thought Alisa was the reason he never married. I figured he was waiting for her to grow up. I was dead wrong."

At that moment, Alisa opened the front door and stepped outside. "Dinner's ready," she said.

Kristina, wondering if she had overheard their conversation, looked at the woman closely. Alisa's placid expression assured Kristina that she hadn't.

Kristina stood, waited for Drake to rise, then walked into the house beside him. She glanced over her shoulder to see if Alisa was following. But Alisa was standing at the porch railing and was looking into the distance. Kristina recalled that she had stood there earlier with her thoughts on Cole. She wondered if Alisa was thinking about Josh. Kristina could fully sympathize with Alisa's unrequited love, for she was sure that Cole didn't love her any more than Josh loved Alisa. If Cole truly cared, he wouldn't stay away so long. She knew if it was the other way around, she could never stay away from him. If he were waiting for her, nothing on this earth could keep her from rushing to his side. It was

161

apparent, however, that Cole didn't share her feelings.

Kristina had been asleep for a couple of hours when she was awakened by a loud rapping on her door, followed by Joseph's voice. "Miz Kristina! Wake up, Miz Kristina!"

Bounding from the bed, she slipped on her robe, hurried to the door, and opened it. "What's wrong?" she asked, gripped with sudden fear.

"It's Mista Drake. He done had another heart attack. I sent one of the ranch hands into town for the doctor."

Kristina's knees weakened, and she had to grip the door for support. "How . . . how bad was the attack."

"I ain't sure. Autumn Moon and Miz Alisa's with Mista Drake. They sent me to get you."

Kristina darted into the hall and to Drake's room. The door was open, and she stepped quietly inside. The two women were standing beside the bed, Autumn Moon on one side, Alisa on the other. Drake's labored breathing filled the room, and it was obvious that he was fighting for each breath.

Kristina moved over and stood at Autumn Moon's side. The woman seemed about to collapse, and Kristina put an arm about her shoulders.

"We're losing him," Autumn Moon moaned wretchedly.

"But he was doing so much better," Kristina cried.

The two women were shocked when, suddenly, Alisa dropped to her knees, grabbed her father's hand, and begged, "Papa, please don't die! I love you, Papa!"

Drake's eyes flitted open. "Alisa," he whispered,

162

his voice so weak he could barely be heard. "Forgive me, Alisa." His strength was failing rapidly, and he was too exhausted to say anything more.

"Oh Papa! Papa!" Alisa cried. Now, in her time of grief, she forgot her self-pity, and love for her father conquered her bitterness. Like a drowning victim, her life flashed before her, and pictures of her childhood crossed her mind. She recalled the tender, loving moments she had shared with her father—the bedtime stories, the birthday parties, the times he had held her in his arms and kissed away her tears. As precious memories continued flooding Alisa's heart, deep, wracking sobs shook her shoulders.

Somehow Drake found the strength to murmur feebly, "Kristina?"

She leaned over the bed, placing her ear close to his lips. "Yes, Drake?"

"Tell Cole . . . tell Cole I love him. I couldn't love him more if he were my own son."

"I'll tell him," she replied in a trembling voice.

"You and Cole be . . . be good to each other. You two belong together. And Kristina . . . ?"

"Yes?" she cried softly. Grief tore at her so painfully that her body ached.

"I love you. You've been like a . . . a daughter to me."

She placed a lingering kiss on his brow. "I love you, too."

"I . . . I want to be alone with Autumn Moon," he rasped weakly.

Kristina went to Alisa, and grasping the grieving woman's shoulders, she helped her rise to a standing position. Keeping her hold, Kristina led Alisa from the room.

Joseph was waiting in the hall. "Is he—?"

"No," Kristina replied. Her voice breaking, she

added, "But, Joseph, I think he's dying."

Alisa suddenly drew away from Kristina, and crying heavily, she fled down the hall to her own room.

Alone with Joseph, Kristina paced back and forth in front of Drake's closed door. A spark of hope burned within her: Drake had survived his first heart attack, maybe he'd overcome this one, too.

Kristina had been pacing only a short time when Autumn Moon emerged from Drake's room.

"He's gone," the woman whispered. She then collapsed into Joseph's arms.

Kristina entered Alisa's room without knocking. She found the young woman lying across the bed and sat beside her.

As the mattress gave a little under Kristina's weight, Alisa asked softly, "Is he dead?"

"Yes," she answered. "He passed away a few minutes ago. Your mother fainted, and Joseph carried her to my room. I think she's all right now, but she's very grief-stricken. She needs you."

Alisa didn't move, and keeping her head buried in her folded arms, she replied, "How can I help Mama when I can't even help myself?"

"She doesn't need your help, just your presence."

Alisa remained unresponsive for a long time, then she sat up and looked at Kristina. Her eyes were glazed with sorrow. "Kristina, I wish I was the one who had died!"

"Don't say that!"

"But it's true! I've always hated my life, but now I hate it even more! How can I live with my conscience? I hurt Papa over and over again!"

"Alisa, listen to me . . ." Kristina began anxiously,

grasping her companion's hands. "You were wrong to hurt Drake, and it's wrong for you to hurt your mother. But they were also to blame. They should have married. It was wrong for them to bring you into this world out of wedlock. But that's all in the past, and it can't be changed. You must get rid of this bitterness that is eating you alive! If you don't, it'll destroy you!"

Alisa shrugged listlessly. "Does it really matter? I have nothing to live for."

"If you'd stop feeling so sorry for yourself, you'd realize that you have everything to live for. You're young, beautiful, and intelligent. Your life can be what you make it."

"That's easy for you to say. You don't know what it's like to be a half-breed."

"Have you ever considered being proud of your Comanche blood? Why do you consider whites so superior to Indians?"

"I could never make you understand," she replied hopelessly. "If you were born and raised here, then you'd know why I feel the way I do."

Withdrawing her hands from Kristina's, she rose from the bed. "I'll go to Mama." She went to the door, then turned back to Kristina. "Thank you for caring."

Leaving the room, Alisa walked slowly down the hall. Josh's image flashed across her mind. She wished he was here to take her into his arms and console her. His embrace would surely ease some of her pain. She loved him, and had never needed him as much as she did now.

Reaching Kristina's room, Alisa stepped inside. Her mother was sitting on the edge of the bed. "Mama!" she cried, going to her and drawing her close.

165

Resting her head on her daughter's shoulder, Autumn Moon wept mournfully.

Needing fresh air, Kristina left Alisa's room, hurried down the staircase and out to the front porch. She wasn't surprised to find Joseph sitting on the top step. She sat beside him.

The night was well lit by a radiant moon, and Kristina could see grief etched on the butler's face. "Do you feel like talking?" she asked.

"Yeah, I reckon maybe I do. It might help some. I's been sittin' here thinkin' 'bout the past, and 'bout Mista Drake."

"I'm a good listener," she murmured. "Tell me your thoughts."

"Miz Kristina, I was born and raised on a plantation outside New Orleans. The masta lost everything durin' the war, and one day he called us house servants together and told us we had to leave. All the field workers had done left. He said he didn't have no money to feed us, clothe us, or nothin' else. I had a woman—she weren't my wife 'cause the masta didn't allow his slaves to marry. Me and my woman, we moved into New Orleans. I was able to get odd jobs, and she took in washin'. But we was barely scrapin' by. We went to bed with empty stomachs more times than I can remember. I knew there weren't no future for us in New Orleans, so I decided to move westward. We was able to make enough money to buy a used wagon and two old mules. Although I didn't know it at the time, we was travelin' across Mista Drake's property when we was stopped by three white men. These men was ex-Confederates, and they was all liquored up and lookin' for a good time. That's why they raped my woman, then killed her. They strung me up to a tree and lashed me with a whip. They left me for dead and rode away. Mista Drake found me hours later. He took me home, and him and Autumn Moon doctored me. I was a breath away from death. It took weeks for my body to heal, even longer for my heart. Back then, Mista Drake didn't have this big house, he lived in a log cabin. Didn't make no difference to him, he still gave me a job as his butler. I knew he didn't need no butler, he was just givin' me work. Well, I's been workin' for Mista Drake ever since. I ain't never respected no man as much as I respect Mista Drake.''

Joseph's voice trembled. "He was more than just a boss, he was a friend."

They glanced up as Dr. Newman's carriage came into sight. Billy Stockton was accompanying him, but he turned his horse to the bunkhouse.

As the doctor arrived, Joseph went down the steps to greet him. The servant's story remained with Kristina for a few moments, and she could easily understand why he had been so fond of Drake.

Dr. Newman's sudden, mournful moan caught Kristina's attention, and looking at him, she could see he was grieving over Drake's death.

Fresh tears stung Kristina's eyes and rolled down her cheeks. Drake Carlson's passing would leave a void in many lives, her own included.

Chapter Fourteen

Kristina awoke slowly, pleased to see her room bathed in sunlight. The day's brightness was a cheerful change, for it had been raining intermittently for the past three days. The dismal weather had arrived the day of Drake's funeral, and the black clouds had lingered.

Propping her pillows against the headboard, Kristina leaned back. She sighed with discontent and uncertainty. She wanted to make future plans, but she couldn't reach any definite decisions until Cole returned.

Although she didn't dare hope that he loved her, she was determined to face him and explain her actions. The upcoming confrontation, however, filled her with dread. Nevertheless, she was anxious to get it over with.

A knock sounded on her door. "Kristina?" Autumn Moon called.

Kristina got up quickly, but as she reached for her robe, a wave of dizziness washed over her. For a moment, she tottered unsteadily. The spell vanished, and as she slipped on her robe, she supposed that rising so abruptly had made her lightheaded.

"Kristina . . ." Autumn Moon began, entering the room. "Mr. Cullen is downstairs."

Kristina had met Mr. Cullen at the funeral and knew that he was Drake's lawyer. "What does he want?" she asked.

"He needs to get in touch with Samantha. I told him that she and her parents are in Europe. He then asked for the name and address of their lawyer."

Kristina went to her vanity, opened a drawer, and took out a sheet of paper. She dipped the pen into the inkwell, then wrote the lawyer's name and address. Taking the paper to Autumn Moon, she asked, "Why does he need this information?"

"He said that it has to do with Drake's will."

Kristina's face paled. "His will!" she gasped. "Oh, no! He never got the chance to change it!"

Autumn Moon was baffled. "What are you saying?"

"Didn't Drake tell you he planned to change his will?"

"No," she replied.

"The title to this ranch goes to Samantha. No wonder Mr. Cullen is anxious to contact her."

"Will she sell the Diamond-C?" Autumn Moon sighed dismally, for she felt she already knew the answer.

"Yes, I'm sure she will," Kristina confirmed.

Not wanting to keep the lawyer waiting, Autumn Moon stepped to the door. "As soon as Mr. Cullen leaves, I'll fix you some breakfast."

Before Kristina could tell her not to bother, she was out of the room.

Kristina removed a set of clothes from the armoire and began to dress. Her thoughts were troubled. The Diamond-C could fall into the hands of strangers. Drake had worked so hard to build his empire, and now it might never belong to his loved ones.

Unless Cole buys it! Kristina suddenly thought. *Surely he will! I'll tell him how much it meant to Drake.*

Her hopes took an abrupt plunge. The Diamond-C was demanding and time-consuming. Would Cole be willing to accept such responsibility? He was accustomed to coming and going at will, but the Diamond-C would tie him down.

She thrust the nagging thoughts aside. Drake had originally left the ranch to Cole, and Cole hadn't seemed to mind. *But maybe Cole no longer feels that way,* she worried. *He might flatly refuse to tie himself down to a ranch.*

Knowing worrying wouldn't bring answers, Kristina cleared her mind. She brushed her hair briskly, and leaving the blond tresses unbound, she hurried from the room.

Finding the parlor unoccupied, she went to the kitchen where Autumn Moon was at the stove, cooking Kristina's breakfast.

"Did Mr. Cullen leave?" she asked, sitting at the table.

"Yes, he left as soon as I gave him the paper."

"Where's Alisa?"

"In her room."

"She spends too much time alone."

"Drake's death weighs heavily on her conscience. She wishes she had been nicer to him."

"Drake understood her bitterness. But she must put all her mistakes behind her and look to the future." Kristina sighed, knowing she must heed her own advice.

"I wish I could help her, but I don't know how."

"She has to help herself," Kristina replied, studying Autumn Moon. She had been curious about the

171

woman for some time. "How did you learn to speak English so fluently?" she asked, hoping Autumn Moon wouldn't mind her prying.

"My people were at peace with the soldiers. When my parents and two brothers died during a cholera epidemic, the fort's doctor, Major Robertson, took me to the fort to live with him and his wife. I was twelve years old at the time. The major's wife was pregnant and needed help with the house-cleaning and cooking. She was a very nice lady, and she took it upon herself to teach me perfect English. She had been a schooteacher before she married the major. I lived with them for seven years, then the major was transferred. However, he found me employment before he left. He and Drake were friends, and he knew Drake was looking for a housekeeper. So he got in touch with him."

Autumn Moon turned away from the stove, and Kristina noticed a trace of tears in the woman's eyes.

"I loved Drake at first sight," Autumn Moon continued. "But he was a married man with a pregnant wife. I thought my love was in vain, and I was resigned to loving him secretly. I hadn't worked for Drake very long, though, before I realized his marriage was an unhappy one. Drake and Mary were as different as night and day. Drake had been in St. Louis visiting his cousin Eva when he met Mary. She was from Philadelphia, but was also in St. Louis visiting a relative. Following a whirlwind courtship, Mary and Drake were married. I suppose Mary was so blinded by her husband's dashing good looks that she didn't consider the hardships she'd face living in the West. She was miserable here, and her constant nagging and complaining destroyed her marriage. Finally, Drake turned to me for love. Although I knew it was wrong, I welcomed him with open arms.

172

Mary found out about us and left Drake. He didn't stop her, for he no longer loved her. By then, he was in love with me."

Autumn Moon turned back to the stove and served breakfast, placing a plate of ham and eggs before Kristina.

The food was cooked to perfection, the ham juicy but crisp, the eggs fried with the yolks unbroken. Two flaky biscuits, dripping with butter, complemented the appetizing fare.

Kristina, however, took one look at the food, pushed back her chair, and darted to the back door. Flinging it open, she caught sight of an empty bucket on the porch and gagged wretchedly into it; then as her stomach began to settle, she turned to find Autumn Moon standing behind her.

"I don't know what's wrong with me," Kristina said weakly. "I've been feeling nauseous for a couple of days, but this is the first time I was actually sick."

The older woman's eyes swept over her knowingly. "Kristina, when was your last monthly?"

At first, Autumn Moon's probing failed to fully register with Kristina. "I'm not sure," she said, thinking back. Had she had her monthly flux since her arrival at the Diamond-C? No, she hadn't! The reason for her nausea suddenly hit her with a shocking force. "Oh, no!" she moaned, her face ashen.

"Are your breasts tender?"

"They seem a little sensitive."

The woman smiled gently. "Kristina, honey, you're going to have a baby."

"But I can't be pregnant!" she cried. "I just can't be!"

"Well, I'm afraid you are," Autumn Moon said kindly.

"But . . . but how . . . ?" Kristina blushed. "I mean, I thought it took more time for a woman to—? How can it happen so quickly?"

"It takes only one time," Autumn Moon said, laughing good-naturedly. Wrapping an arm about Kristina's waist, she led her back into the kitchen. "Sit down," she said, "and I'll fix you a cup of tea. Maybe you can keep that down."

Kristina's head was swirling. A baby! She was pregnant with Cole's child! For a blissful moment she was delighted, but then cold reality struck. Cole wouldn't find the news thrilling but would most certainly view her pregnancy as an added responsibility—one that he could very well do without!

She glanced up to find Autumn Moon watching her with concern, for Kristina's expressive features had revealed her anguish. "Cole won't want this baby," she moaned.

"Of course he will," Autumn Moon was quick to assure her. "Cole loves children."

"Maybe," she said lamely. "But loving them and fathering them isn't the same thing."

At that moment, Joseph barged into the kitchen, a broom in his hand. He had been sweeping the front porch. "Miz Kristina," he said excitedly. "Mista Cole's back! He's ridin' up to the house."

Kristina rose to her feet, but her knees were so weak that she almost sank back onto the chair. "Cole's here?" she gasped.

"Yes, ma'am." Joseph appeared worried. "Miz Kristina, I reckon you best tell him 'bout Mista Drake. I just ain't got the heart to tell him."

Numbly, Kristina reached out and patted the butler's arm. "It's all right, I'll tell him."

She had to force her legs to carry her from the kitchen, down the hall, and to the front door. She

174

wished she could welcome Cole home with smiles, hugs, and kisses. Instead, she had to tell him that his dearest friend had died!

Cole saw Kristina as she stepped onto the front porch. His horse was nearing the house at a slow pace. The animal was as fatigued as its rider! The sight of Kristina revitalized Cole, for she was an enticing vision. Her long blond tresses were cascading freely, and a gentle breeze was ruffling the curly strands, causing them to fall into seductive disarray. Her powder-blue dress, despite its modest design, enhanced Kristina's full bosom and small waist.

Reaching the hitching rail, Cole dismounted. A young drover had seen his arrival, and he now rushed over to take the tired Appaloosa.

As Cole was telling the drover to give the horse extra feed, Kristina was watching him intently. She thought he might have stopped in town before coming to the Diamond-C. If he had, he would already know about Drake. But as she looked closer she could see by Cole's casual manner that he hadn't been in town, nor had he talked to any of the ranch hands who were working on the range.

Kristina dreaded the sad task that lay ahead. A painful sob caught in her throat, and she swallowed it back with difficulty. She watched as Cole came toward her. His presence stirred mixed emotions within her, sending sympathy mingling with hungry desire coursing through her body.

Cole was attired in black trousers and a cream-colored, western-style shirt. The top buttons were open, revealing dark, curly hair. The brim of his black, weatherworn hat was shading his eyes, and Kristina couldn't see his expression. Was he happy to see her? Had he missed her at all?

Cole came slowly up the porch steps, then pausing in front of Kristina, he removed his hat. As he gazed down into her face, his azure eyes reflected his feelings. His gaze was filled with love. He drew her into his arms, bent his head, and kissed her tenderly yet passionately. Although Kristina leaned into his embrace, she was too emotionally torn to fully respond. When Cole finally released her, he did so with reluctance.

"I'm sorry I was gone so long," he said, "but I had to chase Wilkes into Mexico. When I finally caught him, I took him back to Albuquerque and handed him over to the sheriff."

"Albuquerque? But I thought he was wanted here."

"He's wanted in just about every town across the West. But Albuquerque has first claim on him."

"Is he the man—?"

"No," Cole cut in. "The scar on his chest was caused from a knife wound." He slapped his hat against his leg, knocking loose the grimy particles of trail dust that had accumulated on the wide brim. "I need to get out of these dirty clothes, take a bath, then sleep about twelve hours straight." He pitched his hat onto the porch lounge, then looked contritely at Kristina. His face was charmingly boyish yet so sensual that Kristina shivered imperceptibly.

"I should've sent you a wire," he murmured, "but when I'm trackin' someone, I don't think about anything else."

Cole wondered why he was keeping their discussion so casual when all he really wanted was to take her into his arms. He had missed Kristina more than he had thought possible. Now he longed to draw her close and feel her supple curves pressed intimately against him. But there was a certain reserve about her

176

that held him at bay.

Meanwhile, Kristina had achieved a tenuous control over her desire for Cole. This wasn't the time for passion. She had to tell Cole about Drake.

She reached out a trembling hand and grasped his arm. "Cole . . ." she began, tears forming. "Drake . . . Drake is . . . He is . . ." God, she couldn't bring herself to say it!

She didn't need to, for Cole could see the terrible truth on her face. He whirled awkwardly about and stepped to the railing. "Was it another heart attack?"

"Yes," Kristina answered, wishing he hadn't turned away from her. She wanted to hold him close and console him.

"When?" Cole asked raspingly. "When did he die?"

"Three days ago," she answered softly.

Kristina's heart broke when she saw Cole's strong shoulders shake as though a chilling wind had coursed through him.

"God!" he groaned, grief ripping into his voice. "Drake! Drake!"

Kristina continued to watch as Cole mustered a semblance of control. He straightened his shoulders, and his tall frame moved gracefully as he turned back around to face her.

Cole's eyes, however, starkly revealed his anguish. Kristina, sharing his sorrow, was so overcome that her composure crumbled. Covering her face with her hands, she sobbed heavily.

Cole quickly drew her into his arms, holding her close. "I'm sorry, sweetheart," he murmured. "I know how much you loved your father."

Cole's reference to Drake as her father cut sharply into Kristina's grief. Restraining her tears, she moved out of his embrace. "Let's go to the study," she

177

suggested, her voice weak. "There's something I must tell you." Although she dreaded telling him that she wasn't Drake's daughter, she was anxious to get it over with. As her somber thoughts turned to her pregnancy, she glanced up into his watching eyes and said clearly, "I have a couple of things to tell you, and they're very important."

"All right," Cole agreed. Taking her arm, he escorted her into the house. "How's Autumn Moon?" he asked.

"She's holding up remarkably well."

"Is Josh here?"

"No, he didn't come for the funeral. But he did send a wire."

"That's strange," Cole remarked. "I wonder why he stayed away." They reached the study, and as Cole opened the door, he asked about Joseph.

"He's all right," Kristina answered. "But I know he's grieving terribly."

"Where are Autumn Moon and Joseph?"

"In the kitchen," she replied, preceding him into the study. She remembered to tell him that Alisa was at the Diamond-C.

"Did she arrive before Drake died?"

"Yes," Kristina answered. The drapes were drawn, and the dark room was gloomy. Stepping to the windows, Kristina opened the heavy curtains, admitting the sun's cheery brightness. "Would you like a drink?" she asked, gesturing toward the liquor cabinet.

"No, thanks," Cole replied. "But I would like some coffee."

Complying, Kristina started for the kitchen, promising a hasty return.

Cole went to Drake's comfortable leather easy chair and sat down. He closed his eyes, leaned back,

178

and released a long, weary sigh. An infinite sorrow filled his being, and a groan sounded deep in his throat. He hadn't known such grief since losing his parents. Memories of Drake flooded his mind as he reminisced.

Cole was engrossed in his solemn musings when Kristina returned. She carried a tray laden with two cups and a coffee pot. She poured two servings, then sat in the chair facing Cole.

He took a drink of coffee before asking, "Were you with Drake at the last?"

Her wistful gaze met his. "Yes," she murmured.

"Did he leave a message for me?"

"Yes. He said to tell you that he loved you . . . that he couldn't love you more if you were his son."

Cole took another sip of coffee, then following a long moment of silence, asked, "Did he say anything else?"

"Yes . . . yes, he did," she stammered.

When she didn't continue, he coaxed somewhat impatiently, "Go on, what did he say?"

"He said for us to be good to each other . . . and that we belong together."

Feeling a little embarrassed, she lowered her gaze to her lap.

"He was right," Cole remarked.

She glanced up quickly.

"We do belong together." He got to his feet and moved around the desk. Going to Kristina, he grasped her hands and drew her into his embrace.

Lacing her arms about his neck, Kristina nestled her head against his shoulder. She clung desperately, for she feared he might never hold her this way again. When she told him the truth about herself, she might lose him forever.

"You have no idea how much I missed you," Cole

said with deep feeling. "More than once, I was tempted to forget tracking Wilkes and return to the Diamond-C."

She moved so that she could gaze into his eyes. "Why didn't you?"

"Loving a woman the way I love you is new for me. It's going to take me a while to learn how to deal with it. My feelings for you are going to change my whole life, I know that. But the change will have to come about gradually." His expression beseeching, his voice choked with sincerity, he pleaded, "Darlin', please be patient with me."

Cole's vulnerability touched Kristina. She sensed correctly that Cole had never before bared his heart to a woman. She was thrilled to learn that he loved her, but her joy was short-lived, and with a sullen sigh, she moved out of his arms. She must be strong, confess her true identity and then . . . and then would the love in his eyes turn into contempt?

Her obvious doubt worried Cole. Had her feelings changed during his absence? Was she about to reject him? Had he lost the only woman he had ever loved?

The uneasy silence between them was suddenly interrupted by a loud rapping on the door. Kristina was annoyed, for she was determined to tell Cole the truth this time.

Cole admitted Joseph to the room.

"Mista Cole . . ." the butler began. "Excuse me for intrudin', but the sheriff is here. He's got two gentlemans and a lady with him. They's strangers, I ain't never seen 'em before."

Cole turned to Kristina. "I guess we'd better welcome our guests."

"I wonder who they are," she replied, sighing inwardly. As soon as the visitors left, she would tell Cole who she really was if she had to shout from the

180

rooftop to be heard!

Cole took Kristina's hand, then with Joseph leading the way, they left the room and went to the parlor.

The sight of the visitors caused Kristina to halt abruptly. She could hardly believe her own eyes. Her face turned deathly pale, and staring at the woman with disbelief, she gasped chokingly, "Samantha!"

A cold chill ran up Kristina's spine as she forced herself to look at the man who was standing beside the sheriff. It was Raymond Lewis!

Suddenly Samantha pointed an accusing finger at Kristina, looked at the sheriff, and demanded, "I want that impostor arrested!"

Chapter Fifteen

"What the hell's goin' on?" Cole asked gruffly.

"I can explain—" Kristina replied, turning to Cole, her eyes pleading with his.

"Spare us your lies," the man beside Samantha cut in, his accent unmistakably British. He spoke to the sheriff. "Will you please arrest this woman?"

"Who are you?" Kristina asked. She had never seen him before.

Samantha answered her query. "This is Bernard Galsworthy, my fiancé." She slipped her arm into his, then smiled up at him with complete devotion.

Bernard was dressed impeccably, his expensively tailored suit fitting his tall, lanky frame perfectly. He sported a handlebar mustache, its color matching the shade of his reddish-blond hair. The man was neither handsome nor unattractive.

Meanwhile, Sheriff Bickham, uncomfortable with the situation, cleared his throat and said somewhat hesitantly, "I don't think there's any reason to arrest Miss Parker."

Cole's impatience erupted. "Who the hell is Miss Parker?" he demanded.

"I am," Kristina answered softly. Her spirits sank.

Cole's learning the truth about her in this fashion would surely destroy his love. If she had only told him sooner! She drew a long breath, and was about to explain when Raymond Lewis interrupted.

"Miss Parker," he clarified, speaking to Cole, "is Samantha Carlson's maid. She came here impersonating Samantha in order to swindle money from Drake Carlson. I have no tangible proof, but why else would she pretend she was Samantha? Apparently, though, her attempt to defraud failed. Somehow, Drake Carlson learned the truth. Then I suppose she turned on her feminine wiles and convinced the man not to press charges. I'm sure she used her alluring charms to wrap the poor man around her little finger."

Joseph had remained in the doorway, and turning to face him, Cole asked, "Do you know what this man is talking about?"

"The gentleman's wrong 'bout Miz Kristina wantin' to swindle Mista Drake. But, yes suh, I know she ain't Samantha Carlson. It was right after you left that Mista Drake realized she weren't Samantha. It seems that Miz Samantha has got a birthmark on her arm, and Mista Drake noticed that Miz Kristina don't have one."

Kristina clutched at Cole's arm. "Oh, Cole, please let me explain!"

He threw off her hand. "Explain!" he lashed out. "Why, you lying little fraud!"

His harsh words rendered Kristina speechless, and her feelings went numb.

"You must be Cole Barton," Samantha spoke up. She waited, but when Cole didn't respond, she took his silence as verification. "When I heard that Kristina had actually married you under my name, I was totally incredulous." Her eyes traveled furtively over Cole. She found him strikingly handsome, though there was an intimidating aura about him that wasn't to her liking. This man was clearly beyond a woman's control.

Kristina's numbness had passed, and anxious to make Cole understand, she said imploringly, "Please, I must talk to you alone!" If they were sequestered away from the others, then she could explain her side of the story without interruption.

Raymond, afraid Kristina would escape, said firmly to the sheriff, "If you allow her to leave this room, we'll never see her again! She'll talk that gunslinger into running away with her!"

"Who the hell is this ass?" Cole grumbled to no one in particular.

"My name is Raymond Lewis," Raymond remarked huffily. *How dare the man call him an ass! He should call him out for such rudeness!* As Raymond measured his opponent, however, he had second thoughts. The cowboy might be unpardonably rude, but he was also undoubtedly dangerous.

Deciding to overlook Cole's remark, Raymond continued. "I am a good friend of Samantha's. I accompanied her and Bernard on this trip because I'm searching for a wanted man. I'm sure he'll come here looking for Kristina. I heard in town that you are a bounty hunter, so you might be interested to know that I have posted a thousand-dollar reward for him."

"A thousand dollars!" Cole said, amazed. "He must've killed someone mighty important."

"As far as I know, he hasn't killed anyone."

"That's a steep reward for a man who isn't a murderer. What's his name?"

"Ted Cummings."

"Ted!" Kristina cried. "I . . . I don't understand.

185

Why are you looking for Ted?"

"Shortly after you ran away, the bastard tried to kill me. Fortunately, his attempt was thwarted. He did, however, escape arrest."

Cole was confused as well as frustrated. The only thing he knew unquestionably was that Kristina Parker had lied, cheated, and made a fool of him! A simmering rage flared into life.

Cole's hands shot out, grasping Kristina in a viselike grip. "Damn it!" he said furiously. "Did you want Samantha's inheritance so badly that you didn't even draw the line at marriage? You played the loving daughter to the hilt, didn't you? You wouldn't even deny Drake his last request!" His voice filling with contempt, he added, "You acted your role to perfection, Kristina Parker!"

His harshness aroused Kristina's own anger, but before she could say anything, Cole turned to Raymond. "Tell me about Ted Cummings," he ordered.

"Cummings was the Johnsons' coachman. Although no one knew it at the time, it is now apparent that he and Kristina were lovers."

"That's a lie!" Kristina cried sharply. Her gaze flew to Samantha. "Surely you don't believe that Ted and I were anything more than friends!"

"Well, you did spend a lot of time with him," Samantha replied smugly. "He's quite a few years older than you, but I understand that some women prefer older men. And Ted Cummings is attractive in a barbariclike way."

Raymond quickly continued as though the interruption hadn't occurred. "After Samantha and her parents left for Europe, I stopped by their home. Kristina was there alone. I'm a very wealthy man, Mr. Barton, and Kristina offered me a proposition. If I would give her a generous allowance and set her up in her own home, she'd become my mistress. She's a very seductive young woman, and her offer was tempting. I told her I'd consider it but that I didn't intend to buy the merchandise without sampling the goods. She was very willing to agree to that. We were locked in a lover's embrace when Cummings barged into the house. I suppose Kristina feared the man's jealous temper, for she suddenly started fighting me. She pretended, quite convincingly, that I was forcing my intentions upon her. As you already know, she is a very talented actress. Well, she was playing the victim so convincingly that she actually stabbed me with a pair of scissors. I managed to stumble out of the house, reach a doctor, and have my wound treated. I then went to the police, but by the time we arrived at the Johnsons' home, Kristina was gone. So was Ted Cummings."

"Is that the story you gave the police and everyone else?" Kristina demanded harshly. "Why, you vile, contemptible liar!"

"You have no right to call anyone a liar!" Cole interrupted bitterly. His gaze went to Samantha. "Why aren't you in Europe?"

"My father became ill on the passage over." She slipped her hand into her fiancé's as though she needed his reassuring touch. "If it hadn't been for Bernard, I don't know what Mother and I would have done. Bernard and I met on the ship. His home is in London." Samantha leaned against Galsworthy, and he placed an arm about her shoulders. "Father died before we reached England and Mother was too grief-stricken to tour Europe so we booked passage on the next ship back to New York. Bernard accompanied us—we needed him so desperately."

"Why did you decide to visit Drake?" Cole asked.

"It was Raymond's suggestion. He figured we'd find Kristina here, but, of course, we didn't expect to find her using my name. When we arrived in town and learned that she was impersonating me, I was completely shocked."

"I'm not impersonating you," Kristina spoke up.

Samantha cast her a smug expression, but Kristina had turned to Raymond. "Why did you come here looking for me?"

"I'm not looking for you, but I *am* looking for Cummings. He'll show up sooner or later."

Kristina didn't think so. "Ted and I were only friends. There's no reason for him to come here."

Bernard, growing impatient with the proceedings, sighed tediously. "Love . . ." he said to Samantha. "Will you please tell the constable to arrest Miss Parker? I'm dreadfully tired, and I need a nap." He set his arrogant gaze upon Joseph. "Is there a housekeeper?"

"Yes, suh," he answered. "Autumn Moon takes care of the house."

"Summon her, please."

It wasn't necessary, for Autumn Moon and Alisa were in the foyer. They had been standing out of sight, listening. Now they stepped forward and into the parlor.

As Samantha regarded Autumn Moon with disdain, Raymond's lustful scrutiny zeroed in on Alisa. He found Kristina the prettier of the two young women, but he focused his lewd intentions upon Alisa. Someday he was determined to have Kristina at his mercy, but, in the meantime, he'd entertain himself with this dark beauty. It was apparent to Raymond that she was part Indian, and that the older woman was her mother. He didn't think he'd encounter too much difficulty seducing the daughter, for he could remember reading once that Indian women were always anxious to lie with a white man—especially if he bribed her with baubles.

Samantha was still measuring Autumn Moon with scorn. "When Mother learned I was coming here . . ." Samantha began coolly, "she told me all about your dalliance with Drake. On our way to the Diamond-C, we encountered Mr. Cullen. I was very relieved when he informed me that Drake hadn't married you. The lawyer also told me that he plans to read Drake's will early next week. If Drake dared to leave this ranch to you, I'll take you to court."

"I won't inherit the Diamond-C," Autumn Moon replied with quiet dignity.

Kristina's temper flared. "Samantha, you have no right to treat Autumn Moon so rudely!"

"Stay out of this!" Samantha snapped, then turned to Alisa. "Who are you?"

Alisa's anger was smoldering, but keeping it under control, she answered evenly, "My name is Alisa, and I'm your sister."

"Sister!" she gasped, paling. "Heavens above!"

Bernard drew Samantha close, murmuring, "You poor darling. This day has been too trying." He gave her a consoling hug, then said to Autumn Moon, "Prepare a room for your mistress."

"You don't have to obey him!" Alisa told her mother sternly.

"No, it's all right," Autumn Moon replied, her eyes pleading with Alisa to remain calm. She moved to leave, but was detained by Kristina.

"Wait!" she called. Kristina whirled about, expecting to find Cole behind her, but he wasn't there. He had moved across the room and was staring out the open window, his back turned to the group.

Kristina went to his side. Touching his arm, she

said softly, "Cole?"

He didn't respond.

"Cole?" she whispered, her tone pleading. "Please say something."

"What do you want me to say?" he grumbled, turning to look at her.

She studied him closely. She couldn't find any anger in his eyes—they seemed devoid of any emotion. "Will you let me explain?" she implored. "Won't you listen to my side of the story?"

"You have nothing to say that I want to hear." His rebuff was frosty.

A cold chill coursed through Kristina. Desperate, she grasped his arm. "You must listen to me!"

He flung off her hold. "No!" he answered. "You listen to me! Less than an hour ago, I learned that my best friend is dead. Then, a few minutes later, I learn that the woman I thought was my wife is really a fraud! Stay away from me, Kristina Parker, before I say or do something that I might later regret!"

Though Cole's rejection hurt Kristina severely, she understood his anger . . . his pain. She had probably lost Cole for good, and she had no one to blame but herself. She should have told him the truth from the very beginning. Her heart breaking, Kristina moved away from the man she loved. Her gaze swept over the others. Samantha, Bernard, and Raymond were watching her with gloating expressions. They were obviously enjoying her misery. Kristina looked at Joseph, Alisa, and Autumn Moon. Their faces seemed to reflect her own suffering. She turned back to speak to Cole. "I'll not bother you anymore," she said calmly. "But if you should decide to hear what I have to say, I'll be more than willing to tell you everything."

She waited, hoping he might give her some small

encouragement. But when Cole turned his back on her, she lost all hope. Sighing, she remarked calmly to Autumn Moon, "You can prepare my room for Samantha. I won't be needing it."

Kristina was determined to hold on to her pride, and with a proud lift to her chin, she crossed the room with long strides, went to the sheriff, and said, "Sheriff Bickham, arrest me. Please! I'd rather go to jail than spend another minute in this house."

"But, Miss Parker, jail ain't no place for a lady," the lawman objected.

"Haven't you heard?" Kristina replied with a note of bitterness. "I'm not a lady. I'm a fraud." She held out her hands. "Cuff me, and take me to jail."

"But . . . but . . ." the sheriff stammered.

"Do as she says!" Cole suddenly intervened. "If she wants to go to jail take her!" Cole had no intention of leaving her there, but he needed time for his temper to cool, time to sort his thoughts. In the interim, she'd be in good hands with the sheriff and it was clear she didn't want to stay at the Diamond-C anyway.

"Sheriff Bickham!" Bernard spoke up impatiently. "Take the woman to jail. My fiancée is pressing charges against her. We insist that you put her behind bars."

The lawman groaned. "All right, but I don't like doin' it." He turned to Kristina. "These people rented a buckboard from the livery. The driver's out front waitin'. You can ride with him in the wagon. I've got my horse. Do you wanna pack some clothes?"

"Her clothes can be sent later," Samantha insisted. "Just get her out of here."

The sheriff took Kristina's arm in a gentle hold. "Ma'am, are you ready?"

"Yes, I am," she answered firmly. As Kristina

passed Autumn Moon, Alisa, and Joseph, she tried to give them an encouraging smile, but the gesture was pathetically weak.

"I'll go to the hotel and get you a clean set of sheets," Sheriff Bickham said as he escorted Kristina into her confining cell.

Kristina gave the cramped space a cursory glance. It contained a narrow cot and an enamel wash basin chipped and cracked in places. The cell was as dreary as her mood.

"This ain't no place for a lady," the sheriff said, speaking his thoughts aloud. "But, ma'am, I'll try to make it as comfortable as I can. I'll move in a table and a chair so you can have a place to sit when you eat. Also, you can use the bath at the hotel." His latter offer brought a blush to his cheeks, but hidden beneath his full beard, it escaped Kristina's notice.

"Thank you," she murmured. "But why are you being so nice to me?"

"Miss Parker, when Drake was gettin' well, I visited him often. Well, you know that. Anyway, Drake always spoke real highly of you. He never thought you was tryin' to swindle him, and I don't think so, either. And, don't you worry, the judge is gonna agree."

She smiled at the heavyset man warmly. Looking deeply into his kind eyes, she said sincerely, "I appreciate your kindness."

"I'll go for the sheets," he said, leaving the cell.

"Aren't you going to lock me inside?"

"No, ma'am. I sure ain't." With that, he headed toward the front door.

The one cell was attached to the sheriff's office, and Kristina watched as Bickham left, then went to the cot and sat down. She tried not to think about Cole, but she could no more will him from her mind than she could will her heart to stop beating. Tears smarted her eyes as she recalled the angry, unfeeling way in which he had told the sheriff to take her to jail. Did he hate her?

She lay down on the cot. Its coverings were soiled and smelled of unwashed bodies and the offensive odor unsettled her stomach, bringing her pregnancy to mind.

I may have lost Cole, she thought, *but I have his baby.* For a moment she considered using her pregnancy to get Cole back, but she quickly discarded the notion. If she couldn't have Cole's love willingly, then she'd rather not have him at all. She'd not force him into marrying her. Furthermore, living with him for the child's sake, and knowing all along that he despised her, would be more than she could bear.

A heavy curtain of worry suddenly draped her musings. What would become of her and her child? Even if the judge dismissed Samantha's charges, where would she go? How would she support herself and a baby?

Josh! she suddenly thought. *He'll help me!* She began to feel a little better. She wasn't truly alone, for she knew that Josh was a good friend. But he was also Cole's friend. If his loyalty was put to the test, would he side with Cole, perhaps even refuse to help her? She thrust the doubts from her mind. She mustn't let herself get too upset, it wasn't good for the baby.

Kristina moved her hand to her still flat stomach. She wanted this child with all her heart, and she was determined not to let anyone or anything prevent her giving it life.

Chapter Sixteen

Autumn Moon packed Kristina's clothes, prepared the bedroom for Samantha, then went in search of Cole. She found him in the study sitting at Drake's desk, his hand wrapped about a half-empty bottle of bourbon. Cole's eyes were lowered, but, when he heard someone entering the room, he lifted his gaze. He watched as Autumn Moon placed herself in the chair facing him.

A bitter smile came to Cole's face as he lifted the whiskey bottle, as though he were making a toast. "Here's to life," he said, gulping a big swig. "It can be full of surprises."

"Getting drunk isn't going to help," Autumn Moon remarked reproachfully.

"It can't hurt," Cole returned. He put the bottle back on the desk, then murmured with a somber sigh, "Damn! I'm gonna miss Drake."

"So will I," Autumn Moon replied. "But, Cole, I didn't come here to talk about Drake."

An angry glint sparked in Cole's eyes. "If you came here to discuss Miss Parker, then—"

Autumn Moon cut him off sharply. "The way you treated Kristina in front of Samantha and the rest of us was inexcusable."

Cole emitted a scoffing laugh. "The way I treated her? You can't be serious. She's a fraud."

"She isn't a fraud!" Autumn Moon said, rising angrily to her feet. Placing her hands on the desktop, she leaned forward and her eyes met Cole's in open warfare. "She never intended to swindle Drake."

"How can you be so damned sure?" he countered. "She didn't admit to her true identity until after Drake confronted her. If he hadn't realized she was a fake, how long would she have continued her impersonation? Long enough perhaps to get money from Drake? Maybe even long enough to inherit this ranch? Damn it, Autumn Moon! She probably wouldn't have admitted the truth to any of us if Drake hadn't uncovered her!"

"You're wrong!" Autumn Moon replied firmly. "Kristina told Dr. Newman who she was, and she told him before Drake guessed the truth! The doctor asked her to continue her pretense because he was afraid that Drake wasn't strong enough to take the shock."

Cole was taken aback. "She . . . she told Newman?"

Autumn Moon, her anger cooling, returned to her chair. She told Cole that it was Kristina who had written to Drake all those years, then explained why Kristina had been traveling under Samantha's name.

Cole listened raptly.

"She became so entangled that there was no way out," Autumn Moon continued. "She planned to be honest with Drake, but his heart attack made that quite impossible. If you'll recall, on the day she arrived, Dr. Newman warned her not to say anything that might upset Drake."

Cole held his silence as his mind absorbed

everything Autumn Moon had told him. He could understand why Kristina had felt she couldn't be honest with Drake. He couldn't understand, however, why she hadn't told him the truth—or why she had gone so far as to marry him!

Finally, Cole relented. "I guess Kristina didn't plan to swindle Drake, I'll give her that much. I can also understand why she couldn't tell Drake the truth, but that's no excuse for marrying me under Samantha's name. She had plenty of opportunities to be honest with me."

"She was confused. Also, you and Dr. Newman didn't give her a chance to decline. She was pressured into marrying you."

"She wasn't pressured into granting me my husbandly rights!" he grumbled.

"Of course she was!"

He arched a brow quizzically.

"Love, Cole! She was pressured by love! Don't you understand that Kristina loves you?"

"A love born out of lies?" he remarked caustically.

"No," Autumn Moon answered softly. "I'm sure her love comes from the heart."

He waved aside her reply. "You're talking romantic nonsense. The woman lied to me, tricked me, and made a fool of me."

Impatient with Cole's bitterness, Autumn Moon frowned. "Well, regardless of your personal feelings, there's an innocent life involved."

He eyed her dubiously. "What are you saying?"

"Kristina's pregnant."

Concern showed on Cole's face. Autumn Moon had expected him to be shocked, maybe even angry. She was pleased to note that he cared so deeply.

"Why didn't she tell me?" he groaned.

"I suppose she didn't have a chance."

"Damn it!" he mumbled angrily. "She didn't bother to tell me she's Kristina Parker, and she didn't bother to tell me she's pregnant. It would seem that keeping the truth from me is her favorite pastime!"

"Kristina couldn't tell you that Drake was dead and that she was pregnant in the same breath. If Samantha and the others hadn't arrived, she'd have told you about the baby."

Cole helped himself to another swig of bourbon, then pushing back his chair, he rose to his feet. "I'm going to get Kristina."

"You can't bring her back to the Diamond-C, not with Samantha here."

Cole agreed. "I'll take her to Josh's."

Autumn Moon cast him an imploring glance. "Be kind to her, Cole. She loves you."

Cole wasn't sure of Kristina's love, nor did he trust her motives, but he saw no reason to voice his doubts to Autumn Moon.

Raymond was on his way to the kitchen in search of Joseph when he spotted Alisa in the parlor sitting on the sofa with an open book resting on her lap. Her eyes were staring blankly into space.

He entered the room on quiet steps. Pausing, he studied the lovely woman with lustful intent, then he cleared his throat to make his presence known.

Alisa glanced up quickly. "Mr. Lewis," she remarked, closing the book.

"Please call me Raymond," he said warmly, sitting in the wing chair facing her. He was all set to woo her with whatever means he thought necessary and, when she suddenly rose to her feet, he asked a little too sharply, "Why are you leaving?"

She resented his sharp tone, and gave him a hostile look.

"Please forgive me," he apologized, then gestured to the sofa. "Sit back down, won't you? I didn't mean to sound so bossy. I guess my nerves are frayed."

She complied hesitantly.

"I was looking for Joseph when I happened to see you sitting in here. You seemed very deep in thought. Are you worried about Kristina?"

Alisa hadn't been thinking about Kristina—her thoughts had been on Josh. "Actually, I wasn't thinking about Kristina, but, yes, I suppose I am concerned about her."

"Are you two close friends?"

"No, not especially," she answered, eyeing him questioningly.

"Alisa, Kristina is guilty as charged. All those accusations Samantha and I made are true. Kristina is very clever. Her congeniality is only an act. Behind her compassionate facade lies a very wicked young woman. She longs for riches, and she'll use anyone to get what she wants. I'm sure that she was sweet to Drake after he learned the truth because she was planning to win his affections—and I don't mean in a daughterly fashion."

"You mean she intended to seduce him?"

"All the way to the marriage altar."

"But she's married to Cole."

"That marriage isn't legal."

Alisa wondered if Raymond was telling the truth. Had Kristina planned to marry Drake? Thinking of her own failed plan to marry Eva's husband, Alisa didn't find it hard to believe that Kristina could be just as calculating.

Raymond, reading Alisa's suspicions, gloated

inwardly. He had easily surmounted the first obstacle between them. Now he wouldn't let Alisa's friendship with Kristina block his plan to get Alisa into his bed. Pasting a kindly smile on his face, he tackled the second obstacle. "I'm sorry about the way Samantha treated you and your mother," he said tenderly. "Her behavior was uncalled for." He didn't want her to think that he sided with Samantha.

"I'm used to people treating me like that. I even received the same treatment in St. Louis."

"You lived in St. Louis?"

Finding Raymond Lewis an affable companion, Alisa began telling him why she had moved to St. Louis to live with Drake's cousin.

Raymond quickly realized that Alisa couldn't be bought with baubles. She was apparently an educated and willful young lady. Hearing resentment in her voice when she spoke of her Comanche blood, he knew she was far removed from her Indian heritage. Tempting this woman to become his lover was not going to be as easy as he had thought. Knowing he couldn't seduce Alisa with good looks, Raymond decided the most logical way to win her was through his money. He somehow sensed that wealth meant a great deal to her.

Moving to the edge of his chair, he reached over and took her hands into his. He squeezed them gently. "Alisa, I hope you won't find me too forward, but . . . but . . ." He pretended shyness.

"Yes?" she encouraged.

"You are the most beautiful woman I have ever seen. You have me totally enchanted. When I return to Philadelphia, I'd love to have you accompany me. Don't misconstrue my motives. You'll be a guest at my parents' home. I'm certainly not trying to compromise you. And rest assured, my dear, that my fellow Philadelphians won't treat you abhorrently. Quite the contrary. My family is a very important one, for, you see, we're terribly wealthy. As our guest, you'll be accepted into society like visiting royalty." He smiled warmly. "I promise you."

Releasing her hands, he leaned back in his chair. He had no intentions of taking her to Philadelphia. His invitation was merely a ploy to gain her gratitude. He was confident that he'd soon have her in his bed.

Alisa was flattered. Imagining herself socializing with Philadelphia's gentry was exciting. She wasn't ready, however, to commit herself. She wasn't about to make the same mistake she had made three years ago. This time, she was determined to force Josh into revealing his feelings.

During the three years she had spent in St. Louis, she had managed to convince herself that she no longer loved Josh. Having money and marrying an aristocratic husband was all that mattered. True love was an emotion she could live without. When she had returned to the Diamond-C, and seen Josh again, her resolve had crumbled. She still loved him, and she had a feeling that she always would.

"Raymond, I thank you for the invitation, but I can't give you a definite answer. After all, we're practically strangers. When we know each other a little better, then I'll consider your generous offer."

"Of course, my dear. I'll probably be here for quite some time, so I'm sure we'll become the best of friends. Perhaps you'll have dinner with me tonight. Is there a decent restaurant in town?"

"There are a couple of very nice ones."

"Good," he remarked, getting to his feet. "I'll rent a buggy and pick you up at seven."

"Pick me up?" she questioned, confused.

201

"Yes. I plan to move into town. I'll get a room at the hotel. That's why I was looking for Joseph. I was going to ask him if I might have the use of a wagon and a driver. I need to take my luggage to town with me."

"But why don't you want to stay here?"

He chuckled pleasantly. "I'm not the type to live so far away from the comforts of town. I guess I'm too city-bred."

She smiled. "I understand."

"You will have dinner with me, won't you?"

"Yes."

"Until tonight, then," he said, moving away.

Alisa watched him as he left the parlor. A sigh of disappointment passed her lips. If only Raymond was as handsome and dashing as Josh, then maybe he could rout Josh from her heart.

Well, she told herself spiritedly, *Raymond might not be good-looking, but he's a perfect gentleman. He's also very rich. And even more important, my Comanche blood doesn't offend him. I'd be a fool not to encourage his affections. That way, if Josh firmly rejects me, I'll still have Raymond.*

Kristina heard the door to the jail clang open. She was resting on the cot, but the loud noise caused her to sit up with a start. She was surprised to see Cole poised in the doorway, his steely gaze aimed in her direction.

Sheriff Bickham was seated at his desk, but Cole's intrusion sent him bounding to his feet. He watched as Cole remained standing in the open door, staring at Kristina with an expression far from congenial.

"Barton . . ." the sheriff said firmly. "Come the rest of the way inside and close the door."

202

Cole drew his gaze from Kristina, slammed the door shut, and remarked to Bickham, "I'm taking Miss Parker out of here."

Before the sheriff could give his consent, Kristina spoke up. "I'm not going anywhere with you, Cole Barton!"

"She's not locked in there," Bickham told Cole. "Take her with my permission."

As Cole came toward her cell, Kristina moved to the far corner and braced her back against the wall. Folding her arms across her chest, she said defiantly, "I'm staying right here!"

Cole entered the tiny cell, went to Kristina, and grabbed her hand, jerking her to his side. "We're leaving!" he mumbled tersely.

She wrested free. "A few hours ago, you were anxious to see me in jail! Now you want me out of jail! Can't you make up your mind?"

"I never wanted you in jail," he replied.

"Oh?" she countered. "That wasn't the impression I got!"

"You were the one who asked Bickham to arrest you. Did you prefer jail over being in the same house with me?"

"You, Samantha, and, most of all, Raymond Lewis!"

His patience gone, Cole placed his hands on her shoulders, drew her close, and leered down into her defiant eyes. "I'm taking you out of here! You've got a choice, my deceitful beauty—you can either walk or I'll carry you!"

Kristina was piqued. The man had his nerve! This morning he had treated her cruelly, and now he had the gall to come here and order her around!

"Cole . . ." she began reasonably. "If you're willing to listen to my side of the story, then I'll leave with you. But if you intend to continue treating me like I'm a criminal, then I'm not going anyplace with you!"

"I already know your side of the story. Autumn Moon told me everything."

Kristina tensed. Had Autumn Moon also told him about her pregnancy? She tried to find the answer in his face, but his expression was indiscernible. "Wh— what did she tell you?"

"She told me you were the one who had written to Drake."

"What else did she say?"

"She explained why you didn't tell Drake who you really are."

Kristina searched his eyes. "Did you believe her?"

"Well, I didn't disbelieve her."

His misgivings weren't very encouraging. "You want to think the worst of me, don't you?"

He leaned closer to her, and said too softly for the sheriff to overhear, "Kristina Parker, you lied to me, tricked me, and made love to me as my wife. You let me believe that I was married to Samantha Carlson. Now, you want me to believe in your integrity on faith alone. The way I see it, you haven't earned my trust. Just for the record, darlin', I don't trust you any farther than I can see you."

"If you feel that way, why are you taking me out of here? Why don't you just leave me alone?" Tears threatened, but she held them in check. She'd not give him the satisfaction of seeing her cry!

His blue eyes glinted. "I'm taking you out of here because Autumn Moon told me you're pregnant."

His words ripped into Kristina's heart. He didn't care about her, he only cared about his child!

Her sorrow was visible, and Cole was touched. He was about to tell her that her pregnancy wasn't his only reason for being here, but distrust suddenly surfaced again. He knew from experience that Kristina was a talented actress. Was she acting now? Was this deep sadness in her eyes a ploy? Was she still playing him for a fool? Cole knew there were no firm answers to these questions, and his frustration merely refueled his anger. "Let's go!" he grumbled, reaching for her hand.

She recoiled. "Leave me alone! I'm not going!" Kristina's pride was strong. If she couldn't have Cole's love, she would rather not have him at all. She'd not use her pregnancy to entrap him, nor would she allow him to use it to dictate her life.

Cole was through arguing, and taking Kristina by surprise, he scooped her into his arms and carried her from the cell. "Fight me," he warned, "and I'll put you across my lap and give you the spanking you deserve!"

Kristina believed that he'd carry out his threat.

Passing the sheriff's desk, Cole told Bickham, "Thanks for taking care of her. I knew you would."

"It was my pleasure," the man replied.

Carrying Kristina outside, Cole took her to the sorrel mare tied beside his Appaloosa. He swung her up into the saddle, her long skirts flaring.

"We'll have to get you some suitable riding clothes," he said, moving to his own horse.

"Where are we going?" she asked.

"To Josh's ranch."

"Josh!" she exclaimed, smiling radiantly. Thank goodness he wasn't taking her back to the Diamond-C. She didn't want to come into contact with Samantha or Raymond. Her anxieties settled. Staying at Josh's ranch met with her approval. She liked Josh immensely.

She turned to look at Cole. He was mounted and

was watching her intently. Her smile remaining bright, she said cheerfully, "I'm looking forward to seeing Josh. He and I became very close during his visit to the Diamond-C."

Cole was suddenly struck with jealousy. So Kristina and Josh were very close, were they? He wondered just how close! He quickly cast his suspicions aside. Josh was a good friend, and he trusted him.

"I suppose Josh knows you aren't Samantha," Cole muttered.

"Yes, he does."

"It seems I'm the last one to know my wife isn't my wife," he uttered bitterly.

Chapter Seventeen

"There's a town called Sandy Creek," Cole said. "It's about an hour's ride from here. We'll stop there so you can buy some riding clothes. We'll also get a room at the hotel and spend the night. In the morning, if we get an early start, we'll be at Josh's by noon."

They were quite a few miles from San Antonio, and had said little to each other since leaving the jail.

Thinking of the upcoming night, Kristina asked, "Do you plan to get two rooms at the hotel?"

"Is that what you want?"

Was it? She wasn't sure. A part of her longed desperately to be in Cole's embrace, but her pride demanded that she hold on to her self-respect. Cole didn't love her, and if he were to share her bed, he would make love to her body, not to her heart. Her pride won out, and with a lift to her chin, she answered coolly, "I prefer to have my own room. I might be carrying your child, Cole Barton, but that doesn't give you the right to act as though you own me."

Cole suddenly reached over, grabbed Kristina's bridle reins, and brought her horse and his to an abrupt halt.

"Why are we stopping?" she asked.

It was a long moment before he answered, his eyes searching hers in the silence as though he could find the truth in their emerald depths. "Why didn't you tell me you weren't Samantha?" he finally asked. "You had so many opportunities."

"I did try to tell you. I was just about to do so when we were interrupted. Twice by Autumn Moon and once by Joseph." Her tone grew anxious. "Think back, Cole! I kept telling you that I had something important to say! Actually, I did finally tell you." A warm blush colored her cheeks as she continued. "It was after we had made love. I told you everything, but you slept through my confession. The next morning, when you told me you were going after Wilkes, I didn't have the heart to tell you. By then, I was too hurt."

"Hurt?" he asked, confused.

"I didn't want you to leave," she murmured.

"Kristina . . ." he began, "I believe you up to a point. I remember you telling me more than once that you had something important to say. And, you're right, we were interrupted. But, if you had really wanted me to know the truth, you'd have made the opportunity to tell me."

Kristina knew he had a valid argument. She knew why she hadn't forced him to listen. She had feared the truth would alienate her from his affections. It was a foolish excuse, and one she seriously doubted he'd accept. Furthermore, she wasn't about to tell him this and leave herself vulnerable. Protecting her pride, as well as her heart, she replied, "I suppose I didn't make the opportunity because I dreaded your reaction. I was afraid you'd be furious with me."

"You're right. I would have been furious—and

I am."

"Yes, I know," she remarked tartly. "You were so furious that you sent me to jail."

"Going to jail was your idea," he reminded her.

"But you encouraged the sheriff to arrest me."

"I knew he'd take good care of you. Besides, I had no intention of leaving you in jail. I needed time, though, for my temper to cool."

Kristina looked away from him, but he reached over and placed his hand beneath her chin. Slowly he turned her face back to his and studied her thoughtfully. "In the picture of you on Drake's desk . . . ," he began. "There's a look of sadness in your eyes. I used to wonder why such a beautiful young lady would seem so unhappy."

"That picture was taken shortly after my mother died. I hadn't gotten over losing her."

Noticing the sun was slanting westward, Cole decided they should move on. Picking up their pace, they sent their horses into an easy gallop. As they headed toward Sandy Creek, they kept to impersonal topics of conversation.

Sandy Creek was a small, rowdy town that had sprung up on the Shawnee Trail, which ran from San Antonio to Austin and beyond to Kansas City. The boisterous town was doomed to extinction, for it was frequented by unsavory characters, which caused law-abiding citizens to look elsewhere for a place to settle. Its three booming saloons kept the town alive. The barrooms featured gambling and prostitutes, and the good times found in Sandy Creek caused the town to be filled with men—most of them thieves and murderers.

Cole was a little concerned about bringing Kristina

to Sandy Creek, but she needed riding clothes. Also, the town's hotel offered good food and clean beds.

As Kristina rode down the town's dusty street, she looked the place over with misgivings. Music, laughter, and boisterous voices carried from the three saloons, and the wooden walkways were crowded with unkempt and dangerous-looking men. She began to question Cole's decision to bring her here.

They guided their horses to the town's general store. Cole quickly dismounted, then stepped to Kristina and helped her down. Reaching into his pocket, he withdrew some bills and handed them to her. "Go inside and buy some riding clothes while I take the horses to the livery. Wait for me in the store. I don't want you on this street alone."

Kristina assured him that she would. Cole waited until she had gone inside before leaving with the horses.

The general store was filled with merchandise. Four shelves were stacked to their limits, and the front counter was piled with various articles. "Can I help you, ma'am?" the proprietor, a tall, skinny man with a heavy beard, asked.

"I need a set of riding clothes."

"Don't have no women's ridin' attire," he answered, spitting a stream of tobacco juice into a spittoon. "But I got some trousers, shirts, and boots that'll fit you."

Kristina told him the clothes would do fine, and by the time Cole arrived, she had finished her purchase. After the articles were wrapped in brown paper and tied with a string, she followed Cole outside.

As they were crossing the street, heading toward the hotel, Cole reached over to take the package from her but he was suddenly stopped by a man's booming voice.

"Barton! Cole Barton!"

The sound had come from his back, and Cole turned around cautiously. A young gunslinger was poised a few feet down the street, eyeing him hostilely. He had two companions standing off to the side, and they were watching their friend with admiration. The threesome had spotted Cole when he rode into town. Although they had never met Cole, they knew who he was. Two of them had dared the third one to challenge Barton to a draw, but they hadn't believed he'd actually do it. He was fast, true, but everyone in the West knew Barton's reputation with a gun.

"Get out of the street," Cole ordered Kristina. He nodded tersely toward the hotel. "Wait for me over there."

She was frightened for Cole. "Does that man want to . . . to—?"

"Do as I said!" Cole remarked gruffly. He gave her a persuasive push, and she hurried to the front of the hotel. With her heart pounding, she watched fearfully.

The street was quickly deserted, but the walkways were soon crowded with observers. Word passed fast, and in no time at all, people were coming out of the saloons to watch the shootout.

Cole was hoping to talk the young gunslinger into backing down. "I don't want to kill you, kid," he said, his eyes regarding his opponent closely. "Why don't you just keep your gun holstered, walk away, and live a little longer?"

The overzealous gunman wasn't about to concede. He was sure he could take Barton. Killing such a well-known bounty hunter would make him famous. Also, he was determined to impress his two comrades and if he were to chicken out, they would ridicule him.

The young man's eyes turned steely, and taking a

shooting stance, he uttered threateningly, "Barton, I'm gonna give you to the count of five to either draw or walk away like a yellow-bellied coward!"

"Then count to five, 'cause I'm in a hurry to eat dinner." Cole was totally calm.

Kristina gasped. Dear God, surely Cole wasn't going to accept the man's challenge!

The gunfighter smiled coldly and began to count. "One, two, three, four . . . five!" He reached quickly for his Colt revolver.

Cole drew his Peacemaker with blurring speed, and opening fire, he shot his opponent's gunhand, causing him to drop his weapon. The young man, moaning, grabbed his neckerchief and wrapped it about his bleeding hand.

Cole turned his gaze to the gunslinger's two young companions. "Your friend's gonna be eatin' and shootin' left-handed for the next few weeks. Are either of you interested in becomin' maimed?"

"No, sir!" they uttered in unison.

Reholstering his pistol, Cole turned to his wounded victim. "Kid, I could've killed you. If you're smart, you'll keep that gun of yours holstered. The next man you challenge might not be as lenient. I know you think you're good with a gun, but, kid, you're second-rate."

Kristina, her heart still pounding, watched as Cole came to her side. Taking her arm, he guided her to the hotel's front door.

She stared at him wide-eyed and pulled back. "Cole, you purposely aimed for that man's hand!" she exclaimed. "You could've been killed! What if you had missed?"

He grinned wryly, lifting an eyebrow. "I don't miss," he replied.

*   *   *

212

Seated in the hotel dining room, Kristina, impressed with Cole's prowess with a gun, wondered just how well she knew this man who had become such an important part of her life. She had heard that he was fast and an accurate shot, but being an easterner, she hadn't fully understood what that meant.

"What are you thinking about?" Cole questioned.

"I was thinking of how quickly you drew your gun. It must've taken a lot of practice to become so fast."

"Practice and determination."

She smiled warmly. "You spared that young man's life."

"That wasn't the first time I've been confronted by a kid wantin' to make a name for himself. So far I've never had to kill one of 'em." He frowned deeply. "But one of these days . . ."

"If you'd quit bounty hunting and stop wearing your gun, such encounters wouldn't happen."

"I can't quit," he replied dryly.

"Why not?"

"I haven't found my mother's killers."

"Cole, you may never find them!" she pleaded with exasperation.

He knew she was right, for he was acutely aware that his chances were slim and with each passing year, they became slimmer. He changed the subject. "Tell me what really happened between you and Raymond Lewis."

She was skeptical. "If I tell you, will you believe me?"

"Well, I sure as hell don't buy Lewis's story."

They were interrupted by the waiter, who quickly took their order. As the man moved away, Kristina looked intently into Cole's eyes and asked, "Why don't you believe what Raymond said?"

213

"I wouldn't believe that pompous bastard if he swore on a stack of Bibles. I know his type."

Kristina sighed audibly. "I thought you were starting to trust me, but you don't. You merely distrust Raymond more. You've decided to take my word over his, which isn't saying much for me."

Cole probed deeply for an honest reply. He didn't exactly distrust Kristina, he just wasn't certain about her feelings or her motives. He looked into her eyes, and gazing intensely into their green depths, he was suddenly reminded of all the times he had admired her photograph and how her lovely image had enchanted him. As his musings wandered to the letters she had written to Drake, he remained buried in deep thought. Then, suddenly, he grinned at her. "I've been so damned angry at you for deceiving me that I overlooked something vitally important. I forgot how well I know you. Kristina, I've known you since you were eight years old. I've read every letter you've written to Drake."

"I . . . I don't understand . . ."

His azure eyes twinkled. "I've been judging you as the woman who married me under false pretenses. But that woman isn't the real Kristina. The real Kristina is the one who wrote all those letters."

"And?" She was anxious to hear more.

"The real Kristina isn't capable of fraud, nor is she capable of intentional deceit."

Kristina smiled happily. "Cole . . ." she began, her mood suddenly light-hearted. "I think we should start anew." She extended her hand across the table. "My name is Kristina Parker, and I'm very glad to meet you."

Taking her proffered hand, he placed a light kiss upon it. "I'm Cole Barton, ma'am, and meeting you is a pleasure indeed."

214

"Thank you kindly, sir," she replied gaily.

"Now, Miss Parker, suppose you tell me all about yourself."

"Everything?"

"Yes, everything. Start at the beginning and tell me about your childhood, your years with the Johnsons, and what happened between you and Lewis."

"It'll take a long time for me to give you a full account."

His warm grin askew, he replied, "Darlin', we have lots of time."

Much later, as Kristina left the dining room with Cole, her spirits were soaring. During dinner, and, later, over coffee, she and Cole had talked intimately and candidly. Their lengthy discussion had erased their recent hostilities and suspicions. Kristina was sure their friendship was now firm and could withstand whatever the future might bring. She was, however, uncertain if their new-found camaraderie would lead to matrimony, for Cole hadn't mentioned marriage, their child, or love.

They headed toward the front desk as Cole slipped an arm about Kristina's waist, drew her close, and asked, "Do I get one room or two?"

Her steps faltered, and with a short intake of breath, she gazed up into his face. The invitation in his blue eyes was blatantly sensual. A warm, delightful flush came over her, and her body ached for his touch, but, Kristina's consent came from the heart. "One room, Cole."

He was carrying her wrapped package, and handing it to her, he said, "Wait here. I'll get us a room and be right back."

Cole stepped to the desk. He was anxious to be alone with Kristina. God, he had never wanted a woman as desperately as he wanted Kristina Parker. He was head over heels in love. He knew it beyond a doubt. Now that they had settled their differences, he was overjoyed to be so deeply in love. His future was beginning to look bright, and he had every intention of sharing it with Kristina.

After checking in, Cole returned to Kristina, took her arm, and escorted her up the stairs to their room on the second floor. He quickly unlocked the door, and as they went inside, he told her, "I need to go to the stables and pick up my bag." He had left his belongings at the livery. "I'll be back as soon as possible. Lock the door behind me."

He was gone before she had a chance to utter a reply. She secured the door, then placing her package on the dresser, she took stock of the room. She was surprised to find that it was clean, as well as comfortable. A large four-poster bed, covered with a bright quilt, stood in the center of the room. An oak wardrobe occupied one corner, and a wing-back chair was placed in front of the open window. The hardwood floor was bare except for a colorful throw rug located at the foot of the bed. A light southerly breeze drifted through the window, and its gentle caress billowed the white, lace-trimmed curtains.

Moving to the window, Kristina held the curtains aside and looked down on the street below. The sun was making its final descent, and long shadows were falling across the rowdy town. Blaring music, mingling with loud voices, carried from the three saloons, and the sounds of plodding horses and creaking wagons filled the street. She turned away from the window, wondering if it would be possible to get any sleep.

216

A somewhat naughty smile touched her lips. Considering she and Cole planned to share the same bed, she might not care if she got any sleep. She knew she could make love to him all night, and still be greedy for more. As her thoughts dwelled on the subject, she hugged herself with delight and practically danced across the room. Oh, she wanted Cole Barton so desperately! She supposed she should be abashed by her wantonness, but she wasn't even the slightest embarrassed. She loved Cole from the depths of her heart.

She sat down in the comfortable wing chair and eagerly awaited Cole's return. But to her dismay, a cloud of apprehension suddenly shadowed her radiant mood. Was she thinking and behaving foolishly? Should she hold her feelings in check? If she continued this way, was she heading straight for a fall? She and Cole had patched up their differences, true, but he certainly hadn't said anything to make her believe that he loved her or wanted to marry her. He hadn't even spoken of her pregnancy. Did he not want their child?

A wife and child were a big responsibility, and to take proper care of them, Cole would have to give up his way of life. Would he be willing to settle down, hang up his gun, and abandon his search for his mother's killers? Kristina suspected that he might be too set in his ways to change.

Outside, the sun had completely disappeared over the distant horizon, and the landscape grew as dark as Kristina's now dispirited mood.

Chapter Eighteen

Cole bounded up the stairs and hurried down the hall to his and Kristina's room. He knocked on the door. "Darlin', it's me."

Kristina opened the door, then moved back as Cole came inside. He had brought his bag, and pitching it onto the chair, he said, "I'd have been back sooner, but I stopped at the desk and ordered a bath. I thought you might like to soak in a tub of hot water."

"Thank you, Cole," she replied, her tone dour.

Cole sensed her mood immediately. "What's wrong?" he questioned.

"Do you want our child?" she asked point-blank.

Her question took Cole by surprise. Why would she even ask such a thing? "Of course I do."

"Then why haven't you said anything about the baby?"

He thought long and hard before answering. "Kristina, so much has happened in so short a time that your pregnancy hasn't truly had a chance to sink in. Losing Drake, finding out you aren't Samantha, the real Samantha showing up . . ." He brushed his fingers through his dark hair, then said with a sigh," "I'm sorry if I gave you the impression that I don't

219

care about the child."

"Do you care, Cole?" she asked intensely.

He drew her into his arms, holding her close. "Yes, Kristina, I care. I care very much."

"Enough to quit being a bounty hunter?"

"What does that have to do with the child?"

She pushed out of his embrace. "It has everything to do with our baby. If you continue your dangerous lifestyle, this child will most likely lose his father to a desperado's bullet."

A tender grin touched Cole's lips. "Darlin', I know what you're trying to say, and you're right. I should quit my profession and make a home for you and our child."

"You should quit for your own sake, as well as ours!" she insisted.

As Cole gazed at Kristina, he was struck anew with his deep feelings for her. Logic surfaced, telling him if he didn't give up his profession, he might not have a future to share with Kristina and his child. His job was too dangerous.

"All right, sweetheart," he said gently. "I'll become a full-time rancher." But as his thoughts shifted to his mother's murderers, he was compelled to add, "However, I can't completely forget what happened to my mother. I won't go looking for the men who killed her, but if I hear about them, especially the one with the branded chest . . . Well, I can't promise you that I won't go after him."

"I understand, Cole," she replied with sincerity.

He took her arm and led her to the bed. When they were seated, he began explaining his immediate plans. "Kristina, I intend to leave you at Josh's, return to the Diamond-C, and offer Samantha a fair price for the ranch. I'm sure she'll accept my bid, then I'll come back for you, and we'll get married at the

Diamond-C." He grinned disarmingly. "That is, if you'll agree to marry me."

Her face was radiant. "Yes, Cole! I'll marry you!"

His arms went about her, and she clung to him tightly. Kristina had never been happier. Cole wanted her and the baby, and they would live at the Diamond-C! It was almost too wonderful to be true! Her thoughts suddenly sobered, and she began to worry about Autumn Moon and Alisa. The Diamond-C was also their home.

She stirred in the circle of Cole's arms. "What will happen to Autumn Moon and Alisa?" she asked.

"I'm familiar with Drake's will. Although he left the title to the ranch to Samantha, if she should decide to sell, she must give a third to Autumn Moon, a third to Alisa, and keep the remaining third for herself. I'm sure Alisa won't want to remain at the Diamond-C, but Autumn Moon will have a home with us for as long as she wants. So will Joseph. I know you're very fond of those two, so I'm sure you agree with me."

"Yes, I do," she replied. She suddenly flung her arms about his neck. "Cole, everything has worked out so splendidly." All at once, though, a despondent shadow fell over her spirits. "If only Drake was still with us," she murmured sadly.

He held her tightly. "I know, darlin'. Drake's gonna be sorely missed. He was a wonderful man, and a loyal friend. I don't think I'll ever stop missing him."

A loud rapping broke into their somber discussion. "Your bath is here, señor," a man's voice called from the other side of the door.

Cole crossed the room and admitted two Mexican men. The employees of the hotel placed a large tub in the middle of the floor, then left to get buckets of hot water. They returned momentarily and filled the tub.

221

Then a young Mexican woman arrived with towels and a bar of soap. She placed them beside the tub, then followed the men from the room.

Poised in the open doorway, Cole said to Kristina, "I'll leave so you can take your bath. I'll be back soon."

"Wait!" she called. She moved to the tub, looked at it, then, casting Cole an inviting smile, said, "This tub is quite large. In fact, I think it's big enough to accommodate two people. What do you think?"

"I think I'm stayin'," Cole remarked without hesitation. Grinning, he closed the door, then quickly locked it.

Going to him, and turning her back, Kristina asked, "Will you undo my dress, please?"

"My pleasure," he replied.

Her dress fastened in the back, and she lifted her long tresses, giving him free access to the tiny buttons.

Cole managed the buttons with amazing speed. He slipped the gown down past her shoulders, then, bending his head, he placed a kiss on her bare flesh.

The touch of his lips was thrilling, and a delightful chill ran up Kristina's spine. Turning and facing him, she shoved the dress past her hips. The gown fell about her feet, and stepping free, she reached down, lifted the dress, and pitched it onto the chair. Next, she removed her full slip in the same seductive fashion.

Watching raptly, Cole was mesmerized by her sultry beauty. When she was left wearing only her lace undies and chemise, his eyes raked over her with a scorching intent.

"Don't stop now, darlin'," he said in a soft, husky tone.

She smiled pertly, then slipped out of her chemise

222

with a tantalizing slowness. Cole's gaze focused on her delectable breasts. He admired their fullness, their taut peaks—he could hardly wait to relish them completely.

Kristina slipped off her final undergarment. She now stood before Cole totally unclad, her complete beauty his to behold.

His eyes traveled leisurely over every inch of her silky flesh. "Kristina," he murmured throatily, "you're so beautiful." A sensual smile came to life on his lips. "And exciting. You're the most exciting woman I've ever seen."

She returned his smile. "You're not bad yourself, Cole Barton. However, you're wearing too many clothes."

He moved to her, lifted her into his arms, placed a passionate kiss on her mouth, then eased her gently into the tub. Standing before her, he quickly removed his gun belt, then removed his clothes with haste.

Kristina watched his every move, and as his muscular physique was revealed, she scrutinized him intently. She longed to run her hands over his superb body, to touch and caress his male perfection.

He stepped into the tub, and as he sat down to face her, water splashed over the rim and onto the floor. In order for both to fit, they had to draw up their knees, which made it difficult to maneuver.

Taking the cloth, Kristina sudsed it thoroughly and began to bathe, but when it came time to wash her legs, she wasn't sure just how to manage it, for there wasn't much room in the tub.

Cole solved the problem. He lifted her long, slender legs, parted them, and placed her feet on his shoulders. She handed him the cloth, and he tenderly finished the washing. Keeping her legs resting on his wide shoulders, he then moved a hand down to her womanly softness. With her legs parted, she was vulnerable to his passionate fondling, and his finger probed into her feminine depths.

Cole's intimate caress was thrilling, and reveling in ecstasy, Kristina leaned her head back against the back of the tub. Raptuous sighs came from deep within her throat, and she surrendered fervently to the wild pleasure of his touch.

Caressing her rhythmically, Cole took her to the heights of love. Wondrous sensations coursed through her as she climbed to her peak of pleasure. Then, suddenly, she was engulfed with total fulfillment, followed by crashing tremors.

Cole took her gently into his arms, cradling her against his chest.

Kristina, still shaken, held tightly to the man she loved. "Oh, Cole," she whispered timorously, "I never dreamed just your touch could be so wonderfully exciting."

He smiled tenderly and kissed her brow. "My innocent, you have lots to learn about making love."

She smiled at him saucily. "You will teach me everything, won't you?"

"And then some," he chuckled.

"I'm a slow learner. You'll have to show me over and over again."

"I'll be patient," he said teasingly.

Moving out of his embrace, she stepped out of the tub and dried off. Hurrying to the bed, she drew down the covers and slipped beneath them. Glancing provocatively at Cole, she said, "Hurry up and get washed, slowpoke. I'm anxiously awaiting my first lesson."

"You wanton little vixen," he uttered gruffly. Grabbing the cloth, he began to wash with haste, then got out of the tub, and dried off in record time.

As he made a mad dash for the bed, Kristina held back the covers, and he lay beside her, drawing her soft, supple curves against his hard frame. His lips claimed hers in a kiss so passionate and devouring that it left her breathless.

Cole threw back the covers, then moving his lips to her breasts, he kissed their erect nipples. Placing her hand on the nape of his neck, she encouraged him to continue. A hot flush coursed through her body, coming to rest betwen her thighs. Oh, she wanted him to fulfill her again! She needed his hardness deep inside her!

Cole moved to lie on his back, his strong arm bringing Kristina above him. She pressed herself fully against him, her undulating hips driving him wild with passion.

She loved the feel of his aroused body, and while kissing him intimately, she wriggled seductively against his hardness. The glorious friction set their desire to burning hotly, and their bodies longed to become one.

Letting her remain on top, Cole placed his hands on her hips, murmuring huskily, "Darlin', sit up and slide down on me."

Kristina was willing, for she was anxious to experience everything about lovemaking. She hoped Cole would never find her inadequate, for pleasing him meant the world to her.

She lowered herself down onto his stiff member, and the thrill was so electrifying that she cried out with wonder.

Keeping his hands about her waist, Cole guided their movements, and Kristina's eager response soon fanned his desire into a leaping flame.

They made love with a hungry intensity. It seemed as if they were so famished they couldn't get enough of each other.

Finally, their rapturous joining reached a crucial juncture, and Cole quickly slid her body beneath his. Placing her legs about his back, he thrust into her vigorously.

Abandoning herself to a spiraling climax, Kristina arched powerfully beneath him. Then, reaching a feverish pitch, she shuddered with blissful release.

Cole's moment of ecstasy exploded at the same time. He kissed her deeply, then stretched out to lie at her side. "I love you, Kristina," he murmured.

She smiled and snuggled close. "I love you, too, Cole."

"Darlin', from this moment on, I want us to always be totally honest with each other. No more secrets and no more deceptions."

She agreed with no reservations.

He kissed her brow, then asked unexpectedly, "Do you want a boy or a girl?"

She hadn't anticipated the question, and it took a moment for her to reply. "I don't know. Either one will make me happy. What about you?"

"I don't care, either. A son would be nice, but I'd also like a daughter."

"Cole, I want a large family. I was an only child, and I missed not having any brothers or sisters."

"I know, I feel the same way." He smiled tenderly at her. "Then it's settled. We'll have lots of kids." His lips came down on hers, and he kissed her with deep devotion.

Raymond returned his rented buggy to the livery, then headed toward the Branding Iron Saloon. It was a warm, humid night, and he removed his suit coat and draped it over his arm. Walking at a leisurely pace, he reflected on his evening with Alisa. Although his only objective was to get the beautiful lady in his bed, tonight he had behaved the perfect gentleman. It would be a mistake to rush her. First, he would need to wine and dine her, impress her with his riches, and give the impression that he was a lonely bachelor looking for a wife. A smug smile curled Raymond's mouth. Within the week, maybe even less, Alisa Carlson would be his to relish. And when he tired of her, well, he'd simply cast her aside.

Raymond gazed about him as he walked. He liked San Antonio and had decided to remain. The town had great possibilities for a man with his ambition and wealth.

He had to pass the jail to reach the Branding Iron, and he decided to go inside and pay a short visit to Kristina. He hoped incarceration was making her miserable. The little tart deserved it! So far, he hadn't decided how to get even with Kristina, but he'd find a way. The bitch would pay dearly for stabbing him! Before meting out his revenge, however, he'd enjoy the pleasure of her body. He couldn't recall ever desiring a woman as much as he desired Kristina.

Raymond opened the door to the jail and stepped inside. Sheriff Bickham was sitting in his chair, his feet resting on the desktop, his arms folded over his chest. He had been dozing, but at Raymond's entrance he came wide awake.

"What can I do for you, Mr. Lewis?" he asked. He remained seated, and kept his feet on the desk. He didn't like the man, so he wasn't about to relinquish his comfortable position to welcome him.

Raymond, noticing the unoccupied cells, demanded harshly, "Where is Miss Parker?"

"She ain't here," Bickham answered dryly.

"I can see that!" Lewis snapped. "Why isn't she here?"

"Barton came after her."

"You mean, he broke her out of jail?"

"Well . . ." the sheriff drawled. "Actually, he carried her out."

"You didn't try to stop him?"

Bickham smiled insolently. "I ain't Barton's keeper. He can do what he wants, so long as it ain't against the law."

"Taking a prisoner out of jail is against the law!"

"Miss Parker wasn't a prisoner. She was a guest."

"But Samantha Carlson is pressing charges against her."

"Until I receive a warrant for Miss Parker's arrest, she's free to go wherever she damned well pleases."

"Where did Barton take her?"

"I don't know. But I'm sure they ain't in town."

Raymond was fuming. Damn it! He was determined to catch Ted Cummings, and he had planned to use Kristina as bait. Also, if Barton didn't bring her back to San Antonio, he might lose his chance to get even with her.

"Do you think Barton and Miss Parker are gone for good?"

"They'll be back. Barton won't desert the Diamond-C, or Autumn Moon, Alisa, and Joseph. With Drake gone, he'll see that they're taken care of."

Raymond felt somewhat better. Kristina might be his after all. He had to be patient and bide his time.

"How long are you plannin' to stick around?" the sheriff asked.

"Actually, I'm considering staying here permanently. I like your town, Sheriff. And there's something about the West that is quite appealing.

228

Maybe it's the sense of danger that appeals to me. Philadephia is too civilized for my taste."

Bickham frowned. Lewis as a permanent resident didn't meet with his approval. He had a feeling the man was a troublemaker. "If you're gonna settle in my town, then you gotta abide by my laws. All that money you got doesn't impress me. You can't buy your way out of my jail."

Heading for the door, Raymond grinned to himself and called over his shoulder, "Whatever you say, Sheriff."

Raymond firmly believed that for the right price, any man was for sale. And with that in mind, he hurried to the Branding Iron to see the proprietor. Now that he had decided to remain in San Antonio, he needed to establish a business. He'd offer the owner a decent price for the saloon, but if he refused to part with it, he'd simply keep upping the bid until the man agreed to sell. Owning a saloon appealed to Raymond, for he liked barrooms and in Philadelphia he had frequented them often.

Raymond was sure that the Branding Iron's proprietor could be persuaded to sell. He had learned from past experiences that he could buy whatever he wanted. The Branding Iron had a top price, but with his riches, meeting it would pose no hardship.

Chapter Nineteen

As the sun's morning rays filtered into the hotel room, the brightness brought Kristina awake. She was lying on her side with Cole snuggled against her back and she could feel his maleness touching her bare buttocks. He had an arm wrapped firmly about her waist, and one leg was slung across hers. A contented smile curled her lips. Waking up to find Cole pressed so intimately close to her was thrilling.

Slowly, Cole's hand moved up and cupped her breast. "Are you awake, darlin'?" he asked softly.

"Yes, but I thought you were asleep." She sighed blissfully, for his fondling was arousing her passion.

He took his hand from her breast, and his fingers etched a tingling path down her stomach and beyond. Touching her between her thighs, he stroked her gently. "Kristina," he murmured huskily, his desire rising.

She rolled over, and entwining her arms about him, she whispered seductively, "Cole, I want you."

His lips claimed hers in a demanding exchange, then hovering above her, he positioned himself between her parted legs. He thrust forward, and his hardness filled Kristina with ecstasy.

231

Clinging, they made love with a frenzy, and their wildly excited movements carried them to a rapturous zenith. Sated, they shared a love-filled kiss, then moved to lie side by side.

Kristina smiled radiantly. "Cole, I'm so happy, and I can hardly wait to become your wife." She laughed lightly, adding, "This time, *legally* your wife."

Leaning over her, he kissed her softly. "It shouldn't take long to complete my business with Samantha. Then I'll come to Josh's and get you. We'll get married as soon as possible."

He left the bed, and started putting on his clothes. "I'll go to the livery and get our horses. We'll have breakfast and then head out. We should reach the Lazy-J by noon, if not sooner."

Kristina knew Josh had named his ranch the Lazy-J. He had told her that the brand on his cattle was a reclining J, whereas the brand on Drake's cattle was diamond-shaped with a C in the middle. Texas cattle grazed on unfenced pastures and cattle from bordering ranches often mingled. A rancher's brand thus marked an animal for identification of ownership.

Kristina remained in bed until Cole was dressed and gone, then following a long, catlike stretch, she threw back the covers. Getting up, she padded barefoot across the hardwood floor and locked the door. She went to the water pitcher, filled the ceramic bowl, and washed quickly. Forgotten until now, she picked up her package and took it to the bed. Peeling away the paper, she uncovered her new apparel, and once dressed, she hurried to the mirror to take a close look at herself. She had never worn clothing so masculine looking before, and she found her reflection a little startling. As her initial shock passed, however, she began to find the attire to her liking. The suede shirt was soft against her skin, and she knew that, riding astride, the blue denim trousers would indeed be an improvement over her cumbersome dress.

She returned to the bed, wrapped her discarded clothes in the paper, grabbed her hat, and went back to the mirror. Her hair was mussed, and she wished fervently for a brush. She ran her fingers through the curly locks, but to her dismay, the gesture did little to tame the unruly ringlets. Giving up, she placed the hat atop her blond tresses and tied the thongs beneath her chin.

Kristina decided she was suitably attired for the journey to the Lazy-J. She failed to notice, though, that she was also enticingly beautiful. The suede shirt, adhering to her breasts, defined their fullness, and her trousers clung provocatively to the curve of her hips and long, shapely legs. Her blond tresses cascading from beneath the wide-brimmed hat, enhanced her seductive beauty.

Kristina turned away from her reflection, picked up the key, and left the room. As she went to the bath located at the end of the hall, she was oblivious to the two men standing at the other end of the corridor.

They, however, were very aware of her. One man kept a vigilant eye on the stairs, watching for Cole's return, while the other one waited for Kristina to head back to her room.

Soon Kristina left the bath, and as she was nearing her door, the man stepped forward. She was inserting the key when she caught his approach from the corner of her eye. Sensing danger, she was about to dart into her room when the stalker drew his pistol.

"Don't move!" he warned gruffly. "I don't wanna kill ya, lady, but if you scream, I'll put a bullet right between your eyes!"

"Wh—what do you want?" she stammered.

"I want you to take a ride with me and my brother."

The other man came forward, Kristina recognized him. "You're the one who drew against Cole!" she gasped.

He held up his bandaged hand. "Just look what that bastard did to me. The doc said my hand won't never be worth a damn!"

"You're lucky Cole didn't kill you!" she spat.

"Lucky?" he snarled. "You stupid bitch, this is my shootin' hand. Well, my luck"—he spit the word out as though it tasted bitter—"is Barton's misfortune! My brother and me are gonna get even."

"Damn it, Jimmy!" the other one grumbled. "Let's stop yappin' and get the hell out of here." He gestured tersely toward the closed door. "Put the note inside the room where Barton's sure to find it."

Jimmy quickly turned the key and stepped inside.

"Why are you leaving a note?" Kristina asked.

"We want Barton to know where to find you. When he comes after you, we'll be waitin' for him."

The man reached out and grasped Kristina's arm. He was a burly man, and his thick fingers dug painfully into her flesh. His face was covered with an unkempt beard, which was streaked with tobacco stains. He was a loathsome figure, and as he drew Kristina closer, her nostrils picked up the offensive odor coming from his unwashed body.

Jimmy returned from placing the note, and as his gaze swept over Kristina, he said with a grin, "Hey, Ned, didn't I tell you she was a real looker? Are you gonna let me hump her first?"

"We ain't got time for thinkin' 'bout that. Let's go before Barton shows up. I don't wanna tangle with him here. I want him on our own territory."

Forcing Kristina to walk alongside them, they

moved to the other end of the corridor and used the back stairs, which led them through the rear door and into the alley.

Their horses were waiting. Ned lifted Kristina and placed her on his own mount. Swinging up behind her, he wrapped one powerful arm about her waist, then holding the reins in his other hand, he spurred his steed, into a gallop. Jimmy followed close behind.

Staying on the back roads, they headed out of town. The brothers kept their horses at a steady gallop, but when they reached open ground, they urged the animals into a loping run.

The jolting gait was hard on Kristina. She began to fear that the constant jouncing might bring on a miscarriage. The day was already extremely warm, and the hot sun caused her brow to bead with perspiration. The heat, plus the rough pace, caused her stomach to churn.

Despite her own misery, she was worried about Cole. Would these men kill him? How could he possibly save her and himself as well? Would he bring help? The sheriff perhaps? Even a town as lawless as Sandy Creek must have a sheriff! But she wasn't so sure. Yesterday, no law officer had interfered with the shootout.

Swallowing back the sickening taste of bile, she managed to ask Ned, "Where are you taking me?"

"My brother and me have a cabin 'bout five miles from here. That's where we're takin' you."

"Aren't you afraid that Cole will bring the sheriff with him?"

The man guffawed. "Hell, lady, the sheriff is the town's biggest drunk. He's probably in one of his cells sleepin' off last night's drinkin' spree. 'Sides, even if he ain't drunk, he won't help Barton. The

235

sheriff's kin to me and Jimmy. He's our cousin."

"Good Lord! Why did the citizens elect a man like that for sheriff?"

"'Cause the citizens don't want no law and order. We like our town just the way it is."

"But there must be some respectable citizens."

"Some rich ones, but no respectable ones. And the rich ones wouldn't be so rich if Sandy Creek became too civilized."

Kristina was silent for a long moment, then asked, "Why do you want to kill Cole? Don't you realize he spared your brother's life?"

"He crippled Jimmy's shootin' hand. In these parts, that's just as bad as killin' a man."

"What do you plan to do with me?" she asked, although she wasn't sure if she wanted to hear the answer.

"I ain't gonna kill you, lady. That is, if I don't have to. But Jimmy and me are gonna have some fun with you. Don't worry none, you'll have a good time, too. Then, when we're through with you, we'll turn you loose." He chuckled heartily. "Of course, by then you might not want us to turn you loose. You might think you done died and went to heaven. I'm sure lookin' forward to gettin' in between your legs." He moved his hairy hand from her waist and up to her breasts.

Forcefully, she brushed his hand aside. "Don't touch me!"

"Uppity little bitch, ain't you?" he goaded, his foul-smelling breath making Kristina gag.

She leaned forward in the saddle, trying to get as far away from him as possible. God, she felt she'd rather die than have Ned or his brother touch her! She'd fight them to the bitter end!

* * *

236

The small cabin, shaded by cottonwoods, was falling to ruin. The front porch was partially caved in and the door was hanging obliquely on its rusty hinges. Three scroungy, underfed hounds, along with a puppy, were resting in the yard, but as their owners rode up to the cabin, the dogs got up, wagged their tails and barked rapidly. The young pup couldn't quite expel a full-fledged bark, but he did manage a few friendly yaps.

Ned dismounted, then lifted Kristina from the horse. The puppy bounded over and nipped playfully at its master's ankles. Drawing back his foot, Ned booted the small animal, sending him sprawling backward. Yelping painfully, the puppy stuck his tail between his legs and scooted under the cabin for cover.

"You heartless beast!" Kristina raged. "How can you hurt something so small and helpless?"

"It's easy," Ned said laughing. "You wanna see it again?"

"No!" she cried in fury.

He chuckled, shoved her toward the cabin, and ordered, "Get inside!"

For a moment, Kristina's balance was precarious, then, regaining her momentum, she mounted the rotting steps, crossed the porch, and went into the cabin.

The interior was even more dilapidated than the outside. Chipped and partially broken furnitue was scattered sparsely throughout the one-room cabin. The smells of cooking grease, unwashed dishes, and the lingering odor of unclean bodies filled the small space.

Again, Kristina's stomach grew queasy. She went to a straight-backed chair and sat down. She wished she could draw a long breath to ease her nausea, but the air was too fetid to inhale deeply. She watched apprehensively as Ned and Jimmy came inside. She had never imagined such vile creatures existed. They lived worse than animals!

Jimmy carried a rifle, and going to the open window, he laid the barrel across the sill. The area bordering the cabin was open ground, and he would spot Cole long before he arrived.

Meanwhile, Ned went to the cupboard and removed a bottle of whiskey. Taking it with him, he sat down at the table, which was cluttered with dirty dishes. Uncorking the bottle, he took a long, gulping swallow. Following a loud belch, he helped himself to another big swig. He ignored Kristina, and seemed perfectly content to simply drink his liquor.

Kristina relaxed somewhat, for she knew she was in no immediate danger. The front door was halfway open, and she caught sight of a small movement. It was the puppy sneaking into the cabin. Kristina hoped Ned wouldn't spot the pup, for he'd surely abuse it.

Ned, however, was too preoccupied with his whiskey to take note of the puppy, and the little creature seemed to know that. His courage grew, and his strides lengthened. He was hungry, and hoping for food, he scurried to Kristina. Halting at her feet, he sat on his haunches and peered up at her with pleading eyes.

Kristina was touched, for she loved animals. She bent over, picked up the puppy, and placed it on her lap. She rubbed him behind his ears. Her stroking was soothing, and the pup curled up, closed his eyes, and was soon asleep.

Petting the puppy had a calming effect on her shattered nerves, but suddenly, Jimmy broke the peace. "Barton's here!" he called.

Ned jumped to his feet and rushed to the window.

Cole, sitting astride his horse, was safely out of shooting range. Ned whirled about and said gruffly to Kristina, "Get up, woman! We're gonna go outside and greet Barton!"

She put the puppy on the floor, and as she got to her feet, her heart hammered, and a tightness constricted her chest, making it difficult for her to breathe. *God! . . . God!* she prayed. *Please don't let these men kill Cole! Please!*

Ned clutched her arm and dragged her out the door and onto the porch. Holding her so that her back was against his chest, he drew his pistol and placed it at her temple. "Barton!" he yelled. "If you don't come on up here, I'm gonna shoot your woman!"

Cole had Kristina's mare with him, and her belongings were packed on the horse. Leaving it behind, he urged his Appaloosa into a cautious walk. As he approached, he raised a hand to his neckerchief to check the knot. It was still tied securely, hiding the leather thongs beneath it. A sheathed knife was connected to the other end of the thongs, and the small case was concealed at the back of Cole's neck.

Jimmy, his rifle in tow, came onto the porch and took a stance beside his brother and Kristina. Silently, the group watched as Barton drew steadily closer.

Cole dismounted carefully.

"Unbuckle your gunbelt," Ned ordered. "And do it real slow-like. Make one fast move, and I'll blow your woman to hell."

Cole did as he was told.

"Now lower the belt to the ground."

Again, he obeyed without comment.

A large grin spread across Ned's bearded face. "Raise your hands and keep them raised."

Cole did so willingly, for raising his hands

brought them closer to his hidden knife.

Certain he had Barton at his mercy, Ned relaxed. He turned his pistol away from Kristina and aimed it at Cole. "I'm gonna kill you, Barton. But first I'm gonna tie you up and let you watch me and Jimmy poke your woman." He waited, but his goading didn't provoke an outburst. Cole merely stared at him with an expression as fierce as the fires of hell.

Without taking his eyes off Barton, Ned said to Jimmy, "Tie him up, and tie him real tight!"

At that moment, the puppy, looking for Kristina, scurried out the front door. Running clumsily, he collided headfirst into Ned's feet.

Perturbed, Ned made a crucial mistake—he lowered his gaze from Barton's and stepped back to kick the mischievous pup.

Cole's hand went to his sheathed knife, and freeing it with amazing speed, he sent it soaring through the air and into Ned's shoulder.

The man staggered, dropped his pistol, then, as his knees buckled, his heavy body keeled over.

In the meantime, Kristina lunged at Jimmy. Her arm swung out and knocked his rifle aside. Cole moved quickly, and leaping onto the porch, he stepped to Jimmy and slammed his fist across the man's jaw. The blow snapped Jimmy's head backward, and, losing his balance, he fell to his knees.

Taking the rifle, Cole leveled the barrel inches from the man's face. "I oughta kill you!" he growled, cocking the weapon.

"Cole, no!" Kristina cried. She couldn't stand any more violence. "Please let him live!" She cast a glance at Ned, and was relieved to see that his wound wasn't fatal. She turned back to Cole. "There's no reason to kill either of them!"

Keeping the rifle handy, Cole backed up, went to

240

his gun, and strapped it on. He emptied the rifle, and put the bullets in his pocket. Then, stepping to Ned's pistol, he picked it up and stuck it in his belt. He turned to Kristina. "Come on, darlin', let's go."

She started toward the Appaloosa, but catching sight of the puppy, she paused. Kneeling, she coaxed the pup to her side and petted his head. She had an overwhelming urge to pick him up and take him along, however, she didn't think Cole would want to bother with a dog. Giving him a final pat, she straightened and moved to the Appaloosa.

Cole helped her mount, then to Kristina's surprise, he went to the pup and lifted him by the scruff of his neck.

With the pup in hand, he returned to Kristina. "This smelly hound is a beagle," he informed her and gave her the puppy.

"Cole, are we keeping him?" she asked hopefully.

"You want him, don't you?"

"Yes, I certainly do!" she exclaimed.

"After we bathe him and fatten him up, he might not look so damned ugly."

Cradling the puppy close, she replied, "He isn't ugly. And, Cole Barton, you're a softie."

He mounted behind her and spurred the Appaloosa into a fast trot. When they reached the mare, he grabbed the reins and led the horse.

"Why are we riding double?" she asked.

"I want to feel you close," he said, sliding an arm about her waist. "I was worried about you, darlin'. If anything was to happen to you . . ."

"I know," she murmured. "I feel the same way."

He patted her stomach. "By the way, how's our baby?"

"Hungry," she replied.

241

Chapter Twenty

Cole and Kristina reached the Lazy-J a couple of hours after sunset. A meandering drive, bordered with moss-laden oaks, led to the large, two-story home, which was well lit by outside lanterns.

A group of drovers were loafing in front of the bunkhouse, and one of them hurried over to take the visitors' horses.

Dismounting, Cole went to Kristina and helped her down. Cole knew the young drover, and greeted him with a cordial "Good evening, Jake."

"Howdy, Mr. Barton. Do you want me to take the horses to the barn?"

"Please. They also need to be fed and brushed."

"Don't worry, I'll take good care of 'em."

Cole slid an arm about Kristina's waist and guided her up the porch steps. An abundance of yellow jonquils and red roses grew along the front of the house, and their sweet fragrance scented the air. Cole rapped loudly on the door.

Kristina was holding the puppy. She and Cole had bathed him in the river, and his coat was shiny and soft. "Do you think Josh will object to the dog?"

Cole was sure he wouldn't mind.

The door was opened by Josh, whose face registered amazement. He waved them inside. "Come in . . . come in. This is a pleasant surprise."

They stepped into the front foyer—a spacious entrance with a high ceiling and marble floor. Kristina was impressed, and she was anxious to see more of the magnificent home.

Rosa, Josh's housekeeper, arrived from the kitchen.

"Señor Cole!" she said warmly. "It is good to see you again." She cast Kristina an inquisitive look.

Smiling, Cole told the middle-aged servant, "This is Kristina Parker, my fiancée."

Rosa's face brightened with an expansive grin. "It is about time you found yourself a good woman. Does this mean you will settle down and raise a family?"

"A large family, we hope."

"Good!" Rosa remarked cheerfully. She went to Kristina, held out her hands, and said, "Give me the dog, and I will fix him something to eat and a place to sleep in the kitchen."

As Kristina handed over the pet, she looked from Rosa to Josh, saying tentatively, "I hope you don't object to the puppy."

"Of course not," Josh assured her. "What's his name?"

"Lucky," she replied.

Josh arched a brow. "Lucky?"

"Kristina thinks he'll bring us luck," Cole explained.

"He already has," she stated. "It was luck for us that he bounded out of the house and drew Ned's attention."

Josh chuckled. "This sounds like an interesting story. Let's go to my study, and you two can tell me about it over drinks."

Their host led the way down the main hall and to his study. Opening the door, he stepped back for his guests to precede him.

It was an elegant room. The floor was covered with a luxurious carpet, and the glossy-polished mahogany furniture was beautiful.

Josh poured brandy for himself and Cole, and a sherry for Kristina. He served the drinks to his guests, seated on the sofa. Josh took the wing-back chair facing them.

In detail, Cole explained the incident with Ned and Jimmy. Pride flickered in his blue eyes as he told Josh that Kristina had knocked Jimmy's rifle aside, giving him time to reach the porch and put the man out of commission.

Chuckling, Josh said to Kristina, "That's life with Cole—never a dull moment." He took a drink of brandy, then turned to Cole. "Since you're addressing Kristina as Kristina, I assume you know she isn't Samantha."

Cole laughed. "You're real sharp, Josh." He took a drink of brandy, then gave a full account of Samantha's unexpected visit to the Diamond-C.

"If you don't mind," Cole finished, "I want Kristina to stay here until Samantha leaves for Philadelphia."

"She's more than welcome." Josh smiled at Kristina. "I'll enjoy your company."

A moment of silence fell over the threesome, and, Cole, sensing an uneasiness in Josh, studied him curiously. He had a feeling that something was bothering his friend.

"Josh . . ." he began. "Is there a problem?"

Chandler smiled faintly. "You know me too well, Cole. I'm afraid I got on James Kennedy's bad side."

Cole turned to Kristina. "James Kennedy's ranch

borders on the Lazy-J," he explained. "Kennedy is a prominent and influential figure in Texas."

"A couple of weeks ago," Josh resumed, "Kennedy caught his daughter, Laura, and a young man named Juan in a compromising act. Juan and his parents are sharecroppers on my land. His mother is an Indian, but his father is Mexican. In return for produce, I let them farm several fertile acres. Well, when Kennedy caught the pair, Laura claimed rape. Kennedy was about to string up the unfortunate lad when the sheriff got wind of it. He stopped the lynching and put Juan in jail. Juan's trial was today, and I testified in his behalf. I told the court that I caught Laura and Juan in my line cabin on three different occasions, and that two other times I found her there with one of my ranch hands. The young man no longer works for me. The second time I found him with Laura, I fired him. Anyway, due to my testimony, Juan was set free. Now Kennedy's all fired up. I slandered his daughter's reputation, and he'll never forgive me for that."

Josh shrugged limply, but he was obviously disturbed. "The first time I found Laura with Juan, I suppose I should have reported it to her father. But I don't like to stick my nose in other people's business. Besides, Kennedy would have placed the entire blame on Juan. The young man would have paid dearly— probably with his life."

"Kennedy will cool down," Cole replied. His tone, however, lacked conviction. He was acquainted with James Kennedy, and knew he was the type to hold a grudge.

"He might mellow in time," Josh agreed lamely. "But, more than likely, I've made a lifetime enemy."

A knock sounded on the door, then it was opened as Rosa peeked inside. *"Patrón*, Señor Kennedy

246

is here."

Closed inside the study, the group hadn't heard the visitor's arrival.

Josh cursed softly, "Damn!" He got to his feet. "Show him in, Rosa."

In less than a minute, James Kennedy's huge frame came through the open doorway. The man was verging on obesity. Crossing the room, he paused mere inches from Josh. A raging fury glared in his eyes, and his rotund face was livid.

"What do you want, James?" Josh asked calmly.

The man spoke with a distinctive southern accent. "I want to know, suh, why you sacrificed Laura's reputation to save a half-breed Mexican!"

"You might think of Juan as a half-breed, but I see him as a person entitled to his rights."

"Rights?" Kennedy scowled. "What right did you have to ruin my daughter?"

"I didn't ruin Laura, she ruined herself."

The man's face became distorted with rage. "You know what I think, Mista Chandler? I think you lied in court. Laura told me you made up the whole sordid story to get even with her. On several occasions you made advances to her, but she turned you down. You took the witness stand and lied, and you did so out of spite!"

"If Laura told you that I made advances, then she's a liar."

Kennedy's hand shot out, slapping Josh's face. "Suh, I'm callin' you out for insultin' my daughter!"

Josh, his cheek stinging, turned away from the irate father. "Go to hell, James," he mumbled, his voice strangely lacking emotion of any kind.

"Are you refusin' to meet me man to man?"

"Yes, I am."

"Apparently, suh, you are not only a malicious

liar, but a coward as well."

Cole had heard enough, and he approached Kennedy. "James, don't you realize Josh is doing you a favor? Do you really think you could outshoot him?"

"Stay out of this, Cole! It's none of your business!"

"Anything that concerns Josh is my business. Furthermore, you know he wouldn't lie under oath. What he said about your daughter is the truth."

Kennedy conceded with difficulty. It wasn't easy to admit to himself that his daughter was guilty, but, deep down, he believed Josh was a man of his word.

"Why don't you go home," Cole continued, "before you push Josh too far?"

"Very well!" Kennedy snapped. "I'll leave, but first I have something to say."

Josh's back was turned, but he moved about slowly and faced Kennedy. The man's southern drawl had carried him back in time, and he felt as though he were again a humble slave facing his master's wrath. He unthinkingly folded his arms across his chest as if Kennedy's eyes could penetrate his shirt and see the three R's branding him a runaway slave.

"Josh . . ." the man began, his voice barely controlled. "I thought we were friends, as well as neighbors. But a friend wouldn't slander my daughter's reputation, nor would he publicly shame me and my family. My poor wife is beyond consoling."

"James, I'm truly sorry that you and your family have been hurt. But Juan was innocent, and I wasn't going to remain silent and allow him to go to prison for a crime he didn't commit."

Kennedy's already shaky composure crumbled, and his tone grew vicious, "You still don't understand, do you? That half-breed is not as important as my family! That piece of scum is no better than a damned nigger!"

"Get out!" Josh ordered, fuming. "Get out of my house and off my property!"

Kennedy stalked from the room, saying over his shoulder, "Someday I will find a way to even the score, Mista Chandler! You can count on it!"

Josh watched stonily as the man left. Cole, intending to show him to the front door, followed closely.

A cold chill suddenly prickled the back of Josh's neck. If Kennedy knew his secret, he could assuredly even the score. Again, he folded his arms as though his branded R's needed extra protection.

Kristina was worried about Josh, and she moved to his side. "Are you all right?"

He managed a weak smile. "I'm fine."

She didn't think so.

"Alisa, why are you packing a bag?" Autumn Moon asked with surprise. She had come into her daughter's room to tell her that dinner was almost ready. She hadn't expected to find Alisa hastily cramming clothes into a carpetbag.

"Didn't you say that Billy Stockton is leaving in the morning to take Kristina's belongings to Josh's?"

"Yes, he is," Autumn Moon replied. Before taking Kristina to the Lazy-J, Cole had made arrangements with Billy. Because Cole planned for Kristina and him to travel horseback, he had instructed Billy to deliver Kristina's belongings to Josh's ranch.

"When Billy leaves in the morning, I'm going with him," Alisa remarked.

"But why?" Autumn Moon asked, watching her daughter closely. She suspected that Alisa was in love with Josh, and she wholeheartedly approved. She was worried, though, that Josh didn't share Alisa's feelings.

"I need to talk to Josh," Alisa replied. She left it at that, for she didn't care to confide in her mother.

Autumn Moon decided not to pry. "Dinner will be ready soon," she told her.

"I'll be down in a few minutes."

Her mother left, and Alisa finished packing. Closing her bag, she placed it on the floor beside her bed. Then, moving to her vanity, she sat down and perused her reflection. She knew that she was attractive, and although she despised her straight black hair and golden-brown skin, and wished for blond hair and a peaches-and-cream complexion, they nonetheless enhanced her beauty.

A bitter frown hardened her features as her thoughts went to Samantha. Although she didn't consider her half-sister especially pretty, Alisa still envied the woman. Samantha was blonde, and full-blooded white!

Alisa quickly turned her musings to Josh. She intended to confront him, and confess her love. He would probably spurn her affections, but she was determined to give him one last chance. If he rejected her love, then she would cast him from her mind, as well as her heart, and plan a future with Raymond Lewis. She believed that Raymond was quite infatuated with her, and that their relationship might very well lead to matrimony. Raymond had made it apparent that he didn't find her Comanche blood offensive. Quite the contrary, he seemed to find her Indian heritage fascinating.

Her thoughts now filled with Raymond, Alisa left her room and was descending the stairs when, detecting a conversation in the parlor, she recognized

Raymond's voice, along with Samantha's and Bernard's.

The parlor door was open, and catching a glimpse of Alisa, Raymond called to her, "Come in and join us."

She did so somewhat hesitantly, for she preferred to avoid Samantha and her fiancé.

Samantha lavished a cold, contempt-filled gaze upon Alisa. "Go to the kitchen," she said smugly, "and inform your mother that we are having a guest for dinner. Mr. Lewis has accepted my invitation to dine with us."

"Go to the kitchen and tell her yourself," Alisa retorted. "I'm not your servant."

"You don't need to be so rude!" Samantha spat.

Bernard slipped an arm about his fiancée's shoulders. "Don't get upset, love. Come. I'll go to the kitchen with you."

As the pair were leaving, Raymond went to the liquor cabinet and poured Alisa a glass of sherry. Taking it to her, he said with a smile, "Samantha can be a real bitch, can't she?"

His remark pleased Alisa. Raymond was undoubtedly her friend.

"I came here tonight to see you," he continued.

"You did?" she asked, obviously flattered.

"Yes. I wanted to let you know that I bought the Branding Iron."

"You did *what?*" she exclaimed. Her face grew angry. Apparently he had no intention of taking her to Philadelphia! He had coldly lied to her!

Raymond read her thoughts easily. Feigning a tender, understanding smile, he was quick to placate her. "Alisa, this doesn't mean we won't visit Philadelphia. In fact, I hope you and I will travel

251

there frequently. Philadelphia is my home, and I plan to return often."

She felt somewhat better. "But why did you buy a saloon?"

He shrugged casually. "The place has possibilities. I'm also considering investing in a ranch. When I find one that I want, I'll buy it." He was seriously contemplating buying the Diamond-C but hadn't yet made a firm decision.

"Then you're planning to settle in these parts," Alisa murmured sadly.

"I know what you're thinking, Alisa. You were hoping that, through me, you could escape living in Texas. But, sweetheart, it's not where you live that matters, but who you are living with. If you should become mine, believe me, my riches and my power will protect you. No one will dare look down upon you—in fact, you will be treated with the utmost respect." He could tell that she believed his lies, and he gloated inwardly. Soon he would have this beautiful woman in his bed fulfilling his every desire.

Alisa was thrilled, for she trusted Raymond. Her happy mood, however, took a sudden plunge. Although she found marriage to Raymond a pleasant prospect, the possibility didn't douse the old flame still burning in her heart. She still wanted Josh Chandler. Josh was a prominent rancher, and his fellow Texans held him in high regard. As his wife, she'd receive the respect she craved. But even more important, she would be married to the man she loved. Guiltily, she turned her eyes away from Raymond's. He was her second choice, and she inwardly chastised herself for leading him on. He was a kind, compassionate man, and he deserved better. Alisa quickly thrust her guilt aside. Raymond

252

didn't know that he was second choice, and what he didn't know wouldn't hurt him. She wasn't about to say or do anything that might cause her to lose him. Raymond Lewis was her ace in the hole!

Raymond placed a hand beneath her chin and turned her face back to his. "Alisa, is something wrong?" he asked, his kind tone belying his impatience.

She smiled sweetly. "No, everything is fine."

"That's good. Will you have dinner with me tomorrow night?"

"I can't," she replied. "I'll be out of town for a few days."

He was surprised. "Where are you going?"

"To visit a friend," she answered. Hoping to evade further explanation, she said abruptly, "I should go to the kitchen and see if my mother needs any help."

At that moment, however, Joseph came into the parlor and announced that dinner was ready.

As Raymond escorted Alisa into the dining room, he was indeed curious about her trip. He helped her to be seated, then sliding into his own chair, he looked at Samantha and remarked quite casually, "Alisa is taking a trip."

As Raymond had suspected, Samantha's curiosity was aroused. "A trip?" she questioned. She gave Alisa her full attention. "Where are you going?"

"To see a friend," she replied evasively.

Samantha wasn't about to be put off. "Is this friend's name Kristina Parker?"

Raymond smiled to himself. Leave it to Samantha to seek the answers he wanted.

Alisa saw no reason to lie. "Yes, it is Kristina."

"Where is she?" Samantha wanted to know.

When Alisa refused to answer, Raymond took it upon himself to coax her gently. "You can tell us where she is. Kristina isn't wanted by the law."

"She's at Josh Chandler's. He was a good friend of Papa's. He has a ranch outside Austin."

Raymond was satisfied. He wasn't ready yet to get even with Kristina, but when the time came, he now knew where to find her.

Kristina had gone to bed, leaving Cole and Josh sitting on the front porch drinking brandy. Cole, his long legs stretched out in front of him, was reclining on a mahogany glider. Josh was sitting sideways on the porch's sturdy banister.

It was a clear night, and the Texas sky was dotted with a myriad of twinkling stars with a crescent moon nestled among them.

"Cole . . ." Josh began. "I hope you plan to quit your profession." He knew that Cole and Kristina planned to get married. "It wouldn't be fair to your wife for you to be gone all the time."

Cole smiled. He didn't resent Josh's interfering in his business. Their friendship was too deep for that. "I won't be tracking down any more killers," he said matter-of-factly.

"That's good news. You've always known how I feel about your profession."

Cole nodded. "You never kept it a secret, that's for sure." He cast his friend a questioning look. "Tell me, Josh, when are you going to find yourself a wife?"

He shrugged, and, uncomfortable with the subject, he glanced away from Cole. "I guess the right woman hasn't come along."

"Hell, Josh!" Cole remarked good-naturedly. "Do you expect her to suddenly show up at your door, saying, 'Here I am. Take me!' You have to show a little initiative, you know."

"Look who's talking. You never went looking for a wife. Kristina just happened to drop into your lap—you lucky devil."

"Yeah, but it was different with me. You have this ranch, and a well-organized life. Don't you want to share your future with a wife and children?"

Josh wanted a wife and children more than anything on the face of the earth. He believed, however, that such happiness was never to be his. The three R's branded across his chest made that impossible.

He feigned a light-hearted tone. "Cole, just because you're about to tie the knot doesn't mean I'm ready to do likewise. I relish my independence, and I don't intend to relinquish it for a while."

Cole grinned. "You'll change your tune when the right woman comes along. I sure did." He got to his feet. "I guess I'll call it a night. I plan to leave early in the morning."

Josh bid him good night, and Cole went inside the house. He climbed the stairs quickly and started down the hall. As he passed Kristina's room, his long strides halted. Her door was closed, and he lifted a hand to knock softly, but suddenly changed his mind and let his hand drop back to his side. She was probably asleep, and he didn't want to disturb her. The day had been long and tiring, and her experience with Ned and Jimmy had been harrowing. She needed a good night's rest, for her sake as well as the baby's.

Reluctantly, he continued down the hall and to his own room. Later, as he lay in bed, he longed to feel Kristina curled up against him. He craved her closeness with every fiber of his being.

Suddenly, he threw off the covers. His movements

quick and precise, he slipped into his trousers and left the room. Hurrying to Kristina's door, he opened it quietly and went inside. Closing the door soundlessly, he moved furtively to the bed. The outside lanterns illuminated the room with a soft golden light, and he could see Kristina plainly. She was lying on her side, sound asleep. He thought her beautiful in repose, and his love-filled gaze raked her possessively. Due to the warm evening, she merely had a sheet drawn up to her waist. She had borrowed a nightgown from Rosa. The garment was too large and it had fallen away from her shoulders, giving Cole a clear view of her lovely breasts.

Quietly, he removed his trousers, drew back the sheet, and got into bed. Kristina, somewhere between sleep and consciousness, snuggled up against him. "Cole," she murmured softly.

"Go back to sleep, darlin'," he whispered. He drew her to his side. Now content, Cole closed his eyes. With his love at his side, where she belonged, sleep no longer eluded him.

Chapter Twenty-One

Kristina awoke to find herself held snugly in Cole's embrace. They were lying on their sides, facing each other, their arms entwined. Kristina's legs were entangled with Cole's. Her nightgown had worked its way up to her waist, leaving her bare thighs pressed intimately against her lover's.

The room was beginning to lighten with the cresting sun, and the chirpings of early-rising birds carried musically through the open window.

Kristina's eyes fluttered open, and seeing that Cole was awake, she smiled at him, and stifling a yawn murmured, "It's still too early to get up. Let's go back to sleep."

"I can't," he replied. "I want to leave as soon as possible. I intend to travel without stopping so I can reach the Diamond-C some time tonight."

His words brought Kristina wide awake and her arms went about him tightly. "Cole, I'll miss you so much!" She felt like crying.

"I'll only be gone a few days. I'll be back before you know it."

"No chance," she replied. "Time will crawl by, I just know it will."

"Try to enjoy your visit with Josh. And get a lot of rest. You need to take good care of our baby, you know."

"I'll certainly do that. I want this child with all my heart."

"So do I," Cole whispered. "I also want you, Kristina Parker. I love you so fiercely that . . . that my feelings are overwhelming."

"I know," she murmured. She placed her lips against his and expressed her devotion in a long, passionate kiss.

"Kristina," Cole moaned thickly. His desire was raging, and his mouth took hers in another fervent kiss. As she responded ardently, his hand traveled over her body, seeking, and finding, her soft curves and crevices.

Kristina, her passion fully aroused, trembled beneath his touch and his fiery caresses. When his finger probed the entrance of her womanhood, she parted her legs, giving him free access. His rapid, rhythmic strokes sent spasms of desire sweeping through her, and the pleasure was so intense that it was almost an aching torment.

"Cole . . . Cole," she pleaded. "Love me . . . love me."

His mouth suddenly sought hers in a demanding exchange, which left them breathless but hungry for more. Slowly, his hand moved upward to caress the fullness of her breasts.

Returning his intimate fondling, Kristina ran her fingers over his flesh, reveling in the feel of his strength and corded muscles.

Cole's desire was now raging beyond control, and moving over her, he thrust his hardness into her with a thrilling force.

Her legs went about his waist, and his full length

plunged deeply within her. Kristina moaned aloud with unbearable ecstasy, and, clinging tenaciously, she matched Cole's driving hips with equal fervor.

They became wonderfully engulfed in their passionate union, and following more fiery kisses and vigorous thrusting, they reached love's plateau where, together, they achieved total fulfillment.

Cole kissed her softly, then moved to lie at her side. His breathing somewhat labored, he said raspingly, "No woman has ever excited me the way you do."

She rolled over and snuggled against him. "And no woman ever will, for you belong to me, Cole Barton. And don't you ever forget it."

He chuckled lightly. "Are you the jealous type?"

"Yes, but not unreasonably so. What about you?"

"I'm not sure," he replied honestly.

He tried to imagine a situation that might provoke his jealousy, but the thought alone was too maddening to consider. A frown furrowed his brow. "Yeah, I'm the jealous type. Probably too damned jealous."

Suddenly, he pulled her close and kissed her possessively. "You're my woman," he whispered, his tone husky. "And you'll always be mine."

She smiled agreeably. "You'll get no argument from me. I'm yours completely . . . totally."

"Promise?" he murmured, his eyes twinkling playfully.

"Cross my heart," she told him pertly.

He sighed long and reluctantly, then moaning regretfully, he left the bed. "I hate to leave such lovely company, but I've already lingered too long. I still have to eat breakfast and saddle my horse." He put on his trousers and headed for the door. "I'll get my clothes and dress in here. That way, we can be together a little longer."

"But, Cole, don't you want me to go downstairs with you and see you off?"

"I'd rather remember you lying in bed. Besides, it's still too early for you to get up. You need your rest."

He left quickly, and was back in a few minutes, carrying a change of clothes, his boots, hat, and gun belt.

Kristina already missed him, and she watched tearfully as he filled the water bowl, washed hastily, and dried off. Her gaze never wavered from Cole as he started dressing. She admired him fully, and was struck anew with his virile good looks. He was so devilishly handsome that just looking at him sent her heart aflutter.

She continued to watch intently as he slipped into a pair of dark trousers which clung tightly to his strong legs and manly hips. He then donned a fringed, cream-colored shirt, and the soft suede, fitting snugly, clearly defined his muscular chest, and the wide width of his shoulders.

Kristina's gaze followed as Cole moved to the dresser and ran a comb through his sable-brown hair. Despite the grooming, however, a lock went astray and fell across his brow, lending him a boyish but sensual appeal.

Cole was seemingly unaware of Kristina's scrutiny. He moved to a chair, sat down, and reached for his boots. Suddenly, though he glanced up. Their eyes met, locked, and held for a moment. Then a smile crossed his lips, and it was so filled with love that it sent a tingling thrill through Kristina.

He gave her a wink, then returned to putting on his boots. She looked closely at his handsome face. She loved the deep blue of his eyes, and the way in which his well-trimmed mustache gave him a roguish charm.

Kristina knew with a certainty that Cole Barton was the type of man that other men envied and women adored.

She was proud of her man, and adoration welled within her as she held out her arms to him. "Hold me, Cole," she beckoned. "Please hold me close. I love you so much!"

He was beside her in a flash, and taking her into his embrace, he whispered deeply, "I love you, too, darlin'." He kissed her then, and his lips branded hers with a fiery desire. "God!" he groaned. "I'd better leave before I end up undressed and back in bed."

Kristina hated to let him go, but she knew his trip to the Diamond-C was necessary. She had to muster all her willpower to move out of his embrace. "Yes, darling," she finally said persuasively, "you had better leave. Please be careful, and hurry back."

"I will," he murmured, kissing her quickly.

Somehow, Kristina controlled the urge to summon him back into her arms, and she watched silently as he picked up his hat, and carrying it at his side, crossed the room. Pausing at the door, he turned back to face her.

"While I'm away, promise me you'll take good care of yourself and our baby."

She smiled timorously. "I will. I promise."

"I love you both," he said. Then he was gone, closing the door behind him.

Rolling to her side, Kristina grasped Cole's pillow and held it close, as though it were a part of the man she loved.

Cole was surprised to find Josh already at the dining table, eating breakfast.

"You're up early," Cole remarked, pulling out a chair.

"I have some wild mustangs, and the men and I plan to start breaking 'em this morning."

Rosa entered, carrying a fresh pot of coffee. "Señor Cole," she said, "I will bring you a large breakfast, *sí?*"

"*Sí*, Rosa. I'm as hungry as a bear. Also, will you pack me some food? I plan to travel straight through to the Diamond-C."

She agreed, and left quickly to carry out her tasks.

Josh was finished eating, and he pushed aside his plate, then poured coffee for himself and Cole. He spoke somberly. "It's hard to imagine the Diamond-C without Drake there."

"Why didn't you attend his funeral?"

"I couldn't leave. I was afraid I wouldn't be back in time for Juan's trial." Josh's answer was only partially true. He had also stayed away because of Alisa. He was still determined to avoid her whenever possible. He took a sip of coffee, then murmured, "It's hard for me to accept that Drake's gone."

Cole felt the same way. "I know what you mean."

Josh leaned back in his chair. "Let's talk about something cheerful, shall we?" he suggested.

Concurring, Cole asked, "What do you have in mind?"

"Let's talk about you."

"Me?" he questioned.

"Cole, the change in you is remarkable. I've never seen you so happy and so at ease."

He grinned expansively. "I am happy, Josh. Kristina has turned my life completely around. I never dreamed I could give up my way of life so easily. But marrying Kristina, raising a family, and living at the Diamond-C is all that matters to me."

Josh watched him intently. "Does this mean you've given up your quest? Have you decided to stop searching for your mother's killers?"

It was a long moment before Cole answered, during which time he seriously considered his reply.

"I won't look randomly for them, but if I hear about the one with the branded chest, I'll hunt him down. He and his friends murdered my mother, and I can't forget that."

"You never give up, do you, Cole?" Josh sounded exasperated.

"Would you?" Cole asked crankily. "If your mother had been raped and killed, would you just forget about it?"

"No, I guess not," Josh conceded. "However, I wouldn't become obsessed with revenge."

A sudden smile crossed Cole's face. "But I'm no longer obsessed with revenge. The most important thing in my life is Kristina . . . and our child."

Chandler was stunned. "Your child?"

"Kristina's pregnant. She probably doesn't want you to know yet, but I thought I should tell you. You'll see to it, won't you, that she takes care of herself? I want her to get a lot of rest, and please make sure she doesn't overly exert herself."

Josh laughed heartily.

"What's so funny?" Cole asked, baffled.

"You!" his friend replied. "Cole Barton, the most famous bounty hunter in Texas—the man with the deadly draw! Who would imagine that such a legend would turn into a jittering father-to-be!" He laughed again. "Kristina Parker has definitely made a change in you. And one for the better, I might add."

Cole didn't argue.

*   *   *

The three men entered San Antonio and rode slowly down the main street. The scorching rays of the midday sun had driven most of the town's citizens indoors, and the thoroughfare was practically deserted as the men veered their horses toward the Branding Iron.

Dismounting, they looped their bridle reins around the saloon's hitching rail. The rugged threesome exuded an aura of danger, for they moved with the stealth of predators. Each man had a gun strapped to his hip and a knife sheathed at his waist. They were unshaven, their clothes coated with trail dust. Apparently they had ridden a long distance.

Pushing open the saloon's bat-wing doors, they lumbered inside, went to the bar, and ordered shots of whiskey.

The Branding Iron wasn't crowded, and, Raymond Lewis, seated at a far table, had a clear view of the strangers. From his vantage point, he studied them thoughtfully for a few minutes, then beckoned to his bartender.

The man hurried over to see what his boss wanted.

"Joe, who are those men?" Raymond asked, gesturing toward the threesome.

"I don't know, Mr. Lewis. I've never seen them before."

"Ask them to join me, then bring a bottle of our best whiskey."

"Yes, sir," the man replied. He returned, and relayed his employer's message.

The men turned away from the bar and looked at Raymond eyeing him suspiciously. They were curious, however, and wondering about his invitation, they went to his table.

Raymond didn't rise, for he intended to establish from the start that these men were not his equal. His gaze swept fleetingly over the threesome, then he said congenially, "My name is Raymond Lewis, and I own this saloon." He indicated three empty chairs. "Sit down, please."

They complied, and the one in the middle made introductions. He gestured to the man on his left. "This here is Les," then motioned to the one on his right, "this is Tom, and I'm Norman."

"Do you men plan to stay in town, or are you just passing through?"

"What's it to you, mister?" Tom mumbled, his tone guarded.

At that moment, the bartender arrived with the whiskey and three glasses. He put the order on the table, looked at his boss, and asked, "Will this be all, Mr. Lewis?"

"Yes," he replied, waving him away.

Raymond filled the glasses, and handed each man a drink. "I need to hire a few men. Men I can trust. You three might very well qualify. The work will be easy, and the pay will be excellent. I'm a stranger to the West. I guess you could say I'm a greenhorn. I'm not a gunman, in fact, I don't ever carry a weapon. That's why I hope to hire loyal employees—men who can handle a gun and aren't opposed to using it."

"Sounds like a good deal," Norman said. He quaffed down his whiskey, then refilled the glass.

"I'm sure you men can understand why it's important that I question you. I hope you won't take offense."

"Naw, we won't mind," Norman was quick to reply. He was interested in the prospective job. "Go ahead. Ask away."

"Where were you men last employed?"

At this question, the men guffawed. Raymond

bristled inwardly. How dare they laugh at him!

Norman's chuckles abated. "Mr. Lewis, we just spent the last twelve years in prison. Now we ain't headed in no place particular. We're just wanderin', looking for some kind of work. Whether it's honest or not doesn't matter so long as the pay is good."

"Why were you sent to prison?"

"Robbery," Norman answered.

"You spent twelve years in prison for robbery!" Raymond exclaimed.

Les spoke up for the first time. "During the robbery, a man was killed. We're lucky we got only twelve years."

Their prison records didn't dissuade Lewis. In his estimation, they were the kind of men whose loyalties had a price—and he could easily afford it.

"Are you men southerners?" he asked.

Norman grinned knowingly. "Mr. Lewis, I can tell by your accent that you're from up North. Well, you don't have to worry that we're ex-Confederates who are liable to stab you in the back. We didn't fight for the South." He helped himself to a large swig of the whiskey, then continued. "We're originally from Kansas, and we fought for the Union."

"Jayhawkers?" Raymond questioned.

"Yeah, we were Jayhawkers." Norman scowled defensively. "Does our war record matter to you, Mr. Lewis?"

"Not at all. I just wanted to be sure that I'm not hiring three diehard Johnny Rebs."

Norman studied him keenly. "Did you fight in the war, Mr. Lewis?"

"No, I did not." Raymond's answer was firm, as though he were proud of it. "Gentlemen, the Union didn't have my undying loyalty. I am loyal only to myself."

"How did you get out of fightin'?" Les asked. "Were you too young?"

"No, I was twenty years old when the war started. But my family is very wealthy and influential. While the war raged, I was in school abroad. I stayed away until the Confederacy surrendered. If that causes you three to harbor ill feelings, then there's no reason to continue this interview. As I have already emphasized, the men I hire must completely support me."

Norman chuckled gustily. "Mr. Lewis, we don't give a damn whether or not you fought in the war. We were Jayhawkers, true, but we're also deserters. We got tired of puttin' our lives on the line for army pay. We left the goddamn war behind and headed to California."

Raymond smiled complacently. "Gentlemen, you are exactly the kind of men I'm looking for."

"Money can buy our loyalty, that's for damned sure!" Tom remarked emphatically.

Lewis regarded them reflectively. "So you three deserted, went to California, and have been together ever since."

"Actually . . ." Norman began. "When we deserted there was another man ridin' with us. When we got to California, he went his own way. We ain't seen him since. He was a runaway slave who managed to escape into Kansas."

"A Negro?" Raymond queried, his expression distasteful. He thought Negroes far inferior to whites, and, in that respect, he had sided with the South. In his opinion, Negroes should have remained enslaved.

"He was a quadroon," Norman explained. "He didn't look like a Negro. His skin was whiter than mine. He ran three times before he finally got free. Each time he ran, his owner branded an R on his chest. That poor bastard had three of 'em burned into his flesh.''

"I wonder whatever happened to Moses?" Tom pondered.

"Moses?" Raymond repeated.

"Yeah, his name was Moses," Norman replied. "He hated that name. His former owner gave biblical names to all the slaves born on his plantation."

"Moses was a clever nigger," Les put in. "He's probably passin' for a pure-blooded white man."

Norman agreed. "Yeah, and I bet he ain't usin' the name of Moses."

Raymond was growing bored. He wasn't interested in discussing a quadroon. He returned to the matter at hand. "Well, do you want the job or not?"

Norman answered for the group. "Mr. Lewis, you've hired yourself three bodyguards."

"Bodyguards?"

The man grinned slyly. "That's what you're wantin', ain't it?"

"Exactly," Raymond admitted. He refilled their glasses. "Drink up, men. This is my best whiskey. Get used to it. Hereafter, it's what you'll be drinking."

Chapter Twenty-Two

Sitting alone at the dining table, Kristina regarded the midday meal with disinterest. Cole's departure and her pregnancy were playing havoc with her insides. Her heart was aching, and her stomach was churning.

It was obvious that Rosa had gone to great lengths to prepare the scrumptious meal. Not wanting to appear ungrateful, Kristina placed her napkin on her lap, and picking up a fork, she began to eat.

She managed to devour half the food before her stomach revolted. Knowing she'd certainly lose her lunch if she ate any more, she pushed her plate to the side.

She sipped the hot tea that she had asked for in lieu of coffee in hopes it would be less apt to aggravate her squeamish stomach. Her thoughts lingered on Cole. She missed him terribly. He had been gone only a few hours, but to Kristina it seemed much longer.

She decided to shake her melancholy, and picking up her dishes, she carried them toward the kitchen. She'd spend some time with Lucky, for the mischievous pup would surely lift her dispirited mood.

Going into the kitchen, she handed the dishes to

Rosa. Lucky was lying on a blanket in the corner, but at Kristina's arrival, he leapt to his legs, scurried over, and nipped playfully at her long skirt.

Laughing at her delightful pet, she picked him up and told Rosa that she was taking him outside.

Hurrying down the steps, she turned the beagle loose. Then, shading her eyes from the bright sun, she peered into the distance. She could barely make out the corral, where Josh and his men were breaking wild mustangs. Rosa had told her that they had been at the task all morning. Josh hadn't returned to the house for lunch, and the woman had been annoyed. Rosa clucked over the *patrón* like a mother hen, and because she was a firm believer in three meals a day, she was upset over Josh missing one.

Looking away from the distant corral, Kristina turned her full attention to Lucky. The brown-and-white speckled pup was sitting on his haunches, watching her with affectionate eyes.

"You want to play, don't you?"

He wagged his tail, and pricked his long, droopy ears.

Coaxing the puppy to chase her heels, she ran to a tall oak and sat down in its shade. Lucky plopped in her lap and began chewing gently on her fingers.

Enjoying her pet's company, Kristina remained outdoors for quite some time before returning to the kitchen. She placed the tiny beagle on his bed, where he quickly curled up and went to sleep.

Kristina was wondering how to pass the rest of the day when Rosa entered through the back door. She was carrying a clothes basket filled with clean linens.

Kristina offered to help fold the laundry and when the chore was completed, she said she'd take her linen and Josh's to their rooms.

She put away her laundry, then went down the hall

to Josh's quarters. The door was open, and she was impressed with the spacious room. It was furnished elegantly, reflecting fine masculine taste. The mahogany bed had a matching dresser, and a huge wardrobe dominated one side of the room. Lush blue carpet covered the floor, complementing the full-length drapes. There were expensive paintings on the walls, and a set of crisscross sabers hung over the fireplace. Below the swords, a miniature replica of a Spanish sailing vessel sat atop the mantel.

Rosa had instructed Kristina to store the folded laundry in the chamber table, which was located in a corner, on the far side of the bed.

She went to the table and opened the top drawer. It was already filled, so she checked the two lower ones, only to find that they were also full.

Kneeling, she opened the bottom drawer, and seeing that it was empty, she began placing the linen inside.

Josh, meanwhile, had returned to the house and was on his way to his quarters. Breaking wild horses was dirty work, and his clothes were filthy.

As he stepped into his room, he was already unbuttoning his shirt, and, Kristina, still kneeling at the chamber table, did not hear him shut the door. The deep carpet totally muffled his footsteps as he moved toward his wardrobe. Unaware of another's presence, he removed his soiled shirt and pitched it onto a chair.

At that instant, Kristina rose to her full height. She whirled about, saw Josh and, as her gaze flew to the three R's on his naked chest, she gaped with horror.

Josh froze, as though riveted to the floor. He had a fleeting impulse to cross his arms over his exposed chest, like a woman hiding her bare breasts from an unexpected observer. Instead, he did nothing. He merely continued to stand rigidly—every muscle in his body drawn taut, his heart pounding madly.

Kristina's voice was rasping, weak, but undeniably incredulous. "You! My God, it's you! You're the man who killed Cole's mother!"

George Cullen admitted Samantha and Bernard into his private office. Gesturing to the chairs facing his desk, he invited them to be seated.

He hadn't expected their arrival, and wondering why they had called on him, he asked them what could he do for them.

Samantha, dressed fashionably in an expensive gown with a matching bonnet, screwed her face into a pretty pout. "Mr. Cullen, I must insist that you read Father's will tomorrow. Bernard and I are anxious to know my inheritance. We simply can't wait any longer."

The lawyer went to his desk and sat down. "Very well, Miss Carlson. Do you prefer I read the will here in my office or at the Diamond-C?"

Wishing to avoid another trip into town, she replied, "At the ranch, please."

"Ten o'clock tomorrow morning?"

She detested dressing early and was accustomed to having breakfast in bed at that hour. She was, however, very anxious to hear Drake's will, so resigning herself to rising earlier than usual, she replied, "Ten o'clock will be fine."

Cullen sensed there was more to the pair's visit, and he regarded them somewhat expectantly.

Bernard cleared his throat, then said, "Mr. Cullen, I know it isn't ethical for you to discuss Drake's last will and testament, but since Samantha is his daughter, would you be opposed to answering a few questions?"

"Not at all," he replied. "Drake's will is cut and dried, and contains no surprises."

"Mr. Cullen . . ." Samantha began. "Did Father leave me the Diamond-C?"

"Yes, he did. That is, he left you the title. His will stipulates that if you keep the Diamond-C, you are to give one-fourth of its profits to Autumn Moon, one-fourth to Alisa, put one-fourth back into the ranch, and keep the remaining fourth for yourself. I don't want to mislead you—this is not a condition, but your father's wish. However, if you decide to sell the Diamond-C, it was also Drake's wish that you give one-third of the money to Autumn Moon, one-third to Alisa, and, of course, the remaining third is yours."

Samantha frowned. "Are Drake's wishes binding? I mean, must I follow his instructions?"

"You aren't legally bound to do so. If Autumn Moon and her daughter were white women—well, they might have solid grounds to contest your actions. Even so, they would most likely lose their case. Autumn Moon isn't Drake's widow, and since Alisa was born out of wedlock, she isn't Drake's lawful daughter. Legally, you are Drake's only heir."

A beaming smile curled Samantha's lips. "Mr. Cullen, you have been very helpful."

Bernard, studying the lawyer thoughtfully, said, "I have a feeling, Mr. Cullen, that you don't especially like Indians."

The man was taken aback, for he hadn't realized his prejudice was so evident. "Why do you think that?"

"You were too willing to inform Samantha of her rights. Also, you did so with a . . . shall I say, with a cheerful flair? You don't seem at all concerned about

273

Autumn Moon and Alisa."

"I'm not concerned, Mr. Galsworthy. As you have already guessed, I have no use for Indians especially Comanches. I was raised in Texas, and I was a witness to the bloody conflicts between the Comanches and the whites. My younger sister was abducted by a band of Comanche warriors. She was found murdered three days later. She had been raped and scalped. Seven years ago, the murdering savages killed my father. He was working for a government contractor. My father and a group of teamsters were traveling by wagons from Fort Griffin to Fort Richardson when a renegade band of Comanches and Kiowas, truants from the Fort Sill reservation, attacked the wagon train. My father and several others were killed. Their bodies were left behind. Later, when the Army rode to the site, they reported that the bodies had been stripped naked, then mutilated and scalped."

A cold, undying hate radiated in the lawyer's eyes. "I've also lost friends to the Comanches. I can relate several occasions when—"

"Please say no more!" Samantha interrupted. "Tales of such violence unnerve me. I'll have nightmares for sure!"

"I'm sorry, Miss Carlson. I didn't mean to upset you."

She rose and extended her hand. "I'm sure you're a busy man, so we'll take our leave. I'll see you in the morning."

He shook her gloved hand. "Good afternoon, Miss Carlson." Moving from behind his desk, he showed his clients to the door.

Samantha suddenly turned back to the lawyer. "Mr. Cullen, will the Diamond-C sell quickly?"

"It's a very prosperous ranch. Many buyers will

want it, but only a few will be able to afford it. You must hold out for a fair bid. Don't sell the Diamond-C for less than its worth."

She assured him that she wouldn't, then she and Bernard left.

The Diamond-C carriage was parked out front. Bernard assisted his fiancée on to the seat, then climbed up beside her. Releasing the brake, he took up the reins, and turning the horse about, they headed out of town.

With a cunning smile, Samantha said spitefully, "Autumn Moon and Alisa won't get a penny from the Diamond-C. I'll not share my inheritance with them. As far as I'm concerned, they can go to the nearest Indian reservation and live in a wigwam."

"It's where they belong," Bernard declared. "After all, they are kin to the bloody savages."

"Kristina, I didn't kill Cole's mother," Josh said, his voice as calm as though he were denying a trivial accusation. Despite his placid tone, however, his eyes seemed to be pleading with hers, and his tall, muscular frame was still poised rigidly.

Kristina didn't respond. She was too shocked—too filled with horror.

Josh continued, a desperate edge now cutting into his words. "I can explain everything. Won't you please listen? Dear God, Kristina, surely you don't think I'm capable of raping and murdering a helpless woman!"

"I don't know what I think," she murmured weakly. Her knees were shaky, and she moved awkwardly to the bed. Sitting, she made a feeble gesture toward the wardrobe. "Please get a shirt and put it on."

She couldn't bear looking at the three R's branded so blatantly across his chest. The sight was grotesque, yet also pathetic.

Josh slipped quickly into a shirt, then grabbing a small chair, he dragged it over to the bed, sitting, and facing Kristina, he said imploringly, "Will you listen to me?"

"Yes," she whispered, "I'll listen. But, Josh, why . . . why have you kept the truth from Cole?"

"Need you even ask?" he groaned, his face ravaged.

"But if you didn't kill his mother—" she ventured.

"But I didn't stop the others from killing her!" he interrupted thunderously.

"Why didn't you stop them? You're a strong man, and you're good with a gun."

"Back then I wasn't much more than a boy, and I wasn't the marksman I am now. All I knew about guns was what the Army had taught me, which wasn't very much."

Kristina was drained, her emotions exhausted. "Oh, Josh!" she moaned brokenly, lowering her gaze from his.

"I want to tell you everything," he said hastily. "For the first time, I'd like to open up and tell someone the whole story."

She mustered her composure. "All right, Josh," she murmured softly, lifting her eyes to his.

He leaned back in his chair. He was quiet for some time as he gathered his thoughts. Then his deep, pleasant voice broke the stark silence. "I was born on a plantation in Tennessee. My mother was a mulatto slave, and my father was the white master. He was married and had four sons, all of them older than me. His youngest son, William, was born a year before I was. When I was four years old, I was given to William as a playmate. Later, I would become his manservant. We got along well, and until I was seven years old, I was a relatively happy child—I didn't know any better."

Josh suddenly plunged into a deep silence, and Kristina was alarmed to see a furious anger harden his otherwise gentle features.

"What happened then?" she asked.

"My mother was sold because the master found her with another man. She was supposed to be his own personal bedwench. One day he discovered her with the man she loved. He was a slave from another plantation. Out of anger, the master sold her to a slave trader. I loved my mother—she was a gentle, caring woman." Josh's deep voice quivered. "I haven't seen her since the day the slave trader took her away, and I have no idea if she's alive or dead."

Josh could no longer sit still, and he stepped restlessly to the window. Parting the drapes, he stared outside blankly. When he was again in full control of his emotions, he turned and faced Kristina.

"Until William was twelve years old, he had a tutor. Because he'd throw a tantrum if his playmate was out of his sight, I was allowed to sit in on his lessons. I was thirsty for knowledge, and I greedily absorbed everything I could learn. I was no longer a happy, ignorant slave. I knew only through an education would I gain my freedom. I had also become acutely aware that my skin was almost as white as my owners'. You see, it was much easier for a slave to run if he could pass for white.

"When William turned thirteen, he was sent away to school, and I accompanied him as his valet. This time, I wasn't allowed to sit in the classrooms. But William kept his books and lessons in his quarters, and as William slept, I pored over his books and assignments. I educated myself.

"William was eighteen when he graduated, and we returned permanently to the plantation. I was determined to flee my bonds, or die trying. I ran three times, and three times I was caught. Each time, the master branded an R on my chest, marking me a Runner. On my fourth try, I was successful. I managed to escape into Kansas. By then, the war had started. I was living in Lawerence, and I joined the Union Army. They put a gun in my hand, and a uniform on my back. I was no longer a slave—I was now a soldier."

Josh returned to his chair, and with a somewhat scoffing laugh, he said, "I was a soldier on the outside, but inside I was still a scared nigger."

"Please don't degrade yourself!" Kristina entreated.

"But it was true, Kristina! Since the day I was born, I had been honed to fear and obey all whites. It's imperative that you understand that. Otherwise, you won't be able to comprehend why I didn't do more to save Cole's mother."

He waited, watching her closely. Could she, a Yankee, possibly grasp what he was saying?

"I think I understand," she murmured.

"I was assigned to Captain Dickerson's troops. We had been ordered to ride into Missouri to search for Quantrill and his band of guerrillas. The captain knew that the Bartons were southerners, and he sent me and three other men to their homestead. We were supposed to merely question Mrs. Barton and her son.

"When we arrived, Mrs. Barton was alone. Cole was working in the fields. His mother was a very attractive woman. The men with me took one look at her, and made up their minds to rape her. I tried to talk them out of it, but they were beyond listening."

278

Josh paused. When he continued, his tone was self-condemning. "If I had been any kind of a man, I would have fought to the death to save Mrs. Barton! But, damn it, I wasn't a man! I was still a frightened slave! I didn't have the guts to forcefully stop three white men. Inside, I was a scared eighteen-year-old slave who had never dared to raise a hand to a white person.

"Cole heard his mother's screams, and he rushed blindly into the house. One of the soldiers, Norman was his name, knocked Cole unconscious. By this time, I had left the house and wandered into the yard. Imagining what was happening inside the cabin, made me sick to my stomach. I walked to the edge of the woods and vomited until there was nothing left. I swear to God, Kristina, I didn't think they would kill Mrs. Barton!

"After a while, I went back into the house. I saw Norman standing over the woman. He had a knife in his hand and was threatening to kill her. I lunged for him and tried to steal the knife. The other two grabbed me from behind, and I fought them so viciously that my shirt was ripped open. They finally restrained me, and I watched helplessly as Norman murdered that poor woman in cold blood. I was then released, and they went outside, leaving me in the house. Cole was still unconscious. I stepped to his mother's body. The knife was still embedded in her flesh, and I drew it free. It was then that I heard Cole moaning. I turned and looked at him. For a moment, his eyes were open, but then he sank back into unconsciousness. I found a quilt and placed it over Mrs. Barton. Norman and the other two men had come back inside and were setting fire to the house. I carried Cole outside and placed him in the yard. I was about to go back for his mother's body, but Norman wouldn't allow it. He threatened to shoot me if I didn't do as he said."

Josh halted his story to look more closely at Kristina. "You seem tired," he observed. "Perhaps you should go to your room and lie down. I can tell you the rest tonight, after dinner."

She agreed. "I am tired, but I'm also very concerned. Not only for you, but for Cole, too." Her expression grew frantic. "Oh, Josh, I hate to even think what might happen should Cole learn—!"

Josh cut in, his tone soothing. "Kristina, try not to get upset. It isn't good for your condition."

"My condition?" she uttered, surprised.

"Cole told me you're pregnant. He wanted me to know so that I'd make sure you took care of yourself."

He stood, took her hands, and helping her to her feet, he said gently, "I want you to take a long nap. The remainder of my story can wait until tonight."

He guided her down the hall to her room. She closed the door and went quickly to bed. Her feelings were numb as she lay down to stare blankly at the ceiling.

Josh was the man with the branded chest! The man Cole had sworn to kill! A sudden streak of apprehension raced through her, dissolving her numbness. Kristina found it incomprehensible that Josh could indefinitely keep his secret. It was inevitable that Cole would someday learn the shocking truth!

Chapter Twenty-Three

Following dinner, Josh took Kristina to the front porch where they sat on the glider in the pleasant evening, a northern breeze cooling the humid Texas air.

The sun hadn't fully set, and the horizon was a tapestry of red and gold streaks. The fiery colors cast an orange glow over the pastoral landscape.

"Do you mind if I smoke?" Josh asked, ending the silence between them.

She had no objections, and he deftly rolled a cigarette. Kristina watched as he struck a match and lit his smoke. His complexion was olive, his hair a glossy ebony, and his eyes a deep, soft brown. These features, however, didn't particularly reflect his mother's heritage—they simply made him a very attractive man.

An amused smile touched his lips. "You can't tell by looking," he murmured.

Kristina was embarrassed, for she hadn't meant to stare so rudely. "I'm sorry," she apologized.

"It's all right," he assured her. He took a couple of drags from his cigarette, before asking, "Are you ready to hear the rest of my life?"

She sighed. "Yes, as ready as I'll ever be."

"You're very troubled, aren't you?"

"Yes," she admitted. "Josh, learning your secret has placed me in a very awkward position. I know I must protect you, but, in doing so, I'm hiding the truth from Cole. If he ever finds out, he'll never forgive me. I might even lose him."

"You want me to tell him everything, don't you?"

"I'm not sure. In a way, I do. But, in another way, I'm worried about Cole learning the truth."

"Are you afraid he'll kill me?"

"No, of course not," she replied. "Cole could never kill you."

Josh was visibly upset. "Kristina, surely you don't think I'd harm Cole! I would never raise a hand against him, nor would I draw a weapon against him."

"You misunderstood me. I know you'd never fight with Cole. But he thinks of you as his best friend, and he loves you like a brother. When he learns you're the man he's been looking for all these years, it might completely destroy your friendship. He might never forgive you for not telling him."

Josh patted her hand. "Try not to worry so much. Cole and I have been friends for almost thirteen years, and he hasn't learned the truth in all that time."

"It will happen," she predicted somberly. "It's inevitable."

"Perhaps," he gave in reluctantly.

By now the sun had made its full descent and darkness had fallen. Lamps were being lit in the distant bunkhouse, and the voices of the ranch hands carried through their open windows. The corraled mustangs, balking at confinement, pranced back and forth, neighing and snorting.

Kristina was ready to hear the remainder of Josh's

story. "What happened after you and the others rode away from Cole's home?" she asked.

"We deserted," he remarked flatly. "I didn't want to desert, but I didn't think I had any choice in the matter. An innocent woman had been raped and murdered. As Norman very cunningly pointed out, the Union wouldn't believe that I wasn't involved. Now I realize I should have returned to Captain Dickerson and reported what had happened. He was an impartial man, and he probably would have believed me. But, at the time, I still thought like a slave. I didn't think the captain or the Army would accept my story.

"I was scared, so I ran! The four of us managed to make it to California, where I went my own way. I ended up in San Francisco. I changed my name to Josh Chandler, and got a job tending bar in a gambling casino."

"What was your name before you changed it?"

A bitter frown creased his brow. "Moses," he mumbled derisively. "God, how I hated that name! That was it—slaves didn't have last names."

"Why did you choose Josh Chandler?"

"I liked the sound of it."

"So do I," she murmured.

"While I was working at the casino, I became friends with a gambler called Blackie. He was an accurate shot, and a fast draw. I was impressed, and when he offered to teach me to use a handgun, I eagerly accepted. I was still working at the casino when the war ended. One night, Blackie was playing cards with a man who accused him of cheating. Blackie never cheated at cards, he was too damned good. The man left the casino, and waited for Blackie to leave. He shot him down in cold blood. I revenged Blackie, hunted the man down, and killed him.

Afterward I had to get out of town—the man had a lot of friends as sneaky as he, and I was liable to get shot in the back.

"I decided to head for Texas. I was on my way to San Antonio when I came across three men holding Cole at gunpoint. They were planning to steal his horse. I didn't recognize Cole. He was three years older, and also, I had only seen him that one time and I hadn't looked at him all that closely.

"I intervened and saved Cole from the robbers. When Cole learned that I was looking for work, he invited me to ride to Drake's with him. He was sure Drake would give me a job. He told me his name, but I still didn't place him. Barton is a common name, and I never knew Mrs. Barton's son was called Cole. Cole and I had already become friends before he told me what had happened to his mother and that he was determined to track down her killers—especially the one with the branded chest."

Josh rose, crossed the porch, and pitched his cigarette over the banister. He stood still for a moment, immersed in thought, then turned and faced Kristina.

"I should have told Cole the truth right from the beginning. I'm not sure why I didn't. I can think of some reasons, none of them flattering: fear of losing his friendship? Shame, because I was involved in his mother's death? Guilt, because I didn't save her?" Josh shrugged his shoulders. "I'm not sure which one it was—probably all three."

He returned to the glider. "Cole wanted to become expert with a gun, so I began teaching him everything Blackie had taught me. I used to wonder if I was training my future executioner. The thought wasn't a pleasant one, but it didn't dissuade me. I kept on teaching Cole until he eventually surpassed me."

"Josh, I already know that you, Cole, and Drake rounded up longhorns, which led to Drake's improving his ranch and to you building the Lazy-J. I also know Cole put his money away and became a bounty hunter." She turned angry eyes to Josh, and her tone sharpened. "Why did you let him do it? Why did you let Cole risk his life searching for his mother's killers?"

Josh groaned remorsefully. "I kept hoping he'd give up his search. Furthermore, as time passed, I became more and more entangled in my deceit. I was trapped, and I didn't know how to free myself."

Kristina could put herself in his place. "I understand," she said softly, her anger fading. "When I was pretending to be Samantha, I became entangled in a deceit of my own."

"But yours wasn't deliberate," he remarked. "I can't say the same for myself."

She fully sympathized with Josh. "I wish I knew what you should do. Should you tell Cole who you really are, or should you continue to guard your secret and hope that he never finds out?"

"Don't worry about it, Kristina."

"Don't worry!" she exclaimed desperately. "How can I help but worry? Two nights ago I promised Cole I wouldn't keep any secrets from him. Now I'm already breaking that promise. If he finds out I knew about you, and didn't tell him, he might leave me forever!"

"He won't leave you. You're carrying his child."

"He might be too angry to care about me or the baby."

"You don't really believe that," he said gently.

"No, I suppose not," she relented. "He would still care about the baby."

"He'd also care about you," Josh replied, taking her hand and squeezing it encouragingly.

She gave him a smile, rose, and said firmly, "I'll make a decision tonight. Tomorrow, I'll tell you what I think you should do. You aren't obligated to take my advice, but I do hope you'll seriously consider it."

"I will," he promised. "You have my word."

"Good night, Josh. I'll see you in the morning." She moved away.

"Kristina," he called.

She paused at the door and faced him. "Yes?"

"Just for the record, I couldn't love Cole more if he were my own brother."

"I know," she replied wistfully. She went inside, leaving Josh alone with his turbulent thoughts.

Hours later, Josh was in the study sitting at his desk going over his ledgers. He knew he wouldn't be able to sleep, so he had decided to take care of some paperwork. The windows were open, admitting the night's cool breeze. The sound of an approaching wagon carried into the quiet room.

Wondering who was calling so late, he closed his books, left the study and moved to the front door.

On the porch, he watched as Billy Stockton pulled the two-horse team to a halt. Suddenly, Josh remembered Cole's telling him that the young drover would deliver Kristina's belongings, but Stockton's reason for being at the house crossed Josh's mind but fleetingly, for the woman accompanying Billy had his full attention.

Alighting, Billy hastened around the buckboard

and helped Alisa down. She approached Josh hesitantly. She wished she could read his thoughts, but, as always, his expression was inscrutable.

Josh was well-practiced at keeping his feelings hidden. He had learned early in life to mask his emotions. Now he was outwardly composed, though inwardly he was apprehensive. His gaze traveled surreptitiously over Alisa, and the young woman's beauty shook him to the core.

Her long black tresses were unbound, and the straight, silky mane fell to her waist. She was wearing a summer gown, which though modestly cut, complemented her ripe, supple curves. She was such a vision of loveliness that it was difficult for Josh to keep his feelings concealed. He longed to sweep her into his arms and kiss her passionately . . . desperately!

Alisa's resolution hadn't faltered. She was still determined to take a stand with Josh and demand that he express his feelings. If he wasn't romantically attracted to her, then she would bow gracefully out of his life and never bother him again. Believing Raymond Lewis to be in love with her, she had firmly decided that if Josh rejected her love, she would marry Raymond. She wouldn't, however, become Raymond's wife until she was thoroughly convinced about Josh.

Josh tore his gaze from Alisa and looked over at Billy, who was removing Kristina's suitcase and Alisa's carpetbag from the wagon.

Josh opened the door and gestured Billy inside. "Put the luggage in the foyer, then after you tend to the horses, go to the bunkhouse and tell my foreman to find you a place to sleep. Also, if you're hungry, he can fix you some grub."

Billy carried the luggage into the house, then,

anxious to get something to eat and then go to bed, he left quickly.

Josh and Alisa stood in the foyer, staring at each other as though they were strangers.

Josh was the first to speak. "Why did you come here with Billy? Is everything all right at home?"

"Everything is fine," she replied tersely.

"Cole's on his way to the Diamond-C. Did you pass him?"

"Yes, he stopped and ate lunch with us."

"Have you had supper? I can awaken Rosa . . ."

"Don't bother," she declined quickly. "I'm not hungry. But I would like a sherry."

He escorted her to his study, where he poured a brandy for himself and a sherry for Alisa.

Accepting her drink, Alisa sat on the sofa, patting the cushion next to her. "Josh, please join me."

He did so with reservations. Her nearness was more intoxicating than the liquor he held in his hand. He put the glass to his lips and took a long, deep swallow. "Why are you here?" he asked quietly.

"I think you know the reason."

He sighed wretchedly. "Alisa, we've been over this before."

"This will be the last time. I promise." She leaned back against the sofa's high back, took a couple of swallows of sherry, then said calmly, "When I saw you at the Diamond-C, I told you that I had my feelings under control, and that I wouldn't pressure you. Well, in part, it's true. My feelings are under control, but something has come up, and I feel that I must confront you one last time."

He studied her quizzically. "What's come up?"

She didn't intend to tell him about Raymond. For now, she planned to keep her possible marriage to Lewis a secret. After all, the man hadn't even proposed yet! She already knew that Autumn Moon, Cole and Josh would oppose the marriage, for they had befriended Kristina. Also, she was sure they believed that Raymond had tried to rape and kill Kristina. They had all foolishly fallen prey to Kristina's devious maneuvers. Alisa wanted to warn them, to try to make them understand that Kristina was a calculating liar, but she knew her efforts would be a waste of time. They had already decided to believe Kristina's story over Raymond's.

"What's come up?" Josh asked again, his tone impatient.

"It doesn't matter," she answered. "It's something I'm not free to discuss, at least not yet."

"All right," Josh conceded. "Just tell me what you came here to say."

She put her glass on the coffee table, turned to Josh, and gazed unwaveringly into his eyes. "I believe that you desire me, but for some reason you are keeping your feelings in check. Is it because of my age, or is it my Comanche blood?"

Placing his glass beside hers, he got up abruptly, walked to the center of the room, then wheeled about to face her. "Alisa, I have no romantic notions toward you. I love you like a sister."

"No, you don't!" she declared firmly. Rising, she moved to stand before him. "That night at the stable, when I kissed you, your response wasn't brotherly!"

"That was three years ago," he groaned.

"What does time have to do with it?" Her voice was sharp, demanding.

Controlling the need to hold her close, he asked miserably, "What do you want from me?"

"The truth!" she remarked. "Why do you keep rejecting my love?"

"I already told you why," he mumbled.

Alisa's temper flared. "Damn you, Josh! I'm not leaving this room until I get an honest answer!"

Earlier, Josh had lit only the lamp on his desk, and the room was dim, the solitary light flickering softly. Its golden glow fell across Alisa's face, illuminating her features. Her face had mellowed as she awaited his reply. He knew, however, that her expression was capable of turning cold . . . unfeeling. He had seen her bestow that look many times upon her parents, breaking their gentle hearts beyond repair.

If he were to tell her that he was born a slave, would she then turn that icy gaze upon him? He knew how determined she was to marry a rich aristocrat, and he also knew how deeply she despised her mixed blood. Would she still love him if she knew he was not truly an aristocrat but an ex-slave? Would she find his mixed blood as distasteful as she found her own? Josh was certain that "yes" would be the answer to all the questions.

Although he was tempted to confess everything and end her infatuation once and for all, he knew he couldn't do it. If he should decide to make a full confession, he had to make it first to Cole. Then, and only then, would he be free to tell others. He didn't want Cole to learn the truth through someone else—it was his place to tell him.

Alisa, having no inkling of Josh's thoughts, suddenly grasped his arm and asked anxiously, "Are you in love with another woman?"

When he didn't answer, she persisted, "Tell me!"

Still, he offered no reply.

"Who is she?" Alisa asked.

He frowned testily. "Alisa, please!"

"Are you going to marry her?"

All things considered, Josh decided to let her think that he loved another. This way, she would stop pursuing him, find a man who could love her freely, get married, and start a new life.

He didn't answer her questions, for he knew she'd mistake his silence as confirmation. Changing the subject brusquely, he said, "I'll show you to your room. I'm sure you're tired."

Placing a hand on her elbow, he guided her from the study. As they crossed the foyer, he picked up her bag, then led her up the stairs. He took her to a guest room, opened the door, and stepped back for her to enter.

Before she could attempt to detain him, he hastened down the stairs and headed back to his study.

In the past, Josh had overcome a lot of hardships and battled overwhelming odds. Rejecting Alisa, however, was the hardest thing he had ever done. Although he was familiar with her bitterness and her selfishness he still loved her very much. He understood her feelings, for he also suffered inside. Unlike Alisa, though, Josh had learned to live with his bitterness. He hoped that someday Alisa would do the same.

Kristina awoke early, the sun was barely cresting the horizon. She'd spent a restive night, for she had been disturbed with worrisome dreams.

She wondered if Josh was still asleep. Probably not, since activities at the Lazy-J began at sunrise, and Josh always worked alongside his wranglers.

Deciding to talk to him during breakfast, she got out of bed. A few minutes later, she was dressed and ready to leave.

She hurried down the stairs, and as she passed through the foyer, she missed seeing her suitcase. She went straight to the dining room, but not finding Josh, she moved on to the kitchen. Rosa was at the stove, starting breakfast.

"Josh hasn't come down yet?" Kristina asked, stepping to Lucky. The pup's tail was wagging vigorously.

"The *patrón* is in the study," Rosa answered. She turned and looked at Kristina, who was now kneeling beside the beagle, petting him affectionately.

"Señorita . . ." the woman began, her tone tinged with concern. "I am worried about the *patrón*. I think he did not go to bed last night. Also, I think maybe he has been drinking very much."

"I'll talk to him," Kristina replied. She left the kitchen and hastened to the study. The door was closed, and she knocked softly. "Josh, may I come in?" she called.

"Yes, please do," he answered. His voice sounded fatigued.

She went inside, and leaving the door open, she crossed the room. Josh was seated at his desk, but pushing back his chair, he rose and stepped to Kristina.

She gazed caringly up into his tired face. His eyes were bloodshot, his hair mussed, and he needed a shave. "Have you been awake all night?" she asked.

"I got a couple of hours sleep on the sofa." He managed a wry smile. "Did you sleep well?"

"No, I didn't."

"Did you make a decision?"

"Yes," she murmured.

He moved to the desk, leaned back against it, and folded his arms across his chest. "You've decided I should be totally honest with Cole, haven't you?"

"Yes, I have." Her eyes pleaded with his. "Josh,

you must tell him the truth! If he were to find out some other way—!"

"I understand," he replied, sighing deeply.

"Cole will believe you. He knows you aren't capable of rape and murder."

"All right," he conceded reluctantly. "I'll tell Cole everything." A nervous tremor coursed through him. "It won't be easy, but somehow I'll find the courage." He grinned. "I just hope he doesn't shoot first then ask questions later."

"He won't," she assured him, returning his smile.

Josh suddenly changed the subject. "Did you see your suitcase in the foyer?"

She told him she hadn't.

"Billy and Alisa delivered it late last night."

"Alisa is here?" she exclaimed. "How long is she planning to stay?"

"Billy will be leaving this morning, and I'm sure she'll leave with him."

Kristina was puzzled. "Why is she leaving so soon?"

It was a long moment before Josh answered, then deciding to confide in Kristina, he replied, "She came here hoping I would ask her to marry me. You see, Alisa is in love with me."

"Yes, I know."

He was visibly startled.

"Drake was aware of Alisa's feelings. He always hoped that you would fall in love with her."

"I do love her," he said. His declaration sounded hollow . . . hopeless.

"Why haven't you told her how you feel?"

"Alisa loves the man she thinks I am—a rich aristocrat. She wouldn't be so quick to love me if she knew that I was once a slave. Also, considering how much she despises her own mixed blood, how do you think she'd feel about mine?"

"Maybe you're misjudging her," Kristina replied, but with little conviction.

"I know Alisa very well, and, believe me, she wouldn't marry an ex-slave. If my heritage became public, many people would consider me inferior. If Alisa was my wife, she would fall from social grace with me. And belonging to the upper crust means more to Alisa than anything else—including love."

Josh shrugged his shoulders, and the gesture was so hopeless that it went straight to Kristina's heart. "I'm resigned to never having Alisa. But I'll always love her . . . regardless."

Kristina moved to Josh, and when he opened his arms, she went into his embrace.

He held her close, his grip clinging desperately. "Kristina . . . " he declared fervently. "You mean the world to me. I thank God for you. And I promise I'll tell Cole everything."

She tightened her arms about his neck. They embraced firmly, their friendship secure and filled with warmth.

Alisa had also risen early, and had gone downstairs to see Josh. Detecting voices in the study, she headed in that direction. The door had been wide open, and the sight of Kristina in Josh's embrace had rendered Alisa motionless. Shocked, she had listened with disbelief.

"Kristina," she had heard Josh say, "you mean the world to me. I thank God for you. And I promise I'll tell Cole everything."

When Kristina wrapped her arms tightly about Josh's neck, Alisa had whirled about and raced down the hall and outside.

Now, as she walked swiftly toward the bunkhouse, she was raging inwardly. Kristina was the woman Josh loved! Damn Kristina Parker! Wasn't Cole enough, did she have to entrap Josh, too? Between the two men, she had obviously chosen Josh—otherwise, why had he promised to tell Cole everything? Oh, Raymond was right about Miss Parker! She was indeed calculating and devious!

Reaching the bunkhouse, Alisa found Billy and told him to hitch up the buckboard, for they were leaving immediately. Then, returning to the house, she slipped up to her room, packed her bag, went to the window and watched for Billy's arrival. When the buckboard came into sight, she hurried downstairs and outside.

Billy was waiting, and as she climbed onto the wagon seat, she told him to drive away as quickly as possible. She knew Josh would worry that she had left without saying good-bye. Let him worry! She didn't care!

Chapter Twenty-Four

Alisa and Billy spent the night in Sandy Creek, arriving at the Diamond-C shortly before noon. Cole, leaving the house as their buckboard rolled to a stop, hurried down the porch steps and helped Alisa from the wagon.

"I didn't expect you back so soon," he said.

Alisa scowled harshly. "I couldn't leave the Lazy-J fast enough."

Cole was puzzled. "I don't understand. Did something happen?"

"Yes, something happened!" she said sharply. "Let's go inside the house. I need to talk to you."

"I was on my way to the stables to get my horse. I completed my business with Samantha, and I'm leaving for the Lazy-J."

"Well . . ." Alisa began testily, "before you leave, you had better hear what I have to say! It concerns Kristina Parker."

Worried, Cole demanded, "Kristina's all right, isn't she?"

"She's fine," Alisa replied, tugging at Cole's arm. "Let's go into the house."

He followed her to the study. Alisa went to the

liquor cabinet and poured sherry for herself and brandy for Cole.

"I don't want a drink, but thanks anyway," Cole said.

She handed him the brandy, remarking, "Here, take it. When you hear what I have to say, you'll need it."

He accepted the drink, then said impatiently, "Alisa, what's bothering you?"

She took a sip of sherry, regarded Cole closely, and asked, "Are you in love with Kristina?"

"Yes, I am," he answered unhesitantly. "We plan to marry as soon as possible."

Alisa finished her sherry and returned her glass to the liquor cabinet. Whirling around to face Cole, she declared bluntly, "Kristina and Josh are lovers!"

At first Cole stared at her as though she were out of her mind, then, he remarked, "That's ridiculous. Kristina and Josh are only friends."

"Friends?" Alisa questioned, smirking. "Cole, I saw them embracing."

"I'm sure it was simply an embrace between friends."

"I know a friendly embrace when I see one!" Alisa argued. "They were clinging to each other! Josh told her that she meant the world to him. He then said he was going to tell you everything."

Alisa's accusation was staggering, and, for a moment, Cole was too stunned to reply. Suddenly needing the brandy, he placed the glass to his lips and took a generous swallow. "What did Josh mean—he'd tell me everything?" he asked, his voice strained.

Alisa shrugged. "I'm not sure. At this point, I stopped watching them and left the house. They were in Josh's study. The door was open, and I came upon them accidentally. I didn't purposely spy on

298

them, nor did I intentionally eavesdrop."

She poured another glass of sherry. "I'm sure Josh plans to tell you that he loves Kristina. What else could he have meant when he said he was going to tell you everything?"

Cole quickly shook his suspicions. Alisa was talking nonsense. Kristina loved him completely, and Josh was a true friend. He trusted them both.

"Alisa . . ." he began calmly, "I'm sure you misconstrued what you saw and heard."

Her patience flared. "Cole, don't be a fool! Kristina will do anything for money, and she doesn't care who she hurts. She chose Josh over you because she thinks he's richer than you are!"

Cole drank his brandy, then put down the glass. He eyed Alisa sternly. "Kristina is the woman I love, and I'll not tolerate you slandering her character. And Josh is my friend, he would never double-cross me."

Alisa laughed bitterly. "Cole Barton, you're a fool!"

"I don't think so!" he retorted. "And I refuse to listen to your accusations. The subject is closed!"

"Very well, Cole," she conceded. "In time you'll learn the truth. When that happens, just remember I tried to warn you."

Cole's temper flared. "Damn it, Alisa!"

She held up a warding hand, as though she could block his anger. "All right, Cole," she said. "Have it your way. The subject is closed."

Letting the matter rest, he told her, "I bought the Diamond-C from Samantha. Mr. Cullen is handling the final paperwork. When Samantha receives her full payment, she'll give you and Autumn Moon your fair share."

"When will she receive the money?"

"In the morning. She's also leaving on the noon stage."

Alisa smiled. "I'll be glad to see the last of her."

Cole understood, and didn't blame Alisa for feeling the way she did. He headed toward the door, saying, "I'll be back in a few days, and Kristina will be with me." He paused, turned to Alisa, and said sincerely, "You're welcome to live here as long as you want. The Diamond-C is your home."

"I appreciate your offer, but I think I'll be getting married in the near future."

Cole was astounded. "Married! I didn't know there was a special man in your life."

"Well, there is," she answered, a defiant lift to her chin.

"Who is he?"

She smiled secretly. "I'll tell you when the time is right."

Cole was tempted to ask more questions, but deciding it wasn't really his business, he let the matter drop. He bid her a quick good-bye and left.

Samantha, watching from her bedroom window, saw Alisa arrive, and was also aware of Cole's departure. She was eager to talk to Autumn Moon and Alisa, but still, she remained in her room. She wanted to give Cole time to be miles away, otherwise, they might send someone to catch up to him and bring him back. Although Samantha knew Cole couldn't force her to give Autumn Moon and Alisa money from the sale of the Diamond-C, she preferred nonetheless to avoid a confrontation with him. Though she found Cole strikingly handsome and savagely virile, all the same, he was threatening, and she didn't want him to know that she was about to go

300

against his and Drake's wishes. Cole believed that she planned to share her inheritance with Autumn Moon and Alisa, and she hadn't said anything to make him think otherwise. The law was on her side, and she had the legal right to keep all the money. Nevertheless, she had decided to steer away from an altercation with him.

Remaining in her room, Samantha passed several hours with a book. Deciding Cole had been gone long enough, she set out to find Autumn Moon and Alisa. She checked the kitchen first and was pleased to find mother and daughter sitting at the table, drinking coffee.

Samantha, smiling like the proverbial cat who had swallowed the canary, remarked, "I'm glad to find you two together. I have something to tell you."

Autumn Moon gestured to an empty chair. "Sit down and I'll bring you a cup of coffee."

"Let her get her own coffee." Alisa mumbled hatefully.

"Alisa, please . . ." Autumn Moon began.

"I don't want coffee," Samantha spoke up, as she cast her sister a look filled with contempt. "What I have to say will take only a minute. As you know, Bernard and I are leaving tomorrow. I'm sure you two expect me to give you a share of my inheritance before I leave. Well, I'm here to inform you that you'll not get one red cent."

Alisa bounded to her feet in a rage. "Why, you selfish bitch, how dare you refuse us our rightful share!"

"Rightful?" Samantha returned smugly. "You and your mother have no rights! Autumn Moon was never married to my father, and you are his half-breed bastard! The law doesn't recognize either of you as Drake's legal kin!"

"You're lying!" Alisa yelled. "Papa's will stipulates—"

Samantha interrupted, "His will stipulates nothing! It was merely his wish that I give you and your mother a share of the Diamond-C. If you don't believe me, you can ask Mr. Cullen."

"I will!" Alisa replied angrily.

Samantha turned to Autumn Moon and was surprised to find the woman undisturbed. She had just lost a fortune, one would think she'd be terribly upset. "You don't seem at all bothered," Samantha remarked.

"Money isn't as important to me as it is to my daughter."

"Try living without it!" Samantha retorted.

"Cole will take care of Alisa and me."

"I don't want Cole to take care of me!" Alisa cut in. "I refuse to be dependent on his charity!" She glared at Samantha. "Drake was also my father, and I demand that you give me my fair share!"

She laughed. "You can demand all you want, but you'll not get a penny."

"We'll see about that! I'm going to ride into town and talk to Mr. Cullen."

"As you wish," Samantha replied, smiling as she waved her toward the door.

"You both disgust me!" Autumn Moon spoke up, pushing back her chair and rising. "You were Drake's daughters, and he loved you both. Neither of you even care that he's dead, all you care about is his money."

"That isn't true!" Alisa replied. "I loved Papa! But I have a right to my inheritance!" She stormed out of the kitchen and headed to her room to change into riding clothes.

Autumn Moon returned to her chair, heaved a deep

sigh, then said to Samantha, "I'm almost glad your father didn't live to see you. Your selfishness and wicked ways would have broken his heart."

"Surely you don't think I care," was Samantha's riposte as she left the room.

The sun had set, and darkness was cloaking the town as Alisa led her horse down the main street. She was on her way to the Branding Iron, and although she was anxious to see Raymond, her steps were nonetheless sluggish. She moved lethargically, as though putting one foot in front of the other was a tiresome effort. Her spirits were crushed, and she was finding it difficult to hold her tears in check. But Alisa Carlson was not one to cry easily. She was determined to overcome her present situation. She believed firmly that Raymond Lewis was her salvation, that through him, she'd gain the riches she craved so desperately.

A complacent smile touched her lips as she envisioned herself visiting Philadelphia as Mrs. Raymond Lewis. On, wouldn't that irritate Samantha! She'd get the last laugh on her sister!

Alisa's somber mood had lifted considerably by the time she reached the Branding Iron. Everything would work out splendidly. She might have lost her father's inheritance, but she still had Raymond.

She tied her horse to the hitching rail, then eyed the Branding Iron with misgivings. She had never been in a saloon before and was wary about entering. She was, however, eager to see Raymond, so putting her apprehensions aside, she pushed open the swinging doors.

The establishment was crowded, and as Alisa stepped inside, her presence startled the customers.

The men standing at the bar turned to gape at her, and the ones seated at tables stared with disbelief. A lady walking into a saloon was astounding, especially unescorted.

Raymond had three prostitutes working for him, and they were in the crowd soliciting patrons. The sight of Alisa rendered them temporarily speechless, and turning away from their prospective customers, they watched as the beautiful young woman moved to speak to the bartender.

Norman and his two comrades were at the back of the room, and Norman rushed upstairs to Raymond's private quarters.

Meanwhile, pausing at the bar, Alisa asked, "Is Mr. Lewis here?"

The bartender hadn't fully recovered from her presence, and he answered hesitantly, "Yes . . . yes, ma'am. He's . . . he's here."

At that moment, Raymond appeared at the top of the stairs. Seeing Alisa, he sent Norman to get her, and the henchman escorted her up the stairs, and to Raymond's quarters. Norman then left, closing the door behind him.

Going to her side, Raymond took her hands into his, asking anxiously, "Darling, why are you here? Is anything wrong?"

"Oh, Raymond, hold me!" she pleaded, flinging herself into his arms. "Hold me close!"

He embraced her tightly, and her supple curves pressed against him aroused his passion. With extreme difficulty, he kept himself under control. Damn! He wanted this lovely woman, and he was tired of waiting! If she didn't succumb soon, he'd take her without her permission! She might claim rape, but he'd deny any such thing. If necessary, he'd have his men swear to the sheriff that she had also spread her favors to them.

Feigning tenderness, he quizzed her gently. "Alisa, darling, what happened?"

She moved out of his embrace, drew a long breath, then told him what Samantha had done. "I just came from seeing Mr. Cullen," she completed, "and he told me that Samantha isn't bound by Papa's wishes. She can keep all the money, and there's nothing my mother and I can do to stop her."

"Barton bought the Diamond-C?" Raymond exclaimed.

His response surprised Alisa. Didn't he understand why she was distraught? "Yes, Cole bought the ranch. But, Raymond, it's not who bought the Diamond-C that bothers me. I'm upset because Samantha's keeping all the money."

He turned away from Alisa, and, fuming, he began to pace the room. *Damn it, he had planned to buy the Diamond-C!* He cursed himself for not acting sooner. But then he hadn't thought Samantha would find a buyer so quickly.

Well, there are other ranches, he thought, trying to appease himself. He'd find another one, maybe even one larger and more prosperous than the Diamond-C. Suddenly, remembering Alisa, he stopped his pacing and looked at her. She was watching him uncertainly. She had come here expecting his sympathy, and he had been too perturbed to give it to her. A calculating gleam came to his eyes. Alisa was upset, vulnerable, and was obviously hoping he'd take away all her troubles. If she had his money, she wouldn't need her father's. Ah, yes, she thought he was the answer to her prayers! Raymond gloated inwardly. This dark beauty would be in his bed within minutes. She was ripe and ready to be picked!

Moving to stand before her, he masked his true

emotions and said contritely, "Darling, forgive me for acting as though I'm not concerned. Believe me, I'm very concerned. But, you see, I had planned to buy the Diamond-C from Samantha, then give it to you as a gift." There, he thought, that will make her putty in my hands!

Alisa was touched. "Raymond, I don't know what to say! You're . . . you're so wonderful, and I've never known a man so kind and generous."

He drew her into his arms and kissed her. Leaning into his embrace, Alisa waited anxiously for his lips to set fire to her passion. She waited in vain, however, for his kiss didn't ignite her desire. As he released her, she gave an inward, defeated sigh. When she was John's lover, he had also failed to stir her deepest passion. She wondered at her coldness, but as the memory of Josh's kiss flashed across her mind, she knew it wasn't so. Although it happened three years ago, she could still remember it as though it were yesterday. His kiss had set her passion ablaze. She quickly erased the memory. Josh would never be hers, he was in love with Kristina. She must forget him. Raymond Lewis was her future, and although he didn't stir her desires, he was her salvation, her only hope. She would marry him, and try to make him a good wife. Perhaps, in time, she'd even fall in love with him. Regardless, his money and social standing would guarantee happiness.

As Alisa was considering her future, Raymond's eyes were traveling over her with lustful intent. She was exceptionally pretty in her western-style riding clothes. Her black, divided skirt clung seductively to her rounded hips, and the matching blouse, trimmed with gold braid, emphasized the fullness of her breasts. Her dark tresses tumbled past her shoulders and down to her waist in soft, silky waves. She was a beautiful vision, and Raymond could hardly wait to relish her completely.

"Would you like a glass of sherry?" he asked.

"Yes, please," she replied. As he went to the liquor cart, she glanced curiously about the room. The decor was far from elaborate, and she wondered why Raymond was content to live in such drab surroundings. After all, he was used to grandeur. The sofa and two chairs were showing signs of wear, and the tables were scratched and chipped in places. The drapes and rug had once been a royal blue, but time had turned the rug threadbare and the sun had faded the drapes.

Raymond returned with Alisa's sherry. He read her thoughts with ease. "I plan to have my quarters completely redone. This decor is tasteless and dreary." He handed her the filled glass. "Drink it all, darling. It'll make you feel better."

She smiled. "Just being with you makes me feel much better. You're very good for me."

He waited until she finished her sherry, then taking the empty glass, he placed it on the coffee table. He took her into his arms, holding her close. Impatient, and eager to bed her, he played his trump card—the one he was sure would win her full cooperation.

"Alisa, my darling, will you marry me?"

"Yes, Raymond," she answered unhesitantly.

He kissed her deeply, passionately. "We'll be married in Philadelphia. I want my family to meet you and to be at our wedding."

"Philadelphia? When will we leave?" She didn't want to wait, but she could understand his feelings.

"Next month," he replied.

She wrapped her arms about his neck and clung to him tightly. "Oh, Raymond, you have made me so happy!"

As he returned her embrace, he was crowing inwardly. In his opinion, she was gullible and simple-minded. The silly chit actually believed he'd take her to Philadelphia, introduce her to his family, then marry her!

He placed his lips close to her ear, whispering with feigned emotion, "Alisa, my precious darling, I can't wait for our wedding night. Please make love to me. I want you so powerfully, so desperately. I love you so much."

Although she didn't share his passionate fervor, she was indeed fond of him, and she hadn't the heart to turn him away. "Yes, Raymond, I'll make love to you."

She didn't see his cunning grin as he swept her into his arms.

He carried her into his bedroom and laid her on the large feather mattress. As he started to lay beside her, she sat up and said softly, "Before we go any further, there's something I must tell you."

The postponement angered him, and he cursed her inwardly.

Hoping her confession wouldn't destroy his love, she remarked in a shaky voice, "I'm not a virgin. In St. Louis, I became involved with—"

He interrupted strongly, "Your past isn't important. Only the present and the future matter." Hell! He didn't give a damn how many lovers she'd had! He just wanted her to spread her legs for him!

Alisa smiled warmly. "Raymond, you're such a wonderful man. And I promise I'll make you a good wife." She held out her arms to him, "Come to me, darling."

As Lewis went into her embrace, she swore to herself that she would keep her promise. Despite her undying love for Josh Chandler, she'd be a perfect wife to Raymond. It was no more than Raymond Lewis deserved.

Raymond was snoring loudly when Alisa left the bed. Her clothes were scattered on the floor, and she picked them up and carried them into the sitting room. She dressed quickly, then going to the liquor cart, she poured a glass of sherry.

Her hand trembled somewhat as she lifted the glass to her lips. She took a liberal swallow, for she needed the wine's soothing effect. Tears smarted her eyes, but she fought them back. As her thoughts went to Raymond, a shudder ran through her. Making love to him had been a nightmare! His caresses had been rough, almost brutal in their intensity. Her flesh still hurt, and she knew by tomorrow, bruises would attest to his brutality. Penetration had been worse than the foreplay, for he had taken her fiercely. Afterward he had apologized for his cruelty, assuring her that it wouldn't happen again.

Alisa drank the remainder of her sherry, then headed toward the door. Her high opinion of Raymond was beginning to vanish. She wondered if he was really as compassionate as she had believed.

Leaving the room, she decided to avoid the saloon and use the rear stairway. Darting down the narrow hall, she passed the rooms belonging to the prostitutes. Moans and grunts of passion sounded behind the closed doors.

Descending the back stairs quickly, she hurried around the building and to her horse. Mounting, she turned the animal about and headed out of town.

She was halfway home when her desperate need for money and social standing overruled her better judgment and convinced her that Raymond's cruelty was a one-time occurrence. The next time they made love, he'd most certainly be a considerate, compassionate partner.

Alisa saw no reason to break her engagement. Everything would work out fine, she was sure it would. Soon, she'd be Mrs. Raymond Lewis, then no one would ever look down on her again.

Chapter Twenty-Five

Kristina studied Josh thoughtfully as he turned the two-horse team onto the lane leading up to the house. He met her gaze and smiled, then looked away. His full attention seemed to focus on driving the buggy. Kristina knew he was worried about facing Cole. Since the day she had learned the truth, Josh had appeared cheerful and unconcerned, but Kristina was certain that it was merely a facade. Although Kristina was sure Cole would believe in Josh's innocence, she nonetheless knew he would be very angry. He would remember all the years he had searched for the man with the branded R's—believing him to be his mother's murderer—when all along the man he was pursuing was his best friend.

She turned her thoughts to more pleasant matters. It was a beautiful sunny day, and she and Josh were returning home from a picnic. Rosa had fixed them a basket-lunch, and the fare had been delicious. They had taken Lucky with them, and the pup had enjoyed romping in the green meadow where they had stopped to eat.

Kristina suddenly became aware of a tautness in Josh. He was sitting rigidly, and his hands were gripping the reins tightly.

"Josh, what's wrong?" she asked.

He nodded toward the horse tied in front of the house. "That's Cole's Appaloosa."

A bright smile shone on her face. "Cole's back!" she exclaimed joyfully.

"I wasn't expecting him back so soon," Josh remarked, his voice laced with anxiety.

Her exuberance mellowed. Cole's return might not be pleasant for Josh. She swallowed a little nervously, patted his hand, and said with all the encouragement she could muster, "Cole will understand. He loves you, Josh. He'll forgive you, I just know he will."

Chandler smiled wanly. "Maybe, but then he might hate me for the rest of his life. And I sure as hell wouldn't blame him."

Cole had arrived only minutes before. Rosa was in her room taking a nap, and finding no one downstairs, Cole had gone to Kristina's room, hoping to find her there. He had been disappointed to find it unoccupied and was about to leave when he heard a buggy approaching the house. Going to the open window, he watched as Josh drew the horse to a halt. Eager to take Kristina into his arms, Cole started to turn away and rush downstairs, but the sudden sight of Josh placing an arm about Kristina's shoulders and drawing her close, rendered Cole riveted. He looked on with frozen disbelief. Their voices carried to the window.

"Kristina," Josh was saying, "God, how I dread facing Cole!"

She hugged him tightly, then moving out of his embrace, she asked, "Do you want me to be with you when you tell him? Would my presence make it easier for you?"

He forced a chuckle. "Well, he'd be less apt to shoot me."

She knew he was merely trying to lighten a grave situation, and she replied with a smile, "He'll be angry, but he won't shoot you."

Josh slipped his hand into hers, and lifting it to his lips, he kissed it softly. "Kristina, what would I do without you?" He leaned closer to her, and whispered too quietly for Cole to hear, "You're a good friend, and you mean a lot to me."

When she responded by kissing his cheek, the gesture pierced Cole's heart. Had Alisa been right—were Josh and Kristina lovers?

As Cole remained at the window, too shocked to turn away, Josh was telling Kristina that he had to go into town on business.

"I'll be back before dusk," he explained. "After dinner, I'll tell Cole everything."

She squeezed his hand affectionately, then got out of the buggy. She reached inside and picked up the puppy. "You never answered my question. Do you want me to be with you when you talk to him?"

He thought a moment, then answered, "No, I'll face him alone." He managed a carefree shrug, but he was obviously disturbed. "I'm not sure how Cole will react, but I do know he's gonna be madder than hell. There's no reason for you to be a witness to such an unpleasant scene."

"But, Josh, you might need my support."

"Just give me your love, honey, that's all I need."

"You have my love, Josh." She lowered her voice, and her next words eluded Cole. "You're my dearest friend."

He lifted the reins and slapped them against the

team. As the buggy moved away, he said over his shoulder, "I'll see you later."

As Kristina watched Josh's departure, Cole, inside her bedroom, was trying to come to grips with what he had seen and heard. Josh's last remark flashed across his mind. "Just give me your love, honey, that's all I need." Kristina's response had been shattering. "You have my love, Josh."

Cole turned away from the window, and the expression in his eyes was oddly vacant, a sodden dullness had descended, falling over his emotions like a heavy blanket. His heart felt hollow and devoid of feeling. He went numb, and as he headed slowly toward the door, his mind was blank. At the moment, Kristina's and Josh's disloyalty was more than he could grasp. His anger, simmering deeply within him, didn't surface.

Kristina left Lucky on the porch and went into the house. She was anxious to see Cole, and was pleased to find him coming slowly down the stairway. She paused in the foyer, and as her gaze swept over his tall frame, the mere sight of him sent her pulse racing. She was struck anew with deep emotions, for she loved Cole Barton from the depth of her heart. She took a step forward to rush into his arms, but she suddenly sensed a strange coldness about him that held her back.

Cole stopped halfway down the steps as he regarded the woman he loved. Her unfaithfulness was playing havoc with his emotions. Anger, mixed with pain, was coursing through him like a turbulent storm threatening to erupt. He had trusted her, had believed in her love! Alisa had been right—

314

he was a fool!

He controlled his anger, forcing it to remain beneath the surface. This was not the time to confront her. He had to give himself time.

Drawing an inscrutable mask over his feelings, he said calmly, "You need to change into your riding clothes. We're leaving."

"What?" she gasped, surprised.

"I said, we're leaving."

Kristina was totally perplexed. "Cole, is something wrong?"

"What could be wrong?"

Perturbed, she placed her hands on her hips and eyed him testily. "Cole, I refuse to budge until you tell me what's bothering you!"

He descended the remaining steps, then paused in front of her. She looked up into his face, meeting his gaze head-on.

"I'm not going anywhere with you," she argued. "Not until you explain yourself."

"There is no explanation," he replied, his even tone belying his inner turmoil. "I'm just anxious to get back to the Diamond-C."

"We can't leave until Josh returns. He has something very important to talk to you about."

"Oh?" he said, quirking a brow. "Well, whatever it is, I'm sure it can wait."

"It can't wait!" she insisted, her anxiety evident.

Cole considered telling Kristina that he already knew what Josh had to say, and that as far as he was concerned, they could damn well have each other! Playing their game only made him a bigger fool! Why should he insist that she return with him to the Diamond-C? Did he think he could make her love him? Besides, he was sure Josh would come after her, and considering his anger, it was best that his path not cross with Josh's—he might forget their friendship.

It was on Cole's lips to tell Kristina that she could have Josh, but he thought of the baby she was carrying. Could he step aside and let another man raise his child? He knew it was a decision he couldn't make without first giving it a lot of thought.

"I'll go to the stables and saddle your mare while you change clothes," he said, as though she had agreed to their immediate departure.

Kristina's temper exploded. "Damn it, Cole! What in the world is wrong with you?"

"We'll discuss it later," he replied.

She held her ground. "I don't intend to discuss it later!"

Kristina was puzzled to see a note of pleading in his eyes. "Believe me, Kristina, it can wait. I'll tell Rosa to have your belongings sent to the Diamond-C, so pack lightly."

She stamped her foot angrily. "Cole Barton, how dare you clam up on me! I thought you trusted me!" His strange mood had her steaming.

Suddenly, Cole swept her into his arms, his lips branding hers in a kiss so demanding that it stole her breath.

"You're very beautiful when you're angry," he remarked, releasing her. Inwardly, he berated himself for kissing her, but his love for her was more powerful than his pride. He turned on his heel, and walked quickly out of the house. As he headed toward the stables, he curbed the desire coiled within him and managed to still his passion, but the pain of losing Kristina to another man remained.

*   *   *

Entering her room, Kristina slammed the door behind her. She discarded her dress for riding clothes, sat on the bed, and drew on her boots. She tried to make sense out of Cole's mood. Had something happened at the Diamond-C, something terrible? Was his peculiar behavior related perhaps to Samantha?

Kristina went to her carpetbag, and as she filled it to its limit, her anger changed to petulance. She was totally annoyed with Cole, and had every intention of telling him how she felt. She'd not tolerate his moods—not now, not ever!

Finished packing, she picked up the carpetbag and left the room. Her thoughts included Josh as she descended the stairs. Damn Cole for wanting to leave immediately! Josh had finally decided to tell Cole the truth, and now he wouldn't get the chance. She hoped Josh would come to the Diamond-C without delay and tell Cole everything. She was afraid if he kept putting it off, Cole would learn the truth some other way, and, if he did, he might never forgive him.

Rosa appeared at the bottom of the stairs. "Señorita . . ." she began, obviously puzzled, "why are you and Señor Cole leaving so quickly? Señor Cole just came to the kitchen and told me to have your things sent to the Diamond-C. He then told me that you two are leaving. The *patrón* will be disappointed to return and find that you and Señor Cole are gone."

"I don't know why Cole is so anxious to leave," Kristina replied. "Where is he?"

"He said to tell you that he is waiting out front for you."

She hugged Rosa fondly. "I hope I'll see you again soon. Will you give Josh a message for me?"

"*Sí*, of course.

317

"Tell him I think he should come to the Diamond-C and tell Cole everything."

"Everything?" she questioned, confused.

"He'll understand what I mean."

Kristina found Cole waiting on the porch. Her mare was tied at the hitching rail beside the Appaloosa. Lucky was sitting at Cole's feet, but seeing his mistress, he scurried to her side.

Cole took Kristina's carpetbag and attached it behind her saddle. He turned to look at her. "Are you ready?" he asked, holding out an assisting hand.

She picked up the puppy, then with Cole's assistance, she mounted the mare. She watched as he went to his Appaloosa and swung into the saddle.

She kept her horse abreast of his as they galloped away from the house and down the oak-bordered lane. She managed to maintain silence, but, later, when they stopped for the night, Cole would explain himself . . . or else!

Because Lucky was traveling with them, they didn't stop at Sandy Creek to get a room, but instead, made camp. Cole didn't have many provisions packed, but it would be enough for the two of them.

He chose a fertile area, well surrounded by thick foliage. As they pulled up their horses, the sun was setting, its radiance casting a golden glow across the turquoise horizon.

Lucky had fallen asleep in Kristina's arms, and Cole helped her dismount. They had traveled for hours, during which time, Cole's odd behavior had been almost more than Kristina could tolerate. Her patience was frayed, and her temper was about to flare.

Cole wasn't faring any better. His own patience

was straining, and his temper was barely under control. He had been doubled-crossed by his best friend and the woman he loved. He was angry, hurt, and shocked. He had believed in Kristina's love, and would have trusted Josh with his life.

Cole tried to block their betrayal from his mind, and set about bedding down the horses. Kristina watched for a moment, then she gathered twigs for a fire. By the time Cole was finished with the horses, she had a fire burning.

"Do you want something to eat?" he asked. "I have a can of beans—"

"No thanks," she cut in. "I'm not hungry."

He sat across the fire, watching her. The light from the flickering flames shone in his eyes, and Kristina detected a glint of anger shining in their depths.

She stared back at him, her own gaze glazed with fury. She raised her chin defiantly, and sat ramrod straight. She wasn't about to be intimidated, and spoke strongly, "Cole, my patience is at an end. I insist that you tell me what's bothering you. Why are you so angry?"

A cold smile crossed his lips. Kristina Parker was indeed a talented actress. But then, he shouldn't be surprised, she had done a remarkable job impersonating Samantha. She had fooled him completely. But, this time, he wasn't fooled. He was, however, somewhat perplexed. Why was she keeping up a pretense? Why didn't she just tell him she wanted Josh?

"Well?" Kristina asked sharply. "Don't you have anything to say?"

"I have a lot to say," he replied. "But I still need time to think."

Her rage erupted, and leaping to her feet, she declared, "As far as I'm concerned, you can think

319

about it in Hades! I'm leaving! I refuse to remain in your presence one minute longer!"

She moved toward her horse, but he blocked her path. "Where do you think you're going?" he demanded.

"I'm returning to the Lazy-J!" she remarked.

"Over my dead body!" His hard gaze dared her to make one move.

She was about to defy him when a gruff voice sounded from the heavy thicket, "Don't worry, lady, you're gonna be able to step over his dead body, 'cause I'm gonna kill him."

Recognizing the voice, Kristina gasped as she whirled about to see Ned making his way through the bushes. His brother Jimmy followed close behind. Both men were armed with rifles. She instinctively edged closer to Cole.

"I should've killed you two when I had the chance," Cole said, his tone deadly cold. He cursed himself for letting them slip up on him.

"You're gettin' careless, Barton," Ned replied, chuckling. "You should know that men like me and my brother would track you down." He raised his rifle, leveling the barrel at Cole's chest. "Say your prayers, you damned bastard, 'cause you're gonna die!"

Chapter Twenty-Six

Josh drew back on the reins, slowing his palomino to a steady canter. He didn't want the animal to tire, for he was determined to keep traveling until he found Kristina and Cole. Earlier, when he had left the Lazy-J to go into town, he had gotten halfway there before deciding to turn around and head back to the ranch. His business in town could wait. His discussion with Cole was more important! When he returned to find that Cole and Kristina were gone, he was worried that something was seriously wrong. It wasn't like Cole to leave without waiting to see him. Concerned, Josh decided to try to catch up to Kristina and Cole. If trouble was brewing, Cole might need his help.

Now, spotting smoke in the distance, Josh was certain the fire belonged to Kristina and Cole. He had been following their tracks since leaving the Lazy-J. Relieved that he had reached them, he guided his horse toward the campsite. He hadn't gone very far, however, before he sensed something wasn't right. A cold chill pricked the back of his neck, and he reined in cautiously.

Josh had no tangible reason for suspecting

trouble, it was just a feeling. He had learned years ago to trust his intuition, and, dismounting, he drew his Winchester from its holster. Moving stealthily, he slipped up to the campsite with the silence of a hunter. The area was bordered on all sides by shrubbery and prickly barberry bushes. He moved carefully into the foliage and approached the campsite without making a sound.

Josh wasn't surprised to find two men holding Cole at gunpoint—his instincts never steered him wrong.

As Ned was telling Cole to say his prayers, Josh was taking aim.

Kristina barely had time to comprehend Ned's death threat before Josh opened fire. He hit his target, and Ned keeled over, hitting the dirt face-down. A scream lodged in Kristina's throat as Cole, anxious to remove her from the line of fire, pushed her to the side. Thus, she didn't see Cole draw his pistol with lightning speed, nor did she see Jimmy drop to the ground, dead, Cole's bullet buried in his chest.

Cole's unexpected push had caused Kristina to lose her balance, and she had fallen to the ground. Her head grazed a protruding rock, and the blow sent stars flashing before her eyes.

Cole knelt at her side, drawing her into his arms. "Kristina!" he called, his tone gravely worried. "Darlin', are you all right?"

"Yes . . . yes, I think so," she stammered.

"Are you hurt?" he asked.

She cringed painfully. "I hit the back of my head."

He gently checked her injury. A small lump had already arisen.

Josh rushed over, and kneeling beside them, asked, "Does she need a doctor?"

"I'm not sure," Cole replied. "She might have a slight concussion."

"There's no doctor in Sandy Creek. We'll have to take her back to Austin, or else to San Antonio."

"Please . . . ," Kristina managed to murmur. "I don't need a doctor. I'm sure I'll be fine."

"I have a first aid kit with me," Josh said, and hurried to fetch it.

"Kristina," Cole said, "I'm sorry I pushed you, but I wanted to get you out of the way. I was afraid you might get shot."

"Don't blame yourself, Cole. It was an accident. Besides, you didn't push me very hard. I simply wasn't expecting it and lost my balance. What happened to Ned and Jimmy?"

"They're dead."

"Are you sure?"

"I'm sure. Remember, I once told you that I never miss . . . and neither does Josh."

Kristina sighed deeply. She was sorry they were dead, but she knew Cole and Josh had no choice but to shoot to kill. Ned and Jimmy had brought their deaths upon themselves. Twice, Cole spared Jimmy's life, and he had also spared Ned's. This time, the brothers' luck had run out.

Josh returned with the medical kit. He opened it and withdrew a bottle of antiseptic and a wad of cotton.

Cole watched as Kristina smiled at him. "Josh, I had a feeling you'd follow us."

"Kristina . . . " he began, "if you can manage to sit up, I'll clean your wound.

Cole's anger was piqued. He grabbed the antiseptic and cotton from Josh's hand. "I'll take care of

323

her!" he mumbled crankily.

Josh was puzzled by his friend's ill temper, but he didn't question him. He figured when Cole was ready, he'd tell him what was wrong.

As Cole tended to Kristina, Josh went to check on Ned and Jimmy. He came back and confirmed that they both were dead. "I suppose I should take their bodies to Sandy Creek and tell the sheriff what happened," he said.

"You can't do that!" Kristina remarked. "The sheriff is their cousin. He'll probably arrest you for murder."

"I'll go to Austin and deliver them to Sheriff Canton, then." Josh looked at Cole. "When I get this business taken care of, I'm coming to the Diamond-C. It's important that I talk to you."

"Yeah, I know," Cole grumbled. "I have a few things to say to you, too."

Josh hesitated. Something was obviously bothering Cole. He wondered if he should try to get to the bottom of it. Before he reached a decision, however, Cole offered to help put the bodies on the horses.

When they finished the task, Josh returned to Kristina, who had made coffee. She poured him a cup.

"Thanks," he said, and he sat beside her at the fire.

"Josh, you aren't leaving now, are you? It's dark. Don't you think you should wait until morning?"

"I don't mind traveling at night. I know this territory like the back of my hand. Besides, the sooner I take care of this business, the sooner I get to the Diamond-C. Now that I've finally decided to tell Cole the truth, I'm anxious to get it over with."

She touched his arm, her fingers gripping him tightly. "Josh, something is bothering Cole, but I have no idea what it is."

Cole, standing in the distance, watched as they conversed. They spoke in low voices, like two conspirators. He couldn't hear what they were saying, but he was too emotionally beaten to care.

Josh was patting Kristina's hand encouragingly. "Don't worry sweetness. Sometimes Cole finds it difficult to express his feelings. Try to be patient with him."

Kristina considered that easier said then done.

Finishing his coffee, Josh told her he'd see her soon, then walking away from the fire, he went to Cole. "I'll be at the Diamond-C in a couple of days. Then we'll talk. I don't think this is the right time or the right place."

Cole agreed.

Josh went to his palomino and mounted. Grabbing the reins to the horses carrying the bodies, he rode out of camp.

Kristina thought Cole would come to the fire, and she poured him a cup of coffee. Josh was gone, but still, Cole remained standing off to himself. She set the cup aside, and stewed impatiently as the coffee sat untouched, growing cold. Damn him! Why was he being so cantankerous!

Kristina tensed as Cole suddenly moved in her direction. His strides were slow, as though he were reluctant to join her. And she was right, for Cole did dread her closeness. Being near her and knowing she loved another man was hell!

"How are you feeling?" he managed to ask.

"I have a slight headache," she replied.

"I'll fix you a bed." He went to the rolled blankets, picked them up, and carried them close to the fire. He prepared a pallet, then turned to Kristina. "You should rest. Tomorrow we'll stop by Dr. Newman's office and let him have a look at you."

She considered questioning Cole about his peculiar conduct but then decided she was too tired to make the effort. She got to her feet, and a wave of dizziness washed over her, causing her to sway unsteadily.

Cole was beside her in a flash, and sweeping her into his arms, he carried her to the blankets. He laid her down with extreme care.

He had her totally confused. His emotions ran hot and cold.

"I have a bottle of whiskey in my saddlebag," he told her. "A couple of drinks will make you sleep better."

Her face screwed into a frown. "Whiskey? I've never had whiskey, but I don't think I'd like it."

She was delighted to see a smile lighten his grave expression.

"You're drinking it for medicinal purposes, so it isn't supposed to taste good."

He got the whiskey, returned, and sat beside her. He uncorked the bottle, then placing an arm about her shoulders, helped her to sit up.

"Here, take a drink," he said, handing her the whiskey.

She tilted the bottle to her lips. The smell alone was overwhelming, and dreading the taste, she took a tentative sip. "Ugh!" she groaned. "I knew it would be terrible."

"Take a bigger drink," he insisted.

She did so reluctantly. The potent liquor burned her throat, and, coughing, she handed him the bottle.

He took a couple of swigs, recorked the bottle, and placed it at his side. "How do you feel?" he asked.

"Better," she replied, for the whiskey was having a

soothing effect. His arm was still around her shoulders, and enjoying his closeness, she snuggled against his chest.

Their intimacy jolted Cole back to cold reality. For a moment he had forgotten her treachery. His body stiffened, and he quickly moved her out of his arms. Standing, he looked down at her and said tersely, "Get some sleep, we'll be leaving at dawn." With that, he picked up the whiskey bottle and moved to the fire.

Kristina couldn't remember ever being so angry! She rolled to her side, drew up the top blanket, and breathed deeply in an effort to control her rage. She fought back the urge to go to Cole and slap his face. It would be no more than he deserved!

As her anger cooled, she tried to think rationally. There was only one answer that made any sense. He didn't love her, probably had *never* loved her. He had mistaken their passion for love. Now that marriage was looming, he was getting cold feet. He didn't want a wife, nor did he want a child. Cole relished his independence and was apparently averse to giving it up.

Well, she decided heatedly. *I'll not rob him of his precious freedom! I'll find a way to take care of myself and my baby without his help!*

Tears teased her eyes, but she wiped them away. Crying wouldn't solve her problems! Imagining her future without Cole was depressing, and she had a sinking feeling that she would always love him. How could she give her heart to another man when it belonged to Cole Barton?

As Kristina's thoughts were running turbulently, Cole was immersed in his own troublesome reverie. He reflected on his conversation with Alisa. She believed that Kristina was after Josh's money. Cole

327

disagreed. If she was that cold, that calculating, he would have sensed it somehow. No, she wasn't devious, she had simply fallen in love with Josh. It wasn't the first time, nor would it be the last, that a woman thought herself in love with one man, only to fall in love with another.

Josh's image flashed across his mind. He could well imagine Kristina falling for him. He was handsome, intelligent, and his manners were impeccable. Hell, Chandler was a lot more worldly than he was. Also, his reputation was above reproach. Cole couldn't say the same for himself. He was a renowned bounty hunter whose name was known across the West! It was a dangerous reputation, and had probably driven Kristina into another man's arms.

Cole uncorked the bottle and took a long swallow as though his thoughts weren't in turmoil. Should he graciously step aside and let Kristina and Josh have each other? It wouldn't be an easy decision to make, but he doubted if he really had any choice. He couldn't force Kristina to love him.

He knew he might never get over losing the woman he loved—her memory would most likely torture him forever. Then there was the baby to consider. Thoughts of his child drove him to taking another drink, and he continued to drink until, finally, the liquor numbed his aching heart. Putting the bottle aside, he made a pallet and went to sleep.

Kristina and Cole arrived at the Diamond-C shortly before noon. Cole had wanted to stop at Dr. Newman's office, but Kristina had insisted on going straight to the ranch. The lump at the back of her head was still a little sensitive, but otherwise she was fine.

The morning's journey had been an agonizing one for Kristina. Although she and Cole hadn't argued, in fact, had both been overly polite, their formal conduct was more frustrating than an outright quarrel.

The large, columned house, sitting grandly atop the grass-covered hill, was a heart-wrenching sight to Kristina. She loved the Diamond-C dearly, and had looked forward to living in the home that Drake had built. But now that Cole no longer loved her, this home could never be hers.

Her present circumstances were grave. She was pregnant, almost penniless, and had no place to go. She was, however, determined not to be dependent on Cole's charity. Somehow she'd find a way to support herself. How she would accomplish such a feat totally eluded her, and thinking about it was exasperating, but she was a firm believer in the adage—Where's there's a will, there's a way. She had the will, and was resolved to finding a way. Furthermore, Josh was a good friend, and if necessary, she knew she could turn to him for help.

Unknown to Kristina, Cole's feelings were even more dismal than her own. He wondered if he should tell Kristina that he knew she was in love with Josh, or should he say nothing and wait for her and Josh to confront him? Why was he postponing the inevitable? He had been dealt a losing hand, so why in hell didn't he simply fold and leave the game? Why did he keep holding on when there was nothing left to hold on to?

Arriving, they handed their horses and Lucky over to a wrangler and went into the house. Looking for Autumn Moon, they found her in the kitchen.

She hugged both of them eagerly, then insisted they sit at the table and eat lunch. A pot of stew was simmering on the stove, and she quickly dished up two plates along with slices of bread and hot coffee.

Autumn Moon knew her news would take away their appetites, so she waited until they were finished. Then, refilling their cups, she said heavily, "Samantha left, and she took all the money with her."

Cole wasn't sure he understood. "What do you mean, she took all the money?"

"She refused to give Alisa and me our fair share."

"But Drake's will—"

"Drake's requests aren't legally binding," she interrupted. "His will simply stated his wish for Samantha to share her inheritance, and she chose to do otherwise."

"I'm not surprised!" Kristina said harshly. "Samantha has always been selfish beyond belief." She looked at Cole. "This is partly my fault. I should have warned you not to trust her."

"No woman can be trusted!" he grumbled. His eyes bore into her, their expression accusing. He turned away abruptly and said to Autumn Moon, "I told Mr. Cullen to make sure that you and Alisa received your money."

"Legally, there was nothing he could do."

Cole was steaming. "Damn it!"

Autumn Moon smiled wanly. "Don't get upset, Cole. I'm not completely without means to support myself. I have the jewlery Drake bought me."

"You aren't selling your jewels," he remarked. "The Diamond-C is your home, and you'll receive your fair profits from this ranch. And so will Alisa."

"Alisa won't need any money."

"Why not?"

"She's engaged to Raymond Lewis." Autumn Moon's tone reflected her disapproval.

"Raymond Lewis!" Kristina remarked sharply. "She shouldn't trust that man! He won't marry her, he'll only use her!"

"I was afraid of that," Autumn Moon replied. "I tried to warn Alisa, but she won't listen to me." She turned pleading eyes to Cole. "She might listen to you. Please talk to her!"

"Where is she?"

"In town, having lunch with Mr. Lewis."

Cole pushed back his chair and got to his feet. "I need to go into town and order some supplies. I'll ride back with Alisa and try to talk some sense into her."

Cole left, and Kristina offered to help Autumn Moon with the dishes. The woman declined her assistance, and reminding her of her delicate condition, suggested that she take a nap.

Kristina knew that rest was important during pregnancy, and although her body was tired, her mind was restless. Knowing she wouldn't be able to sleep, she wandered aimlessly into the parlor. She sat on the sofa and tried to sort out her thoughts. Losing herself in her jumbled emotions, she wasn't sure how much time had passed when she heard a loud knocking at the front door. Joseph seemed to be nowhere close, so she left to admit the caller.

Opening the door, she was surprised to find Judge Gilbert. She had seen him only once, when he had come to visit while Drake was recovering. He had spoken to her before leaving, and had told her that he was taking a trip to Memphis and would be away for weeks.

She invited him inside.

He removed his hat, revealing a thick mane of snowy-white hair. He had been retired for years but still carried his title.

Gesturing toward the parlor, Kristina said warmly, "Please, have a seat. May I get you a drink, Judge Gilbert?"

"No, thank you, my dear. I can only stay a moment."

"If you came to see Cole, he isn't here." She followed him into the parlor.

"I came to see you," he replied.

"Oh?" she questioned curiously.

He motioned for her to sit beside him on the sofa. He had a briefcase with him, and reaching inside, he drew out a bank statement. He handed it to Kristina. "This belongs to you."

Puzzled, she looked the paper over carefully. "There must be some mistake!" she exclaimed. "This statement says I have a large sum of money deposited in the bank."

"There's no mistake, Miss Parker. Drake had me draw money from his account and put it into an account for you. It was his instruction that should he die, I was to bring you this statement. I'd have delivered it sooner, but I was out of town."

"But . . . but I don't understand. Why did he do this?"

He smiled at her tenderly. "Drake was very fond of you, my dear. He wanted to be sure you were taken care of. He thought of you as a daughter, you know."

Tears welled up in her eyes. "I loved him like a father." Her voice was choked.

He patted her hand consolingly. "Drake was a wonderful man, and he'll be missed by many." He closed up his briefcase, and rose to his feet.

Kristina showed him to the door, then rushed upstairs to her room. She read the bank statement again. She could harldy believe she had just inherited a small fortune.

She sat on the bed and stared into space. It took a while for her shock to wane. As her thoughts settled, she suddenly realized that she was now independent. She could easily support herself and her child. She didn't need Cole's help, or anyone else's.

The revelation was still too new for her to make any firm decisions. She must first give it a lot of consideration. Where should she go? She knew she didn't want to return to Philadelphia. She loved the West and wanted to remain. She had a feeling, though, that she should move a far distance from Cole, for if she remained close to him, seeing him would tear her to pieces.

She took the bank statement to the dresser and put it in a drawer. Then, as her thoughts went to Drake's kind deed, tears filled her eyes. She returned to the bed, fell across it, and wept for Drake Carlson.

Chapter Twenty-Seven

Cole, leading his Appaloosa, was heading toward the Branding Iron Saloon when Raymond pushed aside the swinging doors and escorted Alisa outside. The sight of Alisa coming out of the saloon caused an angry frown to furrow Cole's brow. He damned Lewis for allowing her inside such an establishment. In Cole's opinion, a saloon was no place for a lady.

Raymond was assisting Alisa into the Diamond-C buggy when Cole arrived. The pair looked at him. Alisa's expression dared him to cross her; Raymond merely stared coldly.

"I understand congratulations are in order," Cole said, his tone flat.

Alisa lifted her chin defiantly. "Yes. Raymond and I are getting married next month." Worried that Cole might say something disagreeable which would pique her anger as well as her fiancé's, she quickly changed the subject. "Did Kristina come back with you?"

"Yes, she did."

Cole was watching Alisa, and he didn't see the brief smile that crossed Raymond's face. So Kristina was at the Diamond-C. He was glad she was back—now he wouldn't have to go to Austin to abduct her. He didn't know when he would do it, but he was still determined to have her at his mercy. Not only would he make her pay dearly for stabbing him, he would enjoy her naked beauty to the fullest! He had never in his life lusted after a woman with such intensity!

Cole tied his horse to the rear of the buggy, then leaping up onto the seat, he took the reins from Alisa's hands. "I'll drive," he remarked.

Although she found his boldness perturbing, she saw no reason to argue with him. He had apparently made up his mind to ride home with her. Autumn Moon had probably sent him on this mission, hoping he could talk her out of marrying Raymond. Well, no one was going to dissuade her! She intended to marry Raymond Lewis, and that was that!

She turned to her fiancé and smiled radiantly. "I'll see you tonight."

"Dinner, here, at eight o'clock," he reminded her.

Cole slapped the reins against the horse, and the buggy took off with a jolt. They rode in silence for a couple of minutes, then Cole grumbled, "Dinner in a saloon? Can't he take you someplace respectable?"

"We aren't having dinner in the saloon, but upstairs in his private quarters."

Cole scowled. "I can't believe you actually intend to marry that no-good skunk."

"Raymond happens to be a very kind and considerate man!" she replied querulously.

"Kind and considerate?" he snapped. "He tried to rape and kill Kristina!"

"That's what she says! And if you believe her, then you're a fool! Kristina is a liar!" She cast him a shrewd glance. "You certainly didn't stay very long at the Lazy-J. What happened? Did Josh tell you that he's in love with Kristina?"

336

"No, he didn't. Not yet, anyhow."

"Oh? What does that mean?"

Cole sighed heavily. "You were right about Josh and Kristina. They're in love."

"You mean Josh is in love," she clarified. "Kristina's merely using him."

"Why do you say that? Why are you so sure she doesn't love him?"

"Raymond knows Kristina better than any of us. I told him about her relationship with Josh, and he believes that she's going to inveigle money from him, then run off with Ted Cummings."

"Cummings!" Cole exclaimed. "That's ridiculous!"

Alisa was impatient. "It's your faith in her that's ridiculous! When are you going to remove your blinders and see her for what she is—a selfish liar!"

"That's enough!" Cole said sharply.

"I feel sorry for you, Cole," she smiled in sympathy. "That woman will destroy you."

"No, she won't," he replied.

He had spoken with authority, as though he had his emotions under control, but deep down, he wasn't so sure. He didn't believe Kristina was planning to get money from Josh, then run away with Cummings. He did believe, though, that she was in love with Josh. He had lost her to his best friend, and their betrayal was still playing havoc with his feelings. At times he felt consumed with anger, then at other times he simply felt like gracefully conceding. He was fighting a losing battle, for he couldn't make Kristina love him. He thought about the baby she carried, and knowing he would lose his child filled him with despair.

He found himself speaking his thoughts aloud. "Kristina's pregnant."

Alisa was surprised. "She's pregnant? Is the baby yours or Josh's?"

"Mine, of course."

"How can you be so sure? When Josh came to see Papa, he and Kristina spent a lot of time together. I wasn't at the Diamond-C when Josh arrived, but I heard about their rides and their picnics. They were together all the time—and they were always alone."

"Damn your suspicious mind!" Cole said, his temper erupting. He was more angry with himself, though, than with Alisa. Her accusation had hit a responsive chord, and for a fleeting moment, he had considered the chance that the child wasn't his. But he refused to accept the possibility. *The child was his, damn it!*

"I'm sorry, Cole," Alisa murmured sincerely, reaching over and placing a hand on his arm. "I didn't mean to upset you, we're in this together."

He looked at her with bafflement.

"You love Kristina, and I love Josh."

"I'm not sure I understand."

She smiled pensively. "I've loved Josh since I was a girl."

"Does he know how you feel."

"Yes, he's known for a long time. But he doesn't share my feelings—he never has, and never will."

"If you love Josh, then why are you marrying Lewis?"

"Why not? I have no future with Josh. Raymond loves me and wants to marry me. Why shouldn't I? Surely you don't think I should spend my years pining for an unrequited love. And you should do the same, Cole. You must forget Kristina Parker."

"Even if I were to find a way to forget her, how could I possibly forget my child?"

"If it's your child," she couldn't help from saying.

Cole withdrew into a troubled silence.

Kristina had wept mournfully for Drake, and when her tears abated, she had fallen asleep. It was, however, a restless sleep, for she was dreaming about Cole. He was telling her that he didn't want to be saddled with a wife and child. Although his words were shattering, she was determined to hold on to her pride. She was about to inform him that he was free to leave when a loud knocking sound broke into her dream.

Coming awake, Kristina sat up drowsily. At first she didn't know what had roused her, then when the knocking sounded again, she realized someone was at the bedroom door.

She crossed the room and opened the door.

"Miz Kristina," Joseph said. "There's a gentleman here to see you."

She wondered who it could be. "Did he give his name?"

"Yes'm. He said his name is Ted Cummings."

"Ted!" she exclaimed, surprised. Brushing past the butler, she raced down the hall and descended the stairs quickly.

Hurrying to the parlor, she found Ted sitting in a wing-back chair. He stood at her arrival.

Kristina's gaze swept over him. His clothes were coated with trail dust, and he needed a shave. He appeared tired but otherwise hearty. His tall, robust frame was tense as he regarded her with an expression that made her a little ill at ease. She could read love in his eyes. He had never looked at her in this way before, and his obvious devotion came as a complete surprise to her. She was fond of Ted, but she knew she could never fall in love with him.

Ted no longer saw any reason to hide his feelings, for he planned to be completely honest with Kristina. More than likely, after today he would never see her again. He was heading to San Francisco, where he hoped to resume his former trade.

She was the first to speak. "Ted, what are you doing here?"

"I came to see you," he replied, as though his journey had been no more than crossing a street.

"You came all the way here just to see me?" she questioned, astonished.

"Actually, I'm on my way to San Francisco, so detouring here wasn't that far out of my way."

"Surely you aren't traveling to San Francisco alone!"

"I'll make it." He sounded unconcerned.

She was about to point out all the dangers, but he held up a quieting hand. "Kristina, please don't worry about me."

"But, Ted—" she began.

"I need to talk to you," he interrupted. "It's very important." He indicated the sofa. "Will you sit with me?"

"Of course," she answered.

Ted reached over and took her hand into his. Holding it gently, he gazed deeply into her green eyes. Her curly tresses were unbound, and a few wayward ringlets had fallen over her brow. Using his free hand, he brushed the strands aside, leaned over, and kissed her forehead.

Kristina was startled. In all the months she had known Cummings, he had never displayed this kind of affection. She had believed he liked her simply as a friend. That he might harbor romantic feelings upset her. She liked Ted, and she didn't want to hurt him. But if he had come here to pledge his love, then she had no choice but to disappoint him.

Ted could read her thoughts. He smiled tenderly. "Kristina, when or if I fall in love with a woman, she'll be closer to my own age." He watched her raptly. "I'm old enough to be your father, you know."

She was somewhat embarrassed. She quickly chastised herself for thinking he was in love with her. "I'm sorry," she murmured, blushing.

Ted's hold on her hand tightened. He was tense, and his heart had begun to hammer. God, how was he to tell this lovely young lady that he was her father? Would she hate him for deserting her and her mother? *Of course she will,* he thought gravely. *She already hates me, has hated me for years! She just doesn't know I'm the one she hates.*

For a moment, Ted weakened. Maybe he shouldn't confess. It would be easier to leave for San Francisco knowing Kristina loved him as a friend, than to leave knowing she despised him as a father. The weakness passed, and his resolve strengthened. *Damn it, she was his daughter, and he wanted her to know it!*

He drew a long, nervous breath, squeezed her hand gently, and said, "Kristina, I do love you. But I don't love you as a suitor, I love you like a father."

She smiled fondly. "Having you for a father would be a pleasure."

"Do you really mean that?"

She didn't detect the anxiety in his voice. "Yes, I mean it."

He swallowed heavily. "Kristina, I *am* your father. My name isn't Ted Cummings, it's Theodore Parker."

It took a moment for his words to register, then they hit her with a shocking force. She jerked her hand from his, bounded to her feet, and gaping down at him, she declared hoarsely, "No! You can't be!"

Standing, he reached for her. She stepped back to

341

avoid his touch, but he grabbed her shoulders, his tight grip holding her firm.

"Kristina, please let me explain!"

"Explain?" she uttered bitterly. "How can you explain why you left Mother and me alone and destitute?"

He groaned remorsefully. "I'm not here to excuse my behavior, I only want to tell you why I left you and your mother."

She removed his hands from her shoulders, folded her arms across her chest, and replied flatly, "All right, tell me."

Ted's brawny frame seemed to shrink before her eyes. His posture grew limp, and his wide shoulders slumped. A look of abject misery crossed his face. He spoke raspingly, as though the effort pained his throat. "You sound very unforgiving. You aren't going to listen objectively, are you? You have built a lot of resentment through the years, and now that resentment has made you too biased to hear what I have to say with an open mind and an understanding heart."

Kristina was about to harshly agree when, suddenly Josh Chandler's dark secret came to mind. She compared herself to Cole. Josh would soon tell Cole the truth, and when he did, would Cole react as she was now reacting? Would he refuse to listen to Josh with an open mind and an understanding heart? She had assured Josh over and over that Cole was compassionate and would give him a chance to explain. She had always considered herself compassionate, but now that she was being put to the test, she was failing miserably. She should expect no more of Cole than she expected of herself!

Returning to the sofa, she looked up at Ted, her eyes expressing sincerity. "I'll listen to everything you have to say. And I promise to listen objectively."

Relieved, Ted sat beside her. He smiled shakily. "Although I hope to receive your forgiveness, I know it's probably too much to hope for. But maybe you'll lose all this hostility you feel for me. If my visit here can accomplish that much, then I'll be very pleased."

Kristina regarded him intently. That this man was actually her father was still too startling for her to grasp. She studied his face closely, looking for a resemblance between them. Their eyes were the same color, and his lips were full like her own . . .

"You look more like your mother," he murmured. He had again read her thoughts.

"Mother was a wonderful woman." Her tone grew pleading, "Why did you leave her?"

Cole and Alisa were halfway to the Diamond-C when Cole decided to ride back to town. He brought the buggy to a halt and handed the reins to Alisa. "Tell Autumn Moon I won't be home for dinner," he said. "I'll get something to eat in town."

"Why are you going back to town?"

He leapt to the ground. "I need time to think before seeing Kristina."

A bitter smirk shadowed Alisa's face as she watched Cole untie his horse from the buggy. "If you want my advice, you'll send her packing."

"I don't want your advice," he grumbled as he mounted.

He turned the Appaloosa about and rode away. Alisa slapped the reins against the horse, and the buggy rolled into motion.

She found herself feeling sorry for Cole. In her opinion, he was a fool. Why couldn't he admit that Kristina had used him, just as she was now using Josh? Why were men so blind to a beautiful woman's treachery?

343

She thrust Cole from her thoughts, and with effort, she also cleared her mind of Josh. She set her full concentration upon Raymond. Following lunch, they had made love. This time, Raymond had been a more considerate lover, and although his fondling had been somewhat rough, it hadn't been painful. Alisa had failed to respond fervently, but this hadn't altered her determination to marry him. She felt she could live without passion—wealth and social standing were all that really mattered.

Arriving at the Diamond-C, Alisa left the buggy out front. She knew one of the wranglers would take it and the horse to the stables. She looked curiously at the horse tied at the hitching rail and wondered who was visiting. She entered the house, and was crossing the foyer when she saw Joseph heading toward the kitchen.

"Do we have company?" she asked.

"Mista Ted Cummings is visitin' Miz Kristina. They's in the parlah."

Ted Cummings! She was astounded and glanced at the parlor's closed door. How she wished she could eavesdrop!

As though Joseph had read her thoughts, he stood poised, watching her carefully.

Reluctantly, she went upstairs to her room.

Meanwhile, inside the parlor, Ted was obviously hesitant to answer Kristina's question. Her patience waning, she asked again, "Why did you leave Mother?"

He answered haltingly, "Because I thought she . . . was in love with another man."

Kristina gasped. "No! I don't believe you! If she loved another man, then why didn't she marry him after you left us? What happened to this other man?"

"I killed him."

344

Chapter Twenty-Eight

"You killed him?" Kristina cried. She was shocked. She had always thought Ted was a gentle, peaceful man, but she now stared at him as though she were seeing a complete stranger, one who was dangerous and ruthless. She suddenly remembered Ted's anger the night Raymond attacked her. He had threatened to kill Lewis with his bare hands, and he had apparently tried to carry out his threat, for Raymond had said Ted's attempt to murder him had been thwarted.

"Kristina . . ." Ted began. "Please don't look at me as though I'm a cold-blooded murderer."

She hadn't realized her feelings were so obvious. "I'm sorry," she murmured. "But you said you killed this man, and I know you also tried to kill Raymond Lewis." A shudder coursed through her. "You must be a very violent man."

"I have a bad temper," he replied, and left it at that. He looked at her curiously. "How do you know I tried to kill Lewis?"

"He moved here. He bought a saloon in town called the Branding Iron."

"Why did he come to San Antonio?"

"He was certain you would come here to see me. He intends to get even with you for attacking him."

Ted shrugged calmly. Raymond's presence didn't disturb him.

Kristina waited, thinking he would explain what had taken place between himself and Lewis.

Ted, however, had already dismissed Raymond Lewis. In a soft, plaintive voice, he began to speak of Kristina's mother. "Beth and I knew each other as children. We grew up in the same neighborhood. My parents were shopkeepers, and Beth's father—he was a widower—was a blacksmith." He smiled sadly. "But I suppose you already know this."

Kristina nodded. "Mother told me that her father died shortly before she married, and that your parents were killed in a fire."

"Their shop caught on fire in the middle of the night. By the time it was discovered, it was too late to save them."

"You and Mother married very young, didn't you?"

"She was sixteen, and I was eighteen."

"Why didn't you wait until you were older?"

"We married quickly because Beth was pregnant."

"With me?" she asked. The question had barely passed her lips when she realized it couldn't have been her. Her mother had been eighteen when she was born.

"No, it wasn't you," he answered quietly. "She was pregnant with another man's child. He was a judge's son. His family was rich and very powerful. Richard Jarman was his name."

"Yes, I've heard of the Jarmans. They are among Philadelphia's elite. I also remember reading somewhere that Judge Jarman had a son who was murdered, and that his killer was never apprehended."

346

Her eyes widened accusingly. "It was you, wasn't it? You killed him!"

"I didn't mean to kill him, it was an accident. I only meant to beat him up."

"But why?" she gasped. "Why did you want to fight with him?"

Kristina's emotions were racing. Her mother had married Ted because she was pregnant with Jarman's child? It was almost more than she could absorb.

"Let me start at the beginning," Ted said. "I'll try to make this story as short as possible. Later, if you want, we can discuss it in more detail."

Kristina agreed.

"I loved Beth even when we were still children. As we grew older, my feelings deepened. She liked me, considered me a good friend, but she wasn't in love with me. Richard Jarman's uncle had a law office and living quarters close to our neighborhood. Richard visited him often. One day, he was standing outside his uncle's office, and as I was passing by, we struck up a conversation. Soon after that, we became friends, even though he was a judge's son and I was a shopkeeper's son. I introduced Richard to Beth. I think Beth loved him at first sight. I'm not sure how he felt about her, but I am sure he never intended to marry her. He was a Jarman, and his family would never have accepted Beth—a blacksmith's daughter. They expected Richard to marry a woman of breeding—a rich socialite. Richard never planned to disappoint them. Social standing meant a great deal to him. Also, I'm sure he didn't want to take a chance that he could be disinherited. So when Beth became pregnant, Richard refused to marry her. It was at this time that Beth's father became seriously ill and died. His illness wasn't related to Beth's condition, for he didn't know of it. It was after his funeral that Beth broke down and told me she was with child. Not only was she pregnant out of wedlock, but her father had left her in a financial bind. His blacksmith shop was heavily mortgaged. I was working for my parents, and although I was bringing in an income, I couldn't afford to pay the mortgage. I could, however, afford to take care of Beth. I asked her to marry me, she accepted, and we moved into her father's house. It was a modest home, but comfortable and cozy. Two months after we were married, Beth lost the baby.

"It took a long time, but eventually Beth seemed to forget Richard. When she became pregnant with you, I was overjoyed. From the moment you were born, you were the apple of my eye. I was so proud of my beautiful daughter. Also, I was very happy with my life. I had a wife I loved, a child I adored, and my parents were planning to retire and sign the shop over to me. I thought my family's future was secure.

"Then, suddenly, my life began to fall apart. It started with the fire and my parents' deaths. Their shop wasn't insured, so everything was lost. Jobs were scarce, and most of them temporary, so I had a difficult time earning a living. Shortly after Beth and I married, we heard that Richard had left Philadelphia on a European tour. I don't know how long he had been back before he came to see Beth. The day I lost my job, I went home early and found Beth and Richard in the bedroom. They were . . ." He couldn't continue.

"I understand," she murmured, making it easier for him.

"My temper erupted. I flew into a violent rage and started beating Richard. During the scuffle, he fell and hit his head on the stone hearth. The blow was so severe that it killed him. I was sure the Jarmans

348

would demand my hanging, so I rolled his body in a rug, carried it to my wagon, took it to an alley blocks from the house, and left it there. I was certain Beth would never forgive me for causing Richard's death so I never went home."

Ted sighed dismally. "I ended up in San Francisco, where I got a job on the docks. Years later, I was shocked to run across neighbors who had moved to San Francisco from Philadelphia. They used to live next door to Beth and me. They were good friends, and Beth had told Mrs. Wilson what really happened with Richard."

He rose from the sofa and began to pace the room. "When I barged into the house that day, I thought Richard and Beth were making love, but I was mistaken. Richard was forcing himself on Beth. She tried to tell me, but I was too enraged and too jealous to listen.

"I asked Mrs. Wilson about you and Beth, and she told me that Beth had found employment, and that you were both well. I didn't ask where Beth was working, for I didn't intend to return to Philadelphia. I was too ashamed. I also begged Mrs. Wilson not to write Beth and tell her that she had seen me. After that, I signed on as a sailor and took to the sea."

"Why didn't you want Mother to know that you were alive? You should have let Mrs. Wilson contact her."

"I couldn't!" he groaned. Returning to the sofa, he sat down, covered his face with his hands, and said raspingly, "I felt I could never face her—not after what I had done, what I had accused her of! My God, I deserted my wife when she needed me the most!"

"But you finally came back to Philadelphia. Why?"

"One night there was a terrible storm at sea. The

ship I was on sank, and several men drowned. almost drowned myself. It's true, you know, when a person is drowning, his life flashes before him. In a matter of moments, I relived my entire life. I was rescued by the captain, who, with several others, was in a lifeboat." Ted paused for a long time, gathered his thoughts, then continued. "There was something about reliving my life that compelled me to return home. I knew I had to confront my past, otherwise, would never learn to live with it. Hating myself the way I did, I had become a drunk and a very embittered man.

"We were picked up by another ship, and when it docked in San Francisco, I tried to find the Wilsons. intended to ask them where your mother was staying in Philadelphia, but they had left San Francisco. went back home, returned to the old neighborhood, and asked about you and your mother. That was when I learned that Beth had died and that you were still living with the Johnsons."

"Why didn't you tell me you were my father?"

"I wanted to, but I thought we should get to know each other first. I was about to tell you the truth when you confided in me and told me how much you despised your father. I decided I'd rather have you love me as a friend than hate me as a father."

"But you're telling me the truth now. Why?"

Kristina was touched to see tears in his eyes. "I just felt I had to tell you! You're my daughter, and I want you to know it!"

"Ted . . ." she began, her own tears forming. " don't want you to go to San Francisco, at least no right away. We need time together."

His hopes soared, and his heart began to pound rapidly. "Kristina, does this mean you don't hate me?"

"I don't hate you," she murmured. "What happened between you and Mother was very tragic and very sad. I think you were wrong to run away, but it's not my place to judge you. My own life isn't above reproach. I've certainly made my share of mistakes."

"Would you like to talk about these mistakes? I'm good listener. Maybe I can help."

She could well imagine his reaction if she were to tell him that she was pregnant out of wedlock, and that the father didn't want to marry her. She thought about her mother's first pregnancy, and Richard Barman's refusal to marry her. Yes, indeed, history did repeat itself!

Meanwhile, Alisa, her curiosity racing, had slipped down the stairs and to the parlor door. Opening it a crack, she listened closely.

"We'll talk about me later," she heard Kristina say. "But Ted, you must leave before Raymond finds out you're here. I want you to go to the Lazy-J. It's a ranch outside Austin owned by Josh Chandler. I'll join you there in a few days. Josh will be here at the Diamond-C tomorrow, the day after at the latest. I plan to return to the Lazy-J with him."

Alisa wanted to hear more, but afraid of detection, she closed the door soundlessly and moved away. So Kristina planned to leave with Josh! She was confused. Now that Ted was here, why did she plan to leave with Josh? What wicked scheme was brewing in her calculating mind? Alisa hurried back upstairs. Tonight, at dinner, she'd have a lot to tell Raymond Lewis!

Ted was puzzled. "Why are you leaving the Diamond-C?" he asked Kristina. "Don't you want to stay here with Drake Carlson?"

"Drake is dead," she replied softly.

"I'm sorry. I know you loved him like a father."

351

Kristina didn't want to discuss Drake, for she wa afraid she'd start crying. She still missed him s much. She rose from the sofa, went to the desk, an removed a sheet of paper. "Josh won't be at the Lazy J, so I'll write a letter to Rosa, explaining who yo are. I certainly hope she can read English. If not, yo can have one of the ranch hands read it to her."

Cole rode at a leisurely pace, for he was in no hurr to reach home. He had spent his time in town at th Branding Iron, where he had sat at a corner table drinking.

Although he had consumed a liberal amount o whiskey, he wasn't intoxicated. He had given th matter of Kristina, Josh, and himself his ful concentration. The bottle of whiskey was almos empty before he came to a final decision. It hadn' been an easy decision to make, but now that he ha made it, he was glad that he had waited. If he ha confronted Kristina and Josh earlier, his anger an pain might have caused him to say things h shouldn't. Now, though, with his feelings unde control, he knew he could bow out of Kristina's lif like a gentleman. This decision to let her go however, didn't lessen the hurt. He loved her with al his heart, and he knew that he always would. H wasn't sure how he felt about Josh. There was a par of him that resented Josh's betrayal and though thei friendship had been severed beyond repair, they ha been friends for so long that Cole couldn't brin himself to hate him.

As Cole guided his horse onto the lane leading t the columned home, he maintained his slow pace He planned to go to Kristina and tell her that he wa releasing her from her promise to marry him. H knew it would be the hardest thing he would ever do in his life, and he was in no hurry. He just hoped he could keep his composure and not do something foolish, like begging her not to leave him.

He thought about the baby, and his mood plunged even deeper. He couldn't, wouldn't, sever ties with his child. He planned to insist that Kristina and Josh allow him to be a part of the child's life.

Dusk was descending as Cole rode to the stables, dismounted, and led the horse inside. He unsaddled the Appaloosa, gave him some oats and water, and left.

He entered the house quietly, and, deciding to check Kristina's room, he went upstairs and knocked softly on her door.

It was opened almost immediately. Seeing Cole set Kristina on edge.

"May I come in?" he asked.

She stepped aside for him to enter, then closed the door. She watched him warily. She didn't know what kind of mood he was in, but it didn't really matter. She had made up her mind to tell him she was leaving, and was determined not to be dissuaded.

"Cole, I have something to tell you . . ." she began, her resolve unfaltering. "I'm leaving you. I plan to return to the Lazy-J with Josh. From there—"

She was about to tell him that she didn't know where she'd go from there, but he didn't give her a chance to finish.

"I won't try to stop you from leaving. You aren't bound by your promise to marry me."

Kristina was rankled. Oh, the unfeeling cad! He could set her free so calmly! She cursed herself for loving such a heartless devil!

She stalked to the door, swung it open, and said sharply, "Good-bye, Cole Barton! If our paths never cross again, it'll be too soon for me!''

Moving to her side, he slammed the door closed. ''Not so fast, darlin'! Aren't you forgetting something?'' He was referring to their child.

She lifted her chin and eyed him heatedly. ''Yes, I forgot to tell you what I think of you! You're a lying, despicable rat!''

''If you want to sling mud back and forth, my love, you'll find yourself covered with it.''

Kristina's temper exploded. She drew back a hand to slap his face, but he caught her arm in midair. Gripping her wrist tightly, he said between gritted teeth, ''Listen to me, Kristina, and listen closely! You and Josh can damned well have each other, but the child you're carrying is mine, and I demand my rights! The child will know who his father is, and I will be a part of his life!''

Kristina grew limp, and Cole released his hold on her. Shocked, she could only gape at him as though he had suddenly lost his mind. His accusations whirled through her mind chaotically. Did he think she was in love with Josh? But why? Why? No wonder he had been acting so strangely! Good Lord, he thought he had been betrayed by his fiancée and his best friend!

Her emotions settled, and she gazed deeply into his angry eyes, her own eyes filled with understanding. ''Cole,'' she whispered, ''You love me, don't you?''

He didn't answer. What did she want from him? She already had him down, did she now want to kick him?

''Please answer me.''

''Why?'' he asked quietly. ''Do my feelings matter?''

She smiled radiantly. ''Oh, yes! Your feelings matter a great deal. I love you, Cole Barton! You mean the world to me!"

He was confused. What kind of game was she playing? "I suppose you love Josh and me both!" he uttered bitterly.

"Yes, I love Josh. But I simply love him as a friend."

Cole's confusion changed to anger. "Damn it, Kristina! I know how you two feel about each other!"

"No, you don't!" she came back. "You think we're in love!"

"Arent you?"

"No! We're only friends. Cole, where in the world did you get the idea that he and I were in love?"

It was a long time before Cole answered. He tried to sort his jumbled thoughts in the silence. Kristina wasn't in love with Josh? But then how . . . why?

He drew a deep breath, then told Kristina everything Alisa had seen and heard. He then explained the way he had stood at the window, watching and listening to parts of her conversation with Josh. "If you two aren't in love," Cole resumed, "then what does Josh have to tell me? Apparently it's something very grave, and something he's afraid will make me angry."

Kristina sighed heavily. "I can't tell you. I promised Josh that I wouldn't. He wants to be the one to tell you."

Cole rubbed a hand distractedly through his dark hair. What could Josh possibly want to tell him? He didn't ponder the query very long, for this moment with Kristina was more important. He reached out and placed his hands on her shoulders, gazed deeply into her eyes, and said, "Kristina Parker, I love you from the depth of my soul."

"Cole, my darling!" she cried, flinging herself into his arms.

"Sweetheart, forgive me for the way I treated you. But I was sure that you loved Josh."

"I'll never love any man but you."

She raised her lips to his, sealing her vow with a long, love-filled kiss.

Cole quickly locked the door, then lifting her into his arms, he carried her to the bed and laid her down gently. Moving into her embrace, he lay beside her, holding her close.

Feeling safe and happy, Kristina murmured, "Nothing or no one will come between us again."

Chapter Twenty-Nine

Snuggled into Cole's arms, Kristina couldn't remember being happier. The last two days had been so agonizing. If only Cole hadn't waited so long to tell her what was bothering him. His silence had caused them both so much misery.

She spoke her thoughts aloud. "Cole, why did you keep your suspicions to yourself? Why didn't you confront Josh and me?"

He sighed deeply. "I'm not sure. I guess it's human nature to postpone something you dread. Then, of course, there was the baby to consider. I didn't want to lose our child, but I didn't want to force you into marriage, either. I preferred not to act rashly, so I figured I should give myself time to consider everything rationally." He smiled wryly. "But I was fooling myself. I could never lose you rationally. My emotions were a jumbled mess."

He leaned over and kissed her passionately. "If you have no objections, let's get married while Josh is here. I want him to be my best man."

"I agree wholeheartedly," she murmured. She wanted her father at her wedding, and was getting ready to tell Cole about Ted's visit, but Cole's lips again swooped down on hers.

She wrapped her arms about his neck, and Ted temporarily fled her mind as she surrendered totally to her lover's kiss.

Their desire quickly sparked into a full-fledged flame, and they hastily shed their clothes.

Drawing back the covers, Cole eased her down onto the sheet, then fitted his lean-muscled frame to her soft, feminine contours.

His mouth, warm and demanding, crushed against hers, and his fiery kiss was overpowering. Parting her lips, she gave him full access, and his tongue tasted her sweetness.

Her fingertips traced the smooth planes of his back as he moved to lie at her side. Small moans of passion sounded in her throat as Cole's lips started at her neck, then flickered downward, tracing a heated path over her body.

Returning his fondlings, she ran her hands over the length of his body, then as her excitement became all-consuming, her mouth explored the path her hands had taken.

Their bodies longed for total rapture, and moving between Kristina's legs, Cole entered her deeply. At first, his movements were slow and measured, and she responded to his steady rhythm, but as their passion soared, their thrusting grew demanding. Together they crested love's plateau, finding breathless appeasement.

Cole kissed her softly, then moving to lie beside her, he uttered huskily, "I love you, darlin'."

She cuddled close, resting her head on his shoulder. "I love you, too."

He stifled a yawn. "Damn, I'm tired. I didn't sleep very well last night."

"Neither did I. And it's all your fault." Her small

fist punched his chest playfully. "Cole Barton, don't you ever again clam up on me. If something is bothering you, you had better let me know about it immediately!"

"Yes, ma'am," he replied.

"Promise?"

"I promise." He kissed her endearingly, then Cole extinguished the bedside lamp.

With a blissful sigh, Kristina snuggled close to Cole. She placed a leg over his and an arm across his chest. She was on the brink of sleep when she suddenly remembered Ted. Eager to share her news with Cole, she sat up and was about to tell him that Cummings was her father when she saw that he was sound asleep. A loving, tender smile touched her lips. Her news could wait until morning.

Returning to snuggling against him, she closed her eyes. As she waited for sleep to overtake her, she allowed her thoughts to linger on Ted. She wasn't sure how she felt about his being her father. She liked Ted, and now that she knew who he really was, she supposed she even loved him in a way. But love had to grow and mature. If she and Ted were to spend more time together, then her feelings would most likely deepen until she loved him like a daughter.

She considered trying to convince Ted to remain. If he went to San Francisco, they might never see each other again. However, if he stayed, Raymond's presence would pose a threat. As much as she wished Ted could remain, it was best that he leave.

Kristina's thoughts suddenly raced excitedly. Yes, Ted should leave, but there was no reason for him to travel so far away. Perhaps he could move to a town that was two or three days' ride from San Antonio. That way, she could visit him often. Raymond would never know that Ted was within easy riding distance.

She knew, of course, to ensure Ted's safety, she could never tell Alisa. In fact, the fewer people who knew, the better. It would be a well-guarded secret. Except for herself, only Josh and Cole would know.

Kristina found herself looking forward to having her father close by, but a worrisome cloud suddenly darkened her mood. She was sure he didn't have much money. How would he support himself? How was he to earn a living in a western town? She considered the dilemma for a long time, then came up with a solution. Ted was also a shopkeeper, for he had worked in his parents' store. Maybe, with the help of Cole and Josh he could find a store for sale. She thought about the bank statement in her dresser drawer. She had enough money to stake her father. If he refused to accept it as a gift, then he could consider it a loan.

Hopeful that everything would work out, she put her mind to rest, and remaining snuggled against Cole, she soon drifted into a restful sleep.

Alisa could barely restrain her excitement as she waited for Raymond to open the door. She had come into town alone to meet him for dinner, and using the back entrance at the Branding Iron, had climbed the rear stairway to Lewis's private quarters.

Admitting his caller, Raymond invited her inside. Lust gleamed in his eyes as he ogled Alisa's soft curves clearly enhanced by her mauve, off-the-shoulder gown. "I'm having dinner catered from the hotel," he said. "But it'll be another hour or so before it's delivered."

"That's fine," she assured him. Anxious to deliver her news, she continued rapidly. "Raymond, you'll never guess who came to see Kristina."

His interest was immediately piqued. His expression inscrutable, he asked, "Who came to see Kristina?"

"Ted Cummings!" she answered.

"Are you sure?" He was obviously excited.

"Yes, I'm sure. When I returned home this afternoon, Joseph told me that Ted Cummings was in the parlor with Kristina. I wanted to eavesdrop, but it wasn't possible. I went to my room, but later I slipped downstairs and to the parlor door. I heard Kristina tell Mr. Cummings that she wanted him to go to the Lazy-J. She told him she would join him there later."

"The Lazy-J? Isn't that Josh Chandler's ranch?"

Raymond was curious about the Lazy-J. Because he planned to buy his own ranch, he had asked several people to name the best ranches in the San Antonio and Austin areas. The Lazy-J was always among the ones mentioned.

He moved away from Alisa, went to the liquor cart, and poured a glass of brandy. He considered sending Norman and his other two men in pursuit of Cummings. If they traveled quickly, they could catch him before he reached the Lazy-J. He thought about it for a few moments, then decided that wasn't necessary. He would bide his time, wait for Kristina to go to the Lazy-J, then follow and find a way to abduct her and Cummings at the same time. He would then have them both at his mercy.

He took a large drink of brandy. Apparently he had been right about Kristina and Cummings. They were indeed lovers, and most likely were planning to swindle money from Chandler. Why else would they plan to meet at the Lazy-J? He wondered what kind of game they were playing. He smiled. Well, they would soon be playing their game in the hereafter, for he intended to kill them both.

"Raymond?" Alisa asked, gaining his attention. "Don't you think you should capture Cummings and take him back to Philadelphia? He tried to murder you. He should stand trial."

Lewis laughed inwardly. He found Alisa as transparent as glass. No wonder she was so anxious to tell him about Cummings. She was sure he'd take the man to Philadelphia immediately, and, of course, take her with him—which would mean they'd marry that much sooner! He downed his brandy, eyeing her over the rim of the glass. The simple little chit! It'd be a cold day in hell before he'd marry an Indian half-breed. The mere thought of her being the mother of his children sickened him. Mix Comanche blood with Lewis blood? Never! He would sever their relationship right now if he didn't still need her. But living at the Diamond-C, she could bring him important information—for instance, about Cummings's arrival.

He refilled his glass. Although he was bored with Alisa, he still found her desirable. But she had been an easy conquest, and now that he had her at his beck and call, the thrill of the chase was over. Furthermore, she kept insisting that he be a gentle lover, which always left him unsatisfied. He had to treat a woman roughly to reach complete fulfillment.

A lewd twinkle shone in his eyes as he finished his drink. It wouldn't be long now till he had Kristina Parker naked and beneath him! Then he would unleash his passion and let it run rampant. Imagining Kristina at his mercy excited him, and his sudden erection, confined in his tight-fitting trousers, demanded release.

He put down his glass, moved to Alisa, and drew her into his arms. Wishing she was Kristina, he held her so tightly that her slim body was molded to his hard frame.

He lied cleverly. "Darling, my men and I will go to Austin, apprehend Cummings, and take him to Philadelphia. You will come with us, of course. I'll inform my family that we want to be married as quickly as possible. Mother will arrange everything."

Alisa smiled shrewdly. "She will send a wedding invitation to Samantha, won't she?"

"If you want," he replied.

"Oh, that's what I want!"

He lifted her into his arms and headed for the bedroom.

Kristina stretched gracefully as she came slowly awake. The window curtains were open, and the morning sun shone brightly into the room. Halfway between sleep and consciousness, she rolled to Cole's side of the bed, expecting to find him there. His absence brought her wide awake.

Flinging back the covers, she got out of bed, slipped on her robe, and hurried from the room, hoping to find him in the kitchen. She was disappointed to find only Autumn Moon.

The woman welcomed her with a warm smile. "You slept late, which is good. Expectant mothers need a lot of rest."

"What time is it?"

"It's almost ten o'clock."

"My goodness, I did sleep late." Kristina sat down on a kitchen chair. "Where's Cole?"

"He left early this morning with the ranch hands. He plans to work all day. He said to tell you that he'll be home at dinnertime."

Kristina sighed. Dinnertime was hours away, and she longed to see Cole right now, this very minute! A warm flush coursed through her as a delightfully wicked smile crossed her lips. What she really wanted was to take Cole back to her bedroom and make love to him until she was breathlessly exhausted. She shrugged her shoulders and resigned herself to waiting until this evening.

"I'll fix you some breakfast," Autumn Moon said, disrupting Kristina's intimate thoughts.

"Did Joseph tell you that Ted Cummings visited me yesterday?"

"Yes, he did." She turned to the stove and began frying a slice of ham.

"Does Alisa know that Ted was here?"

"I didn't tell her."

"Did Joseph?"

"I don't know."

"Where is Joseph? I'll go ask him."

"He left with Cole. He gets bored staying around the house. He prefers to work with the wranglers."

"Autumn Moon, will you please not say anything to Alisa, or to anyone else, about Ted's visit?"

"I won't say anything if you don't want me to. But have you told Cole?"

"Not yet, but I'll tell him tonight." She considered letting Autumn Moon know that Ted was her father, but then decided to talk to Cole about it first.

Autumn Moon soon had Kristina's breakfast cooked. Hungry, she did the meal justice, then, after helping with the dishes, she returned to her room.

She drew out a sheet of paper from her vanity. She intended to write a note to Ted and have Josh deliver it. Now that she had decided to keep her father close to her, she was eager for him to agree. Dipping the pen into the inkwell, she began writing:

364

Dear Ted,

I plan to go into town today and draw money from my bank account. Yesterday, when you were here, I should have told you about this money, but, as you know, we had more important things to discuss. This money is like a miracle, for it will make it possible for us to build a loving and lasting relationship . . .

Kristina put down the pen and grumbled. "Darn it!" The inkwell had run dry. She supposed she could go downstairs and get another bottle, but she decided instead to finish the letter later.

Leaving the paper on the vanity, she went to her wardrobe and removed a set of riding clothes. The outfit was one that she had borrowed from Alisa and hadn't yet returned.

Kristina dressed quickly. She had decided to ride into town, go to the bank, and get the money for Ted. She would send it to him in the letter.

She stepped to the mirror and brushed her blond tresses briskly. She left her hair unbound, and the tight curls fell about her shoulders in seductive disarray. Kristina was indeed a fetching vision. The cream-colored divided skirt, made of soft suede, hugged her curved hips, and the matching fringed blouse emphasized the fullness of her breasts. The leather boots, their tops touching the hem of her skirt, added a tasteful touch. She put on her wide-brimmed western hat for emphasis. She was halfway down the stairs when she heard someone at the front door. The rapping was loud and demanding.

Descending the remaining steps, she went to the door and was shocked to see Ted. "What are you doing here?" she cried. "You're supposed to be on your way to the Lazy-J!"

365

"I turned around and came back. Kristina, I must talk to you."

Worried that Alisa might see him, Kristina stepped outside, closing the door behind her. She untied Ted's horse from the hitching rail, and handed him the reins, then steered him toward the stables.

"I'm on my way to town. We can talk while I saddle my horse, then you must leave. If Raymond knew you were here, there's no telling what he might do."

They moved quickly to the stables. Ted insisted on saddling Kristina's mare. He talked as he carried out the task. "I felt I had to come back. Yesterday, we didn't get anything settled. Your only concern was getting me away from here."

"That's because I'm afraid Raymond will try to kill you."

"I'm not worried about Lewis."

"Well, I am! He's an evil, heartless scoundrel, and I wouldn't put anything past him."

Ted finished saddling the mare, then turned to Kristina and said with a warm smile, "You wouldn't be so concerned about me if you didn't care."

"Yes, I care," she murmured. She moved closer and into his arms.

He held her tightly. "Does this mean you've forgiven me?"

Tears came to her eyes. "I forgive you."

She pushed gently out of his embrace. "You can ride part way to town with me. I have much to tell you. But then I want you to go to the Lazy-J. Promise me you will."

He agreed without hesitation, then helped Kristina mount, went to his own horse, and swung into the saddle.

They were riding out of the stables when Lucky,

who had been romping in the back yard, turned the corner of the house and caught the scent of his mistress.

Running as fast as his short legs could carry him, he began yapping rapidly as he headed toward Kristina. She pulled up her horse and waited.

She wanted to send him back, but he was still too young to obey commands. If she carried him inside the house, she might meet with Alisa, and until Ted was safely away, she thought it wise to avoid Alisa.

Deciding her best choice was to take the dog with her, Kristina dismounted. She scooped Lucky into her arms, then before Ted could get down to assist her, she was back on her horse.

Ted smiled with pride. "The way you handle yourself, one would think you were raised on a horse."

"Riding has always come easy to me." She slapped the reins against the mare's neck, and the animal took off at a steady canter.

Ted spurred his steed onward, caught up to Kristina, and rode beside her.

Chapter Thirty

Alisa dreaded facing her mother. She knew Autumn Moon would be furious at her for staying out all night. She had never spent the night with Raymond, and she wasn't sure why she had. It certainly wasn't passion that had tempted her to stay, for Raymond's lovemaking still left her unresponsive. She supposed that it was because she was so unhappy at home. The old resentment she felt for her father and mother was still very real. Maturity had dimmed it somewhat, but the terms "half-breed" and "bastard" hadn't lost their power to wound. She blamed her misery on Drake and Autumn Moon. She had loved her father, and she loved her mother, yet, she was still filled with bitterness, and was holding firm to her belief that wealth and social standing would somehow erase the slate. Marriage to Raymond would raise her so far above the disparaging terms that no one would dare use them in her presence or behind her back. Not even Samantha Carlson!

Alisa was traveling in the Diamond-C buggy, and Raymond, on horseback, was riding beside her. Norman and his two comrades were accompanying

369

them, but they had ridden ahead.

Raymond had insisted on escorting Alisa home, making her believe that he was too concerned to allow her to face her mother's disapproval alone. His true reason for escorting her, however, was to see Kristina. If he went into the house with Alisa, he would surely come across Kristina. He hadn't seen her in quite some time, and she was still an obsession. He had never wanted a woman as much as he wanted Kristina. She was so seductively beautiful that just thinking about her was sexually arousing. He almost wished he didn't have to kill her, but he knew she would leave him no other choice. Unlike Alisa, she would never succumb to his charms, nor would she become his mistress. Kristina would fight him all the way, giving him no choice but to force her to submit. If he let her live, she'd convince Barton to kill him. Raymond wasn't about to cross swords with Cole. He was familiar with the bounty hunter's reputation, and knew he could be dangerous when riled. Although Raymond had three bodyguards, he wasn't sure they could protect him from Barton.

Alisa and Raymond were engulfed in their own thoughts when Norman, Les, and Tom rode back to join them.

"Mr. Lewis . . ." Norman began, pointing toward a hill in the distance. "There's two people over that rise. A man and a woman. They're sittin' under a tree, talkin'."

They were on Diamond-C land, and Raymond wondered if the woman could possibly be Kristina. If she was, then the man was probably Barton. He preferred to avoid Cole.

"Did they see you?" he asked Norman.

"No, sir. They were too busy talkin'."

"I think I'll have a look." If the couple turned out

370

to be Kristina and Cole, he would let Alisa go the rest of the way alone and he'd return to town. Although he longed to see Kristina, he wanted to steer clear of Barton.

Leaving Les and Tom with Alisa, Raymond rode to the hill with Norman. Their horses ascended the grassy slope, and reaching the top, Lewis looked down at the pair below. When he saw Kristina and Ted, he could hardly believe his own eyes. Afraid they might spot him, he turned his horse about, and with Norman following, he trotted back to the buggy.

"I want everyone to remain silent!" Raymond ordered gruffly. "I must think, and think quickly!"

Alisa and the men, though confused, did as Lewis commanded. They watched curiously as Raymond withdrew into deep thought.

Lewis's heart was thumping excitedly, and his nerves were at full stretch. Finding Kristina and Cummings together, and within his grasp, was almost too good to be true. His evil mind running rapidly, he came up with a plan, a plan so perfect that it caused him to smile.

He turned to Alisa, who was still watching him with puzzlement. Using his most charming tone, he said, "Darling, I need your help."

"Of course, Raymond."

"Kristina and Cummings are at the bottom of that hill. I want you to ride by, speak to them for a moment, then go on home. Later, when Kristina comes up missing, you are to tell Barton and others that you saw her with Cummings and that you got the feeling that they were running away together."

"Are you planning to apprehend both of them?"

"Naturally."

"But I thought you were after Ted Cummings."

"If you'll remember, my dear, Kristina tried to kill me. She's wanted by the Philadelphia police."

Alisa's reluctance to help capture Kristina was obvious.

"Darling . . ." Raymond began, forcing his voice to remain on an even keel. "Kristina is a calculating liar. If Barton and Chandler are truly your friends, you'll see to it that Kristina's plan to swindle them is thwarted."

Alisa was convinced, for she still believed Kristina was after Josh's money, and it was quite obvious that Cummings was her partner in crime.

"All right," she replied. "I'll do as you say. But, Raymond, you won't hurt Kristina, will you? I mean, she may be a criminal of sorts, but she—" Alisa was about to tell him that Kristina was pregnant and must not be harmed.

Before she could, however, Raymond cut in and assured her that she wouldn't be hurt. "I would never dream of injuring a woman, regardless of her crime." He smiled to himself.

Satisfied, Alisa started to slap the reins against the horse, but turned back to Raymond and asked, "When will I see you again?"

"Soon," he answered. "We'll leave for Philadelphia in a couple of days."

Alisa left, and as Raymond watched the buggy approaching the hill, a frown furrowed his brow. He didn't know what to do about Alisa. When he severed their ties, she would most assuredly run to Cole Barton and, out of anger, tell him everything. Barton would then come after him to avenge Kristina.

The only way to ensure Alisa's silence was to kill her. Raymond shrugged. He found Alisa's death of no importance whatsoever.

*　　　*　　　*

Kristina and Ted had decided to dismount and converse leisurely. Their horses were grazing nearby, and seated beneath a large cottonwood, they were discussing the possibility of Ted's buying a store when Alisa's buggy came into view.

Surprised, Kristina bounded to her feet. Alisa! She had thought she was home. Had she spent the night in town with Raymond?

Standing beside her, Ted asked about the young woman.

"She's Alisa Carlson. Drake's daughter."

"You mean, he has another daughter besides Samantha?"

"Yes," she replied. She hadn't yet told Ted about Alisa and Autumn Moon.

Bringing the buggy to a stop, Alisa looked at Kristina and smiled. She turned her eyes to Ted. "You're a stranger in these parts, aren't you?"

"Yes, ma'am. My name's Ted Cummings."

Kristina's heart sank. Why hadn't she realized Ted was about to introduce himself and stopped him? She spoke pleadingly to Alisa. "Please don't tell Raymond that you saw Ted."

"I won't say anything," she replied. "Besides, Raymond is no longer interested in finding Mr. Cummings. He's more concerned with buying a ranch and settling down with me. Well, I'll see you back home." She laid the reins against the horse, and the buggy took off with a sudden jerk.

Kristina watched her with misgivings as the carriage rolled into the distance. She didn't believe that Raymond wasn't still interested in finding Ted. She was certain that Alisa had lied.

Clutching Ted's arm, she said, "You must leave right away!"

The words had barely passed her lips when Lucky began barking, followed immediately by the sounds of charging horses.

Kristina watched with stunning fear as Raymond and his men rode swiftly toward them. Ted wasn't wearing a gun. Though he did have a rifle on his horse, she knew he could never reach it in time.

Reining in, Raymond greeted the pair with a complacent smile. "I knew if I bided my time and waited patiently, someday I would have you both right where I want you." He dismounted, motioning for his men to do likewise.

Ted placed an arm about Kristina's shoulders and drew her close.

Raymond laughed. "Your gesture's pathetic, Cummings! How do you intend to protect her? With your bare hands? Can they stop bullets?"

"No, but they can break your neck!"

"Maybe, but you'll never get the chance to find out." He spoke to Norman. "I want you to destroy all tracks around this area. Barton's liable to come looking for Kristina."

With a jerk of his head, Norman indicated the darkening horizon. "See them clouds coming. The rain will ruin any tracks left behind."

"Good!" Raymond declared. "It seems everything is working out splendidly. Even Mother Nature is cooperating."

Lucky was pawing at Kristina's legs. She reached down and picked him up, then looking at Raymond, she asked, "What do you intend to do with us?"

"You'll find out in due time," he uttered, his lust filled eyes crawling over her.

His scrutiny sent a shudder through her.

"We'd better get movin'," Norman said, "before someone sees us. A spread as big as the Diamond-C is full of wranglers, and one or more of 'em is liable to ride by."

Raymond agreed. Moving incredibly fast, his hand snaked out, snatching Lucky from Kristina's grasp. Throwing the dog to the ground, he told Norman, "Shoot the mutt, then pitch it in the shrubbery."

"No!" Kristina cried. Drawing away from Ted's hold, she made a lurch to grab her pet, but Norman pulled his gun and shot the puppy before she could reach it.

Norman lifted the dog by its hind legs, then swung it into a clump of nearby bushes.

Kristina turned on Raymond like a crazed woman. Taking him unawares, her fists pounded against his chest and her foot kicked him sharply in the shin. "You unfeeling bastard!" she raved.

Moving quickly, Tom captured Kristina's arms and pulled her away from his boss.

Raymond's shin was throbbing. "You damned little bitch! You'll pay for this!" His eyes bore into hers with a vengeance. "I'll get even with you later! You can count on it!" He told his men to put the captives on their horses.

As Norman and Les led Ted to his horse, he cursed his own inadequacy. Kristina had fallen prey to Lewis, and he was helpless to protect her. His thoughts went to Barton. Kristina had told him about Cole, and that they were deeply in love. He hoped, prayed, that Cole would find Kristina before Lewis used her to vent his revenge.

Raymond was in the Branding Iron sitting at his favorite table when Josh Chandler entered. He paid scant attention to the tall, handsome stranger who went to the bar.

As Raymond filled his glass with whiskey, a delighted smile was on his lips. He was indeed pleased that everything had worked out so perfectly. His smile grew even wider as he thought about his captives, who were safely incarcerated in the storm cellar out back. It was the ideal place to keep them, for the cellar had been closed up for years, and few people even knew of its existence. When the saloon's former owner was giving Raymond a tour of the property, he had shown him the cellar, warning him that it was unsafe. The shelter was underground, and the supportive beams were rotting in places. Fearing a cave-in, the owner had boarded up the trapdoors, and through the years, weeds and brambles had taken over. Now, nature's camouflage had the cellar well concealed.

Bringing Kristina and Ted into town had been relatively easy. While Raymond and the others waited outside town in a secluded area, Norman had gone to the stables behind the Branding Iron and hitched up the buckboard. When he returned, Kristina and Ted, tied and gagged, were forced to lie in the bed of the wagon, and were then covered with blankets. Later, as Raymond stood guard, his men took the captives into the storm cellar.

Disposing of Kristina and Ted's horses had been more difficult. It was Norman who found a solution. He was vaguely acquainted with two Mexicans who were visiting San Antonio. He knew they were leaving that day for Mexico. He asked them to take the two horses, and they were so pleased with their gifts that they asked no questions.

Raymond's thoughts wandered to Barton. He wondered if Cole would believe that Kristina had run away with Cummings. He was sure Alisa would do her part in convincing him. Raymond's confidence soared. Alisa had kept him well informed, and he knew Cole was unsure of Kristina. Alisa shouldn' have a problem persuading Cole that Kristina had left with Cummings.

Norman came in the saloon through the back entrance and sat at the table with his boss.

"Did you see to our guests' comfort?" Raymond asked, grinning.

"Yes, sir. I took 'em some food and blankets and left Les to guard 'em." An extra glass was on the table, and Norman poured a drink. "How long are you plannin' to keep 'em down there in the cellar?"

"I'm not sure," Raymond replied. "I intend to enjoy Kristina more than once. When I finally tire of her . . ." He shrugged. "Well, the cellar has a dirt floor, and digging two graves there shouldn't pose a problem. In fact, I'll bestow that honor upon Cummings. He's a strong man, so we might as well put him to work."

Norman chuckled. "Makin' the bastard dig his own grave is a good idea." He hesitated, then asked haltingly, "Mr. Lewis . . . when you're finished with the woman . . . would you mind if me and my men poked her?"

"Be my guest," he replied.

At that moment, the bartender walked over. "Excuse me, Mr. Lewis. I know you're thinkin' 'bout buyin' a ranch, and the other day you asked me 'bout the Lazy-J." He pointed at Josh, who was still standing at the bar. "That man owns the Lazy-J. His name's Josh Chandler."

"Thanks," Raymond replied. He then dismissed his employee with a wave of his hand.

"Well, I'll be goddamned!" Norman uttered, gaping at Josh with disbelief.

"What is it?" Raymond asked.

Norman chuckled. "Josh Chandler, my ass! You know who that is? That's Moses!"

"The quadroon?" Raymond was astounded.

"In the flesh!" he answered. "Why, that light-skinned nigger's passin' for white. Hell, I ain't surprised! I always knew he was too damned smart for his own good. I bet his Texas neighbors don't know he was born a slave."

"I'm sure they don't," Raymond agreed. "Texas is filled with southerners." Lewis's mind ran swiftly and cleverly. "Norman, slip out the back door. I don't want Chandler to see you. Stay out back."

Raymond waited for Norman to leave, then catching the bartender's eyes, he motioned for him.

The man hurried over. "Yes, Mr. Lewis?"

"Ask Mr. Chandler to join me, then bring another glass."

Josh stared vacantly at the half-empty glass before him. A bitter smirk touched his lips. He hated himself for being such a coward. Why didn't he ride straight to the Diamond-C, tell Cole the truth, and get it over with? Why did he need whiskey to muster his courage?

He tipped the glass to his lips, emptying it, then refilled it. God, why had he let himself become so entangled in deceit? If only he had been honest with Cole right from the start!

His thoughts drifted back in time, and he remembered the day Cole told him about his mother's death. He had come so close to telling Cole that he was the man with the branded chest. But his own shame had caused the words to stick in his throat. He couldn't bring himself to admit to Cole that he had let his mother die—had stood by meekly as his companions raped her, had watched helplessly as Norman killed her in cold blood! He should have saved her, or

378

died trying!

He downed his whiskey and set the glass on the bar with a solid bang. He reached for the bottle, hesitated, then decided against it. He would face Cole sober!

He was turning to leave when the bartender caught his attention. "Mr. Chandler?" The man pointed in his boss's direction. "Mr. Lewis wants you to join him."

Josh looked at Lewis, his gaze far from friendly. Kristina had told him about Raymond. He was tempted to ignore the invitation and walk outside, but concern drove him to Lewis's table. He couldn't imagine why the man wanted to see him, but there was a chance that it might involve Kristina.

Raymond stood, drew out a chair, and said affably, "Please sit down, Mr. Chandler."

Josh complied, and Lewis returned to his own chair. The bartender brought the extra glass.

Raymond picked up the bottle and was about to pour his guest a drink, but Josh placed a hand over the glass.

"I don't intend to drink with you, Lewis. I only accept drinks from people I like."

Raymond wasn't offended. Before this conversation was over, Chandler wouldn't be so imperious. Quite the contrary, he would be groveling!

"How can you dislike me when you don't even know me?" Lewis asked, smiling shrewdly.

"I've heard about you."

He quirked a brow. "Of course. From Kristina Parker, no doubt. Well, Mr. Chandler, I didn't invite you over to discuss my character."

"What do you want?" Josh grumbled, impatient with the man's hedging.

"I think you should know that I plan to own

379

the Lazy-J."

"It's not for sale."

"I didn't say I plan to buy it. You will sign the title over to me free and clear. No money will change hands. My silence will be sufficient payment."

"What the hell are you talkin' about?" Josh's anger was surfacing.

"There's an old friend of yours out back. I'm sure you'd like to see him." He got to his feet. "Wait here, Mr. Chandler."

Raymond went quickly to the back door, opened it, and gestured for Norman to come inside. Together, they returned to the table.

Josh's body grew rigid, and an icy chill ran up his spine. His worst nightmare had come to life and was now standing before him.

Grinning at Josh, Norman said, "How ya doin', Moses?"

Chapter Thirty-One

A streak of lightning zigzagging across the sky was followed by a powerful clap of thunder. Its force vibrated the saloon's foundation, as if a freight train had passed. Solid sheets of rain fell from the dark clouds and splashed onto the town's dusty streets, sending people scurrying for shelter.

Inside the Branding Iron, Josh wasn't aware of the storm raging outdoors. Norman's presence had rendered his mind blank and his senses numb. He sat rigid, staring at his ex-comrade as though the man were an apparition.

Norman spoke again. "Ain't you got anything to say, Moses?"

The man's question seemed to jolt Josh out of his benumbed state and he responded coldly. "Call me Moses again and I'll kill you."

"Is that any way to welcome your old army buddy?" Norman goaded.

Raymond intervened, "Now, gentlemen, there's no reason for hostility. I'm sure we can settle everything peacefully." He sat down, gesturing for Norman to do the same.

"What do you want from me, Lewis?" Josh asked.

He smiled cunningly. "You already know what I want. I intend to own the Lazy-J."

"It's not for sale."

"Whether or not it's for sale is immaterial," Raymond answered impatiently. "I don't plan to buy it—you are going to give it to me."

"And if I don't?"

"Then Norman will tell your neighbors and associates that you are an escaped slave. Your Texas confederates won't take the news kindly."

Josh wasn't daunted. "Tell 'em! You can tell the whole state of Texas, but you'll never get my ranch, Lewis. I'll see you dead first!"

"Don't threaten me, Chandler! And don't underestimate me. If you don't give me the Lazy-J, I'll convince your neighbors and the townspeople to run you out of Austin, tarred and feathered!"

"Some people will turn on me because of my past, but you're misjudging most of 'em. The majority won't care."

"I think they will," Norman spoke up. He turned to his boss. "Durin' the war, right before we deserted, the captain sent us to question some southern sympathizers. Tom, Les, and me, we stopped at this farm, but Moses went on to the next farm. When we caught up to him at this farm, he had raped and killed a white woman." Norman turned back to Josh. "I think people will find this piece of news very interestin', don't you?"

"You lying son of a bitch!" Josh raged.

Raymond grinned delightedly. "My, my! I take back what I said earlier. Your southern associates won' tar and feather you, they'll string you up."

Josh indicated Norman with a jerk of his head. "They won't believe this lyin' piece of trash. It's jus his word against mine."

"You're wrong," Raymond answered. "Tom and
Les are also working for me. It's three against one."
He shrugged. "Maybe some people won't take their
word over yours, but it doesn't matter. The ones who
believe you're guilty will string you up and hang you
by the neck until you're dead."

"And I suppose you'll be leading this lynch mob."

"Naturally." Lewis was complacent.

"I oughta kill you right now," Josh uttered
furiously, his eyes boring into Raymond's.

Norman chuckled. "Don't try it. I got a gun under
this table, and it's aimed right at ya!"

Raymond's patience was at an end. "Chandler, I'm
through dickering. You have forty-eight hours to
sign the Lazy-J over to me. If you don't, I will
personally see to it that you hang."

"You still won't get my ranch. It's mine free and
clear, and, in case of my death, it goes to Cole Barton.
He'd never sell it to you. So what can you gain from
my death?"

"Satisfaction," he replied flatly.

Josh got to his feet. "If you blackmail me, Lewis,
I'll kill you. That's not a threat, but a fact."

Raymond wasn't intimidated. "I'll be in Austin,
waiting for your decision. You have forty-eight hours
to bring me the title." He grinned confidently. "I
think you'll cooperate. I understand that hanging is
a very painful way to die."

"I'll see you in hell, Lewis," Josh remarked. With
that, he whirled about and walked out of the saloon.

The storm was still unleashing torrents of rain,
and the downpour had turned the streets muddy.
Josh's boots sunk in the wet slush as he mounted his
palomino and headed for the Diamond-C.

In no time at all, his clothes were soaked, and rain poured off his hat's wide brim. But the wetness didn' faze him, for he was too enraged to feel anything.

Cole paused at the back door to shake the rain from his hat. As he stepped into the kitchen, he saw Autumn Moon standing at the stove. He and the wranglers had been caught in the storm, and Cole's clothes were dripping.

Grinning wryly, he glanced down at his muddy boots. "I guess I better take these off so I don't track up the house," he said.

Autumn Moon rushed to stand before him. "Cole . . " she began, visibly upset. "Kristina's missing!"

Fear cut into Cole like a sharp lance. "Missing?"

"She left the house some time late this morning. didn't see her leave, but I know she took her horse because it's gone. I've been worried sick."

"I'll search for her," Cole said. He made a half turn to leave, but Autumn Moon detained him.

"Cole, she's with Ted Cummings."

"What do you mean, she's with Cummings? thought you said you didn't see her leave."

"I didn't. But Alisa saw her and Mr. Cummings together. She was on her way home when she came upon them."

Cole's fear was now mingled with puzzlement. "Cummings? What the hell is he doin' in these parts?"

"I don't know. But, Cole, he was here yesterday. He came to see Kristina."

Anger now swirled through Cole's emotions. "She didn't bother to tell me about his visit!"

384

At that moment, Alisa came into the kitchen holding Kristina's partially written letter in her hand. She looked at Cole. "Did Mother tell you about Kristina?"

She didn't give him time to answer. "Yes, I can see by your face that she told you." She went to him and handed him the letter. "I found this in Kristina's room. I think you should read it."

Although Cole's eyes scanned the note hastily, his mind absorbed every word. The last line hit him the hardest: "This money is like a miracle, for it will make it possible for us to build a loving and lasting relationship." My God, was there truth to Lewis's accusations? Was Kristina in love with Cummings? No! Cole refused to even consider it.

"Where do you suppose Kristina got all this money?" Alisa asked Cole, watching him closely.

"I have no idea."

"Well, I do," she remarked. "Raymond was right about her. She inveigled money from Josh, and now she and Cummings have taken it and have run off together." Alisa believed what she said was partly true. She was sure that Kristina had gotten money from Josh, for she couldn't imagine her getting it any other way.

"What makes you think she's run away with Cummings?" Cole demanded.

Cleverly, Alisa carried out Raymond's ploy. "It's just a feeling I have. When I came across them this morning, Kristina acted very nervous and guilty. I had a hunch she was up to something."

"I'll saddle a fresh horse and go after her."

Alisa grabbed his arm. "Cole, you can't be serious! Why don't you just let her go? She obviously wants Ted Cummings! She has apparently been in love with him all along. She merely used you, Papa, and Josh. All she's ever wanted is money so that she and Cummings can live in style. Cole if you chase after her, you're a fool!"

He flung off her grip. "I found Kristina guilty twice before when she was innocent. I'll not make the same mistake again! As for being a fool, *you* are the fool! Surely to God, you don't believe Lewis will marry you!"

Anger flared in Alisa's dark eyes. "He loves me!"

"Lewis loves no one but himself!" Without further words, Cole swung open the back door and left.

Autumn Moon turned on her daughter angrily. "How dare you say such horrible things about Kristina!"

"Why not? They're true!"

"There isn't a crooked bone in her body! You're judging her by yourself!"

"Are you insinuating that I'm devious?"

"Aren't you? You tried to inveigle Cousin Eva's husband into marriage, and now you're doing the same thing with Mr. Lewis! That's why you spent the night with him, isn't it? You're using your body to buy a wedding ring!"

"If I'm devious, it's all your fault! Yours and Papa's! You brought me into this world with two strikes against me!"

The anger went out of Autumn Moon's eyes and she looked at her daughter sympathetically. "I feel sorry for you, Alisa. You are so immersed in self-pity that you will eventually drown in it."

"We'll see about that!" she retorted. She cast her mother a defiant look, then left the kitchen in a huff.

*　　　*　　　*

Alisa sat alone in the parlor, her thoughts flowing. Cole was a fool and her mother was blind to Kristina's character. Why couldn't they see that Kristina was a fraud?

An angry frown creased her brow. Cole was wrong about Raymond! He loved her and he did intend to marry her! Futhermore, how dare her mother pass judgment on her! Her own life certainly wasn't above reproach! She had lived with Drake Carlson and had borne him a child out of wedlock!

Alisa's anger intensified as her thoughts wandered to Josh. She suddenly wondered if she was wrong to blame her parents for all her unhappiness. It was more Josh's fault than theirs. As though it had happened yesterday, she remembered the night she and Josh had kissed. Three years hadn't dimmed the memory. Josh had wanted her that night, she knew it beyond a doubt. Passion had been in his kiss, true. In his eyes, however, she had seen love. Yet he had turned away.

His rejection had broken her heart, for she had firmly believed he was opposed to her mixed blood and that her age had nothing to do with it. If Josh had overcome his prejudice and asked her to marry him, then she would never have gone to St. Louis. The affair with John would never have happened, nor would she now be planning to marry Raymond. If she were a devious woman, as her mother claimed, then it was because of Josh. The man she loved had turned her away because of her Comanche blood. She supposed she should hate Josh, for he wasn't worthy of her undying love. But she couldn't bring herself to hate him, for her heart had a will of its own—and it was still obsessed with loving him.

A loud rapping at the front door broke into Alisa's

sullen reverie. She left the parlor to receive the caller.

Outside, the storm was still raging full force, and, as she opened the door, the wind blew sheets of rain into the foyer. As she stepped back to avoid the wet onslaught, Josh crossed the portal, closing the door behind him.

Alisa knew, of course, that Josh was expected at the Diamond-C, for she had overheard Kristina telling Ted about his arrival. But she certainly hadn't been expecting him tonight, especially in this downpour.

Josh was soaking wet, and drops of water were rolling down his clothes and spilling onto the floor. He carried a carpetbag, and indicating it with a slight lift, he said, "I need to change into some dry clothes."

"You can use Cole's room."

"Is Cole here?"

"No," she replied.

"Kristina?"

"She isn't here, either," Alisa said somewhat tartly. She could well imagine how anxious he was to see Kristina!

"Where are they?"

"Why don't you change clothes, then we'll talk. I think you'll be very interested in what I have to say."

"Alisa, if something is wrong, I want you to tell me about it now."

"Honestly, Josh. If you don't get out of those wet clothes, you'll end up sick. I'll wait for you in the study."

Agreeing, he hurried up the stairs to Cole's room. As he undressed, his mind was racing turbulently. He hoped nothing was wrong with Cole and Kristina. He had enough problems without his two best friends adding their problems to the list. A murderous rage filled his eyes as his thoughts went to

Raymond Lewis. He was sure Lewis would carry out his threat. The man certainly wasn't above black-mail, and would use whatever means available to take possession of the Lazy-J.

Dressed, he descended the stairs swiftly, and went to the study. Alisa had a brandy poured, and she handed it to him.

He took a deep swallow, welcoming the liquor's warmth. He eased his tired body into the large, comfortable chair at the desk, looked at Alisa, and asked, "Where are Cole and Kristina?"

"I'm surprised you didn't come across Cole. He's out there somewhere, looking for Kristina."

Josh sat up straight. "What do you mean, he's look-ing for Kristina?"

Alisa could read concern in his eyes. "I can see you're worried about your darling Kristina!" she said with resentment. "Well, you needn't concern your-self. She's in good hands! She's with the man she truly loves—Ted Cummings! They have run away together!"

Josh bounded to his feet. "What the hell are you saying?"

As quickly as possible, she told him the same story she had given Cole, and also repeated the contents of Kristina's letter to Ted.

"I don't believe Kristina's in love with Cum-mings!" he remarked strongly.

"I suppose you think she loves you!" Alisa spat.

"Why would I think that? She loves Cole."

Alisa was confused. "Are you telling me that you actually fell in love with her, gave her money, and all along you thought she loved Cole? Good Lord, what kind of fool are you?"

"In the first place, I'm not in love with Kristina,

389

and in the second place, I never gave her money. Where did you get such crazy notions?"

"Don't lie to me, Josh Chandler! I know how you feel about her! I saw you two together!" She told him about the morning she had seen them in his study, embracing.

"Futhermore," she continued, "Cole knows about you and Kristina!"

"Cole thinks that Kristina and I are in love?" Josh was incredulous.

"Yes, he does."

"No wonder he was acting so strangely," Josh murmured, but he was speaking to himself. He put down his drink and moved from behind the desk.

As he brushed past Alisa, she reached out and grasped his arm. "Where are you going?"

"To find Cole and tell him he's wrong about Kristina and me. Then I'll help him find her and Cummings."

Alisa's temper blazed. "Leave! See if I care! Run after Kristina if you want! Your're as big a fool as Cole! She's pulled the wool over your eyes as well as his! Well, I'm through trying to warn either of you about her. To hell with both of you! I have my own life to consider." She raised her chin smugly. "Raymond Lewis and I are getting married."

Alisa was astounded to see rage flicker in Josh's eyes. "You aren't marrying that son of a bitch!"

"Oh?" she questioned sharply. "Why not? Are you willing to marry me?"

"My feelings toward you have nothing to do with it. Lewis is a pompous, calculating ass!"

"And you are a prejudiced bastard!"

"Prejudiced?" he repeated archly.

"Yes! You think my Comanche blood places me

390

far below you! Well, Raymond doesn't find my mixed blood distasteful."

"Your Comanche blood has never been a factor."

"Well, I can't believe it's my age. I'm no longer a child!"

Josh sighed deeply. His past would soon be public knowledge, for he didn't plan to give in to Lewis's blackmail. He wondered if he should tell Alisa himself or let her hear about it through Lewis. At the moment, however, he felt he didn't have a choice in the matter. He needed to catch up to Cole, and time was of the essence.

He moved closer to Alisa, placed a hand beneath her chin, and tilted her face up to his. He gazed thoughtfully into her watching eyes. Her feelings were mirrored there, and he could see her desire. A small, bitter smirk played across his lips. When she learned the truth, she would no longer want him. Quite the contrary, she would probably loathe him. She would despise his mixed blood more than she despised her own.

He spoke huskily. "It's not your Comanche blood, nor is it your age that has kept us apart. You have your own prejudice to blame."

"I . . . I don't understand," she murmured.

"You will," he replied tersely.

"Tell me what you mean."

"I don't have time." He turned and walked away.

Alisa, perplexed, watched as Josh went to the door. He stopped abruptly, and taking her completely by surprise, he came back, took her in his arms, and uttered thickly, "I've been wanting to do this for years!"

His lips seized hers in a kiss filled with longing. Alisa's response was immediate, and as she slid her hands about his neck, she pressed her thighs intimately to his. Her skirt and petticoat didn't prevent her from feeling how powerfully he wanted her. With a shuddering sigh, she surrendered to her own fervent passion.

He released her so abruptly that she tottered backward. His eyes searched hers with deep torment. "I love you, Alisa. I've loved you for a long time." He whirled about and headed toward the door.

"Josh!" she called desperately. "If you love me, then why . . . ?"

"Ask your fiancé."

He walked out of the room, leaving Alisa stunned.

Chapter Thirty-Two

The storm unleashed its fury and passed over, leaving the terrain soaked. Cole was wet, chilled, and miserable. He had failed to pick up Kristina and Ted's tracks, for the rain had washed away all signs. Sighing, he pulled up his horse, and drew out a cheroot and a match from his inside pocket.

He glanced overhead. The rain clouds had moved on and the moon, surrounded by twinkling stars, was now dominating the sky.

He struck the match with a flick of his thumbnail, and as it flared into life, he cupped his hands about the flame and lit his cheroot. He took a long drag, blew out the match, and pitched it to the ground.

A worried frown fell across his face. Where was Kristina? Cole couldn't, wouldn't, believe that she had run away with Cummings. He had her letter to Ted tucked in his shirt pocket, yet, despite her own written words, he refused to find her guilty. His better judgment played havoc with his emotions, flooding him with questions he couldn't answer: Where had Kristina gotten money? Was Alisa right, did she inveigle money from Josh? Why didn't Kristina tell him about Cummings's visit? What

393

exactly were her feelings for the man? Love? Did she love him?

Cole wiped the questions from his mind. To hell with logic, he would listen to his emotions, for deep in his heart, he knew he was the man Kristina loved.

The sound of an approaching horse grabbed Cole's full attention, and he quickly dropped his cheroot. Drawing his pistol, he rode to a nearby cottonwood. Concealed under the tree's sweeping branches, he watched as the rider came into view. The moon's golden rays made the man easy to see and holstering his gun, Cole called out, "Josh, I'm over here!"

Chandler rode to the cottonwood. "I'm glad I found you."

"Were you at the house? Has Kristina returned?"

"I'm afraid not."

"Damn!" Cole cursed softly.

"I talked to Alisa, and she told me that you think Kristina and I are in love. Cole, I think the world of Kristina, but—"

He cut in, "I know you two aren't in love. I feel like a fool for thinking you were."

"Where do you suppose Kristina is?"

"I have no idea, but since I can't find any tracks, guess I'll ride into town. Maybe she and Cummings are there."

"I'm going with you."

They were about to leave when, suddenly, Cole detected a small whimper. It was almost inaudible, and, when he didn't hear it again, he decided it must have been a trick of the wind. Then, vaguely, the whimper sounded once more.

This time, Josh heard it also. "What was that?"

"I don't know, but it seems to be coming from those bushes."

The men dismounted and hurried over. As Cole parted the heavy foliage, the whimper became a low, painful whine. Looking down, he saw Lucky. The puppy was lying on his side, his coat matted with blood.

Kneeling, Cole reached out a hand and placed it lightly on Lucky's head. "Easy boy," he said soothingly.

"Has he been shot?" Josh asked.

"Yeah. He's hurt bad. I'm surprised he's still alive." His tone affectionate, he said to Lucky, "You're a tough little fella, aren't you?"

Gently, Cole lifted the puppy and carried him to his horse. Josh took the dog as Cole mounted, then handing him up, he said, "Kristina loves this pup. She'd never allow anyone to shoot him. Something has happened to her."

"I know," Cole replied gravely. He feared for Kristina's life.

"Are we still going to town?" Josh asked, mounting.

Cole nodded. "We'll take Lucky to Dr. Newman's, then pay a visit to Lewis."

Josh was filled with foreboding. Lewis! Would he mention his blackmail threat in front of Cole? God, he had to tell Cole the truth! But, damn it, there wasn't time!

Josh's consternation was visible, and Cole asked, "What's wrong?"

"Nothing," he replied evasively. "Do you think Lewis is behind Kristina's disappearance?"

"He's the most likely candidate."

They spurred their horses into a fast gallop and headed toward San Antonio.

*　　　*　　　*

The storm cellar was damp and chilly. Kristina sat close to Ted, huddled in the blanket draped over her shoulders. They were seated on the dirt floor, leaning back against the wall. She was so tired that simply moving was an effort. She needed rest but could not sleep, for every nerve in her body was taut, and a fearful knot was lodged in her stomach. She kept watching the trapdoors, dreading Raymond's appearance. Would he come for her, take her to his quarters, and use her for his own enjoyment? The possibility wasn't only terrifying but sickening as well. The mere thought of Raymond's hands touching her made her skin crawl. She felt she would rather die than suffer his abuse. If she weren't pregnant, she would find a way to kill herself before submitting. Or better yet, she decided, she'd find a way to kill him! It was an encouraging thought, but not a very practical one, for she knew the chance would never present itself. And, even if it did, she wasn't sure if she was capable of murder. Before, when Raymond had attacked her, she hadn't sent the scissors into his heart but had only stabbed him in the shoulder.

With effort, she routed Lewis from her mind. Thinking about him only worsened her fear. She glanced about, taking stock of her surroundings. The underground cellar was musty, and the lone kerosene lantern did little to lighten its gloom. It was a dreary place and made her think of a dungeon. Her gaze went to Les, who was guarding them. He was sitting on a hard chair. It was placed at the end of the stairs leading up to the doors.

Ted had also taken close stock of the area. Kristina hadn't noticed that the beams were unsafe, but Ted had seen the hazard immediately. Lewis wasn't the only threat to their lives—this cellar could cave in a any moment. The weakest studs were the ones lodged in the floor, supporting the overhead crossbeams. But the stud beside the stairs was still sturdy. If the ground above was to cave in, the dirt roof over the stairs would most likely remain intact.

Ted knew he had to come up with an escape plan, for he couldn't sit back and do nothing to save his daughter. He glanced once again at the deteriorated beams. The worst one was directly in front of him. If he could find a way to get Les over here, and Kristina to the stairs, then he could throw himself against the stud. The force should make it topple, which would send the ground above plunging down over him and Les. Kristina, however, should be able to scramble up the steps to safety. If that part of the ceiling were to give way, it wouldn't happen immediately. She would have time to get out.

Ted sighed inwardly. It was a risky plan and might backfire, killing Kristina as well as himself and Les. But it was Kristina's only chance. He was certain that Lewis would eventually kill her. He wrestled with the ropes binding his hands. If only he could break loose, then he could rush Les and kill him. He was tied securely, though, and the knots held firm.

Kristina, aware of his movements, turned to him. Her hands had been bound when she was brought into the cellar, but apparently she wasn't considered a threat, for she had been untied. Ted's hands were restrained behind his back, and she knew the position had to be uncomfortable.

A small, wistful smile touched her lips. "Are you all right?"

"I'm fine," he replied, returning her smile.

"Ted . . ." she began. "What happened when you tried to kill Raymond?"

"I waylaid him one night when he was coming out of his favorite bar. I dragged him to the alley and was choking him when a group of his drinking buddies spotted us. I had no choice but to run. They chased me, but I lost them."

"Your violence worries me."

"I'm not usually a violent man. But Lewis tried to kill you. I was too enraged to act rationally."

"I should think Richard Jarman's death would've taught you to control your rage."

He groaned remorsefully, "I know what you're saying. And you're right. But you're my little girl, and Lewis tried to rape and kill you. I was mad enough to tear him to pieces."

Their discussion was interrupted by the trapdoors swinging open. "Les, we're coming down!" Raymond called out.

Kristina, her heart pounding fearfully, watched as Raymond and Norman descended the steps.

A large grin was spread across Lewis's homely face as he went to Kristina, grasped her hands, and drew her roughly to her feet. He glanced about the cellar, then turned back to Kristina. "Are you finding your accommodations pleasant, my love?"

"I was, until you arrived!" she retorted, dislike for Raymond overcoming her fear.

He laughed coldly. "Your spirit is admirable, but, in this case, worthless. Don't you know when you are beaten? It would be to your advantage to treat me nicely."

"I'd rather be nice to a rattlesnake!"

He arched a brow. "You're as stubborn as you are beautiful. It's going to be a pleasure to break you. Before I'm through with you, I'll have you groveling at my feet."

"Don't count on it!" she spat.

"But I am counting on it, and I always get what I want . . . one way or another. I'd give you an example of what I mean, but a business matter has come up, and I'm leaving town for a few days. When I return, you and I have a date." He shoved her so hard that she fell backward, landing against Ted. Leering at her, Raymond said with a cruel grin, "I'm sure you'll anxiously await my return."

Without saying anything to Cummings, he wheeled about and moved quickly to his men. He spoke to Les in a hushed tone, then he and Norman left.

"I wonder where he's going," Ted said quietly.

"To hell, I hope."

"We wouldn't be so lucky." For a moment, he wondered if he should temporarily discard his plan for Kristina's escape. Lewis's departure had given her a short reprieve. As his eyes went to the decayed beams, however, he decided to go through with his plan as soon as possible. Kristina had been granted a reprieve from Lewis but not from this cellar. Earlier, he had heard rain hitting against the doors, and he knew the wet ground above would put even a heavier load on the rotted beams. How long could they support the weight? Indefinitely? Weeks? Days? Hours? One of the studs creaked. Minutes?

A small clump of dirt fell from the roof, hitting the floor soundlessly. Only Ted saw its descent, and it made him even more uneasy.

Alisa knocked rapidly on Raymond's door. When her knock went unanswered, she tried turning the knob. Finding the door unlocked, she went inside. The sitting room was empty, and wondering if Raymond could be in his bedroom sleeping, she hurried to check. She was disappointed to find he wasn't there.

Deciding to wait, she sat on the bed. She was tense, and trying to relax, she expelled a long sigh. She hoped Raymond would show up soon, for she was anxious to talk to him. She was also thoroughly confused. What could Raymond possibly have to do with her and Josh? What did Raymond know that she didn't?

Determined to find these answers, Alisa had left the Diamond-C immediately after Josh. Changing quickly into riding clothes, she had rushed to the stables, saddled her horse, and raced into town.

Now, as she waited, she thought about Josh's kiss and his declaration of love. His kiss had stirred her deepest passion. Only Josh had the power to arouse these fervent feelings. A trace of tears dampened her eyes as she recalled his words. "I love you, Alisa," he had said. "I've loved you for a long time." *Then why . . . why?* her heart cried. *Why does he turn away from me?* More of his words surfaced. "It's not your Comanche blood, nor is it your age that has kept us apart. You have your own prejudice to blame." Prejudice? What did he mean? It made no sense whatsoever!

Suddenly, she heard the living-room door open, and she jumped to her feet. Hopeful that Raymond could solve the puzzle, she started across the room, but Raymond's words brought her strides to an abrupt halt.

"As soon as we get back from Austin, we have to find a way to kill Alisa," Raymond was saying to Norman. "We'll have to make it look like an accident."

Norman was a little surprised. "I thought she could be trusted."

"She can, up to a point. But I've grown tired of her, and when I send her packing, she'll run straight to Barton. The only way to guarantee her silence is to kill her." He chuckled heartily. "Did you know the stupid bitch actually thought I was going to marry her? Can you imagine anyone being that gullible?"

Norman laughed along with him. "Well, no one ever said Indians were smart."

"Go find Tom. Tell him to go to his room and get some sleep. He'll have to relieve Les in a few hours." A worried scowl crossed his face. "I hope I can trust those two to do their job. I don't want to come back and find that Kristina and Ted escaped."

"You can depend on 'em boss. They're good men."

"I have no choice but to depend on them. Right now, taking possession of the Lazy-J comes before Kristina and Cummings."

In the bedroom, listening, Alisa stood motionless. She could hardly believe what she was hearing.

"I sure hope we won't need Tom and Les to back up my story," Norman said. "I mean, if Chandler doesn't hand over the title to the Lazy-J, I'm gonna have to tell everyone 'bout him rapin' and killin' that woman. What if nobody believes me?"

"They'll believe you," Raymond said with certainty. "They won't take his word over yours. Those three R's branded on Chandler's chest prove he's a liar. What better proof do we need?"

Norman grinned. "None, I reckon."

Raymond eyed Norman. "Chandler didn't really rape and kill that woman, did he?" He spoke too softly for Alisa to hear.

"What makes you say that?"

"He isn't the type." He dismissed the discussion. "Find Tom, then pack a bag. I want to leave right away."

As Norman left, Raymond headed toward his bedroom to pack. But he changed his mind, and his course veered to the liquor cart. He poured brandy into a large snifter.

Meanwhile, Alisa, certain Raymond would come into his bedroom, was looking about frantically for a place to hide. Her eyes flew to the closed window, and knowing a narrow ledge ran beneath it, she crept quietly across the room.

Carefully, she eased the window open, parted the curtain, and eyed the ledge with misgivings. It was dangerously narrow, and she wasn't sure if it was sturdy enough to support her weight. She felt, however, that she had no choice but to take the risk. If Raymond were to find her, he would certainly kill her.

Mustering her courage, she carefully slid a leg through the window, then gingerly placed one foot on the ledge. Straddling the sill, letting it support most of her weight, she eased her other leg outside, putting her foot down carefully. She drew a deep breath, uttered a silent prayer, and stood. The ledge held. Turning cautiously, she closed the window, then placing her back flush to the building, she began taking tiny steps, moving as far away from the window as the short ledge allowed.

Raymond, his drink in hand, entered his bedroom. Alisa's heart pounded against her rib cage as she heard him moving about. It took him only minutes to pack, but to Alisa it seemed to be taking forever. She hoped, prayed, he wouldn't check the window and decide to lock it. She was already terrified, but if she were to find herself stranded on the narrow ledge, she might lose control and panic.

From her position, she had a side view of the window, and when she saw the lamp go out, she breathed a sigh of relief. Raymond was leaving, and he hadn't locked her outside.

She forced herself to wait for several minutes before venturing back inside. She wanted to give Raymond ample time to be gone.

Inching her way back down the ledge, she eased the window open and crawled through to the bedroom.

She stood still for a moment, listening. Met with silence, she moved furtively to the closed door leading to the sitting room. She opened it a crack and peeked inside. The room was unlit, but the curtains that usually covered the windows were open. The moon's rays shining inside assured her that the room was unoccupied.

Alisa's knees shook as she lit the lamp. Moving to the sofa, she sat down and leaned her head into her hands. She was on the verge of tears. God, Raymond was as heartless as everyone said. Heartless? He was an unfeeling monster!

Her troubled mind went over Raymond's conversation with Norman. He was apparently hoping to own the Lazy-J. But Josh would never sell his ranch!

Good Lord! she suddenly exclaimed to herself. *He isn't planning to buy it! He must be blackmailing Josh!*

Alisa's face paled. Earlier, she had been too scared, too confused, for Raymond's reference to Josh's three R's to sink into her consciousness. Now, though, the words came to mind, shocking her with a tremendous force. Was Josh the man Cole had been pursuing for years? The man who killed his mother? Was Josh the killer with the R's branded across his chest? The runaway slave?

"No!" she cried brokenly. "Dear God, no!"

Dr. Newman's office was adjacent to his house, and he had been preparing for bed when Cole and Josh arrived with the wounded puppy.

Newman wasn't too surprised to find that his patient was a dog. It wasn't the first time he had been asked to use his medical skills to save a pet.

Showing the men into his office, he had Cole lay the puppy on the examining table. He checked the gaping wound, then getting his stethoscope, he listened to Lucky's heartbeat. It was weak and irregular.

"I don't know if I can save him," Newman told Cole. "But I'll try. How did he get shot?"

"I don't know. Kristina's missing, and whoever's behind her disappearance probably did this to the dog."

"Kristina's missing?" The doctor was alarmed.

"Josh and I are lookin' for her. I'm sorry about dropping the dog off like this and leaving, but . . ."

"Don't worry. I'll tend to the dog, you just find Kristina. God, I hope she's all right."

Cole motioned to Josh. "Let's go."

The doctor's house was located at the end of town, and they galloped down the street to the Branding Iron. Reining in, they dismounted, looped their reins over the hitching rail, and went inside the saloon.

Looking about, and failing to spot Lewis or his men, they darted up the stairway and to Raymond's quarters. Cole tried the door, it was locked. He stepped back, then kicked the door with such force that it flew open.

Alisa, still on the sofa, bounded to her feet. With a surprised gasp, she looked at Cole, and then at Josh.

"Where's Lewis?" Cole demanded.

"He's gone to Austin," she replied.

"Austin!" Cole exclaimed. "Why in the hell did he go there?"

Alisa didn't answer but looked down at the floor, unable to meet Cole's eyes, or Josh's.

"Answer me!" Cole insisted angrily. "Why did Lewis go to Austin?"

Josh swallowed heavily, touched Cole's arm, and murmured, "I know why."

Chapter Thirty-Three

Cole looked questioningly at Josh. "What do you know about Lewis? Does his trip to Austin have anything to do with you?"

"He wants the Lazy-J."

"You aren't selling, are you?"

"Of course not."

"Then what the hell's goin' on?"

"It's a long story, but I guess this is as good a time as any to tell you. I keep waiting for the right time, but it never seems to get here."

Cole was too concerned about Kristina to listen to a long story. "Sorry, Josh. But you're gonna have to tell me about it later." He turned to Alisa. "Lewis has Kristina and Cummings, doesn't he?"

She sank back onto the sofa, and answered listlessly, "Yes, he does. He told me he was taking them back to Philadelphia to stand trial for attempted murder. But it was a lie. Everything he's told me has been a lie."

"Where's Kristina?"

"I don't know."

Cole moved swiftly to Alisa, and grabbing her arm, he jerked her to her feet. "Alisa, if you're lying to me,

405

so help me God . . . !"

"I'm not lying!" she cried pleadingly. "I don't know where Raymond is keeping Kristina!" Suddenly, remembering, she said excitedly, "But Tom knows! He's one of Raymond's men, and he has a room down the hall. He's probably there now. Raymond left him and Les behind to guard Kristina and Cummings."

Cole's fingers remained locked about Alisa's arm. "Let's go. You're gonna get Tom to open his door."

She drew free from his firm hold. "You don't have to force me, Cole. I'll gladly help you. I'm no longer loyal to Raymond. He not only used me, but he's also planning to kill me. I overheard a conversation between him and Norman."

Josh spoke up, "Exactly what did you overhear?" His eyes searched hers anxiously.

She looked away from his questing gaze and didn't answer.

She knows! Josh thought desperately. *She knows who I am, and that's why she can't look at me. God, she must hate me!*

Cole was too involved with finding Kristina to catch the tense interplay between Josh and Alisa. He took Alisa's arm again, but this time his grip was gentle. He ushered her to the door, and with Josh following, they went down the hall to Tom's room.

Josh's nerves were stretched tightly. He didn't know what to expect from Tom. Would the man call him Moses? Would he mention their past relationship? He wanted Cole to learn the truth but not like this! He had to tell Cole himself, friend to friend, man to man!

Cole placed Alisa in front of the door, then he stepped to one side, gesturing for Josh to cover the other side. The men drew their pistols, then Cole motioned for Alisa to knock.

"Who's there?" Tom called out.

"Alisa," she replied.

"What do you want?" They could detect a note of surprise in his voice.

"I'm lonesome," she said, her tone unmistakably inviting.

"In that case," Tom said loudly, "I'll be right with you, sweetheart."

Tom didn't expect trouble, and leaving his holster hanging on the bedpost, he threw open the door.

Cole's pistol greeted him. Keeping it aimed between Tom's bulging eyes, Cole entered the room. "Where's Kristina?"

"I . . . I don't know what you're talkin' about," he stammered.

Josh told Alisa to remain in the hall, then closing the door, he listened as Cole threatened coldly, "You've got five seconds to tell me where she is."

"Go to hell, you bastard!" Tom uttered, sounding more brave than he felt.

Cole shrugged as though unconcerned. "All right, have it your way."

Tom watched as Cole opened the Peacemaker's chamber and emptied bullets into his hand. He wondered what the man was up to.

Moving quickly, Cole closed the chamber, spun it, then put the barrel to Tom's temple, saying gruffly, "There's still one bullet left. I don't know which chamber it's in, but I do know you've got one chance in six that it's not about to scramble your brains." Cole pulled the trigger. A thudding, dull click.

Tom's knees weakened, and heavy perspiration beaded up on his brow.

"Feel lucky?" Cole asked, his eyes chilling. He pulled the trigger again. Click!

"God!" Tom groaned.

"Talk, you bastard!" He spun the chamber, pulled the trigger. Click! He repeated the procedure three more times. Click! Click! Click!

Tom could stand no more, and, breaking, he dropped to his knees, groveling. "She's in the storm cellar out back!"

"Get up, you pathetic bastard!"

Shakily, he got to his feet. He watched as Cole opened the gun's chamber to reload it. He looked at the bullets in Cole's hand, and counted six of them. The son of a bitch had gotten him to talk with an empty gun!

Tom had been too scared to notice Josh standing at the door, and believing he and Cole were alone, he decided to go for his gun. Determined to kill Barton, he made a mad dash for his holstered pistol. He moved incredibly fast, and actually had the weapon drawn before Josh's bullet slammed into his chest. The powerful force sent him sprawling against the wall before he fell over, dead.

Frightened by the gunshot, Alisa barged into the room. Finding Cole and Josh unharmed, she sighed gratefully.

"Alisa . . ." Cole began briskly. "There's a storm cellar somewhere out back. That's where Raymond's holding Kristina. Get the sheriff and meet us there."

She left at once. Cole turned to Josh, a deadly cold edge to his voice. "If Kristina's been harmed, I'll kill Lewis with my bare hands!"

Josh didn't doubt it.

Kristina was concerned about Ted. He had been immersed in his own thoughts for a long time. She wondered if his silence was the stillness before the storm. Was he contemplating some kind of escape?

She was about to question him, but before she could, he spoke to her in a whisper, "I want you to pretend you're sick. Les will come over to check on you. When he does, I want you to make a dash for the stairs. Don't look back and don't stop. Get those doors open and get out as fast as you can."

"What are you planning to do?" she asked quietly.

"Never mind. You just do as I say."

"Ted, please tell me—"

He interrupted softly, "Can't you obey your father without giving him a difficult time?"

She smiled faintly. "It's still so hard for me to think of you as my father."

"I understand," he murmured sadly. His expression grew wistfully reflective. "When you were a little girl, you called me Daddy. Do you remember?"

"Yes, I do."

He grinned timorously. "I suppose now you're too grown up to call me Daddy."

"Yes, I suppose," she murmured. For a moment, years faded into the distance, and she could remember her childhood memories with clarity. Bitterness had placed these memories into the far recesses of her mind, but, now, with her father so close, she could recall the special relationship they had once shared. Oh, yes, she remembered calling him Daddy, and she also remembered how much she had idolized him. But his desertion had filled her heart with resentment. The resentment had now vanished, but the lost years could never be returned.

Ted, sensing her thoughts, whispered. "I'm sorry, Kristina. I wish I could go back in time and change everything. I failed you miserably."

But I won't fail this time! he thought determinedly. *I'll get my little girl out of here safely!*

Keeping his voice low, he said quickly, "Start acting sick, and remember what I said. Once you head for those stairs, don't stop and don't look back."

"All right," she promised.

He smiled encouragingly. "Now let's see if you're an actress."

"Cole would tell you that I'm a very talented one," she answered.

He eyed her dubiously.

"I'll explain later," she replied, praying there would indeed be a later time.

Kristina drew a deep breath, mentally prepared herself for a convincing performance, then doubling over, she moaned loudly, "Oh, God, it hurts! It hurts!"

She stumbled to her feet, still bent over, and heaved.

Les went to her. "What's wrong with you, woman? Sit back down, damn it!"

"Please, you've got to help me!" she pleaded. "I . . . I'm in terrible pain!"

He doubled a fist. "You're gonna be in worse pain if you don't shut up and sit down!"

Kristina swayed precariously. "I think . . . I think I'm going to faint!" she cried weakly.

Les reached for her. As he did, however, Kristina shoved him forcefully aside, and made a beeline for the stairs.

"Come back, you bitch!" Les grumbled.

Meanwhile, Ted had managed to scramble to his feet. With his hands tied behind him, it hadn't been easy.

Les didn't see Ted rise, for he was watching Kristina. He moved to grab her before she could reach the stairs. At the same time, Ted's powerful shoulder slammed into the deteriorated beam. The stud creaked, gave way, and tumbled to the floor. Several overhead crossbeams bent beneath the full weight pressing down upon them. Suddenly two beams cracked completely in two, letting a dark mass of dirt fall through and into the cellar.

Les looked up in time to see part of the roof caving in, sending massive amounts of dirt and mud down upon him and Ted. More beams creaked in protest, then one by one, several began to fall from the ceiling.

Kristina was halfway up the steps when the avalanche occurred. She looked back frantically for Ted. A mound of dirt covered the area where she had last seen him and Les.

She couldn't leave Ted! Dear God, he was her father! She loved him! Although she knew the cellar could continue caving in, burying her along with Ted, she nonetheless turned around to rush back and help him.

She had barely descended one step when the trapdoors were suddenly opened. A pair of strong arms found her and swept her off her feet. She was carried up the remaining steps and into the night air.

"Kristina!" Cole moaned gratefully, holding her tightly against his chest.

She wrapped her arms about his neck, clinging desperately. "Cole! Thank God!"

Gently, he placed her on her feet. He was surprised when she unexpectedly pushed out of his arms.

"Cole!" she cried, terror in her eyes. "Ted! He's still down there! The roof caved in on him! We have to help him!" Tears poured down her cheeks, and her expression was one of panic.

Cole was taken aback. Apparently Kristina's feelings for Cummings were very strong.

He placed his hands on her trembling shoulders.

"All right, Kristina. I'll try to save Cummings for you."

"I'll go with you," she replied.

"No, you stay here." He looked at Josh, who was standing close by. "Stay with her."

"It's gonna take both of us to dig him out."

"The rest of the cellar's liable to cave in at any moment," Cole warned.

"Yeah, I know. So let's quit wasting time talking."

Kristina's heart pounded with fear as she watched Cole and Josh descend into the hazardous cellar. *Oh God, what if there was another cave-in! She might lose Cole as well as her father. And Josh! God, help them!* she prayed. *Help them! Please!*

Weakened by fear, Kristina sank to her knees, her eyes fixed on the trapdoors. Thoughts swirled through her mind like fleeting shadows. Why hadn't she told her father that she loved him? Now she might never get the chance! Also, he had longed to hear her call him Daddy.

Only minutes passed, but it seemed forever to Kristina. *Cole! Cole!* she moaned inwardly. *Oh darling, please come back up!*

Alisa arrived with the sheriff, but Kristina was too frightened, to notice their presence.

She could wait no longer and was considering going back into the cellar when she heard footsteps climbing the stairs. She rose slowly to her feet, her heart hammering, her eyes glued to the entrance.

Josh was the first to emerge, then Cole, Ted was last. Though his clothes were covered with dirt, his hair and face filthy, he seemed to be perfectly fine.

Ted looked about for his daughter, and seeing her, he held out his arms.

She rushed into his embrace, and holding him tightly, she cried tearfully, "I love you! I love you!"

Cole was stunned. He turned to leave, his emotions a wreck, but Kristina's next words caused him to pause in midstride.

"Daddy, thank God, you're alive!"

Ted's heart felt like it was about to burst with joy. "Kristina, my baby!"

She kissed her father's cheek, then moved to Cole. He was dumbstruck.

She smiled happily. "Ted's my father."

"Your father?" he repeated. A large grin spread across his face. "Then you aren't in love . . . I mean, you love him because he's your father!"

"Of course. Cole, did you think—?"

"Never mind what I thought," he replied, drawing her into his arms and kissing her soundly.

The sheriff walked over to Josh. "Alisa said Lewis's man was in the cellar. Where is he?"

"He's still down there. One of the beams fell on top of him. He's dead."

Cole and Josh decided it was too late to start for Austin. Furthermore, they needed fresh horses and provisions. They would spend the night at the Diamond-C, then leave in the morning.

Before heading for the ranch, Cole and the others stopped at Dr. Newman's house. Kristina had been delighted to learn that Lucky was still alive. Cole had cautioned her, however, not to get her hopes too high, for her pet's condition was very serious.

The doctor's prognosis was encouraging, though. Lucky was doing better than expected, and if he could hold on for the next twenty-four hours, he should make a complete recovery. Kristina left her pet with Newman, for it would be too dangerous to move him.

When they arrived at the Diamond-C, Autumn Moon insisted that everyone have a hot meal. Over dinner, she and Joseph learned about Kristina and Ted's abduction. They also learned that Ted was Kristina's father.

Alisa admitted to her mother that she had been right about Raymond. The man merely used her, and was even planning to kill her to ensure her silence. She thought Autumn Moon would respond with an "I told you so" attitude, but to Alisa's surprise, Autumn Moon drew her into her arms, kissed her, and assured her that she loved her very much.

Autumn Moon had prepared a delicious dinner, but Josh was too uneasy to eat much. He planned to talk to Cole before retiring. Although he was anxious to get the truth in the open, he was dreading doing so. Cole, however, wasn't his only worry. Lewis's blackmail threat hung over him like a dark cloud, threatening impending doom. Would his friends and associates turn on him? Would he become an outcast? Then, of course, there was Alisa. Josh suspected that she already knew about him. After talking to Cole, he would go to Alisa. He had a depressing feeling that she would greet him with contempt.

When everyone had finished eating, Josh said to Cole, "We need to talk."

"After I see Kristina upstairs, I'll meet you in the study." Cole helped Kristina rise from her chair. "Darlin', you need a good night's sleep."

Kristina looked at the table, laden with dishes. "I should help Autumn Moon clean up."

"Nonsense," Autumn Moon replied. "Joseph will help me. You've been through a trying ordeal, and you need your rest."

414

Kristina agreed, told everyone good night, and allowed Cole to take her upstairs to her room. She watched with a smile as Cole went to the wardrobe and removed a nightgown. He placed it on the bed. Then, moving to her side, he brought her into his arms, kissing her deeply.

"I love you, Kristina," he murmured.

She hugged him tightly. "I love you, too."

He released her reluctantly. "I guess I'd better go to the study. Josh is probably waiting for me."

A worried frown crossed her face.

Cole looked at her closely. "You know what he's going to talk about, don't you?"

"Yes."

"Am I about to hear the news that's going to arouse my anger?" Cole was smiling. He couldn't imagine Josh saying anything that could ignite his wrath.

"You'll be angry at first," she replied, her tone unmistakably grave.

Cole's smile faded.

"When you and Josh are finished talking, please come to me. I'll wait up for you."

"You say that like I'm going to need you."

Tears came to her eyes. "Yes, you'll need me."

Josh waited nervously. He poured a brandy for himself and one for Cole. He would give it to him when he came into the study. With his own drink in hand, he began to pace the room.

He hadn't paced very long before Cole opened the door and came inside.

Josh went to the liquor cabinet, picked up Cole's brandy, and handed it to him. "Here. Drink up. You'll need it."

"Josh . . ." Cole began impatiently. "What's goin on? Tell me this deep, dark secret you and Kristina share."

"I'll do better than tell you. I'll show you."

Josh put down his glass, then turned about, faced Cole, and unbuttoned his shirt.

At that moment, Alisa came into the kitchen holding Kristina's partially written letter in her hand. She looked at Cole. "Did Mother tell you about

Chapter Thirty-Four

Alisa paused at Kristina's door, hesitated, then knocked softly. She was wary about facing Kristina and asking her forgiveness. She wouldn't blame her if she refused even to talk to her, let alone accept her apology.

Kristina invited Alisa inside and gestured to a chair.

Alisa was too nervous to sit. Standing, wringing her hands anxiously, she said to Kristina. "I'm sorry for distrusting you, and I'm sorry for all the trouble I caused. I suppose you hate me."

"No, I don't hate you," Kristina answered sincerely. "I'm sure you believed everything Raymond told you about me."

"Oh, I did! I did!" Alisa exclaimed. "I was such a fool! I honestly thought you were as calculating as Raymond claimed. Mother said that I found you guilty because I was judging you by myself." Alisa's voice dropped to a whisper. "She was right. I am the one who is devious, and . . . and I got what was coming to me. I don't deserve happiness, nor do I deserve a good man's love."

"Alisa, don't be so hard on yourself," Kristina

417

answered warmly. "You most certainly deserve happiness, and you already have a good man's love."

She was surprised. "You know about Josh and me?"

"I know he loves you. And I think you love him."

The tension went out of Alisa, and moving to the chair she sat down. "Yes, I love him, but . . . but . . ." She didn't finish. Instead, looking carefully at Kristina, she asked, "Exactly how well do you know Josh?"

"What do you mean?"

She sensed that Kristina knew Josh very well indeed. "You two are very close, aren't you? In fact, you are so close that he told you about his past."

Kristina sat on the edge of the bed. "What do you know about Josh's past?"

"Enough," she replied flatly. "I overheard a conversation between Raymond and Norman. I know Raymond is blackmailing Josh. He wants the Lazy-J."

Kristina studied her keenly. "What else do you know?"

"I know Josh is the man with the three R's branded on his chest, the man Cole has been pursuing for years."

Bounding to her feet, Kristina said angrily, "Damn Raymond! I wonder how he learned about Josh."

"I'm not sure, but I think Norman knew him a long time ago. He mentioned Josh raping and killing a woman. He was referring to Cole's mother, wasn't he?"

"I suppose. But surely you don't believe Josh committed such a horrid crime!"

"No, of course I don't."

"How do you feel about Josh, now that you know he was born a slave?"

"I still love him, I'll always love him. But . . ."

"But what?"

"If Raymond carries out his blackmail, everyone will know about Josh. He'll be an outcast." She swallowed heavily. "Just like I am."

Her temper piqued, Kristina eyed Alisa angrily and said, "In the first place, you aren't an outcast, except in your own mind. In the second place, Josh's true friends won't turn on him. And the ones who do were never really his friends, so he's better off without them."

"Oh, that's easy for you to say!" Alisa responded, rising to her feet. "You weren't born in the West, you don't know what it's like!"

"It's not necessary to be born in these parts to understand human nature. It's the same all over the country. In Philadelphia, I met with prejudice because my mother was a domestic servant. There will always be those who look down on others. But, Alisa, don't you realize that those kind of people don't matter? They are the Raymonds and the Samanthas of this world. And why should you or I care what they think?"

Alisa sank back onto the chair. "I wish I had your attitude, your strength. But I don't."

"Then why don't you lean on Josh? Use his strength—he has enough for both of you."

"If he's so strong, then why hasn't he told Cole the truth?"

"He's telling Cole the truth right now."

Alisa grew rigid. "Do . . . do you think Cole will forgive him?"

"Yes, I do," she answered firmly.

A worried scowl crossed Alisa's face. "God, what a terrible shock for Cole! All those years he spent searching for the man he thought killed his mother,

419

and, all along, it was Josh he was hunting . . . Cole might not be as forgiving as you think," she added gravely.

One lamp burned in the study, and its glow barely lit the room. Neither man bothered to light another one, for the gloomy atmosphere seemed appropriate. Their dispositions were low, and the tension between them was electric.

They were on their third drink, but the brandy was doing little to calm their charged emotions. Josh, his shirt rebuttoned, was sitting behind the desk. Cole was standing at the window, gazing blankly outside.

Josh had finished his confession and had withdrawn into silence, waiting for Cole's response. He knew there was a chance that Cole might never forgive him, and he wouldn't blame him.

Cole continued to stare into the night, as though the darkness was riveting. It was his thoughts, however, that held him motionless. He couldn't move, he couldn't speak. It was as though he were in some kind of trance.

He had seen the R's branded across Josh's chest, had listened to Josh's story, yet the full impact hadn't hit him.

Slowly, steadily, Cole's feelings emerged, and he took a large drink of brandy, turned away from the window to meet Josh's intense gaze. "My God, Josh! Why did you wait so long to tell me?"

"When we first met, I was afraid you wouldn't believe me. I decided to wait until we knew each other better. Later, I could never seem to find the right time. Well, as more time passed, I became so entangled in deceit that I couldn't find a way out. I kept hoping you'd quit searching for your mother's killers. Every time I saw you, I tried to talk you into quitting."

Cole went to the desk, put down his glass, and eyed Josh angrily. "You aren't telling me the whole truth, damn it! There's more to it! Why did you keep silent so damned long?"

"I have no choice now but to tell you. Lewis is blackmailing me. He knows who I am."

Cole's demeanor was accusing. "You were planning to tell me before Lewis's threat. Alisa overheard you telling Kristina that you'd tell me everything. And I heard you and Kristina discussing it."

"Kristina convinced me to be honest with you. She made me realize that I had to tell you before you found out some other way."

"All right," Cole conceded. "I believe you up to that point. Now, damn it, I want you to tell me why you didn't tell me the truth before now!"

"I already told you why."

"Bull! You're evading the truth! Tell me! Damn it to hell, Josh, tell me!" Cole was livid.

Chandler bounded to his feet, shouting wretchedly, "I was too ashamed to tell you! My God, I stood by helplessly as your mother was raped and killed! May God have mercy on my cowardly soul! That's why I never told you! I was too ashamed!" He dropped back into the chair, leaned his head into his hands, and groaned, "I should've saved your mother, or died trying." He smirked with bitterness. "I did finally make a feeble attempt to save her."

"Why do you say a feeble attempt?"

"I had a gun strapped to my hip. I didn't use it."

"Why didn't you?"

Josh shrugged. "I'm not sure. Maybe I was still thinking like a slave, or maybe I was too inexperienced. The Union put a gun in my hand and

421

showed me how to shoot it. But I couldn't hit the broad side of a barn."

"You aren't the only one who failed my mother," Cole said quietly. "I didn't protect her, either. I was a fool to rush blindly into the house. I had a rifle, but I left it in the fields. When I heard my mother's screams, I panicked. I just took off running like a bat out of hell! I was an ignorant kid who failed at a man's job. For the past sixteen years, we have both carried the same guilt. We let my mother die!"

"I never knew you felt guilty."

"This is the first time I ever admitted it to anyone. I could never bring myself to talk about it. Like you, I kept it buried deep inside." Cole groaned in anguish. "I should've saved my mother."

"But, Cole, you were only fifteen."

"And you were eighteen. We were both too young and too inexperienced." Cole's eyes hardened like granite. "My guilt drove me to pursue my mother's killers for sixteen long years!" He placed his hands on the desktop, leaned close to Josh, and demanded, "Where are they? Where are the men who attacked my mother?"

"Two of them are dead. Les and Tom."

Cole drew a sharp breath. "Norman! He's the third one, isn't he?"

"Yes, and he's the one who stabbed your mother."

"I'm gonna kill him!" He spoke firmly yet with an undertone of calmness, as though he were making a simple statement.

"I hope you don't plan to shoot him down in cold blood. He killed your mother, true, but that happened sixteen years ago, and it happened in Missouri. This is Texas. If you kill him, the law will arrest you."

Glowering, Cole replied, "I don't give a damn!

That bastard killed my mother!"

Josh stood, meeting Cole's gaze head on. "Damn it, Cole! Put your revenge to rest! When we get to Austin, let Sheriff Canton tend to Norman, Kristina and your child are more important than avenging a murder that happened sixteen years ago!" Chandler hurried around the desk to Cole's side. He placed a hand on his friend's shoulder. "I want to kill that bastard as much as you do. But we can't just murder him."

"Then what do we do?"

"We play it by ear, Cole."

"I'll try, but I'm not makin' any promises."

Josh didn't press the issue. He was too grateful that Cole seemed to have forgiven him. Picking up their glasses, he handed Cole his and toasted, "Here's to burying the past, and looking to the future."

Cole shook his head. "There's too much in our past that I don't want to bury. We go back a long way, Josh. We've shared some remarkable times together, and you saved my life more than once."

"You reciprocated more than once. But who's keeping count?"

Cole lifted his glass. "Here's to friendship."

"I'll drink to that!"

They downed their brandy.

Kristina was pacing her room nervously when Cole suddenly opened the door. She froze in place, watching him expectantly. She hoped desperately that he and Josh were still friends. She tried to find the answer in his expression, but it was inscrutable.

Cole shut the door, locked it, then going to Kristina, he drew her into his arms. Keeping her close, he murmured, "Hold me tight, darlin'. I want

423

to feel your arms about me."

She embraced him with all her might. "Oh, Cole, my love! Are you all right?"

"I'm fine."

"Are you sure?"

He kissed her softly. "Darlin', I'm all right," he assured her. "Believe me, I am."

She took his hand and led him to the bed. Urging him to sit beside her, she asked. "Are you and Josh still friends?"

"What do you think?"

Detecting a warm twinkle in his blue eyes, she replied "I knew you would understand."

"I understand guilt. Josh blames himself for my mother's death. His guilt drove him into silence. Mine drove me to pursuing killers, especially those who assaulted women."

"Why do you feel guilty?"

"I didn't save my mother, either," he said heavily.

She slipped her hand into his, squeezing gently. "Cole did Josh tell you that Raymond is blackmailing him?"

Cole nodded.

"Does Norman know about Josh's past?"

"Yes, he does."

A cold chill suddenly prickled the back of Kristina's neck. "Good Lord! It was Norman and his two friends who attacked your mother, wasn't it?"

"Yeah, it was them. Norman is the one who killed her."

"I'm going to Austin with you!" Kristina remarked at once.

"You're staying here," he replied, placing a hand on her abdomen. "Considering your condition, you need to stay home and rest."

"Rest!" she exclaimed. "How can I rest knowing

you're in the same town with the man who murdered your mother?"

Cole relented, up to a point. "All right, you can come with me. But you're staying at the Lazy-J."

She didn't argue, pleased that he gave in that much. "What do you plan to do with Norman and Raymond?"

"Well, right now, I'm going to ride to town and have the judge write arrest warrants against Lewis and Norman for kidnapping you and Ted. Then I'll ask the sheriff to deputize me so I can bring them back to San Antonio to stand trial. Which means you'll have to remain at the Lazy-J. After I deliver them here to the sheriff, I'll come back for you."

She studied him warily. "Cole, do you really plan just to deliver them to the sheriff? I mean, you've been after Norman for a long time. Can you turn him over to the law, then just walk away?"

"Do you want an honest answer?"

"Of course I do."

"I don't know." He sighed deeply. "Darlin', I just don't know."

Josh rapped softly on Alisa's door. When she didn't respond immediately, he figured she was asleep, then, suddenly, the door opened.

Alisa stood poised, watching Josh intently. She had changed into a nightgown, and the silk garment enhanced her provocative curves. The luminous glow from the lamp silhouetted her nudity, which was barely concealed beneath the gown's thin material.

Josh's eyes raked over her hungrily. With a husky groan, he said, "Alisa, you're so beautiful!"

Disregarding his compliment, she waved him

425

inside. Closing the door, she asked, "What do you want, Josh?"

"You know who I am don't you?"

"Yes, I do."

"I'd like to explain everything."

She went to the bed, sat on the edge and said crisply. "Go ahead, I'm listening."

Her icy disposition angered him. "Forget it! Why should I explain anything to you? You apparently don't give a damn!"

"Oh, I give a damn all right!" she came back. "But I'm mad, good and mad! All these years, you let me believe you didn't care, when you really did! Because of you, I suffered more humiliation than you can imagine!"

"Humiliation?" he questioned, confused.

"Yes! In St. Louis I had an affair with a man who merely used me! Then I made the same mistake with Raymond! And it's all your fault!"

Josh stalked to the bed, grabbed her arms, and jerked her to her feet. "Don't blame me for your own foolishness! If I had told you the truth, would it have changed anything? Hell, no! You would still have made the same mistakes! You were dead set on marrying a rich aristocrat, not an ex-slave!"

Alisa broke into tears, but they failed to mellow Josh's rage. He continued harshly. "You're always blaming someone else for your misery. Drake, Autumn Moon, and now me! When are you going to grow up and realize you have no one to blame but yourself?"

He released her abruptly, wheeled about to leave but was detained by Alisa's hand clutching his arm.

Sobbing, she cried, "Oh, Josh, I know I've made a terrible mess of my life! But you don't understand what it's like to be . . . to be—"

426

"To be an outcast?" he said loudly. "To be different? To be ridiculed? Believe me, Alisa, a slave knows more about humiliation than you'll ever know!" His anger waned somewhat. "You're bitter, and I can fully understand your feelings. But there's one big difference between us, Alisa. I learned to live with my bitterness and not let it rule my life. You hold on to yours like its a lifeline! Lifeline, hell! It's going to drown you!"

"Maybe it already has," she murmured listlessly.

"I don't think so," he replied. Without warning, he pulled her into his arms and captured her lips in a demanding exchange.

"Alisa," he declared thickly, "I love you! Darling, let me take care of you! Together, we can overcome whatever the future might bring."

Alisa wasn't so sure their love could work miracles. She was sure, however, that she wanted to experience love's passion. And only in Josh's embrace could she find such fulfillment.

She locked her hands about his neck, urging his mouth down to hers. "Make love to me, Josh," she purred as her lips touched his.

Later, Alisa lay snuggled in Josh's arms. His lovemaking had evoked a response in her that was almost wanton. She had clung to him passionately, her hips equaling his driving thrusts. Achieving her first climax, she had cried aloud with intense pleasure as Josh, finding complete satisfaction, had spilled his seed deep within her.

Josh chuckled softly. "If you don't put some clothes on, you're gonna find out it's better the second time around."

"Promise?" she teased.

"Do you want me to prove it to you?"

"Go ahead, I dare you."

"In that case . . ." he said, leaning over her. He kissed her fervently, his tongue entwining with hers. Their hands feathered over each other until their bodies yearned for total fulfillment.

He hovered above her, and she arched to meet him. They came together with a passionate urgency, and were soon lost in love's paradise.

Afterward, they lay in a dreamlike haze. Their lovemaking had been a perfect joining of bodies and hearts.

They knew, however, that their newfound harmony was uncertain, for the real world was still outside the bedroom door, waiting for them.

Chapter Thirty-Five

When Alisa learned that Kristina was accompanying Cole to the Lazy-J, she insisted on Josh taking her. He agreed with Cole that she remain at his ranch. A shootout might ensue when they faced Raymond and Norman, and they didn't want the women close.

Kristina, wary of her father's hot temper, convinced him to stay at the Diamond-C. She was afraid Ted might take one look at Raymond and attack him.

The travelers spent the night in Sandy Creek, left early the next morning, and arrived at the Lazy-J about noon. After lunch, Cole and Josh decided to go into Austin.

Kristina was apprehensive as she watched the men ride away. She wondered if it were possible for Cole to confront the man who had raped and murdered his mother and not kill him. She hoped he could arrest him, deliver him safely to San Antonio, and let the law deal with him. Not that she cared about Norman's life, for the man was an unfeeling monster, but, she knew Cole had vowed years ago to kill his mother's attacker. She prayed he would put his revenge to rest and bury the past.

Late-afternoon shadows were falling across the town as Cole and Josh rode down the main street of Austin. When they reached Ramón's Cantina, Josh pulled up, and Cole continued to the sheriff's office.

Earlier, when Josh had mentioned waiting for Cole and the sheriff at the Cantina, Cole had tried to talk him out of it. He knew Lewis and Norman might be at Ramón's, and they were likely to confront Josh. But Chandler had been adamant. He wasn't intimidated by Lewis's threat.

Now, dismounting, Josh draped the reins over the hitching rail and walked into the crowded cantina.

Josh ordered whiskey, then looking about, he saw Raymond and Norman sitting at a back table. James Kennedy was with them. A frown furrowed Josh's brow. Kennedy still hadn't forgiven him for testifying against his daughter. Josh looked away, picked up his glass, and took a big swig. He didn't know how many friends he'd have left when the truth was known, but he did know if an angry mob erupted, Kennedy would be leading it.

Meanwhile, at the back table, the three men were unaware of Josh's presence. Kennedy had finished his drink, and Raymond promptly refilled his glass.

"Mista Lewis, if I drink any more, I'll be tipsy when I get home, and my wife will nag like a shrew. She's a teetotaler."

"One more drink won't matter," Lewis encouraged.

Kennedy enjoyed his liquor, and said politely, "Thank you, suh."

Raymond smiled outwardly, however, inside he cringed. The man's distinctive southern drawl grated on his nerves. In fact, everything about Kennedy rubbed him the wrong way. But he might need James

Kennedy and had purposefully befriended him. The man was obviously a die-hard southerner, and would certainly turn on Chandler with a vengeance.

Lewis had every intention of carrying out his threat. If Josh refused to cooperate, he'd reveal his secret, and watch spitefully as the town's Confederates, incited by Kennedy, lynched Chandler. That wouldn't give him the Lazy-J, but it would give him great satisfaction. There were other ranches— he'd keep searching until he found one that was to his liking.

Kennedy was about to take a large swallow when, glancing toward the bar, he spotted Josh. A scowl crossed his beefy face, and his heavy lips drooped into a pout.

"Is something wrong, Mr. Kennedy?" Lewis asked.

He indicated Josh with a nod of his head. "I hate that son of a bitch!" The liquor was magnifying his anger. Kennedy didn't feel especially friendly toward Josh, but, sober, he certainly didn't hate him.

Raymond was facing the bar, and he glanced over his shoulder to see who had aroused his companion's wrath. Seeing Chandler put a large grin on his face. He turned back to Kennedy. "What have you got against Chandler?"

"So you know that bastard, huh?" His words were slurring drunkenly. "My daughter was violated by a half-breed Mexican, and Chandler got on the witness stand and testified in that bastard's behalf. He ruined my little girl's reputation." Kennedy downed his drink, clumsily spilling most of it down the front of his shirt.

Raymond was feeling exceptionally good. His eyes met Norman's, and they smiled secretly. The men had an ally in Kennedy.

Standing, Raymond faced the bar, caught Josh's

431

attention, and waved to him. "Mr. Chandler, won't you join us?" he called loudly.

Kennedy was insulted. "Why's he invitin' him over here?" he asked Norman.

Norman refilled Kennedy's drained glass. "Have another drink, sir."

He did just that.

Josh had been expecting the invitation, and was more than ready to face Raymond. He walked away from the bar and went to the back table.

"Won't you sit down?" Lewis asked, a cold smile spreading across his face.

"No, but *you'd* better sit down before I knock you down."

"There's no reason for violence, Chandler. Did you bring me the title?"

"No, but I brought you something else."

"Oh? What's that?"

"This!" Josh said as his fist plowed into Raymond's face, sending him sprawling back into his chair.

Norman, drawing his gun, leapt to his feet.

"Drop it!" Cole's voice sounded from behind. He had slipped inside through the back door. At the same time, the sheriff had used the front entrance.

Norman whirled about, and seeing that Cole had him at gunpoint, he was hesitant.

"Do as he said!" Sheriff Canton ordered.

He placed his weapon on the table.

"You men are under arrest," the lawman continued.

"Arrest!" Raymond exclaimed, bounding to his feet. His nose was bleeding, and blotting it with a handkerchief, he demanded, "What right do you have to arrest us?"

"You're both wanted for kidnapping. Cole's been

deputized and has the legal right to take you back to San Antonio."

Lewis cursed fiercely. Goddamn Les and Tom! The idiots had botched their job! Losing Kristina was infuriating. He wasn't too concerned about his arrest, for he was sure his money could buy him out of this jam. He cast Josh a spiteful glare. His nose was hurting badly, and he wondered if it was broken. He knew how to get even. With a semblance of composure, Raymond said calmly, "Sheriff, before you take us to jail, I have something to say."

The cantina was quiet, for everyone was watching with keen interest.

"Why don't I say it for you?" Josh spoke up. He turned away from Lewis, faced the onlookers and said clearly, "This man was blackmailing me. If I didn't give him the title to my ranch, he threatened to expose my past. My mother was a mulatto slave. I was born into slavery, and escaped into Kansas when I was eighteen."

Kennedy heaved his huge frame from the chair, and swaying drunkenly, he uttered, "Are you tellin' us that you're colored?"

"He's a quadroon!" Raymond declared. "He's been passing for a white man, making fools of all of you!"

Voices rumbled through the crowd, some unmistakably condemning, others raised in Josh's favor.

"That's not all!" Raymond shouted. He looked at Norman. "Tell them the rest!"

Cole slipped up behind Norman, placed the pistol against the man's head, and said too quietly to be overheard, "It was my mother you killed sixteen years ago, and I'm itchin' to put a bullet through your thick skull. You utter one lie about Josh, and I'm gonna scratch my itch."

"Tell them!" Raymond repeated impatiently. "Tell them about the woman he raped and killed!"

Cole drew back the hammer on his gun, Norman broke out in a cold sweat.

"He didn't attack no woman," Norman said shakily. "I lied to you, Mr. Lewis."

Raymond stared at Norman, his mouth agape. Of course he had lied! What difference did that make?

Sheriff Canton stepped to Lewis and took his arm. "Let's go."

"Wait a minute," Kennedy interfered. "Sheriff, Mr. Lewis is a gentleman and an upstanding citizen!" Still drunk, he tottered unsteadily.

"Go home, Kennedy, and sleep it off!" Canton replied gruffly.

Enraged, Kennedy's eyes scanned the spectators. "I demand a town meeting!" He waved a hand in Josh's direction. "We don't need unsavory characters dirtying our streets!"

A voice from the crowd rang out strongly. "Shut up, Kennedy!"

"No, let him talk!" another voice responded.

Anger buzzed, tones grew loud and argumentative.

Sheriff Canton was uneasy, sensing trouble brewing. He glanced at Cole. "Let's get these two to jail. First thing in the morning, I want you to get them out of my town."

Norman was struck with fear. "You ain't gonna hand us over to Barton, are you? The son of a bitch will kill me! He won't take me back to San Antonio!"

Cole chuckled coldly. "You might be right, Norman. I've still got that itch."

The sheriff was through talking, and keeping a firm hold on Raymond's arm, he began leading him through the congested crowd. Cole, his gun aimed at

434

Norman's back, followed. Josh brought up the rear.

Once outside, Norman and Raymond were told to walk in front. The sheriff and Josh had their guns holstered, and as Norman glanced over his shoulder, Cole met his gaze and sheathed his own gun.

Norman turned his eyes forward. He was sure Barton was just biding his time. At the first opportunity, he'd shoot him down in cold blood. He had to make a run for it! He thought about the pistol hidden beneath his shirt. He had to use it now! At the jail, the sheriff might decide to frisk him. The three men had their guns holstered, so he could easily get the drop on them. He'd kill Barton and Chandler, then take the sheriff as hostage. Lewis could run with him or stay behind!

Stealthily, Norman moved his hand to his concealed weapon, and freed it with amazing speed. As he spun about, Cole's hand, moving faster than the eye could see, drew his gun and opened fire.

Norman was hit in the chest, and as he was falling, his finger released the trigger, sending a wild bullet slamming into Raymond. He didn't see his boss keel over, for he was dead before his body hit the ground.

Cole, reholstering his gun, watched as the sheriff went to Norman to see if he was still alive. He turned back to Cole. "This one is dead." A curious frown creased his brow. "How the hell did you know that bastard was drawing a gun?"

"Men like him always carry a gun hidden beneath their shirts."

"If you knew he had a gun hidden, then why . . . ?" Canton shook his head. "Never mind, I don't wanna know why." He moved to Raymond.

Josh stepped to Cole and said quietly, "You were

435

hoping Norman would draw his gun, weren't you?"

"Let's just say, I had an itch that needed scratchin'."

Lewis's insides felt like they were on fire, and grimacing against the pain, he groaned to the sheriff, "Get a doctor. I don't want to die. Please get a doctor. Don't let me die. A doctor . . . get me a . . ." His pleas faded.

"I'll find the doctor," Josh offered, turning to leave.

"Don't bother," Canton replied. "He doesn't need a doctor, he needs an undertaker." He placed his hand on Raymond's lifeless eyes, closing them for eternity.

Josh stood at the parlor window, keeping a vigil. The sun had retired, and murky shadows of dusk were blanketing the landscape. He moved a hand to the back of his neck, massaging his tense muscles. He expected an angry mob to arrive at any moment. By now, Kennedy had certainly incited enough men to follow him.

Alisa, Kristina, and Cole were also in the parlor. The women were seated, and Cole was standing behind Kristina's chair.

No one had spoken for a long time, and it was Alisa who finally broke the silent tension. "Josh, if Kennedy arrives with a large crowd, how can you and Cole possibly hold them off?"

"Won't the ranch hands help?" Kristina asked.

Josh shrugged. "I don't know. The ones who were at Ramón's came back a short time ago and went straight to the bunkhouse. By now, I imagine most of the wranglers are packing. Quite a few of them fought for the Confederacy."

Alisa sighed heavily. "Josh, what are you going to do?"

He whirled away from the window and said determinedly, "This is my home, and no one is going to make me leave! They'll have to kill me to get me off my land!"

"They will if you leave them no other choice!" Alisa cried, bounding to her feet. "I know how these people are, how they think! They ran me out of Texas, and they'll run you out, too!"

"Never!" Josh seethed. The sounds of horses sent him whirling back to the window. "Here they come." He inhaled sharply. "God, there's more than I expected!" He started for the front door.

Cole and the women followed.

Stepping outside, Josh moved down the porch steps to await the riders. Cole told Alisa and Kristina to stay put, then he hurried to take a stance beside Chandler.

The group watched tensely as the large crowd drew closer. Josh had expected to see Kennedy leading the mob, and was surprised to find the sheriff instead. He relaxed a little but was still worried.

Cole smiled. "At least it's not a lynch mob, not with Canton riding along," he said.

"He might be here to try and keep peace. Maybe he intends to ask me politely to leave his jurisdiction."

As the men were arriving, the ranch hands came out of the bunkhouse and walked over. Josh eyed them uncertainly. He didn't know if they were friends or foes.

The sheriff told everyone to remain mounted, then getting down from his horse, he stepped to Josh and Cole. A broad grin was on his face. "Josh . . ." he began. "The others have asked me to be the spokesman. We rode out here to tell you that we

437

Texans don't judge a man by his past. Hell, the whole state was pioneered by men who left their pasts behind for a brand-new start. Furthermore, you're an upstanding citizen and a good neighbor. Quite a few of the men here with me owe their homes to you. When we had that drought a few years back, the smaller ranchers and farmers lost everything they had. The bank wouldn't loan 'em the money to rebuild, but you loaned it to 'em. And most of 'em ain't even paid you back yet." Canton paused, took a breath, then continued. "I could go on and on about how you've helped your neighbors, but I ain't much of a talker. In fact, this is the longest speech I ever made. We just want you to know that you don't need to worry about Kennedy or his kind. Who gives a damn what they think?" He turned to the others. "Ain't that right, men?"

Their voices rang out, concurring unanimously.

"I don't know what to say," Josh replied, his tone choked.

"You don't have to say anything."

"Yes, I do. I thank each and every one of you. This is one of the happiest moments of my life. It's a wonderful feeling to know I have so many friends."

The sheriff moved back to his horse and swung into the saddle. "Well, we won't keep you any longer." He glanced over at Alisa and Kristina, tipped his wide-brimmed hat, and said, "Evenin' ladies."

They turned their horses about and galloped down the lane.

"Mr. Chandler?"

Josh looked over at his foreman. "Yes, Phil?"

"Me and the men, we came out here 'cause we thought there might be trouble. We were gonna back you up." Noting Josh's surprise, he said with a

438

smile, "I bet you thought me and the others were packin' to leave, didn't you?"

"It crossed my mind."

"Ain't nobody leavin', except for those two drifters you hired last week. They packed up and high-tailed it out of here. But they weren't worth a damn anyhow. Mr. Chandler, you're a fair boss and you pay top wages. You don't have to worry about losin' any of us." With that, he turned about and left, followed by the rest of the wranglers.

Cole chuckled heartily and patted Josh's shoulder. "Well, it seems you have more friends than you thought. Congratulations," he said and shook Josh's hand, then went to Kristina and led her into the house.

Alone with Josh, Alisa moved to his side. Tears in her eyes, she said softly, "This night has taught me so much. And it has made me remember."

"What do you remember?"

She spoke reflectively, "When I was in school, there were two girls who made my life miserable. They were sisters. Papa's lawyer, Mr. Cullen, is their father. These girls used to mock me and call me names. Now, as I think back, the other children didn't cheer them on. In fact, most of them would stick up for me. But, Josh, I didn't count the friends I had, I only counted my enemies. I was so hurt by my enemies that I forgot my friends. I let two mean sisters destroy me. If I hadn't been so bitter, I might have turned to those who cared about me. But, instead, I built a wall of self-pity around myself, and I wouldn't let anyone penetrate it. I brought all my misery upon myself. I never had the strength to fight back. I was all alone, and I had no one to blame but myself. As time passed, I judged everyone by those sisters, and I blamed my Comanche blood for all my

439

unhappiness. I also blamed my parents. They aren't without fault—they should have married. But I'm at fault, too. I let money and social standing become more important than common decency and compassion. It all started with the Cullen sisters and became worse as time passed."

Josh slipped an arm about her shoulders and drew her close. "Thank God people like the Cullen sisters are few and far between." He kissed her forehead. "Our friends greatly outnumber our foes."

"I know that now," she whispered.

"Alisa, will you marry me?"

"Yes, Josh, I'll marry you."

"It won't always be easy, you know. Our enemies are still out there."

"But so are our friends," she replied. She laced her arms about his neck and murmured, "I love you, Josh Chandler. And you were right, together we can face whatever the future might bring."

They sealed their commitment with a long, love-filled kiss.

Chapter Thirty-Six

It was Kristina's wedding day, and she stood in front of her mirror, gazing at her reflection with wonderment. She had never worn such a beautiful gown. She turned away from the vanity and looked at the other dress placed neatly at the foot of the bed. Because she and Cole were anxious to marry quickly, she didn't have time to make a new gown, and she had planned to be married in that one. It had been among the clothes Samantha had given her before leaving for Europe. It was pretty, but it couldn't compare to the gown she was now wearing.

Earlier, Kristina had just finished her bath when Alisa and Autumn Moon came into her room with a large box inside of which was a beautiful wedding gown. The women insisted that Kristina try it on.

Now, turning back to the mirror, Kristina admired the gown of white brocaded silk, with its chemisette of lighter silk, and rows upon rows of appliqué lace trimming the garment's flowing hem.

"It fits perfectly!" Alisa exclaimed. "Oh, Kristina, you're such a beautiful bride!"

She couldn't tear her eyes away from the reflection, and still staring into the mirror, she asked, "Where did this dress come from? To whom did it belong?"

"It was in the attic," Alisa answered. "And it belonged to my grandmother."

Kristina turned to Alisa. "But surely you don't expect me to wear it! You should wear it at your wedding!"

"Josh and I aren't getting married until next month, so I'll have plenty of time to have a gown made."

"But wouldn't you rather wear this one?"

"No. I want a new gown for the new me. I'm about to embark on a brand-new life. It's like starting over, only this time I hope to be a much nicer person."

Autumn Moon smiled as happy tears stung her eyes. She went to her daughter and hugged her tightly. "Alisa, I'm so proud of you."

She returned her mother's hug, then turning back to Kristina, she said briskly, "We need to fix your hair, then you can put on the veil."

Kristina was still hesitant. "Alisa, are you sure you want me to wear this dress?"

"I'm very sure." She smiled warmly. "Papa would want you to wear his mother's wedding gown. He loved you like a daughter. And he wanted you to marry Cole. This day would have made him very happy."

There was a moment of sad silence as each woman thought of Drake in her own way. Then keeping with the spirit of the day, their dispositions grew cheery as they busied themselves completing the bride's toilette.

Autumn Moon arranged Kristina's hair into an upsweep style, then she went to the box and returned with a wreath of orange buds and white roses. She placed it atop Kristina's blond curls, and turned to Alisa. "Now for the veil."

Alisa hurried to the box and withdrew the bridal gown's final accessory. She took it to Autumn Moon, who attached it to the wreath. The simple tulle veil was indeed the crowning touch.

"Kristina, you're a breathtaking bride!" Autumn Moon exclaimed.

"I can't wait to see Cole's face when he sees you in that dress," Alisa said. "He'll be overwhelmed by your beauty."

Kristina hadn't seen Cole since the night before. Adhering to the custom that it was bad luck for the groom to see the bride on their wedding day, she had stayed closed in her room. "How is Cole?" she asked Alisa. "Does he seem excited?"

Alisa laughed lightly. "I've never seen Cole so jittery. You know him, he's usually so calm. But he's behaving like a nervous groom."

"Cole nervous?" Kristina questioned, smiling. "That's hard to imagine."

Josh handed Cole a tumbler of brandy. "Here, drink this, sit down, and stop pacing back and forth."

"I can't help it. I'm nervous."

They were in the study, and taking Cole's arm, Josh led him to the sofa and handed him the brandy.

"What time is it?" Cole asked.

"Two minutes later than the last time you asked."

"Are you sure? Maybe your watch stopped."

Josh pointed to the clock on the wall. "If my watch has stopped, then so has the clock. They read the same time."

The study door opened and Joseph came inside. "The guests have all arrived. We're just waitin' on the reverend."

"The reverend!" Cole exclaimed, leaping to his feet. "You mean he's not here yet?"

"Calm down, Cole," Josh said, laughing. "He'll be here. Damn, I've never seen a man so anxious to get married." His eyes twinkling, he continued. "This is your last chance to make a run for freedom, you know."

Cole frowned good-naturedly. "Just wait until next month when you're in my place. I'm gonna give you as hard a time as you're givin' me."

"I don't doubt it."

At that moment, Ted entered the study. Dressed to give away the bride, he was wearing a dark suit with a white, ruffled shirt. He went to the liquor cabinet, poured a glass of bourbon, then smiled admiringly at Cole. He wholeheartedly approved of his future son-in-law. "Are you nervous?" he asked.

Cole began pacing the room. "No . . . no, I'm not all that nervous."

Again, the door opened. This time, it was Dr. Newman. He watched Cole pace for a time, then said, "You know, Cole, if you keep that up, you're gonna wear yourself out. A bridegroom should be well rested. There's the wedding night to consider."

Cole took a big drink of brandy, eyed his companions, and grumbled. "You guys are a big help!"

The doctor looked over at Ted. "I understand you're thinking about buying a store."

"I'd like to, if I can find one for sale."

"The mercantile in town just came up for sale. The Thurstons, who own it, are planning to move to California."

"That's great!" Ted replied, obviously pleased. "Now I can live close to Kristina. I'll go to town in the morning and talk to the Thurstons."

444

Newman looked back at Cole. "How's Lucky?"

"He's not up to chasing chickens yet, but he soon will be."

"Oh, by the way," Newman said, "Reverend Scott has arrived."

"He's here?" Cole remarked. "Why didn't you say so?"

"I just did."

"Well . . ." Ted began. "I guess I'll go upstairs and see if Kristina is ready."

Except for Josh, the others followed him out of the room.

"Do I look all right?" Cole asked, straightening his suit jacket.

"You look better than I've ever seen you," Josh replied, smiling. Cole was indeed a handsome groom. His off-white jacket and matching trousers fit flawlessly. He wore a black linen shirt with a white cravat. His dark hair and well-trimmed mustache complemented the stylish attire.

Joseph stuck his head in the door. "Mista Cole, the Reverend's ready to start the ceremony."

"It's about time," Cole replied and left the room eagerly.

The day had been a happy one for Autumn Moon, but nonetheless it had been tiring. Now she sighed wearily as she put away the last of the crystal. The china had already been washed, dried, and placed in the mahogany cabinet in the dining room.

Alisa had been helpful. Ted and Joseph had also tried to help, but their large hands had been clumsy handling such delicate dishes, and Autumn Moon had found them more suitable chores.

Taking a cup of coffee with her, she sat down at the

kitchen table. She looked up as Ted came into th
room. "Is there anything else I can help you with?
he asked.

"No, thank you. Everything is done." She smile
fondly. She liked Kristina's father. In some ways, h
reminded her of Drake. They were both powerfu.
straightforward men.

Ted poured a cup of coffee, then joined Autum
Moon. Taking a drink, he studied her over the rim c
his cup. He found her exceptionally attractive.

Lucky was on his bed in the corner. Movin
gingerly, he walked over to the table, sat down on hi
haunches, looked up at Ted and then to Autum
Moon. Hoping to be picked up, he whined pleadingl

They reached for Lucky at the same time, causin
their hands to touch. Their eyes met, held for
moment, then Autumn Moon looked away.

Ted smiled inwardly. When their eyes met, he ha
seen a spark of desire in Autumn Moon's gaze. It wa
gone as quick as it materialized, but it was indeed
positive sign. He knew it was too soon for her t
consider him a suitor, for she was still mournin
Drake Carlson. But that was all right. He was
patient man.

Kristina sat in front of her vanity, brushing he
curly blond tresses. Her green eyes shone wit
vitality, and her face was aglow. She glanced down a
her left hand, studying the gold wedding banc
Smiling, she vividly remembered how carefully Col
had placed the ring on her finger as he vowed to lov
her forever.

Anxious for her husband to join her, she put dow
the brush and rose to her feet. She looked into th
mirror, turning this way and that, trying to se

446

erself at different angles. She was wearing a pink ightgown that was shockingly transparent—a wedding gift from Alisa.

Shortly before, Alisa had helped Kristina remove er wedding dress and prepare for bed, then told ristina she'd inform Cole that he could now join his ride.

Kristina was wondering if the nightgown was a ttle too transparent for good taste when Cole uddenly opened the door and came inside. He put a ottle of champagne and two glasses on the bedside able.

He faced Kristina, and his eyes raked over her educive attire. A love-filled smile curled his lips. You're more beautiful than words.''

They both moved at the same time, and meeting alfway, they went into each other's arms. Cole's lips ame down on hers, and clasping her hands behind is neck, she returned his ardor passionately.

"I adore you, Mrs. Barton," he murmured. For a ong moment, he gazed into her sparkling green eyes, hen he grinned wryly.

"What are you thinking about?" she asked, miling curiously.

"I was remembering the first time we were harried—you fainted."

"I'm not going to faint this time, Cole Barton. I ave something much better in mind."

He quirked an anticipating brow. "Like what?"

"Like this," she replied, raising her lips to his. She issed him fervently, setting his passion afire.

He drew her close, pinning her against his hasculine frame. She could feel his hardness, and she ressed her thighs intimately to his.

Cole, his desire flaming, took off her gown with mazing speed. As the delicate garment dropped about her feet, he swept her into his arms and carried her carefully to the bed.

Eager to possess her completely, he shed his own clothes, letting them fall to the floor in a disorderly pile.

He went into his wife's outstretched arms, and she could feel the thundering of his heart pounding against her breasts. He moved to lie at her side, and she turned to him, molding her naked flesh to his. Their lips met in a wild, hungry exchange.

"Kristina, I love you so much," Cole uttered huskily.

"And I love you, my darling."

"I want to thank you, sweetheart."

"Thank me for what?"

"For loving me, for coming into my life and making it complete. I never dreamed I could be so happy."

"I know," she murmured. "I feel the same way."

She kissed him fiercely. Then her hands, stroking his flesh, began working magic on his senses. He returned her caresses, his touch arousing her deepest passion.

Soon thereafter their bodies came together as one, consummating their marriage and uniting their love for now and for always.